6-30-21   LP

Penner, Sarah
The Lost Apothecary

The Lost Apothecary

THE LOST APOTHECARY

SARAH PENNER

THORNDIKE PRESS
A part of Gale, a Cengage Company

LIBRARY OF CONGRESS CIP DATA ON FILE.
CATALOGUING IN PUBLICATION FOR THIS BOOK
IS AVAILABLE FROM THE LIBRARY OF CONGRESS.

ISBN-13: 978-1-4328-8570-0 (hardcover alk. paper)

Published in 2021 by arrangement with Harlequin Books S.A.

Printed in Mexico
Print Number: 04   Print Year: 2021

For my parents

"I SWEAR AND PROMISE BEFORE GOD, AUTHOR AND CREATOR OF ALL THINGS . . .

NEVER TO TEACH UNGRATEFUL PERSONS OR FOOLS THE SECRETS AND MYSTERIES OF THE TRADE . . .

NEVER TO DIVULGE THE SECRETS CONFIDED TO ME . . . NEVER TO ADMINISTER POISONS . . .

TO DISAVOW AND SHUN AS A PESTILENCE THE SCANDALOUS AND PERNICIOUS PRACTICES OF QUACKS, EMPIRICS AND ALCHYMISTS . . .

AND TO KEEP NO STALE OR BAD DRUG IN MY SHOP.

MAY GOD CONTINUE TO BLESS ME SO LONG AS I CONTINUE TO OBEY THESE THINGS!"

— ANCIENT APOTHECARY'S OATH

1
NELLA

She would come at daybreak — the woman whose letter I held in my hands, the woman whose name I did not yet know.

I knew neither her age nor where she lived. I did not know her rank in society nor the dark things of which she dreamed when night fell. She could be a victim or a transgressor. A new wife or a vengeful widow. A nursemaid or a courtesan.

But despite all that I did not know, I understood this: the woman knew exactly who she wanted dead.

I lifted the blush-colored paper, illuminated by the dying flame of a single rush wick candle. I ran my fingers over the ink of her words, imagining what despair brought the woman to seek out someone like me. Not just an apothecary, but a murderer. A master of disguise.

Her request was simple and straightforward. *For my mistress's husband, with his breakfast. Daybreak, 4 Feb.* At once, I drew to mind a middle-aged housemaid, called to do the bidding of her mistress. And with an instinct perfected over the last two decades, I knew immediately the remedy most suited to this request: a chicken egg laced with *nux vomica.*

The preparation would take mere minutes; the poison was within reach. But for a reason yet unknown to me, something about the letter left me unsettled. It was not the subtle, woodsy odor of the parchment or the way the lower left corner curled forward slightly, as though once damp with tears. Instead, the disquiet brewed inside of *me.* An intuitive understanding that something must be avoided.

But what unwritten warning could reside on a single sheet of parchment, shrouded beneath pen strokes? None at all, I assured myself; this letter was no omen. My troubling thoughts were merely the result of my fatigue — the hour was late — and the persistent discomfort in my joints.

I drew my attention to my calfskin register on the table in front of me. My precious register was a record of life and death; an inventory of the many women who sought potions from here, the darkest of apothecary shops.

In the front pages of my register, the ink was soft, written with a lighter hand, void of grief and resistance. These faded, worn entries belonged to my mother. This apothecary shop for women's maladies, situated at 3 Back Alley, was hers long before it was mine.

On occasion I read her entries — *23 Mar 1767, Mrs. R. Ranford, Yarrow Milfoil 15 dr. 3x* — and the words evoked memories of her: the way her hair fell against the back of her neck as she ground the yarrow stem with the pestle, or the taut, papery skin of her hand as she plucked seeds from the flower's head. But my mother had not disguised her shop behind a false wall, and she had not slipped her remedies into vessels of dark red wine. She'd had no need to hide. The tinctures she dispensed were meant only for good: soothing the raw, tender parts of a new mother, or bringing menses upon a barren wife. Thus, she filled her register pages with the most benign of herbal remedies. They would raise no suspicion.

On my register pages, I wrote things such as nettle and hyssop and amaranth, yes, but also remedies more sinister: nightshade and hellebore and arsenic. Beneath the ink strokes of my register hid betrayal, anguish . . . and dark secrets.

Secrets about the vigorous young man who suffered an ailing heart on the eve of his wedding, or how it came to pass that a healthy new father fell victim to a sudden fever. My register laid it all bare: these were not weak hearts and fevers at all, but thorn apple juice and nightshade slipped into wines and pies by cunning women whose names now stained my register.

Oh, but if only the register told my own secret, the truth about how this all began. For I had documented every victim in these pages, all but one: *Frederick.* The sharp, black lines of his name defaced only my sullen heart, my scarred womb.

I gently closed the register, for I had no use of it tonight, and returned my attention to the letter. What worried me so? The edge of the parchment continued to catch my eye, as though something crawled beneath it. And the longer I remained at my table, the more my belly ached and my fingers trembled. In the distance, beyond the walls of the shop, the bells on a carriage sounded frighteningly similar to the chains on a constable's belt. But I assured myself that the bailiffs would not come tonight, just as they had not come for the last two decades. My shop, like my poisons, was too cleverly disguised. No man would find this place; it was buried deep behind a cupboard wall at the base of a twisted alleyway in the darkest depths of London.

I drew my eyes to the soot-stained wall that I had not the heart, nor the strength, to scrub clean. An empty bottle on a shelf caught my reflection. My eyes, once bright green like my mother's, now held little life within them. My cheeks, too, once flushed with vitality, were sallow and sunken. I had the appearance of a ghost, much older than my forty-one years of age.

Tenderly, I began to rub the round bone in my left wrist, swollen with heat like a stone left in the fire and forgotten. The discomfort in my joints had crawled through my body for years; it had grown so severe, I lived not a waking hour without pain. Every poison I dispensed brought a new wave of it upon me; some evenings, my fingers were so distended and stiff, I felt sure the skin would split open and expose what lay underneath.

Killing and secret-keeping had done this to me. It had begun to rot me from the inside out, and something inside meant to tear me open.

At once, the air grew stagnant, and smoke began to curl into the low stone ceiling of my hidden room. The candle was nearly spent, and soon the laudanum drops would wrap me in their heavy warmth. Night had long ago fallen, and she would arrive in just a few hours: the woman whose name I would add to my register and whose mystery I would begin to unravel, no matter the unease it brewed inside of me.

2
CAROLINE
PRESENT DAY, MONDAY

I wasn't supposed to be in London alone.

Celebratory anniversary trips are meant for two, not one, yet as I stepped out of the hotel into the bright light of a summer afternoon in London, the empty space next to me said otherwise. Today — our tenth wedding anniversary — James and I should have been together, making our way to the London Eye, the observation wheel overlooking the River Thames. We'd booked a nighttime ride in a VIP capsule, replete with a bottle of sparkling wine and a private host. For weeks, I'd imagined the dimly lit capsule swaying under the starry sky, our laughter punctuated only by the clinking of our champagne glasses and the touching of our lips.

But James was an ocean away. And I was in London alone, grieving and furious and jet-lagged, with a life-changing decision to make.

15

Instead of turning south toward the London Eye and the river, I headed in the opposite direction toward St. Paul's and Ludgate Hill. Keeping my eyes open for the nearest pub, I felt every bit a tourist in my gray sneakers and crossbody tote bag. My notebook rested inside, the pages covered in blue ink and doodled hearts with an outline of our ten-day itinerary. I'd only just arrived, and yet I couldn't bear to read through our made-for-two agenda and the playful notes we'd written to one another. *Southwark, couples' garden tour,* I'd written on one of the pages.

Practice making baby behind a tree, James had scribbled next to it. I'd planned to wear a dress, just in case.

Now I no longer needed the notebook, and I'd discarded every plan within. The back of my throat began to burn, tears approaching, as I wondered what else may soon be discarded. Our marriage? James was my college sweetheart; I didn't know life without him. I didn't know myself without him. Would I lose, too, my hopes for a baby? The idea of it made my stomach ache with want of more than just a decent meal. I longed to be a mother — to kiss those tiny, perfect toes and blow raspberries on the round belly of my baby.

I'd walked only a block when I spotted the entrance of a pub, The Old Fleet Tavern. But before I could venture inside, a rugged-looking fellow with a clipboard and stained khakis waved me down as I passed him on the sidewalk. With a wide grin on his face, the fiftysomething-year-old said, "Fancy joining us for mudlarking?"

Mudlarking? I thought. Is that some kind of dirt-nesting bird? I forced a smile and shook my head. "No, thank you."

He wasn't so easily deterred. "Ever read any Victorian authors?" he asked, his voice barely audible over the screech of a red tour bus.

At this, I stopped in my tracks. A decade ago, in college, I'd graduated with a degree in British history. I'd passed my coursework with decent grades, but I'd always been most interested in what lay *outside* the textbooks. The dry, formulaic chapters simply didn't interest me as much as the musty, antiquated albums stored in the archives of old buildings, or the digitized images of faded ephemera — playbills, census records, passenger manifest lists — I found online. I could lose myself for hours in these seemingly meaningless documents, while my classmates met at coffee shops to study. I couldn't attribute my unconventional interests to anything specific, I only knew that classroom debates about civil revolution and power-hungry world leaders left me yawning. To me, the allure of history lay in the minutiae of life long ago, the untold secrets of ordinary people.

"I have read a bit, yes," I said. Of course, I loved many of the classic British novels and read voraciously through school. At times, I had wished I'd pursued a degree in literature, as it seemed better suited to my interests. What I didn't tell him was that I hadn't read any Victorian literature — or any of my old British favorites, for that matter — in years. If this conversation resulted in a pop quiz, I'd fail miserably.

"Well, they wrote all about the mudlarkers — those countless souls scrounging about in the river for something old, something valuable. Might get your shoes a bit wet, but there's no better way to immerse yourself in the past. Tide comes in, tide goes out, overturning something new each time. You're welcome to join us on the tour, if you're up for the adventure. First time is always free. We'll be just on the other side of those brick buildings you see there . . ." He pointed. "Look for the stairs going to the river. Group's meeting at half two, as the tide's going out."

I smiled at him. Despite his unkempt appearance, his hazel eyes radiated warmth. Behind him, the wooden plaque reading The Old Fleet Tavern swung on a squeaky hinge, tempting me inside. "Thank you," I said, "but I'm headed to a . . . another appointment."

Truth was, I needed a drink.

He nodded slowly. "Very well, but if you change your mind, we'll be exploring until half five or so."

"Enjoy," I mumbled, transferring my bag to the other shoulder, expecting to never see the man again.

I stepped inside the darkened, damp taproom and nestled into a tall leather chair at the bar. Leaning forward to look at the beers on tap, I cringed as my arms landed in something wet — whatever sweat and ale had been left before me. I ordered a Boddingtons and waited impatiently for the cream-colored foam to rise to the surface and settle. At last, I took a deep drink, too worn-out to care that I had the beginning of a headache, the ale was lukewarm and a cramp had begun to tug on the left side of my abdomen.

The Victorians. I thought again about Charles Dickens, the author's name echoing in my ears like that of an ex-boyfriend, fondly forgotten; an interesting guy, but not promising enough for the long haul. I'd read many of his works — *Oliver Twist* had been a favorite, followed closely by *Great Expectations* — but I felt a subtle flash of embarrassment.

According to the man I'd met outside, the Victorians wrote "all about" this thing called mudlarking, and yet I didn't even know what the word meant. If James were here next to me, he'd most certainly tease me over the gaffe. He'd always joked that I "book-clubbed" my way through college reading gothic fairy tales late into the night when, according to him, I should have spent more time analyzing academic journals and developing my own theses about historical and political unrest. Such research, he'd said, was the only way a history degree could benefit anyone, because then I could pursue academia, a doctorate degree, a professorship.

In some ways, James had been right. Ten years ago, after graduation, I quickly realized my undergraduate history degree didn't offer the same career prospects as James's accounting degree. While my fruitless job search dragged on, he easily secured a high-paying job at a Big Four accounting firm in Cincinnati. I applied for several teaching roles at local high schools and community colleges, but as James had predicted, they all preferred an advanced degree.

Undeterred, I considered this an opportunity to delve further into my studies. With a sense of nervous excitement, I began the application process to attend graduate school at the University of Cambridge, just an hour north of London. James had been adamantly against the idea, and I soon knew why: just a few months after graduation, he walked me to the end of a pier overlooking the Ohio River, fell to a knee and tearfully asked me to be his wife.

Cambridge could have fallen off the map, for all I cared — Cambridge and advanced degrees and every novel ever written by Charles Dickens. From the moment I wrapped my arms around James's neck at the end of that pier and whispered *yes*, my identity as an aspiring historian rusted away, replaced with my identity as his soon-to-be wife. I tossed my graduate school application into the trash and eagerly thrust myself into the whirlwind of wedding planning, preoccupied with letterpress fonts on invitations and shades of pink for our peony centerpieces. And when the wedding was but a sparkling, riverfront memory, I poured my energy into shopping for our first home. We eventually settled on the Perfect Place: a three-bed, two-bath home at the end of a cul-de-sac in a neighborhood of young families.

The routine of married life fell evenly into place, as straight and predictable as the rows of dogwood trees lining the streets of our new neighborhood. And as James began to settle onto the first rung of the corporate ladder, my parents — who owned farmland just east of Cincinnati — presented me with an enticing offer: a salaried job at the family farm, handling basic accounting and administrative tasks. It would be stable, secure. *No unknowns.*

I'd considered the decision over the course of a few days, thinking only briefly of the boxes still in our basement, packed away with the dozens of books I'd adored in school. *Northanger Abbey. Rebecca. Mrs. Dalloway.* What good had they done me? James had been right: burying myself in antiquated documents and tales of haunted manors hadn't resulted in a single job offer. On the contrary, it had cost me tens of thousands of dollars in student loans. I began to resent the books that lay inside those boxes and felt sure my notion about studying at Cambridge had been the wild idea of a restless, unemployed college graduate.

Besides, with James's secure job, the right thing to do — the *mature* thing to do — was to stay put in Cincinnati with my new husband and our new home.

I accepted the offer at the family farm, much to James's delight. And Brontë and Dickens and everything else I'd adored for so many years remained in boxes, hidden in the far corner of our basement, unopened and eventually forgotten.

In the darkened pub, I took a long, deep drink of my ale. It was a wonder James agreed to come to London at all. While deciding on anniversary destinations, he'd made his preference known: a beachfront resort in the Virgin Islands, where he could waste away the days napping beside an empty cocktail glass. But we'd done a version of this daiquiri-drenched vacation last Christmas, so I begged James to consider something different, like England or Ireland. On the condition that we not waste time on anything too academic, like the rare book restoration workshop I'd briefly mentioned, he finally agreed to London. He relented, he said, because he knew visiting England had once been a dream of mine.

A dream which, only days ago, he'd lifted into the air like a crystal glass of champagne

23

and shattered between his fingers.

The bartender motioned to my half-empty glass, but I shook my head; one was enough. Feeling restless, I pulled out my phone and opened Facebook Messenger. Rose — my lifelong best friend — had sent me a message. You doing okay? Love you.

Then: Here's a pic of little Ainsley. She loves you, too. <3

And there she was, newborn Ainsley, swaddled in gray linen. A perfect, seven-pound newborn, my goddaughter, sleeping sweetly in the arms of my dear friend. I felt grateful she'd been born before I learned of James's secret; I'd been able to spend many sweet, content moments with the baby already. In spite of my grief, I smiled. If I lost all else, at least I'd have these two.

If social media was any indication, James and I seemed like the only ones in our circle of friends who were not yet pushing strollers and kissing mac-and-cheese-covered cheeks. And although waiting had been tough, it had been right for us: the accounting firm where James worked expected associates to wine and dine clients, often logging eighty-some hours per week. Though I'd wanted kids early in our marriage, James didn't want to deal with the stress of long hours and a young family. And so just as he had climbed the corporate ladder every day for a decade, so too did I put that little pink pill on the tip of my tongue and think to myself, *Someday*.

I glanced at today's date on my phone: June 2. Nearly four months had passed since James's firm had promoted him and put him on the partner track — which meant his long days onsite with clients were behind him.

Four months since we decided to try for a baby.

Four months since my *someday* had arrived.

But no baby yet.

I chewed at my thumbnail and closed my eyes. For the first time in four months, I felt glad that we hadn't gotten pregnant. Days ago, our marriage had begun to crumble under the crushing weight of what I'd discovered: our relationship no longer consisted of just two people. Another woman had intruded on us. What baby deserved such a predicament? No baby deserved it — not mine, not anyone's.

There was one problem: my period was due yesterday, and it had not yet shown. I hoped with all my might that jet lag and stress were to blame.

I took a final look at my best friend's new

child, feeling not envy but unease about the future. I would have loved for my child to be Ainsley's lifelong best friend, to have a connection just like the one I had with Rose. Yet after learning James's secret, I wasn't sure marriage remained in the cards for me, let alone motherhood.

For the first time in ten years, I considered that maybe I'd made a mistake at the edge of that pier, when I told James yes. What if I'd said no, or not yet? I highly doubted I'd still be in Ohio, spending my days at a job I didn't love and my marriage teetering precariously over the edge of a cliff. Would I have lived somewhere in London instead, teaching or researching? Maybe I would have my head stuck in fairy tales, as James liked to joke, but wouldn't that still be better than the nightmare in which I now found myself?

I'd always valued my husband's pragmatism and calculated nature. For much of our marriage, I viewed this as James's way of keeping me grounded, safe. When I ventured a spontaneous idea — anything falling outside of his predetermined goals and desires — he'd quickly bring me back to earth with his outline of the risks, the downside. This rationality was, after all, what had propelled him forward at his firm.

But now, a world away from James, I wondered for the first time if the dreams I once chased had been little more than an accounting problem to him. He'd been more concerned with *return on investment* and *risk management* than he'd been with my own happiness. And what I'd always considered sensible in James seemed, for the first time, something else: stifling and subtly manipulative.

I shifted in my seat, pulled my sticky thighs from the leather and flicked off my phone. Dwelling on home and the what-could-have-been would do me no good in London.

Thankfully, the few patrons inside The Old Fleet Tavern found nothing amiss about a thirty-four-year-old woman alone at the bar. I appreciated the lack of attention, and the Boddingtons had begun to ease its way through my aching, travel-worn body. I wrapped my hands tightly around the mug, the ring on my left hand pressing uncomfortably against the glass, and finished my drink.

As I stepped outside and considered where to go next — a nap at the hotel seemed much-deserved — I approached the place where the gentleman in khakis had stopped me earlier, inviting me to go . . .

27

what was it, mudlurking? No, mud*larking*. He'd said the group planned to meet just ahead, at the base of the steps, at half-past two. I pulled out my phone and checked the time: it showed 2:35 p.m. I quickened my step, suddenly rejuvenated. Ten years ago, this was exactly the sort of adventure I might have loved, following a kind old British fellow to the River Thames to learn about the Victorians and *mudlarkers*. No doubt James would have resisted this spontaneous adventure, but he wasn't here to hold me back.

Alone, I could do whatever I damn well pleased.

On my way, I passed the La Grande — our stay at the swanky hotel had been an anniversary gift from my parents — but hardly gave it a second glance. I approached the river, easily spotting the concrete steps leading down to the water. The muddy, opaque current in the deepest part of the channel churned as though something toiled underneath, agitated. I stepped forward, the pedestrians around me moving on to more predictable ventures.

The steps were steeper and in much worse condition than I would have believed in the center of an otherwise modernized city. They were at least eighteen inches deep and made of crushed stone, like an ancient concrete. I took them slowly, grateful for my sneakers and my easy-to-carry bag. At the bottom of the steps, I paused, noticing the silence around me. Across the river on the south bank, cars and pedestrians rushed past — but I could hear none of it from this distance. I heard only the soft lapping of the waves at the river's edge, the chime-like sound of pebbles swirling in the water and, above me, the lonely call of a seagull.

The mudlarking tour group stood a short distance away, listening attentively to their guide — the man I'd met on the street earlier. Steeling myself, I stepped forward, moving carefully amid the loose stones and muddy puddles. As I approached the group, I willed myself to leave all thoughts of home behind: James, the secret I'd uncovered, our unfulfilled desire for a baby. I needed a break from the grief suffocating me, the thorns of fury so sharp and unexpected they took my breath away. No matter how I decided to spend the next ten days, there was no use remembering and reliving what I'd learned about James forty-eight hours ago.

Here in London on this "celebratory" anniversary trip, I needed to discover what *I* truly wanted, and whether the life I desired still included James and the children we'd hoped to raise together.

But to do that, I needed to unbury a few truths of my own.

3
NELLA

FEBRUARY 4, 1791

When 3 Back Alley was a reputable women's apothecary shop belonging to my mother, it consisted of a single room. Alight with the flame of countless candles and often teeming with customers and their babies, the little shop gave a sense of warmth and safety. In those days, it seemed everyone in London knew of the shop for women's maladies, and the heavy oak door at the front of the shop rarely stayed shut for long.

But many years ago — after my mother's death, after Frederick's betrayal and after I began dispensing poisons to women across London — it became necessary to divide the space into two separate, distinct sections. This was easily accomplished with the installation of a wall of shelves, which split the room in two.

The first room, situated in the front, remained directly accessible from Back Alley. Anyone could open the front door — it

31

was nearly always unlocked — but most would assume they had arrived at the wrong destination. I now kept nothing in the room except an old grain barrel, and who had any interest in a bin of half-rotted pearl barley? Sometimes, if I was lucky, a nest of rats toiled away at one corner of the room, and this gave further impression of disuse and neglect. This room was my first disguise.

Indeed, many customers ceased coming. They had heard of my mother's death, and after seeing this empty room, they merely assumed the shop had closed for good.

The more curious or nefarious sort — like young boys with sticky fingers — were not deterred by the emptiness. Seeking something to snatch, they'd push deeper into the room, inspecting the shelves for wares or books. But they would find nothing, because I left nothing to steal, nothing of interest at all. And so onward they would go. Onward they always went.

What fools they were — all of them but the women who'd been told where to look by their friends, their sisters, their mothers. Only they knew that the bin of pearl barley served a very important function: it was a means of communication, a hiding place for letters whose contents dared not be uttered aloud. Only they knew that hidden within the wall of shelves, invisible, stood a door leading to my apothecary shop for women's maladies. Only they knew that I waited silently behind the wall, my fingers stained with the residue of poison.

It was where I now waited for the woman, my new patron, at daybreak.

Hearing the slow creak of the storage room door, I knew she had arrived. I peered through the nearly imperceptible cleft in the column of shelves, aiming to get my first dim look at her.

Taken aback, I covered my mouth with trembling fingers. Was it some mistake? This was no woman at all; it was a mere *girl,* not more than twelve or thirteen, dressed in a gray woolen gown with a threadbare navy cloak draped over her shoulders. Had she come to the wrong place? Perhaps she was one of those little thieves who was not fooled by my storage room, and she sought something to steal. If that were the case, she'd be better suited at a baker's shop, stealing cherry buns so she could fatten up a bit.

But the girl, for her youth, arrived at exactly daybreak. She stood still and sure of herself in the storage room, her gaze directed at the false wall of shelves behind which I stood.

No, this was no accidental visitor.

At once, I prepared to send her away on account of her age, but I stopped myself. In her note, she had said she needed something for her mistress's husband. What might become of my legacy if this mistress was well-known about town, and word got out that I sent a child away? Besides, as I continued to peek at the young girl through the cleft, she held high her head of thick black hair. Her eyes were round and bright, but she did not look down at her feet or back at the front door to the alley. She shivered slightly, but I felt sure it was on account of the cool air rather than her nerves. The girl stood too tall, too proud, for me to think her fearful.

With what did she brew her courage? The strict command of her mistress, or something more sinister?

I maneuvered the latch out of its hold, swung the column of shelves inward and motioned for the girl to come inside. Her eyes took in the tiny space in an instant, without need to even blink; the room was so small that if the girl and I stood together and spread our arms wide, we could nearly touch the opposite sides of it.

I followed her gaze across the shelves at

the back wall, littered with glass vials and tin funnels, gallipots and grinding stones. On a second wall, as far as possible from the fire, my mother's oaken cupboard held an assortment of earthenware and porcelain jars, meant for the tinctures and herbs that frayed and decayed in even the faintest light. On the wall nearest the door stood a long narrow counter as tall as the girl's shoulders; on it rested a collection of metal scales, glass and stone weights, and a few bound reference guides on women's maladies. And if the girl were to pry inside the drawers beneath the counter, she would find spoons, corks, candlesticks, pewter plates and dozens of sheets of parchment, many of them spoiled with hurried notes and calculations.

Treading carefully around her and latching the door, my most immediate concern was providing my new customer with a sense of safety and discretion. But my fears were unwarranted, for she plopped into one of my two chairs as though she'd been at my shop a hundred times. I could see her better now that she sat in the light. Her figure was a slender one, and she had clear, hazel eyes, almost too large for her oval-shaped face. Intertwining her fingers and setting her hands on the table, she looked at me and smiled. "Hello."

"Hello," I replied, surprised by her manner. In an instant, I felt a fool for having sensed any doom in the blush-colored letter written by this child. I wondered, too, about her beautiful penmanship at such a young age. As my sense of worry diminished, it was replaced with a relaxed curiosity; I desired to know more of the girl.

I turned to the hearth, which claimed one corner of the room. The pot of water that I had set over the fire a short time ago spewed entrails of steam. "I've hot-brewed some leaves," I said to the girl. I filled two mugs with the brew and set one of them in front of her.

She thanked me and pulled her mug toward her. Her gaze came to settle on the table, on which rested our mugs, a single lit candle, my register and the letter she'd left in the bin of pearl barley: *For my mistress's husband, with his breakfast. Daybreak, 4 Feb.* The girl's cheeks, pink upon her arrival, remained flushed with youth, life. "What kind of leaves?"

"Valerian," I told her, "spiced with cinnamon bark. A few sips to warm the body, a few more to brighten and relax the mind."

We were quiet, then, for a minute or so, but it was not uncomfortable in the way that it can be between adults. I supposed the girl

36

to be grateful, foremost, to be out of the cold. I gave her a few moments to warm herself, while I went to my counter and busied myself with a few small black stones. They needed smoothing along the grinding board, after which they would make ideal vial stoppers. Aware of the girl watching me, I lifted the first stone and, pressing down with my palm, rolled it, spun it around and rolled it again. Ten or fifteen seconds was all I could manage before I had to stop and slow my breath.

A year ago, I was stronger, and my strength was such that I could roll and smooth these stones in a matter of minutes, without so much as brushing a hair from my face. But on this day, with the child watching me, I could not go on — my shoulder ached too badly. Oh, how I did not understand this ailment; months ago it had been borne in my elbow, and then shifted into the opposite wrist, and only very recently, the heat had begun to slip into the joints of my fingers.

The girl remained still, her fingers wrapped tightly around her mug. "What's that bowl of creamy stuff, over there by the fire?"

I turned away from the stones to look at the hearth. "A salve," I said, "of hog's lard and purple foxglove."

"You're warming it, then, for it's too hard."

I paused at her quick understanding. "Yes, that's right."

"What is the salve for?"

Heat rose in my face. I could not tell her that the leaves of purple foxglove, when dried and crushed, sucked the heat and blood from the skin, and therefore assisted a great deal in the days after a woman had birthed a child — an experience unknown to girls the age of this one. "It is for a tear in the skin," I offered, taking a seat.

"Oh, a poisonous salve for a tear in the skin?"

Shaking my head, I said, "No poison in this, child."

Her little shoulders tensed. "But Mrs. Amwell — my mistress — told me you sell poison."

"I do, but poison is not *all* I sell. The women who have been here for deadly remedies have seen the extent of my shelves, and some have whispered of it to their most trusted friends. I dispense all sorts of oils and tinctures and draughts — anything an honorable apothecary might require in her shop."

Indeed, when I began dispensing poisons

many years ago, I did not simply clear my shelves of all but arsenic and opium. I continued to keep the ingredients needed to remedy most afflictions, supplies as benign as clary or tamarisk. Just because a woman has rid herself of one malady — a devious husband, for instance — does not mean she is immune to all other maladies. My register was proof of it; interspersed among the deadly tonics were also many healing ones.

"And only girls come here," the child said.

"Did your mistress tell you that, too?"

"Yes'm."

"Well, she was not mistaken. Only girls come here." With the exception of one long ago, no man had ever stepped foot in my shop of poisons. I *only* aided women.

My mother had held tight to this principle, instilling in me from an early age the importance of providing a safe haven — a place of healing — for women. London grants little to women in need of tender care; instead, it crawls with gentlemen's doctors, each as unprincipled and corrupt as the next. My mother committed to giving women a place of refuge, a place where they might be vulnerable and forthcoming about their ailments without the lascivious appraisal of a man.

The ideals of gentlemen's medicine did

not align with my mother's, either. She believed in the proven remedies of the sweet, fertile earth, not the schemes diagrammed in books and studied by bespectacled gentlemen with brandy on their tongues.

The young girl in my shop looked around, the light of the flame in her eyes. "How clever. I like this place, though it is a bit dark. How do you know when it is morning? There are no windows."

I pointed at the clock on the wall. "There is more than one way to tell the time," I said, "and a window would do me no service at all."

"You must grow tired of the dark, then."

Some days, I could not distinguish night from day, as I had lost the intuitive sense of wakefulness long ago. My body seemed always in a state of fatigue. "I am accustomed to it," I said.

How strange it was, sitting across from this child. The last child to sit in this very room was *me,* decades ago, observing my own mother as she worked. But I was not this girl's mother, and her presence began to pull at me in an uncomfortable way. Though her naivety was endearing, she was very young. No matter what she thought of my shop, she could not need anything else I dispensed — the fertility aids, the cramp barks. She was here only for poison, so I aimed to bring us back to the subject at hand. "You have not touched your hot brew."

She looked at it skeptically. "I do not mean to be rude, but Mrs. Amwell told me to be very careful —"

I held up my hand to stop her. She was a smart girl. I took her mug into my own hands, drank deeply from it and set it back down in front of her.

At once, she grabbed the mug and lifted it to her own lips, emptying the entire thing. "I was *parched,*" she said. "Oh, thank you, how delicious! May I have more?"

I maneuvered myself out of the chair, taking two small steps to the hearth. I tried not to wince as I lifted the heavy pot to refill her mug.

"What is the matter with your hand?" she asked from behind me.

"What do you mean?"

"You've been holding it funny this whole time, as though it hurts. Did you injure it?"

"No," I said, "and it is rude to pry." But I regretted my tone with her instantly. She was merely inquisitive, just as I was once. "How old are you?" I asked her in a softer tone.

41

"Twelve."

I nodded, having expected something thereabouts. "Quite young."

She hesitated and, by the rhythmic movement of her skirts, I presumed she was tapping her foot on the floor. "I have never —" She paused. "I have never killed anyone."

I nearly laughed. "You're only a child. I wouldn't expect you to have killed many people in your short life." My eyes fell on a shelf behind her where there rested a small porcelain dish the color of milk. Inside the dish lay four brown hen's eggs, poison disguised within. "And what is your name?"

"Eliza. Eliza Fanning."

"Eliza Fanning," I repeated, "aged twelve."

"Yes, miss."

"And your mistress sent you here today, is that right?" The arrangement told me that Eliza's mistress must trust her greatly.

But the child paused and furrowed her brow, and what she said next surprised me. "It was her idea initially, yes, but I was the one to suggest the breakfast table. My master fancies the chophouses for supper with his friends, and sometimes is gone for a full night or two. I thought breakfast might be the best idea."

I looked to Eliza's letter on the table and ran my thumb across one edge. Given her youth, I felt it necessary to remind her of something. "And you understand that this will not just harm him? This will not just make him *ill*, but —" I slowed my words. "This will *kill* him, as surely as it would kill an animal? That is what you and your mistress intend?"

Little Eliza looked up at me, her eyes sharp. She folded her hands neatly in front of her. "Yes, miss." As she said it, she did not so much as flinch.

4
CAROLINE
PRESENT DAY, MONDAY

"Couldn't resist the old call of the river, eh?" said a familiar voice. Just ahead, the guide split off from the tour group and stepped toward me, wearing oversize, knee-high galoshes and blue cleaning gloves.

"I guess not." Truth be told, I still didn't even know what we were doing in the riverbed, but that was part of the appeal of it. I couldn't help but grin at him. "Do I need some of those?" I nodded at his boots.

He shook his head. "Your sneakers will be fine, but take a pair of these." From a backpack, he withdrew a pair of used, mud-stained rubber gloves, not unlike his own. "Wouldn't want to cut yourself. Come on, we're down here." He started off, then turned back to me. "Oh, I'm Alfred, by the way. But they all call me 'Bachelor Alf.' Funny, too, seeing as how I've been married going on forty years. Nah, the old nickname's on account of the fact that I've

44

found so many of them bent-up rings."

Seeing the confused look on my face as I tugged on my gloves, he went on. "Hundreds of years ago, men would bend metal rings to display their strength before asking a lady for her hand. But if the lady didn't want to marry the man, you see, she threw the ring off the bridge and told him off. I've found hundreds of the rings. Seems plenty of gentlemen walked away from this river as bachelors, if you gather what I'm saying. Strange tradition anyhow."

I looked down at my hands. My own ring was now hidden beneath a filthy rubber glove. Tradition hadn't done much good for me, either. A few weeks ago, before my life came to a shuddering halt, I bought James a vintage box for his new business cards. The box was made of tin, the traditional gift on a tenth anniversary, meant to signify durability in a marriage. I'd had it engraved with James's initials, and it arrived in the mail the evening before our planned trip to London — right on time.

But not much else had gone right since then.

As soon as the box had arrived, I took it upstairs to hide in my suitcase. As I rummaged about in the closet, I grabbed a few additional items I hadn't yet packed: an assortment of lingerie, a strappy pair of heels, a few essential oils. I sorted and set aside the lavender, absolute rose and sweet orange, among others. James particularly liked the sweet orange.

Sitting cross-legged on the walk-in closet floor, I held up a piece of lingerie I was undecided on, a mess of bright red string that, somehow, fit around one's butt and between one's legs. Shrugging, I tossed it into my suitcase next to a drugstore pregnancy test which, at the time, I desperately hoped to use in London if my period didn't show. Which reminded me — the prenatal vitamins. At my doctor's recommendation, I'd begun taking them as soon as we started trying to conceive.

As I walked to the bathroom to grab the vitamins, a buzzing sound — James's cell phone on the dresser — caught my attention. I gave it a disinterested, passing glance, but it buzzed a second time and two letters caught my eye: XO.

Trembling, I leaned forward to read the messages. They'd been sent by someone listed in James's contacts as B.

I'm going to miss you so much, read the first one. Then:

Don't drink so much bubbly that you forget about last Friday. XO.

The second message, to my horror, included a picture of black panties inside a desk drawer. Beneath the panties, I recognized a colorful pamphlet with the logo of James's employer. The picture must have been taken at his workplace.

I stared at the phone, stunned. Last Friday, I'd spent the night at the hospital with Rose and her husband while Rose was in labor. James had been at the office, working. Or *not* working, I now suspected.

No, no, it must be some mistake. My palms grew clammy. Downstairs, I heard James moving about the kitchen. I took several steadying breaths and grabbed the phone, my fingers clutching it like a weapon.

I rushed down the steps. "Who's B?" I demanded, holding up the phone to show James.

The look in his eyes said it all.

"Caroline," he said steadily, as though I was a client and he meant to present me with a root cause analysis. "It isn't what you think."

With a shaky hand, I navigated to the first message. " 'I'm going to miss you so much'?" I read aloud.

James placed his hands on the counter, leaning forward. "It's just a coworker. She's had a thing for me for a few months. We joke about it at the office. Seriously, Caroline, it's nothing."

A downright lie. I didn't reveal — yet — the contents of the second text message. "Has anything ever happened between you two?" I asked, willing my voice to remain calm.

He exhaled slowly, running his hand through his hair. "We met at the promotion event a few months ago," he finally said. His firm had hosted a dinner cruise in Chicago for new promotees; spouses were welcome to attend on their own dime, but we were saving diligently for London and I'd thought nothing of skipping out. "We kissed that night, just once, after too much to drink. I could barely see straight." He stepped toward me, his eyes soft, pleading. "It was a terrible lapse in judgment. Nothing else has happened, and I haven't seen her since —"

Another lie. I pushed the phone forward again, pointing to the pair of black panties in the desk drawer. "You sure? Because she just sent this picture, telling you not to forget about last Friday. Seems she keeps her underwear in your desk now?"

A sheen of sweat formed on his forehead as he scrambled for an explanation. "It's just a prank, Car —"

"Bullshit," I interrupted, tears spilling down my face. A nameless figure took form in my mind — the woman who owned those tiny black panties — and I understood, for the first time in my life, the incalculable fury that drives some people to murder. "You didn't get much work done at the office on Friday, did you?"

James didn't reply; his silence was as damning as an admission.

I knew then I couldn't trust anything else he said. I suspected he'd not only seen the black panties with his own eyes, but he'd probably pulled them off her. James rarely found himself short for words; if nothing serious had happened between the two of them, he'd be adamantly defending himself now. Instead, he remained mute, guilt written all over his crestfallen face.

The secret — his actual infidelity — was bad enough. But in this exact moment, the raw, ugly questions about *her,* and the extent of their relationship, seemed less critical than his harboring of the secret for months. What if I hadn't found the phone? How long would he have hidden this from me? Just last night, we'd made love. How dare he bring that woman's ghost to our bed, the sacred place where we'd been trying to conceive a child.

My shoulders shook, my hands trembled. "All these nights trying for a baby. Were you thinking of her, instead of —" But I gasped over my own words, unable to say the word *me.* I couldn't bear to attach this travesty to *us,* to *my* marriage.

Before he could answer, the nausea pressed upward, relentless, and I made a run for the toilet, slamming the bathroom door behind me and locking it. I heaved five, seven, ten times, until there remained nothing left inside of me.

The roar of a boat engine nearby on the river jolted me out of the memory. I looked up to find Bachelor Alf watching me, his hands spread open. "Are you ready?" he asked.

Embarrassed, I nodded and followed him to a group of five or six others. A few of them knelt among the rocks, sifting through pebbles. I stepped closer to my guide and spoke in a hushed voice. "I'm sorry, but I don't entirely understand what mudlarking *is.* Are we searching for something?"

He looked at me and chuckled, his belly trembling. "I never did tell you, did I! Well, here's all you need to know — the Thames runs straight through the city of London, and for a long way, at that. Little remnants of history, all the way back to the Roman era, can be found right here in the mud if you go searching long enough. Long ago, mudlarkers found old coins, rings, pottery, and they'd go on to sell it. That's what the Victorians wrote about, them poor kids trying to buy bread. But here today, we're just searching because we love it. You keep what you find, too, that's our rule. Look, right there," he said, pointing at my foot. "You're about standing on a clay pipe." He leaned over and picked it up. It looked like a narrow stone to me, but Bachelor Alf wore a mile-wide smile. "You'll find a thousand of these in a day. No big deal, unless it's your first time. This would have been stuffed with tobacco leaves. See, here, the ridges running up the barrel? I'd date this sometime between 1780 and 1820." He paused, waiting for my reaction.

I raised my eyebrows and looked closer at the clay pipe, suddenly overcome with the thrill of holding in my hands an object last touched centuries ago. Earlier, Bachelor Alf had said the tide turns over new mysteries each time it advances and recedes. What other old artifacts might be within close

51

reach? I checked my gloves to ensure they were pulled taut around my hands, then knelt down; perhaps I would find a few more clay pipes, or a coin or bent ring, as Bachelor Alf said. Or maybe I could remove my own ring, bend it in half and toss it into the water to join all the other emblems of failed love.

Slowly, I scanned my eyes over the rocks and ran my fingertips across the glistening, rust-colored pebbles. But after a minute of doing this, I frowned; it all looked very much the same. Even if a diamond ring were buried in the silt, I doubted that I would spot it.

"Do you have any tips," I shouted to Bachelor Alf, "or a shovel, perhaps?" He stood a few meters away, inspecting an egg-shaped thing that one of the others had found.

He laughed. "The Port of London Authority prohibits shovels, unfortunately, or any digging at all. We're only allowed to search the surface. So it's a bit like fate if you find something, or at least I like to think so."

Fate, or a colossal waste of time. But it was the riverbed or a cold, empty king-size bed at the hotel, so I took a few steps forward, closer to the waterline, and knelt down again, waving away a swarm of gnats that hovered at my feet. I scanned my eyes slowly over the pebbles and caught a glimmer of something shiny and reflective. I gasped, ready to call Bachelor Alf over to inspect my find. But as I stepped closer to pull the thin, shiny object toward me, I realized I'd merely grasped the pearlescent, rotting tail of a dead fish.

"Ugh," I groaned. "Gross."

Suddenly, there came an excited shriek behind me. I turned to see one of the others — a middle-aged woman bent down low, the tips of her hair almost touching a sandy puddle beneath her — holding up a whitish, sharp-edged rock. She scrubbed furiously at the front of it with her gloved hand and then held it up proudly.

"Ah, a bit of delftware!" Bachelor Alf exclaimed. "Be-*auti*-ful, too, I might add. Can't find a blue like that anymore. Cerulean, discovered late eighteenth century. Nowadays, it's a cheap dye. See there —" He pointed, tracing the pattern for the excited woman. "It appears to be the edge of a canoe, perhaps a dragon boat."

The woman happily dropped the fragment into a bag and everyone resumed their search.

"Listen here, folks," Bachelor Alf explained. "The hint is to let your subconscious find the anomaly. Our brains are meant to identify breaks in a pattern. We evolved that way, many millions of years ago. You are not searching for a *thing* so much as you are searching for an inconsistency of things, or an absence."

Well, there were a number of things absent for me at the moment, not the least of which was any security or surety about what the rest of my life might entail. Following James's news, after I'd locked myself in the bathroom, he'd tried to break his way inside where I lay curled up on the bath mat. I begged him to leave me alone; each time I asked, he responded with some plea, a variation of *Let me make this up to you* or *I will spend my life fixing this.* All I'd wanted was for him to go away.

I'd called Rose, too, and shared the entire, miserable thing with her. Aghast and with a crying infant in the background, she'd patiently listened as I told her I couldn't imagine going to London with him the next day to celebrate our anniversary.

"Then don't go *with* him," she said. "Go alone." Our lives might have looked vastly different at that moment, but in my moment of despair, Rose could clearly see what I could not: I needed to be far, far away from James. I couldn't bear to be so near his hands, his lips; they stirred my imagination, made my stomach churn yet again. In this way, my impending flight to London had been a life vest thrown overboard. I reached for it eagerly, desperately.

A few hours before the flight, when James saw me packing the last of my clothes into my suitcase, he looked at me and shook his head in silence, visibly broken, while fury ran hot through my sob-wracked, sleep-deprived body.

But while I needed time and distance, I had been reminded of James's absence at every turn. The airport check-in attendant looked strangely at me, clicking her bright orange nails against the desk while asking the whereabouts of Mr. Parcewell, the second individual on the reservation. The lady at the hotel desk frowned when I stated that only one room key would be necessary. And now, of course, I found myself in a place I never expected: a muddy riverbed, searching for artifacts and, as Alf had said, *inconsistencies*.

"You must trust your instinct more than your eyes," Bachelor Alf went on.

As I considered his words, I caught the sulfuric odor of sewage from somewhere downriver, and an unexpected wave of nausea rolled over me. Apparently I wasn't the only one bothered by the smell, as a few others let out an audible groan.

"That's another reason we don't dig with shovels," Bachelor Alf explained. "The odors down here, they're none too pleasant."

As I continued to make my way along the edge of the water, searching for an area undisturbed by the others, I took a misstep and ended up ankle-deep in a murky puddle. Gasping at the sudden shock of cold water inside my shoe, I considered what Bachelor Alf might say if I bailed early on the tour. Unpleasant smells aside, the adventure had done little to lift my mood.

I checked my phone and decided to give it twelve more minutes, until 3:00 p.m. If things hadn't perked up by then — a small find, even mildly interesting — I'd kindly excuse myself.

Twelve minutes. A fraction of a lifetime, yet enough to alter the course of it.

5
NELLA
FEBRUARY 4, 1791

I walked to the shelf behind Eliza and retrieved the small, milk-colored dish. Resting inside were the four brown hen's eggs, two of them slightly larger than the others. I set the dish of eggs onto the table.

Leaning forward as though badly wanting to reach for the dish, Eliza set her hands on the table, her palms leaving a damp residue.

In truth, I saw much of my own childhood self in her — the wide-eyed curiosity about something novel, something that most other children don't get to experience — though that part of me felt a thousand years dead. The difference was that I had first seen the contents of this shop — the vials and scales and stone weights — at a much younger age than twelve. My mother introduced them to me as soon as I had the ability to lift and sort objects, to distinguish one from another, to order and rearrange.

When I was only six or seven and my at-

57

tention span was fleeting, my mother taught me simple, easy things, like colors: the vials of blue and black oil must stay on this shelf, and the red and yellow on that shelf. As I entered adolescence and became more skilled, more discerning, the tasks grew in difficulty. She might, for instance, dump an entire jar of hops onto the table, spread out the dry, bitter cones and ask me to re-arrange them according to complexion. As I worked, my mother would toil beside me with her tinctures and brews, explaining to me the difference between scruples and drachms, gallipots and cauldrons.

These were my playthings. Whereas other children amused themselves with blocks and sticks and cards in muddy alleyways, I spent my entire childhood in this very room. I came to know the color, consistency and flavor of hundreds of ingredients. I studied the great herbalists and memorized the Latin names within the pharmacopoeias. Indeed, there existed little doubt that someday, I would preserve my mother's shop and carry on her legacy of goodwill to women.

I never intended to stain that legacy — to leave it twisted and tarnished.

"Eggs," Eliza whispered, jolting me from my reverie. She looked up at me, confused.

"You have a chicken that lays poisonous eggs?"

Despite the seriousness of my meeting with Eliza, I could not help but laugh. It was a perfectly logical thing for a child to say, and I leaned back in my chair. "No, not quite." I lifted one of the eggs, showed it to her and returned it to the dish. "You see here, if we look at these four eggs together, can you tell me which two are the largest?"

Eliza furrowed her brow, bent down until the table was level with her eyes and studied the eggs for several seconds. Then abruptly she sat up, a proud look on her face, and pointed. "These two," she declared.

"Good." I nodded. "The *larger* two. You must remember that. The larger two, they are the poisonous ones."

"The large ones," she repeated. She took a sip of her tea. "But how?"

I put three of the eggs back in the dish, but kept one of the larger ones out. I turned it in my hand so that my palm cupped the fat base of the egg. "What you can't see, Eliza, is a tiny hole here at the top of the egg. It is covered, now, with a matching wax, but if you'd been here yesterday, you would have seen a tiny black dot where I inserted the poison with a needle."

"It did not break!" she exclaimed, as

59

though I had demonstrated a magick trick. "And I cannot even see the wax."

"Precisely. And yet, there is poison inside — enough to kill someone."

Eliza nodded, gazing at the egg. "What kind of poison is it?"

"*Nux vomica,* rat poison. An egg is the ideal place for the crushed seed, as the yolk — viscous and cool — preserves it, no different than if there were a baby chicken inside." I returned the egg to the dish with the others. "You'll be using the eggs soon?"

"Tomorrow morning," Eliza said. "When he is home, my mistress and her husband eat together." She paused, as though imagining the breakfast table laid out before her. "I will give my mistress the two smaller eggs."

"And how will you tell them apart, after you have dumped them into the pan?"

This stumped her, but only briefly. "I will cook the smaller eggs first, set them on the plate meant for my mistress and then cook the larger eggs."

"Very good," I said. "It will not take long. Within seconds, he may complain of a burning sensation in his mouth. Be sure to serve the eggs as hot as you can so he does not know any better — perhaps underneath a gravy or pepper sauce. He will think he's

60

only burned his tongue with the heat. Soon after, he will feel nauseous, and he will most certainly want to lie down." I leaned forward, making sure Eliza clearly understood what I was to say next. "I suggest you do not permit yourself to see him after this."

"Because he will be dead, you mean," she said, expressionless.

"Not immediately," I explained. "In the hours after ingesting *nux vomica,* most victims suffer a rigid spine. They may arch backward, like their body has been strung into a bow. I have never seen it myself, but I have been told it is horrifying. Indeed, the cause of a lifetime of nightmares." I leaned back into my chair, softening my gaze. "When he dies, of course, this rigidity will release. He will look much more peaceful then."

"And later, if someone asks to inspect the kitchen or the pans?"

"They will find nothing," I assured her.

"Because of the magick?"

Placing my hands in my lap, I shook my head. "Little Eliza, let me make it very clear — this is not magick. These are not spells and incantations. These are earthly things, as real as the smudge of dust there on your cheek." I licked the pad of my thumb, bent forward and ran it across her cheek. Satisfied, I sat back in my chair. "Magick and disguise may achieve the same end, but I assure you, they are very different things." A look of confusion crossed her face. "Do you know the meaning of *disguise*?" I added.

She shook her head, shrugged one shoulder.

I motioned to the hidden door through which Eliza had come. "When you came into the storage room this morning on the other side of where we sit now, did you know that I watched you from a tiny hole set into the wall?" I pointed to the entrance of my hidden room.

"No," she said. "I had no idea you were back *here*. When I first came in and found it empty, I thought you would come in off the alley, behind me. I would very much like one of these hidden rooms in a house someday."

I tilted my head toward her. "Well, if you have something to hide, you very well might need to build yourself a hidden room."

"Has it been here always?"

"No. When I was a child and worked here with my mother, there was no need for this room. We did not have poisons back then."

The girl frowned. "You have not always sold poisons?"

"Not always, no." Though there was little sense in sharing the details with young Eliza, the admission unfurled a painful memory.

Twenty years ago, my mother developed a cough at the start of the week, a fever by midweek, and was dead by Sunday. Gone in the short span of six days. At the age of twenty-one, I had lost my only family, my only friend, my great teacher. My mother's work had become my work, and our tinctures were all I knew about the world. I wished, at the time, that I had died with her.

I could hardly keep the shop afloat, such was the sea of grief pulling me under. I couldn't call on my father, having never known him. Decades ago, as a boatman, he'd lived in London several months — just long enough to seduce my mother — before his crew set sail again. I had no siblings, few friends to speak of. The life of an apothecary is a strange, solitary one. The very nature of my mother's business meant we spent more time in the companionship of potions than people. After she left me, I believed my heart had fractured, and I feared my mother's legacy — and the shop — would also meet their demise.

But like an elixir splashed onto the very

flame of my grief, a young, dark-haired man named Frederick entered my life. At the time, I'd thought the chance encounter a blessing; his presence began to cool and soften so much that had gone awry. He was a meat merchant, making quick work of the mess I'd accumulated since my mother's death: debts I had not paid, dyes I had not inventoried, dues I had not collected. And even after the shop's figures had been fixed, Frederick remained. He did not want to be apart from me, nor me from him.

Whereas I'd once thought myself skilled in only the intricacies of my apothecary shop, I soon realized my expertise in other techniques, the release between two bodies, a remedy that couldn't be found in the vials lining my walls. In the weeks to follow, we fell terribly, wonderfully in love. My sea of grief grew shallower; I could breathe again, and I could envision the future — a future with Frederick.

I couldn't have known that mere months after falling in love with him, I would dispense a fatal dose of rat poison to kill him.

The first betrayal. The first victim. The beginning of a stained legacy.

"The shop must not have been very amusing back then," Eliza said, turning her head

64

away as though disappointed. "No poisons, and no hidden room? Humph. Anyone should like a secret room."

Though her innocence was enviable, she was too young to understand the curse of a once-loved place — hidden room or not — that had been marred by loss. "It is not about amusement, Eliza. It is about *concealment.* That is what it means to disguise something. Anyone can buy poison, but you cannot simply drop a pellet of it into one's scrambled eggs, because the officials may find residue or the box of poison in the trash. No, it must be so cleverly disguised that it is untraceable. The poison is disguised in that egg just as my shop is disguised within the bowels of an old storage room. That way, anyone not meant to be here will undoubtedly turn around and leave. The storage room at the front is a measure of protection for me, you might say."

Eliza nodded, her bun bobbing at the base of her neck. She would soon be a beautiful young woman, more handsome than most, with her long eyelashes and the sharp angles of her face. She hugged the dish of eggs to her chest. "I suppose this is all I need, then." She pulled several coins from her pocket and set them on the table. I counted them quickly: four shillings, sixpence.

She stood, then touched her lips with her fingertips. "But how shall I transport them? I fear they may break inside the pocket of my gown."

I had sold poison to women three times her age who thought nothing of the vials snapping inside their pocket; Eliza, it seemed, was wiser than all of them put together. I handed her a reddish glass jar and, together, we carefully placed each egg in the jar, then covered it with a centimeter of wood ash, before placing the next egg on top. "You must still handle it carefully," I warned. "And —" I placed a hand softly over one of hers. "One egg will do the trick if it must."

Her look darkened, and in that moment I sensed that, despite the youthfulness and buoyancy she had demonstrated thus far, she did indeed understand the gravity of what she meant to do. "Thank you, Miss, ah —"

"Nella," I said. "Nella Clavinger. And what is *his* name?"

"Thompson Amwell," she said confidently. "Of Warwick Lane, near the cathedral." She lifted up the jar to ensure the eggs were properly nestled within, but then she frowned. "A bear," she observed, gazing at the small image etched onto the jar. My mother had decided upon the bear etching long ago, as there were countless Back Alleys in London, but only ours ran next to a Bear Alley. The little etching on the jar was harmless enough, and recognized only by those who needed to know.

"Yes," I urged, "so you do not mix up the jar with another one."

Eliza stepped to the door. With a steady hand, she ran a single finger down one of the blackened stones near the entrance. It left a sharp line in the soot, revealing a finger-width band of unblemished stone. She smiled, amused as if she'd just drawn me a picture on a spare sheet of paper. "Thank you, Miss Nella. I must say that I loved your tea and I love this hidden shop, and I very much hope we meet again."

I raised my eyebrows. Most of my customers were not killers by trade and, unless she returned needing a medicinal remedy, I did not expect to see her again. But I merely smiled at the inquisitive girl. "Yes," I said, "perhaps we will meet again." I unlatched the door, swung it in and watched as Eliza exited through the storage room and out onto the alley, her small frame melting into the shadows outside.

Once she had gone, I spent a few minutes

thinking about the girl's visit. She was a strange young thing. I had no doubt she would accomplish her task, and I was grateful for the momentary gaiety she brought into my otherwise cheerless shop of poisons. I was glad I had not refused her, glad I had not heeded the ominous feeling first brought on by her letter.

Taking my seat once again at the table, I pulled my register close. I turned to the back, locating the next empty space, and prepared to write my entry.

Then, dipping the nib into the well of ink, I put it to the paper and wrote:

Thompson Amwell. Egg prep NV. 4 Feb 1791. On account of Ms. Eliza Fanning, aged twelve.

6

CAROLINE

I shook off the mud from my wet shoe and continued along the edge of the water. As I distanced myself from the rest of the mud-larking tour group, their quiet chatter disappeared, and the soft lapping of the gentle river waves urged me toward the waterline. I glanced upward to the sky; a bruised-looking cloud moved overhead. I shivered and waited for it to pass, but more followed close behind. I feared a storm was fast approaching.

Crossing my arms, I glanced at the ground around my feet, an unvarying band of gray- and copper-colored rocks. *Look for inconsistencies,* Bachelor Alf had said. I stepped closer to the water, observing the way the low waves seeped toward me and withdrew in a steady, even rhythm, until a boat rushed past, forcing a gush of water close. Then I heard it: a hollow popping sound, like water bubbles caught in a bottle.

As the water receded, I stepped closer to the sound and spotted a glass container, bluish in color, nestled between two stones. An old soda bottle, perhaps.

I knelt down to inspect it and tugged at the narrow neck of the bottle, but its base was lodged firmly between the stones. While I maneuvered it out, I spotted a tiny image on one side of the bottle. A trademark or company logo, perhaps? I pulled one of the larger rocks away, freeing the object at last and allowing me to lift it from its crevice.

The bottle stood no more than five inches tall — more of a vial, given its small size — and was made of translucent, sky blue glass, hidden beneath a layer of caked-on mud. I dipped the vial into the water and used my rubber-gloved thumb to scrub away the dirt, then held it up to inspect it more closely. The image on the side seemed a rudimentary etching, likely done by hand rather than with a machine, and appeared to be an animal of some kind.

Though I had no idea what I'd found, I thought it sufficiently interesting to hail Bachelor Alf. But he'd already begun walking toward me. "Whatcha got?" he asked.

"Not sure," I said. "Some kind of vial with a little animal etched onto it."

Bachelor Alf took the vial, lifting it up to

his face. He turned the bottle over and scratched his fingernail against the glass. "How odd. Very much like an apothecary's vial, but typically we'd see other markings — a company name, date, address. Perhaps this is just a household item, then. A way for someone to practice his etching skills. I do hope they improved a bit from this." He stood silent a moment as he studied the bottom of the vial. "The glass is quite uneven in places, too. It's not factory-made, that's for sure, so it must be quite old. It's yours to keep if you'd like." He spread his hands wide. "Fascinating, isn't it? This is the best job in the world, if I don't say so myself."

I forced a half smile, somewhat envious that I couldn't say the same about my own job. Admittedly, plugging numbers into outdated software on an outdated PC at the family farm didn't often leave me smiling as big as Bachelor Alf did now. Instead, I spent day after day at a wretched yellow oak desk, the same at which my mother worked for more than three decades. Ten years ago, unemployed with a new home, the job opportunity at the farm had seemed too good to pass up — but I sometimes wondered why I'd stayed so long. Just because I couldn't teach history at a local school didn't mean I was out of options; surely

71

something more interesting existed than administrative work at the farm.

But *kids.* With children someday in the picture, the stability of my job was paramount, as James often liked to remind me. And so I'd stayed put, and I'd grown to tolerate the frustration and uncomfortable musings about whether I'd missed out on something bigger. Maybe even something altogether different.

As I stood in the riverbed with Bachelor Alf, I considered the possibility that long ago, he also used to work an uninteresting desk job. Did he finally decide that life was too short to be miserable forty hours a week? Or maybe he was braver than that and bolder than me, and he'd turned his passion — mudlarking — into a career. I considered asking him, but before I had the chance, another member of the tour called him over to inspect a find.

I took the vial back from him and leaned forward, intending to put it back in its spot, but a sentimental, wistful part of me refused. I felt a strange connection with whomever last held the vial in their hands — an inherent kinship with the person whose fingerprints last impressed on the glass as mine did now. What tincture had they blended within this sky blue bottle?

And who did they mean to help, to heal?

My eyes began to sting as I considered the odds of finding this object in the river-bed: a historical artifact, probably once belonging to a person of little significance, someone whose name wasn't recorded in a textbook, but whose life was fascinating all the same. This was precisely what I found so enchanting about history: centuries might separate me from whomever last held the vial, but we shared in the exact sensation of its cool glass between our fingers. It felt as though the universe, in her strange and nonsensical way, meant to reach out to me, to remind me of the enthusiasm I once had for the trifling bits of bygone eras, if only I could look beneath the dirt that had accumulated over time.

It dawned on me then that since touching down at Heathrow this morning, I hadn't cried once over James. And wasn't that exactly why I ran off to London, anyway? To cut away, if only for a few minutes, the malignant mass of grief? I fled to London to breathe and that was damn well what I'd done, even if some of that time had been spent in a veritable mud pit.

I knew that keeping the vial was exactly what I should do. Not only because I felt a subtle attachment to whomever this vial once belonged, but because I'd found it on a mudlarking tour that wasn't even part of the original, fated itinerary with James. I'd come to this riverbed alone. I'd stuck my hands into the muddy crevice of two rocks. I'd staved off tears. This glass object — delicate and yet still intact, somewhat like myself — was proof that I could be brave, adventurous, and do hard things on my own. I dropped the vial into my pocket.

The clouds above us continued to build, and lightning struck somewhere to the west of the bend in the river. Bachelor Alf called us over to him. "Sorry, folks," he hollered, "but we can't go on after a lightning strike. Let's pack it up. We'll be back out tomorrow, same time, if anyone wants to join again."

Pulling off my gloves, I walked over to Bachelor Alf. Now that I'd grown somewhat accustomed to my surroundings, I couldn't help a sense of disappointment about the tour ending early. After all, I'd just had my first real find, and I felt a growing curiosity and the urge to keep looking. I could see how such a pastime might become addictive.

"If you were me," I asked Alf, "where would you go to learn more about the vial?" Even though it didn't have the markings Alf expected on a typical apothecary vial, perhaps I could still glean some information about it — especially given the tiny animal etched onto the side, which I thought resembled a bear walking on all fours.

Giving me a warm smile, he shook off my gloves and threw them in a bucket with the others. "Oh, I suppose you could take it to a hobbyist or collector who studies glassmaking. Polishes and molds and techniques change over time, so perhaps someone could help you date it."

I nodded my head, having not the slightest idea how to find a "hobbyist" glassmaker. "Do you think it's from here, somewhere in London?" Earlier, I'd overheard Bachelor Alf telling another tour participant that Windsor Castle was about forty kilometers to the west. Who knew how far the vial had traveled, and from where?

He raised an eyebrow. "Without an address or any text to help us? Almost impossible to determine." Above us, a roll of thunder warned. Bachelor Alf hesitated, torn between wanting to help an inquisitive novice like myself and keeping us both dry — and safe. "Look," he said. "Try headin' over to the British Library and ask for Gaynor at the Maps desk. You can tell her I sent you." He checked his watch. "Not open much longer today, so you best get moving. Take the Underground, Thameslink to St. Pancras. It'll be fastest — and driest. Plus, it's not a bad place to wait out a storm."

I thanked him and hurried off, hoping I still had a few minutes left before the storm let loose. I pulled out my phone, sighed in relief that the station was only a few blocks away, and resigned myself to the fact that if I'd be spending ten days alone in the city, it was due time to learn how to use the Underground trains.

Leaving the train station amid a downpour, I spotted the British Library just ahead. I started jogging, tugging at my collar in a futile attempt to air out the inside of my shirt. And to make matters worse, my shoe — which had filled with water when I stepped in the puddle along the river — remained soaked through. When I finally stepped into the library, I took one look at my reflection in the window and sighed, fearing that Gaynor may send me away on account of my disheveled appearance.

Pedestrians, tourists and students filled the foyer of the library, all of us taking shelter from the rain. And yet, I felt like the only one without a real reason to be there. Whereas many others carried backpacks and cameras, I'd arrived with only a piece of unidentified glass in my pocket and the first name of someone who may or may not be an actual employee. For a moment, I considered the idea of throwing in the towel; maybe it was time to find a sandwich and plan a real itinerary.

The moment this thought crossed my mind, I shook my head. That sounded exactly like something James would say. As rain continued to batter the glass windows of the library, I willed myself to ignore this voice of reason — the same one that had told me to rip up my Cambridge application and encouraged me to take a job at the family farm. Instead, I asked myself what the old Caroline would do — the Caroline of a decade ago, the zealous student not yet dazzled by a diamond on her finger.

I stepped toward the staircase where a group of wide-eyed tourists milled about, a brochure spread wide in front of them and umbrella bags scattered at their feet. Near the staircase was a desk with a young female attendant; I approached her, relieved when she showed no dismay at my wet, unkempt clothes.

I told her that I needed to speak with Gaynor, but the attendant chuckled. "We have more than a thousand employees," she said. "Do you know which department she works in?"

"Maps," I said, at once feeling slightly more legitimate than I did a moment ago. The attendant checked her computer, nodded her head and confirmed that a Gaynor Baymont worked at the Enquiry Desk, Maps Reading Room, Third Floor. She pointed me to the elevators.

A few minutes later, I stood at the Enquiry Desk in the Maps Room, watching as an attractive thirtysomething woman with wavy auburn hair leaned over a black-and-white map with a magnifying glass in one hand and a pencil in the other, her brow twisted in deep concentration. After a minute or two, she stood to stretch her back, startling when she saw me.

"I'm sorry to bother you," I whispered in the near-silent room. "I'm looking for Gaynor?"

Her eyes met mine and she smiled. "You came to the right place. *I'm* Gaynor." She set down the magnifying glass and brushed aside a loose hair. "How can I help you?"

Now that I stood in front of her, my request seemed ridiculous. Clearly, the map in front of her — a haphazard mess of tangled lines and minuscule labels — was an important point of research for her at the moment. "I can come back," I offered, halfway hoping she would seize the idea, send me off and thereby force me to do something more productive with this day.

"Oh, don't be silly. This map is a hundred and fifty years old. Nothing's going to change in the next five minutes."

I reached into my pocket, drawing a confused look from Gaynor: she was probably more accustomed to students hauling in long tubes of parchment rather than rain-soaked women reaching for small objects in their pocket. "I found this a bit ago at the river. I was mudlarking with a group — led by someone named Alf — and he told me to come see you. Do you know him?"

Gaynor grinned widely. "He's my dad, actually."

"Oh!" I exclaimed, drawing an irritated look from a nearby patron. How sneaky of Bachelor Alf to not tell me. "Well, there's a small image on the side here —" I pointed "— and it's the only marking on the vial. I think it's a bear. I couldn't help but wonder where it might have come from."

She tilted her head, curious. "Most people would have no interest in such a thing." Gaynor extended her palm, and I handed her the vial. "You must be a historian, or a researcher?"

I smiled. "Not professionally, no. But I do have some interest in history."

Gaynor glanced up at me. "We're kindred spirits. I see all sorts of maps at my job, but the old, obscure ones are my favorite. Always a bit of room for interpretation, as places evolve quite a bit over time."

Places *and* people, I thought to myself. I could feel the change in myself at this very moment: the discontent within me seizing the possibility of adventure, an excursion into my long-lost enthusiasm for eras past.

Gaynor lifted the vial to the light. "I've seen a few antiquated vials like this, though normally they're a bit larger. I always thought them rather off-putting, as you don't really know what was once inside. Blood or arsenic, I imagined as a child." She looked more closely at the etching, running her finger over the miniature animal. "It does look like a little bear. Strange there are no other markings, but safe to say it probably belonged to a shop owner at one time, likely an apothecary." She sighed, handing the vial back to me. "My dad has a heart of gold, but I don't know why he sent you to me. I really have no idea what this vial is, or where it's from." She looked back down at the map in front of her, a gentle way to tell me that our short conversation was over.

It was a dead end, and my face fell as disappointment crept in. I thanked Gaynor for her time, pocketed the vial and stepped away from the desk. But as I turned, she called out after me. "Pardon, miss, I didn't catch your name?"

"Caroline. Caroline Parcewell."

"Are you visiting from the States?"

I smiled. "My accent gives me away, I'm sure. Yes, I'm visiting."

Gaynor picked up a pen and leaned over her map. "Well, Caroline, if there's anything else I can help with, or if you learn something about the vial, I'd love to know."

"Of course," I said, then I pocketed the vial. Somewhat discouraged, I resolved to forget the object and the mudlarking adventure altogether. I didn't much believe in the fate of finding things, anyway.

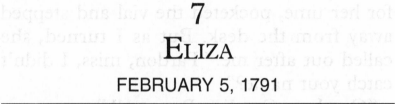

7

ELIZA

FEBRUARY 5, 1791

I woke to a pain in my belly unlike any I
had felt before. I placed my hands underneath my night shift and pressed my fingers
into my skin. Beneath them, my skin felt
warm and swollen, and I clenched my teeth
as a dull ache began to spread itself wide.

It was not the same bellyache I might have
had after too many sweets, or after spinning
'round in the summer garden with the
fireflies back home. This ache was lower,
like I needed to relieve myself. I rushed over
to my chamber pot, but the heaviness still
did not go away.

Oh, but what an important task lay ahead
of me! The most important one my mistress
had ever given me. It was more important
than any dish I had scoured, or pudding I
had baked, or envelope I had sealed. I could
not disappoint her by saying I did not feel
well and would like to stay in bed. Those
excuses might have worked on the farm with

my parents on a day when the horses needed brushing or the beans were ready to be plucked from their stalks. But not today, not in the towering brick house belonging to the Amwells.

Wiggling out of my night shift and walking to the washbasin, I resolved to ignore the discomfort. As I washed, as I tidied my garret room and as I stroked the nameless fat tabby cat who slept at the end of my cot, I whispered quietly to myself, as though saying it aloud made it more believable: "This morning, I will give him the poisonous eggs."

The eggs. They remained nestled in the jar of ash, tucked into the pocket of my gown hanging near the bed. I removed the jar and pulled it to my chest, the coolness of the glass reaching me even through my nightgown. As I clutched the jar more tightly, my hands did not shake, not one bit.

I was a brave girl, at least about some things.

Two years ago at the age of ten, I rode with my mother from our small village of Swindon to the great, sprawling city of London. I had never been to London and had heard only rumors of its filth and its wealth. "An inhospitable place for people like us," my father, a farmer, had always muttered.

But my mother disagreed. Privately, she would tell me of London's bright colors — the golden steeples of the churches, the peacock blues of the gowns — and of the many peculiar shops and stores in the city. She described exotic animals wearing waistcoats, their handlers ushering them through the city streets, and market stands selling hot almond-cherry buns to a line of customers three dozen deep.

For a girl like me, surrounded by livestock and wild shrubs bearing little more than bitter fruit, such a place was unthinkable.

With four older brothers to help on the farm, my mother had insisted on finding a placement for me in London once I reached the proper age. She knew if I did not leave the countryside at a tender age, I would never see a life outside the pastures and pigpens. My parents had argued about it for months, but my mother would not relent, not even a bit.

The morning of my departure was a tearful, tense one. My father hated to lose two good hands on the farm; my mother hated the separation from her youngest child. "I feel as though I'm slicing off a piece of my heart," she sobbed, smoothing out the lap quilt she'd just placed into my case. "But I will not let it doom you to a life like mine."

Our destination was the servant's registry office. As we rode into town, my mother leaned close, the sadness in her voice now replaced with exhilaration. "You must begin where life has slotted you," she said, gripping my knee, "and move upward from there. There is nothing wrong with starting as a scullery maid or housemaid. Besides, London is a magickal place."

"What do you mean by *magickal,* mother?" I'd asked, my eyes wide as the city began to come into view. The day was clear and blue; already, I imagined the calluses on my hands growing smaller.

"I mean that you can be anything you want in London," she replied. "Nothing great awaits you in the farm fields. The fences would have kept you in, as they do the pigs and as they've done to me. But in London? Well, in time, if you are clever about it, you can wield your own power like a magician. In a city so grand, even a poor girl can transform into whatever she desires to be."

"Like an indigo butterfly," I said, thinking of the glassy cocoons I'd seen in the moorland during summer. In a matter of days, the cocoons would turn black as soot, as if

85

the animal inside had shriveled up to die. But then, the darkness would lift, revealing the butterfly's striking blue wings within the papery encasement. Soon after, the wings would pierce the cocoon, and the butterfly would take flight.

"Yes, like a butterfly," my mother agreed. "Even powerful men cannot explain what happens inside a cocoon. It is magick, surely, just like that which happens inside London."

From that moment forward, I desired to know more of this thing called *magick,* and I could hardly wait to explore the city in which we'd just arrived.

At the servant's registry office, my mother stood patiently aside while a pair of women looked me over; one of them was Mrs. Amwell, in a pink satin gown and a cap bordered with lace. I could hardly keep from staring: I had never in all my life seen a pink satin gown.

Mrs. Amwell seemed to take an instant liking to me. She bent forward to speak to me, crouching low so our faces almost touched, and soon after she placed her arm around my mother, whose eyes were brimming again with tears. I was delighted when Mrs. Amwell finally took my hand in hers, walked me to the broad mahogany desk at the front of the office and asked the attendant for the papers.

As she filled in the required information, I noticed that Mrs. Amwell's hand shook badly as she wrote, and it seemed a great effort to keep the nib of the pen steady. Her words were jagged and bent at odd angles, but it meant little to me. I had been unable to read in those days, and all handwriting looked as illegible as the next.

After a tearful goodbye with my mother, my new mistress and I took a coach to the house she shared with Mr. Amwell, her husband. I was to work first in the scullery, and so Mrs. Amwell introduced me to Sally, the cook and kitchenmaid.

In the weeks to follow, Sally minced no words: according to her, I did not know the proper way to scour a pot or how to pick roots from a potato without damaging the flesh. As she showed me the "right" way of doing things, I put up no complaint, for I enjoyed my placement with the Amwells. I had my own room in the attic, which was more than my mother had told me to expect, and from there I could watch the amusing, ever-present activity on the street below: the sedan chairs rushing past, the porters bearing enormous boxes of unseen goods, the comings and goings of a young couple who I believed newly in love.

Eventually, Sally grew comfortable with my abilities and began allowing me to assist in the preparation of meals. It felt a small movement upward, just as my mother had said, and it gave me hope; someday, I, too, hoped to be toiling about in the magnificent streets of London, in pursuit of something greater than potatoes and pots.

One morning, while I was carefully arranging dried herbs on a platter, a housemaid rushed downstairs. Mrs. Amwell wanted to see me in her drawing room. Terror struck me at once. I felt sure I had done something wrong, and I ascended the stairs slowly, held back by a sense of dread. I had been at the Amwell house not even two months; my mother would be horrified if I were dismissed in such a short time.

But when I stepped into my mistress's pale blue drawing room and she closed the door behind me, she merely smiled and asked me to sit down next to her at her writing desk. Here, she opened a book and produced a blank sheet of paper, a pen and an inkwell. She pointed at several words in the book and asked me to write them down.

I was not comfortable holding a pen, not at all, but I pulled the page close and steadily copied the words as best I could.

Mrs. Amwell watched me closely as I worked, her brow knit together, her chin in her hands. When I finished the first few words, she selected several more, and almost immediately I noticed an improvement in my own pen strokes. My mistress must have noticed it, too, for she nodded approvingly.

Next, she pushed aside the sheet of paper and lifted the book. She asked if I understood any of the words, and I shook my head. She then pointed at several of the shorter words — *she, cart, plum* — and explained how each letter made its own sound, and how words strung together on paper could convey an idea, a story.

Like magick, I thought. It was everywhere, if only one knew to look.

That afternoon in the drawing room was our first lesson. Our first of countless lessons, sometimes twice a day — for my mistress's condition, which I'd first noticed at the registry office, had worsened. The tremor in her hand had grown so severe, she could no longer write her own correspondence, and she needed me to do it for her.

In time, I worked in the kitchen less and less, and Mrs. Amwell called me often to her drawing room. This was not well received by the other household staff, Sally most of all. But I didn't worry myself over it: Mrs. Amwell was my mistress, not Sally, and I couldn't refuse the ganache balls and ribbons and penmanship lessons by the drawing room hearth, now, could I?

It took me many months to learn to read and write, and even longer to learn how to speak like a child who had not come from the country. But Mrs. Amwell was a wonderful tutor: gentle and soft-spoken, wrapping my hand in hers to form the letters, laughing with me when the pen slipped. Any lingering thoughts of home vanished; it shamed me to admit, but I did not want to see the farm, not ever again. I wanted to remain in London, in the grandeur of my mistress's drawing room. Those long afternoons at her writing desk, when I was burdened only by the gazes of the jealous servants, were some of my best memories.

Then something changed. A year ago, when the roundness of my face began to fall away and the edge of my bodice grew tight, I could ignore it no longer: the feeling of another gaze, a new one, and the sensation that someone watched me too closely.

It was Mr. Amwell, my mistress's husband. He had, for reasons I could only faintly understand, begun to pay attention to me. And I felt sure my mistress sensed it, too.

■ ■ ■

It was almost time. My bellyache was not so bad anymore; moving about the kitchen seemed to help. I was grateful for it, as following Nella's instructions would require me to be careful and steady. A slip of my hand, which might be laughed about in my mistress's drawing room, would be very bad today.

The two smaller eggs sizzled in the pan. The fat spit onto my apron while the white edges of the egg bubbled and curled. I remained still, concentrating, and spooned the eggs from the pan when the edges reached the color of honey, just as the mistress liked. I placed her eggs on a plate, covered them with a cloth and set them far aside. I then spent a few minutes tending to the gravy, which was Nella's suggestion.

As the gravy thickened, I realized it was the final moment to undo what I had not yet done, to strip out the thread which had not yet been sewn in. If I followed through, I would be like one of those men at Tyburn that I'd heard about at the hanging day fairs: a criminal. Gooseflesh scurried across my skin as I thought of it, and I considered briefly the idea of lying to my mistress —

telling her that the poisoned egg must have been too weak.

I shook my head. Such a lie would be cowardly, and Mr. Amwell would remain alive. The plan — which Mrs. Amwell had set into motion — would fail because of me.

I wasn't meant to be in the kitchen at all today. Last week, Sally had asked Mrs. Amwell for a few days away to visit her ailing mother. My mistress had readily approved and, afterward, called me to her drawing room for another lesson. But this lesson was not about penmanship or letter-writing; it was about the hidden apothecary shop. She told me that I was to leave a note in the bin of pearl barley just inside the door of 3 Back Alley, and that the note should specify the date and time I meant to return for the remedy — which was, of course, a deadly one.

I did not ask my mistress why she meant to harm her husband; I suspected it was because of what happened a month ago, just after the new year, when my mistress left the house and spent the day at the winter gardens near Lambeth.

That day, Mrs. Amwell had asked me to organize a pile of her letters, giving me several dozen to sort before leaving for the gardens, but I could not complete my task because of a headache. Midmorning, Mr. Amwell stumbled upon me with tears on my cheeks; the pressure behind my eyes had become almost unbearable. He insisted that I retire to my room and sleep. A few minutes later, he offered me a drink that he said would help, and I sucked down the sharp, honey-colored liquid as quickly as I could even though it made me cough and gasp. It looked like the brandy my mistress sometimes sipped from the bottle, though I could not fathom why anyone would willingly drink such a thing.

I slept away the headache in the quiet, sunny comfort of my room. Eventually, I woke to the smell of animal fat — a tallow candle — and my mistress's cool touch on my forehead. The ache in my head had gone. Mrs. Amwell asked me how long I had been asleep, and I told her truthfully that I did not know — that I had lain down midmorning. *It is now half ten at night,* she told me, meaning I had slept for nearly twelve hours.

Mrs. Amwell asked if I had had any dreams. Although I shook my head, the truth was that a faint memory had begun to form, one I felt sure was a dream I'd had only a few hours ago. It was a memory of Mr. Amwell in my garret room; he had lifted the fat tabby cat from her place on my cot and set her into the corridor, then closed the door and approached me. He took a seat next to me, placing his hand on my stomach, and we began to talk. Try as I might, I could not remember what we discussed in the dream. He then began to move his hand upward, sliding it along my navel, when one of the footmen made a commotion down-stairs; a pair of gentlemen had arrived, need-ing to speak urgently with Mr. Amwell.

I admitted this story to my mistress, but I said that I did not know whether it had been a dream or real. Afterward, she remained at my side, a concerned look on her face. She pointed at the empty brandy glass and asked if Mr. Amwell had given it to me. I told her yes. She then leaned in close and placed one of her hands on mine. "Is it the first time he has done so?"

I nodded.

"And you are well now? Nothing hurts?"

I shook my head. Nothing hurt.

My mistress eyed the glass carefully, tucked the blankets in close around me and wished me goodnight.

It was only after she had gone that I heard the soft cry of the tabby cat outside my room. She was in the corridor, mewing to be let inside.

Now, I handled each of the larger eggs like they were made of glass. It was a tricky thing, to be sure, and I had never given so much thought to the pressure with which I cracked an egg. The pan was still very hot, and the yolks began to cook almost instantly. I feared to stand too close, lest I breathe in any poisonous odors, so I tended the eggs with a long, outstretched arm, and soon my shoulder ached like it did when I used to climb trees in the country.

Once cooked, I removed the two larger eggs to a second plate. I smothered them in gravy and threw the four eggshells into the rubbish bin, straightened my apron, and — being very sure to place the poisoned eggs on the right side of the tray — I left the kitchen.

The master and mistress were already seated, engaged in a quiet discussion about an upcoming banquet. "Mr. Batford says there will be a display of sculptures," Mrs. Amwell said. "Procured from all over the world."

Mr. Amwell grunted in response, looking up at me as I entered the dining room. "Aha," he said. "Here we are."

"Beautiful things, he's promised." My mistress rubbed at her collarbone; where her fingers touched, the skin was red and splotchy. She seemed jittery, even though I carried the tray of poisonous eggs, and this annoyed me somewhat. She had been too scared to retrieve the eggs herself, and now she seemed unable to calm her nerves.

"Mmm-hmm," he said to her, his eyes never leaving me. "Bring that over here. Quickly now, girl."

Stepping close to him from behind, I lifted his plate from the right side of the tray and carefully set it in front of him. As I did so, he reached his hand behind my legs and delicately pulled the heavy fabric of my skirt upward. He ran his hand over the back of my knee and upward to my lower thigh.

"Lovely," he said, finally pulling his hand away and lifting his fork. My leg itched where he touched it, an invisible rash beneath my skin. I stepped away from him and set the second plate in front of the mistress.

She nodded at me, her collarbone still flushed. Her eyes were sad and dark, as dim as the maroon rosettes on the papered wall behind her.

I took my place at the edge of the dining

room and waited, still as stone, for what would come next.

8

CAROLINE

PRESENT DAY, MONDAY

When I woke later that night, the nightstand clock showed 3:00 a.m. I groaned and turned away from the dim red light, but as I tried to fall back asleep, my stomach began to churn and an unsettled sensation left my skin damp and hot to the touch. I pushed the covers back, wiped sweat from my upper lip and stood to check the thermostat. It was programmed in Celsius, not Fahrenheit, so perhaps I'd accidentally set it too warm the day before. I shuffled my feet along the carpeted floors, stopped to steady myself and threw my hand against the wall.

Suddenly, I heaved.

I dashed for the bathroom, hardly making it to the toilet before vomiting up everything I'd eaten the day prior. Once, twice, three times I retched, my body limp over the toilet.

Afterward, as my stomach unclenched and I caught my breath, I reached for a washcloth on the counter. My hand knocked over something small and solid. The vial. After I'd returned to the hotel, I'd taken it out of my purse and set it on the bathroom counter. Now, to prevent myself from nearly shattering it, I tucked the vial safely at the bottom of my suitcase and returned to the bathroom to brush my teeth.

Food poisoning in a foreign country, I thought to myself, groaning. But then I covered my mouth with trembling, damp fingers. *Food poisoning, or . . . something else.* Hadn't I been queasy a couple times yesterday, too? I'd hardly eaten anything, so I couldn't blame that nausea on bad food.

It felt, at once, like a terrible joke — if I was indeed pregnant, this was not how I imagined it happening. I'd long dreamed about the moment that James and I learned the news together: the happy tears, the celebratory kiss, rushing out to buy our first baby book. The two of us, *together,* celebrating what we'd made. And yet here I was, alone in a hotel bathroom in the wee hours of the morning, hoping that we hadn't made anything at all. I didn't want James's baby, not right now. I only wanted to feel the uncomfortable, heavy ache of my imminent period.

I fixed myself a cup of hot chamomile tea.

Sipping it slowly, I lay in bed for a half hour, wide-awake and waiting for the nausea to pass. I couldn't bring myself to consider the idea of taking a pregnancy test. I'd give it a few more days. I prayed travel and stress were to blame — perhaps my period would start later tonight, or tomorrow.

My stomach began to settle, but the jet lag left me awake and alert. I spread my hand over the right side of the bed, where James should have been, and twisted the cool sheets in my fingers. For a brief moment, I couldn't resist the truth: a part of me missed him terribly.

No. I released the sheets from my grip and turned onto my left side, away from the empty space next to me. I would not let myself miss him. Not yet.

As if James's secret hadn't burdened me enough, there was something more: so far, I'd only told my best friend, Rose, about my husband's infidelity. Now, awake in the middle of the night, I considered calling my parents and revealing everything. But my parents had paid for the nonrefundable hotel stay, and I didn't have the courage to tell them that only one of us had checked into the suite. I'd tell them when I returned, after I'd had time to think things through — after I'd decided what the future of my marriage looked like.

At last I gave up on sleep and turned on the nightstand lamp, then pulled my cell phone off the charger. I opened up my internet app and hovered my fingers over the keyboard, tempted to search London attractions. But the big sights, like Westminster and Buckingham Palace, were already listed inside my notebook with opening times and entry fees — and still, none of it appealed to me. I could hardly stomach James's absence in the spacious hotel room; how could I possibly stroll the winding paths of Hyde Park and *not* feel the empty space beside me? I'd rather not go at all.

Instead, I navigated to the website for the British Library. While chatting with Gaynor in the Maps Room, I'd seen a small card advertising the online database search. Now, jet-lagged and feeling unwell, I burrowed deeper into the cotton bedsheets and decided to do a bit of digging.

Tapping my finger on Search the Main Catalogue, I typed two words: vial bear. Several results appeared, varying widely in subject matter: a recent article from a biomechanics journal; a seventeenth-century book on apocalyptic prophecies; and a collection of papers retrieved in the early nineteenth century from St. Thomas'

101

Hospital. Clicking on the third result, I waited for the page to load.

A few additional details appeared, namely the creation date of the documents — 1815 to 1818 — and the acquisition information about the documents. The site noted the papers were acquired from the south wing of the hospital and included documents belonging to both staff and patients of the ward.

Toward the top of the search result was a link to request the document. I clicked the link and sighed, expecting that I'd be required to register with the library and request the physical document. But to my surprise, several sample pages within the document had been digitized. In moments, they began to materialize on the screen of my phone.

It had been a decade since I'd last done this sort of digging, and I couldn't help the sudden rush of adrenaline in my chest. To think that Gaynor spent day after day in the British Library with full access to archives like this left me nearly writhing in envy.

As the image sharpened, my screen flashed with an incoming call. I didn't recognize the number, but my caller ID said the call originated from Minneapolis. I frowned, trying to remember if I knew anyone from

Minnesota. I shook my head; must be a tele-marketer. I declined the call, settled deeper into the pillow and began to read the sample pages of the document.

The first several pages were irrelevant: names of hospital administrators, a lease document and a signed copy of a will — perhaps signed while the patient was on their deathbed. But on the fourth page, something caught my eye: the word *bear.*

It was a digitized image of a short, hand-written note, the writing jagged and faded in several places:

22 October 1816

To men, a maze. I could have show'd them all they wish'd to see at Bear Alley.

That a killer need not lift her long, delicate hand. She need not touch him as he dies.

There are other, wiser ways: vials and victuals.

The apothecary was a friend to all of us women, the brewer of our secret: the men are dead because of us.

Only, it did not happen as I intend'd.

It was not her fault, the apothecary. It was not even mine.

I lay blame unto my husband, and his thirst for that which was not meant for him.

The note was unsigned. My hands began to shake; the words *bear* and *vial* were present, meaning this was definitely the page that hit my search keywords. And the author of this note, whoever she was, clearly meant to share a heavy secret while she was indisposed at the hospital. Could this have been a deathbed confession of some kind?

And what of the line *all they wish'd to see at Bear Alley?* The author of the note alluded to a maze, implying she knew the way through. And if there *was* a maze, it seemed only logical that something valuable — or secretive — would be at the end of it.

I chewed at a fingernail, at a complete loss over the meaning of this strange wording.

But it was something else that struck me the most: mention of the apothecary. The author of the note said the apothecary was a "friend" and a "brewer" of secrets. If the secret was that men were dead — and clearly not by accident — it seemed the apothecary was the common thread among their deaths. Like a serial killer. A chill ran through me as I pulled the sheets closer.

As I examined the note again, an unread message notification on my email inbox flashed. I ignored it, instead jumping over to Google Maps and quickly typing Bear Alley, London, as mentioned in the first phrase of the note.

In an instant, a single result displayed: there was, indeed, a Bear Alley in London. And to my utter disbelief, it was close — very close — to my hotel. A ten-minute walk, no more. But was it the same Bear Alley referenced in the note? Surely some streets had been renamed in the last two hundred years.

The satellite view of Google Maps indicated the Bear Alley area in London was built up with massive concrete buildings, and the businesses listed on the map consisted mostly of investment banks and accounting firms. Which meant that even if this *were* the right Bear Alley, I wouldn't find much beyond crowds of men moving about in suits. Crowds of men like James.

I glanced over at my suitcase, inside of which I'd placed the vial. Gaynor had agreed the image etched on its side was a bear. Could the vial be tied to Bear Alley? The idea of it — unlikely, though not impossible — was like bait on a hook. I

couldn't resist the pull of the mystery —
the *what if,* the *unknown.*

I checked the time; it was nearly 4:00 a.m.
As soon as the sun came up, I'd grab a coffee and venture over to Bear Alley.

Before setting my phone aside, I jumped
over to the unread email waiting in my inbox and gasped: the email was from James.
My jaw clenched as I began to read.

Tried calling from MSP. I can hardly
breathe, Caroline. The other half of my
heart is in London. Must see you. I'm
about to board for Heathrow. I land at 9
am, your time. Will take a bit to get thru
customs. Meet me at the hotel, 11ish?

In stunned silence, I read the email a
second time. James was on his way to
London. He didn't even ask me if I wanted
to see him, nor was he allowing me the
solitude and distance I so badly needed. The
unknown call a few minutes ago must have
been from James at the airport, perhaps
from a payphone — he likely knew I
wouldn't pick up if I had seen his caller ID.

My hands began to shake; it felt like I'd
just learned about his affair all over again. I
hovered my finger over Reply, prepared to
tell James, *No, don't you dare come here.* But

I'd known him long enough; tell him he couldn't have something, and he would work twice as hard to get it. Besides, he knew the name of the hotel, and even if I refused to meet with him, I had no doubt he would wait in the lobby for as long as it took. And I couldn't stay holed up in my room forever.

Sleep would now be impossible. If James meant to arrive at eleven o'clock, there were just a few hours left without the burden of his presence, his excuses. A few hours left to avoid dealing with our damaged marriage. A few hours left to venture over to Bear Alley.

I stood from the bed and began to pace by the window, checking the sky every few minutes, searching desperately for the first early rays of light.

The sun could not rise soon enough.

9

ELIZA

As a minute passed, then another, with no change in Mr. Amwell's demeanor at the breakfast table, my bravery began to wane. I wished badly for another warm cup of Nella's valerian hot brew, which had left me so relaxed at her little shop with the secret room.

The deed itself had not been so bad — the cracking of the eggs, dropping them into the sizzling pan. I did not even fear the angry words Mr. Amwell might spout at me as the poisoned eggs churned in his belly, nor the rigid, bent form that his body might take, which Nella warned might cause a lifetime of nightmares.

But while I was brave about some things, I was not brave about *all* things. What I feared was his ghost, his unharnessed spirit after death. The unseen movement of it through walls, through skin.

My fear of spirits was recent, beginning a

108

few months ago when Sally pulled me into the cold, dark cellar and told me a story about a girl named Johanna.

I was not so brave after that day, knowing that magick could sour and go bad.

According to Sally, Johanna worked at the Amwell estate just a short time before I arrived. Only a year or two older than me, Johanna had fallen ill — so ill that she could not leave her room. And during her isolation, whispers flew through the corridors: rumors that she was not ill at all, but carrying a little baby and soon to give birth.

Sally said that on a cold morning in November, one of the upstairs maids sat with Johanna while she strained a whole day with the baby. Pushing and pushing, all of that effort but never a cry. The baby never did come out, and Johanna fell into a sleep from which she never woke.

The attic room where I slept — with its cobwebbed, drafty corners — was next to the one where Johanna and her baby had died. And after Sally told me this story, I began to hear Johanna cry out through the walls, late at night. It sounded like she was crying for *me,* crying my name. On occasion, I heard what sounded like rushing water, and a *thumping,* like the baby inside her belly was trying to break his way out

109

with his little balled-up fists.

"Who was the father?" I had asked Sally in the cellar.

She looked hard at me, like I should already know.

Eventually, I worked up the courage to reveal to Mrs. Amwell some of what Sally had told me of Johanna, but my mistress insisted no girl was pregnant in the house, and certainly no girl had died. She tried to tell me that Sally was envious of my place in the house, and the thumping was my own terrified heart — little more than bad dreams.

I did not argue with Mrs. Amwell. But I knew what I heard late at night. How can one mistake the cry of their own name?

Now, as I waited in the dining room with my back to the wall, watching Mr. Amwell chew away at his eggs, it was this set of events that left me unsteady — so much so that I had to place my palms against the wall to balance myself. I did not regret what I'd done; I only hoped the poisonous eggs would kill Mr. Amwell quickly, and in daylight, for I could not bear the idea of another voice calling my name through the walls. I prayed Mr. Amwell's wretched spirit would not release in this very room, or if it did, that it would not dwell long.

I didn't understand this kind of magick. I didn't understand why Johanna's spirit was still stuck or why she haunted me as she did, and I feared Mr. Amwell's spirit might soon accompany her in the hallways.

I was brave about some things, yes, and poisons didn't scare me. But unchained, angry spirits could bring me to my knees.

He clutched his throat halfway through the second egg. "My God," he cried. "What is in the gravy? I've a furious thirst." He downed half the pitcher of water while I remained at the edge of the dining room, waiting to remove the plates.

The mistress's eyes grew wide. She touched the pale yellow ribbing of her bodice; did I imagine the tremble in her wrist? "Dear, are you quite all right?" she asked him.

"Do I look it?" Mr. Amwell snapped. He tugged at his bottom lip, which had begun to swell and redden. "My mouth is so hot, did you use a pepper?" He dabbed at a bead of gravy stuck to his chin, and his napkin fell to the floor as if he had lost his grip on it. I could see it, then, so clearly: his fury curdling into something like fear.

"No, sir," I said. "I made it just the same

as I always have. The milk was to go bad soon."

"I believe it's bloody gone bad already." He began to cough and clutched his throat again.

The mistress picked at her own gravy and eggs, then took a cautious bite.

"Damn this!" He pushed the plate away and stood, his chair tumbling to the floor behind him, rustling the pristine, daisy-print curtains. "I'm to be sick, girl! Take this away!"

I rushed forward and grabbed the plate, pleased to find that he had, indeed, finished the entire first egg and much of the second. Nella had promised one would do, if it must.

Mr. Amwell ascended the staircase, his footsteps echoing through the dining room. The mistress and I looked at one another in silence, and I must admit a part of me was surprised the plan had worked at all. I made my way to the kitchen, quickly wiping the plate, which I then thrust into murky old water.

In the dining room, my mistress still picked at her food. She seemed perfectly well, thank God, but Mr. Amwell's retching from the floor above was so loud, I wondered if the effort of it would kill him before the poison itself. I had never heard such vomiting, such groaning. How long might it take? Nella did not tell me that, and I had not thought to ask.

Two hours passed. It would have been suspicious if Mrs. Amwell continued to hide at her writing desk downstairs, the two of us working on letters that didn't need writing, acting as though nothing was awry.

Everyone knew that Mr. Amwell was fond of the drink and had suffered many a period of days and nights with his head shoved deep into the chamber pot. But the truth was that he had never moaned in agony like this; this was something different, and I thought a few others of the household must realize it. The mistress and I went to see him together and, when she realized her husband had lost his ability to speak, she directed one of the staff to fetch the physician.

Immediately, the physician declared Mr. Amwell's condition to be dire, noting that his patient's abdomen swelled and convulsed in a way he had never before seen. The doctor attempted to explain this to my mistress in strange medical words I did not understand, but anyone could see the convulsions, like an animal writhed inside of Mr. Amwell's belly. His eyes were bloodshot, and he could not even keep his gaze on the candlelight.

As the physician and my mistress stood together in hushed conversation, Mr. Amwell turned his head and those hollow black holes looked right at me, right into my soul, and I swear in that moment he *knew*. Biting back a scream, I rushed out of the room just as the physician palpated his patient's groin, drawing from him a howl so deep and primal that I feared Mr. Amwell's spirit had just released.

Only his raspy, stuttering breaths — audible from the corridor, where I stood trembling — told me it had not.

"His bladder is near rupture," the physician told Mrs. Amwell as I left the room. "This type of episode has happened before, you say?"

"Many times," my mistress said. It was not a lie, and yet she was lying. I leaned against the wall of the hallway, just outside the door in the cool, inky darkness, listening closely to the words of my mistress and the haggard breaths of her dying husband. "The drink is his vice."

"The swelling in his abdomen is unusual, though . . ." The doctor trailed off, and I imagined him considering the strange case before him and whether to call for the

114

bailiff. The dying man, his pretty wife. Had the physician seen the empty bourbon bottles we scattered about downstairs in an effort to fool him?

I took a step forward, unable to restrain my curiosity, and peeked around the open door. The doctor crossed his arms, drummed his finger and stifled a yawn. I wondered if he had his own pretty wife waiting for him at home with supper nearly ready. The doctor hesitated, then said, "You ought to send for a pastor, Mrs. Amwell. Straightaway. He will not survive the night."

My mistress covered her mouth with her hand. "Heavens," she breathed, true surprise in her voice.

At my mistress's command, I showed the doctor the exit. Afterward, as I shut the door at the front of the house and turned around, she stood waiting for me.

"Let's sit by the fire together," she whispered, and we went to the place we had always gone. She wrapped a blanket around our legs, withdrew a notebook and began to dictate a letter to her mother, in Norwich. "Mother," she began, "my husband has fallen terribly ill . . ."

I wrote each word exactly as she said, even though I knew they were not all true. And even when the letter was finished — for I wrote six pages, and then eight, and it was all a repetition of things she had already said — she continued speaking, and I continued writing. Neither of us wanted to move; neither of us wanted to go upstairs. The clock showed nearly midnight. Daylight had left long ago.

But we did not go on forever, for all at once, I felt something strange: something sticky and wet between my legs. At the same time, a servant descended the stairs, taking them two by two, his eyes wide and damp. "Mrs. Amwell," he cried, "I am s-sorry to say it, but he has stopped breathing."

Mrs. Amwell threw the blanket off her lap and stood, and I took her lead and did the same. But to my great horror, the warm and concave spot upon which I'd been sitting was now streaked with a band of crimson, bright as a fresh-picked apple. My mouth dropped open; was death about to find me, too? I sucked in each breath of air, willing it not to leave me.

Mrs. Amwell began to make her way to the staircase, but I cried out. "Wait —" I pleaded, "p-please don't leave me here, alone."

There could be no doubt about it: some terrible magick had found me again. Mr. Amwell's spirit may have exited his body upstairs, but like that of Johanna's, it had not gone entirely. What else could draw blood from my body at his moment of death?

I crumbled to the floor on my knees, fat tears falling down my face. "Don't leave me," I begged her again.

My mistress looked strangely at me, for she had left me alone in the room a thousand times before, but I could feel the wet warmth leaking from me even at that moment. From my place on the floor, I pointed to the sofa where we'd been seated together. My eyes settled on the blood-stained cushion upon which we'd been sitting, and all around us, the shadows of the candlelight danced closer, taunting me, Mr. Amwell hiding in every one of them.

10
NELLA

On the seventh day of February, yet another note was left in the barrel of pearl barley.

Before I read it, I lifted the fine parchment — thin as the skin on my tired hands — and inhaled the scent of perfume. Cherries, with undertones of lavender and rose water.

Like Eliza's letter, I knew immediately, by the steady curls and even loops of the ink, that the author was well mannered, literate. I drew to mind a woman of my own age: the mistress of her own household, the wife of a merchant. I imagined a warm and loyal friend, but not a socialite, one who fancied pleasure gardens and the theaters, but not in the way of a courtesan. I imagined a full bosom, broad hips. A mother.

But as I set aside my own imagination and proceeded to read the words carefully penned onto the paper, my tongue grew dry. The note was very curious. As though the author were hesitant to state what she wanted and preferred instead subtle intimation. I let the note fall onto the table. I lifted the candle above the parchment and read it yet again:

The footman found them together, in the gatehouse.

We've a gathering in two days, and she will be in attendance. Perchance you've something to incite lust? I will come to your shop, tomorrow at ten.

Oh, to die in the arms of a lover as I lie alone, waiting, the corridors silent.

I dissected each verse like the entrails of a rat, looking for some clue buried deep within. The woman's household entailed a footman and a gatehouse, so I presumed her well-off. This concerned me, for I had no interest in meddling in the motives of the wealthy, who I had found over the years to be unpredictable and unstable. And the woman wanted something to *incite lust,* so that he — presumably her husband — might die in the arms of his lover — presumably his mistress. The arrangement struck me as a bit perverted, and the letter did not

119

sit well with me.

And the preparation must be ready in two days. It was hardly enough time.

But Eliza's letter had not settled well with me, either, and all had turned out perfectly well. I felt sure that my unease about this letter, too, could be explained by my ailing body and my weary spirit. Perhaps every letter, from this point forward, would raise alarm. I might as well grow used to it, just as I'd grown used to the absence of light inside my shop.

Besides, this woman's letter implied betrayal, and betrayal was why I began to dispense poisons in the first place — why I began to carry the secrets of these women, to record them in my register, to protect and aid them. The best apothecary was one who knows intimately the despair felt by her patient, whether in body or heart. And though I could not relate to this woman's place in society — for there were no gate-houses or footmen to be seen in Back Alley — I knew, firsthand, her inner turmoil. Heartache is shared by all, and favors no rank.

So, in spite of myself, I readied my things to leave for the day. I threw on my heaviest coat and packed an extra pair of socks. Although the fields where I meant to go were damp and uninviting, it was the place I would find the blister beetles — the remedy most suited to this woman's peculiar request.

I made my way quickly, expertly, through the winding alleys of my city, avoiding the sedan chairs and horse dung, pushing against the oppressive mass of bodies moving in and out of shops and homes on my way to the fields near Walworth, in Southwark, where I would find the beetles. I paid visits to the river often and could walk to Blackfriars Bridge with my eyes closed, but on this day the loose stones underfoot posed a hazard. I watched my step, avoiding such nuisances as a mongrel gnawing on something dead, and a half-wrapped parcel of smelly, fly-covered fish.

As I rushed down Water Street, the open river just ahead, women on either side of me brushed the debris and filth from their doorsteps, forming a cloud of ash and dust. I let out a little cough and was seized, all at once, with a hacking fit. I doubled over, placing my hands on my knees.

No one paid me any attention, thank God; the last thing I needed were questions of my destination, my name. No, everyone else was too busy minding their own chores, merchandise and children.

My lungs continued to suck in air until at last I felt the heat in my throat subsiding. I wiped the moisture from my lips, horrified by the plug of greenish mucus that came away on my palm, like I had just plunged my hand into the river and come away with a slither of algae attached to my skin. I flung the mucus onto the ground, stomped it into nothingness with my shoe and straightened my shoulders, moving ahead to the river.

Coming to the steps at the base of Blackfriars Bridge, I noticed a man and woman approaching from across the road. His eyes were narrow and determined as he looked in my direction, and I prayed that he had recognized someone directly behind me. The woman next to him struggled under the weight of an infant slung to her bosom, and from my distance I could just make out the baby's soft, egg-shaped head. A beautiful, cream-colored blanket was tucked neatly around the child.

I looked to the ground and quickened my pace, but as I reached the bottom step of the bridge, I felt a light hand on my shoulder.

"Miss?" I turned, and there they stood, the three of them in perfect formation: father, mother, child. "Are you quite well?"

The man pushed his hat away from his face and pulled down the scarf wrapped around his neck.

"I — I am all right, yes," I stammered. The handrail was like ice underneath my fingers, but I did not loosen my grip.

He sighed in relief. "My God, we saw you o'er there, coughing. You oughta get off this cold road and get in by a fire." He looked up the staircase, where I was headed. "Not really thinking of crossing this bridge over to Southwark, are you? The exertion in this cold . . ."

I tried to keep my eyes off the dimpled, tightly swaddled infant. "It is no issue, I assure you."

The woman tilted her head in pity. "Oh, do come with us, we'll hire a boatman. This little one is far too heavy for walking." She looked down at her baby, then nodded to one of the several men waiting along the nearby riverbank.

"Thank you, but I'm perfectly well, really," I insisted, lifting my foot to ascend the staircase. I smiled at the nice couple, wishing they'd take their leave, but another cough tugged at my throat and my effort to stifle it was futile. I could not help but turn my head to cough again and, as I did so, I felt another grip on my shoulder — firmer

123

this time.

It was the woman, and her look was fierce. "If you must be out, I insist you come with us on the boat. You won't make it up this staircase, I assure you, much less across the bridge. Come on, just this way." She tugged me along, one hand on the head of her infant and the other hand on my back, and led me to one of the waiting boatmen by the river.

I relented, and once we were settled into the boat with thick, woolen blankets on our laps, I felt instantly grateful for the respite.

The baby began to fuss the moment the boat pushed away from the riverbank. The mother pulled out her breast, and the boat began to bump and roll in the icy waters. I leaned over slightly, hoping I would not lose my stomach on the ride across the river to Southwark. For a moment, I forgot altogether my reason for being in the boat, on the river, with this beautiful family. And then I remembered: the beetles. The gatehouse. The footman. Something to *incite lust.*

"You feel sick?" the man asked. "The water is a bit rough today, but I assure you, it is still better than walking."

I nodded in agreement with him. Besides, the feeling was not foreign to me; it felt much like morning sickness, which I still remembered despite the passage of two decades. The rolling waves of nausea had struck me early, even before I missed my monthly course, and the fatigue came soon after. But I had known it was not just any fatigue; as well as I could hold two seeds side by side and declare which was borne of a yellow lily and which of a white, I knew without doubt that I carried a child inside of me. Despite the sickness and fatigue, one would think I had discovered the secret to all happiness, for never in my life had I been more gleeful than I was in those early days, carrying Frederick's child.

The mother smiled at me and pulled the sleeping baby off her nipple. "You would like to hold her?" she asked. I flushed, having not realized that I was staring at the child.

"Yes," I whispered before I knew what I was saying. "Yes."

She handed me the child, telling me that her name was Beatrice. "Bringer of joy," she said.

But as the weight of the child filled my arms and her warmth carried through the layers of fabric to my skin, I felt anything but joy. The bundle of peach skin and tiny breath settled in my arms like a gravestone, a marker of loss, of having had something special ripped away. A knot formed in my throat, and I instantly regretted this means of passage to Southwark.

To die in the arms of a lover as I lie alone, waiting, the corridors silent. The words in the letter that brought me here seemed a curse already.

The baby must have sensed my discontent, for she startled awake and looked around, disoriented. Even with her full belly, her brow crumbled as though she was about to wail.

Instinct told me to bounce her up and down, up and down, and hold her tighter. "Shhh," I whispered to her, aware of the mother and father watching me. "Shhh, little one, there now, nothing to fuss over." Beatrice calmed and locked her gaze on mine like she meant to see into the depths of me, to peek at my secrets and all that made me ache.

If only she could see what rotted within. If only her little heart could understand the heaviness that had plagued me for two decades, kindling the trail of vengeance that now blazed across London and burdened me with a lifetime of other people's secrets.

It was on this that I dwelt as our boat rolled over the waves and we crossed to the other side. And yet, even with beautiful baby Beatrice, the bringer of joy, in my arms, I could not help but turn my gaze to Blackfriars Bridge. Looking up at the stone arches that supported the structure and lifted it high above the water, I allowed myself to dream for a moment about the release and freedom that could be so easily seized with a single step off the bridge.

A moment of free fall, a blast of frigid water. Just a moment to be done with this curse, and all the others — to seal the secrets inside and protect what had been entrusted to me. Just a moment to suck the loss and rot out of my bones. Just a moment to join my own little one, wherever she was.

I continued to bounce Beatrice up and down in my arms, and I made a silent plea that she would never think thoughts as dark and terrible as my own. And I felt sure if my own baby had lived — she would then be nineteen years old, a young woman — I would not have entertained such things. I certainly would not look so longingly to the black shadow of the bridge a short distance away.

I pulled my gaze down to Beatrice's face. There was not a flaw on her, not so much as a birth blemish. I tugged the cream-colored blanket away slightly so that I might better see the little folds of skin around her chin and neck. By the softness of the wool against my thumb, I believed the blanket swaddling the child cost more than the clothes on both the mother and father put together. *Beatrice,* I said silently, hoping to somehow communicate the meaning to her with only my eyes, *your mother and father love you very much.*

As I said it, I could have cried out; my womb had never felt so hollow, so void. I wished I could have said the same thing to my own lost child — that her mother and father loved her very much — but I could not have said it, because it would only have been half true.

Trembling, I handed Beatrice back to her mother as the boatman began to navigate us to shore.

Early the next morning, after harvesting the beetles from the field and roasting them over the hearth, I could hardly lift myself from my place on the floor. The frigid air of the day prior had left my knees stiff, and the long walk after the boat journey made my ankles swell. My fingers, too, were raw and bloodied, but that was expected; I'd dug more than a hundred blister beetles out of the fields near Walworth, plucking each one from its nest, removing each one from its beloved kin.

Amid this discomfort, relief was provided by the low flame and the opium-laced water boiling over it. I had an hour to rest until the wealthy customer — whose imminent visit still left me with a palpable sense of unease — arrived.

And yet, I was made a fool of; just as I leaned my head back against the hearth, there came a knock on the hidden door, so sudden, so startling, I almost cried out. Quickly, quickly, I scoured my thoughts. Was I so exhausted that I had forgotten an appointment? Had I missed a letter? It was too early for the lady arriving at ten; too early to be blamed on mismatched clocks.

God be damned, it must be a woman needing wormwood or feverfew, the every-day remedies. I groaned and began to heave myself from the floor, but my own weight was like quicksand, sucking me down. Then came another knock, louder this time. Silently, I cursed the intruder, the person bringing more pain upon me.

I went to the door and peered through the narrow cleft in order to view my visitor.

It was Eliza.

11

ELIZA

When Nella opened the door, swinging it toward her small body, she looked frightened out of her wits. "I'm sorry for catching you by surprise," I offered.

"Oh, do come in," she breathed, hand on her chest. I stomped my wet feet and stepped inside. The room looked exactly as it had several days ago, but the odor had changed; the air smelled earthy, like moist, healthy dirt. Curious, I peered around the shelves.

"I read the papers yesterday," Nella said, catching my gaze. The shadows of her sunken cheeks were darker today, and wisps of her charcoal, wiry hair stuck out at odd angles around her face. "About Mr. Amwell, finally succumbing to the drink. Everything went as planned, it seems."

I nodded, pride blooming inside of me. I could hardly wait to tell her how well the poisoned egg had worked, and I wished that she hadn't read of it before I had the chance to tell her myself. "He fell ill instantly," I said, "and he never did improve, not even a bit."

There was only one problem. My hand found its way to my lower belly, which had ached since the hour of Mr. Amwell's death. He might have succumbed to the poison as planned, but I had begun bleeding at the very moment his spirit was released into the house. Returning to Nella's shop seemed my only option; surely one of her tinctures could remove his ghost.

Besides, her vials and potions fascinated me. She might not think them magickal, but I mightily disagreed. I knew that Mr. Amwell had not merely died; something in him had transformed, just like the butterflies in their cocoons. He had taken new form, and I felt sure Nella's elixirs were the only way to reverse it, the only way to stop the bleeding from my belly.

But I could not share this with Nella, not yet, for she'd denied magick during my first visit. I did not want her to think me tiresome — or downright mad — so I'd come prepared with another tactic.

Nella crossed her arms, looking me up and down. Her knuckles, just inches in front of my face, appeared swollen, round and red as cherries. "I'm very glad the egg worked," she said, "but given that you accomplished your task, I am curious what brought you back here. Without warning, I should add." Her tone was not a punishing one, but I sensed she was not pleased with me. "I presume you did not return to issue the same fate to your mistress?"

"Of course not," I said, shaking my head. "She has been lovely to me, always." A sudden draft swirled through the air, and I caught a strong whiff of the damp, earthy odor. "What is that smell?"

"Come here," Nella said, waving me to an earthenware pot on the floor, near the hearth. The pot stood as high as my waist and was filled with loose black dirt. I followed eagerly, but she held out her hand. "No closer," she said. Then she took a pair of crude leather mitts and, with a small, spade-like instrument, she parted some of the dirt toward the edge of the pot to reveal, hiding within, a hard, whitish object. "Wolfsbane root," she said.

"Wolfs . . . bane," I repeated slowly. The object looked like a rock, but, craning my neck, I could just barely make out a few little knots protruding from it, similar to a potato or carrot. "For killing wolves?"

"At one time, yes. The Greeks used to

extract the poison and place it on their arrows while hunting wild dogs. But nothing of that sort will be done here."

"Because it will kill men, not wolves," I said, eager to show my understanding.

Nella raised her eyebrows at me. "You are unlike any twelve-year-old I have met," she said. She turned back to the pot and gently brushed the dirt back over the root. "In a month's time, I will shred this root into a thousand pieces. A pinch of it, mixed well into an otherwise bitter horseradish sauce, will stop the heart within an hour." She tilted her head at me. "You still haven't answered my question. Is there something else you're needing from me?" She took off her mitts and intertwined her fingers in her lap.

"I do not want to remain at the Amwell house," I muttered. It was not untruthful, even if it was not the *whole* truth. I let out a cough and felt the sticky, wet sensation of blood leaking from me. Yesterday, I'd snatched a thin cloth from the laundry and cut it into pieces, just to keep the blood from soiling my undergarments.

Nella cocked her head to one side, confused. "What of your mistress? Your work?"

"She has gone north for a few weeks to be with her family in Norwich. She left this morning, her carriage dressed in black, on account of needing to be with family while she —" I paused, repeating what she had asked me to write in several letters before she left. "While she is in mourning."

"There must be plenty of household work to keep you busy, then."

I shook my head. With my mistress gone, her husband dead and Sally returned from her visit with her mother, there was little for me to do. "I only write her letters, so Mrs. Amwell said I did not need to remain at the house while she was gone."

"You write her letters? That explains your penmanship."

"She has shaky hands. She cannot write much of anything anymore."

"I see," Nella said. "And so she dismissed you for a time."

"She suggested I visit my parents in the country — in Swindon. She thought perhaps a rest would be good for me."

Nella raised her eyebrows at this, but it was true; after I fell sobbing to the floor and Mrs. Amwell found my streak of blood on her chair, she took me in her arms. I had been inconsolable about Mr. Amwell's released spirit, unable to quiet my hiccups, but she seemed unperturbed, even calm. How could she not see the truth? I began

134

bleeding the very same hour that Mr. Amwell died; how could she not see that his spirit had done it to me? His ugly ghost wrapped itself around my belly that night.

No tears over this, my mistress had whispered, *for this is as natural as the moon moving across the sky.*

But there was nothing natural about this death-blood that still had not stopped, despite the passage of two days. My mistress had been wrong about Johanna — I *knew* she died in the room next to me — and she was wrong about this, too.

"And yet you did not go to Swindon," Nella said, bringing my attention back to her.

"It is a long journey."

Nella crossed her arms, a look of disbelief on her face. She knew I was lying; she knew there was something else, some other reason for not returning home. Nella looked to the clock, then the door. Whether she was waiting for someone to arrive or waiting for me to leave, I did not know — but if I could not tell her about my bleeding, I needed to find another way to stay, and quick.

I clenched my hands, ready to say what I'd practiced on my walk here. My voice trembled; I could not fail, or she would send me away. "I'd like to stay with you and help

135

with your shop." The words rushed from me in a single breath. "I would like to learn how to shred roots that kill wolves and how to put poison into an egg without cracking it." I waited, judging Nella's reaction, but her face remained blank and this gave me a surge of courage. "Like an apprenticeship, only for a short while. Until Mrs. Amwell has returned from Norwich. I promise to be of great help to you."

Nella smiled at me, her eyes creasing at the edges. Whereas I believed, a moment ago, that she was hardly older than my mistress, now I wondered if perhaps Nella wasn't forty, or even fifty years old. "I do not need help with my tinctures, child."

Undeterred, I sat up taller. I'd come prepared with a second idea, in case my first plea did not work. "Then I can help you with your vials," I said, motioning to one of her shelves. "Some of the labels are faded, and I have seen the way you hold your arm funny. I can darken the ink, so you do not hurt yourself." I thought of my many hours and days spent with Mrs. Amwell in the drawing room, perfecting my penmanship. "You will not be disappointed with my work," I added.

"No, little Eliza," she said. "No, I cannot agree to that."

My heart almost burst, and I realized I never dreamed she would say no to this, too. "Why not?"

She laughed in disbelief. "You want to be an apprentice, an assistant, and learn to brew poisons so middling women can kill their husbands? Their masters? Their brothers and suitors and drivers and sons? This is not a shop of sweets, girl. These are not vials of chocolate into which we place crushed raspberries."

I bit my tongue, resisting the urge to remind her that only days ago, I cracked a poisoned egg into a skillet and served it to my master. But I knew from writing Mrs. Amwell's letters that the things a person most wanted to say were often the things they should keep tucked away inside. I paused, then said calmly, "I know this is not a shop of sweets."

Her face was serious now. "What interest do you have in meddling with this business, child? My heart is black, as black as the ash beneath that fire, for reasons you are too young to understand. What has harmed you so, in merely twelve years, that leaves you wanting more of this?" She waved her arms around the room, her gaze falling at last on the pot of soil, with the wolfsbane hidden underneath.

"And have you considered what it might be like to sleep on a cot in a room hardly large enough for one of us, much less two of us? Have you considered that there is not a bit of privacy in here? There is no rest, Eliza — something is always steaming, brewing, stewing, soaking. I wake at all hours of the night to tend the things you see around us. This is no grand house of nighttime quiet and pink papers on the wall. You may be just a servant, but I suspect your quarters are much nicer even than this." Nella took a breath and placed a gentle hand on mine. "Do not tell me that you dream of working in a place like this, girl. Do you not wish for something more?"

"Oh, yes," I told her. "I wish to live near the sea. I have seen paintings of Brighton, of castles in the sand. I would like to live there, I think." I pulled my hand away and ran my fingers over my chin; a small, itchy boil had formed there, hardly larger than the tip of a needle. Out of other ideas, I exhaled, resigned to telling Nella the rest of the story. "Mr. Amwell's spirit haunts me. I fear that if I remain at the house without Mrs. Amwell, he will harm me more than he has already."

"Nonsense, child." Nella vehemently shook her head back and forth.

"I swear it! The house has another spirit, too, of a young girl who was there before me, named Johanna. She died in the room next to mine, and I hear her crying at night."

Nella's palms splayed open as though she could not believe my words, like I was mad.

But I went on, resolute. "I very much want to remain in the service of Mrs. Amwell. And I promise, I will return to my post as soon as she has come back to London. I do not mean to inconvenience you. I only thought perhaps you could teach me how to brew something that will remove the spirits from the house, so I mustn't listen to Johanna's incessant crying anymore, and so that Mr. Amwell will leave me alone, once and for all. I could learn other things besides, and perhaps help you some while I am here."

Nella looked me hard in the eye. "You listen here, Eliza. No potion has the power to remove spirits from the empty air we breathe. If one did exist, and if I had been the one to brew and bottle such a tincture, I would be a rich woman, living in a manor somewhere." She traced a fingernail over a scratch on the table where we sat. "Bravery you have in telling me the truth. But I'm sorry, child. I cannot help you and you cannot stay here."

Discouragement coursed through me; no matter my pleas, Nella had not offered to help me in any way, not even by offering a place to stay until Mrs. Amwell returned. And yet, I clung to the tremor in her voice. "Do you believe in spirits? Mrs. Amwell does not believe me, not even a bit."

"I do not believe in ghosts, if that is what you're asking of me. Little clouds of evil that children, like you, fear in the night. Think of it — if we become a ghost when we die, and if we haunt the places we once lived, would not all of London be in a perpetual fog?" She paused as the fire crackled loudly behind her. "But I do believe that sometimes, we feel remnants of those who lived before. These are not spirits, but rather creations of our own desperate imaginations."

"So Johanna, who cries in the room next to mine . . . you think I am imagining her?" It was impossible; I'd never even met the girl.

Nella shrugged. "I cannot say, child. I have not known you long, but you are young, and therefore prone to wild ideas."

"I am twelve," I snapped back, my patience finally gone. "I am not so young."

Meeting my eyes, Nella stood at last, grimacing, and made her way to the large

140

cupboard at the back of the room. She ran her finger along the spines of several books, clicking her tongue against her teeth. Not finding what she wanted, she opened one of the cupboard doors and searched another stack of books, this one more disorderly than the last. Toward the bottom of the pile, she tugged on the spine of a small book and withdrew it.

It was very thin, more a pamphlet than a book, and the soft cover was torn at one corner. "This belonged to my mother," she said, handing the book to me. "Though I never saw her open it, and I have seen no need myself."

Peeling open the faded burgundy cover, I gasped at the frontispiece; it was an image of a woman giving birth to a bounty of fresh harvest, turnips and strawberries and mushrooms. Scattered around her bare breasts were several fish and a newborn pig. "What is this?" I asked Nella, my cheeks flushing.

"Someone gave it to my mother long ago, only a year or so before she died. It's a book claiming to be filled with magick, intended for use by midwives and healers."

"But she did not believe in magick, either," I guessed.

Nella shook her head, then walked to her register and turned the pages backward, furrowing her brow as she searched the dates. Skimming her finger along the entries, she nodded. "Ah, yes. Take a look here." She spun the register around to face me, then pointed at the entry:

6 Apr 1764, Ms Breyley, aus. wild honey, 1/2x pound, topical.

"A half pound of wild honey," Nella read aloud.

I widened my eyes. "To eat?"

She pointed at the word *topical.* "No, to spread onto the skin." She cleared her throat as she explained, "Ms. Breyley was hardly older than me. Hardly older than *you.* She came to my mother's shop after midnight. Her cries woke us from sleep. An infant lay in her arms . . . She said that a few days prior, the little boy had been badly scalded by a kettle of hot water. My mother did not ask how. It did not matter so much as the poor boy's condition. The wound had begun to fester and pus. Worse still, a rash was forming on other parts of his body, as though the wound had begun to crawl its way through the rest of him.

"My mother took the boy in her arms, felt the heat of him against her breast, then laid him onto this table and stripped off his clothes. She opened the jar of wild honey and slathered it onto his body. The infant began to cry and my mother, too. She knew how much it must have pained his new, delicate skin. It is the most distressing thing, Eliza, to issue pain to someone, even when you know it is for the best."

Nella dabbed at her eye. "My mother would not let the young woman and her child leave, not for three days. They stayed with us, in the shop, so the honey could be applied every two hours. My mother did not miss a single treatment — she was not so much as a minute late in brushing the honey onto the baby's skin for three entire days. She treated the boy as though he were her own." She closed the register. "The pus dried. The spreading rash disappeared. The festering wound healed, with almost no scar." She motioned to the book of magick she'd just given me. "That is why my mother never opened the book in your hands. Because saving lives with the gifts of the earth, Eliza, is as good as magick."

I thought of the honey-covered baby that had once lain on the table where I now sat, and suddenly I felt ashamed of having mentioned magick at all.

"But I understand your curiosity about ghosts," Nella went on, "and this is not about saving lives, anyhow. Inside the back cover is the name of a bookstore, and the street on which it's located. I forget it now — something like Basing Lane. They have all sorts of books on magick, or so I've heard. The shop may not even exist anymore, but seeing as how you'd like a potion to remove spirits from the house, I think it as good a place to start as any." She closed the cupboard door. "Better than here, anyway."

I held the book in my hands, feeling the cool heft of it against my damp palms. A book of magick, I thought contentedly, with the address of a shop that sold more. Perhaps my visit to her today had not been as fruitless as I'd feared a moment ago. Anticipation beat inside my chest. I would go at once to this bookshop.

Suddenly, there was a light rapping, four soft clips, on the door. Nella looked again at the clock and groaned. I stood from my chair, ready to leave. But as Nella moved to the door, she placed a light hand on my shoulder and gently pushed me back into my seat.

My heart surged, and Nella lowered her voice to a whisper. "My hand is not steady, and I could not bottle up the powder that I am to sell to the woman who has just arrived. I could use your help, this once, if you would not mind."

I nodded eagerly — the magick bookshop could wait. Then, her knuckles still swollen and red, Nella opened the door.

12

CAROLINE

Just after six o'clock, with a coffee in hand and enough early sunlight to see by, I left the hotel and made my way toward Bear Alley. I sucked in deep, cleansing breaths and considered how best to handle James's impending arrival. I could ask him to book a room at a different hotel, preferably in another city, or print out our vows and tell me what, exactly, he didn't understand about the words *I will remain faithful.* Whatever I asked him to do, one thing remained very clear: when I finally saw him, he wouldn't much like what I had to say.

Distracted by my thoughts, I missed the crosswalk light and a taxi nearly ran me over as I crossed Farringdon Street. I waved my hand to the driver in a futile apology and silently cursed James for almost getting me killed.

On either side of Farringdon Street, imposing concrete-and-glass buildings rose high into the sky; as I'd feared, most of the area around Bear Alley looked to be taken up by mega corporations, and it seemed unlikely that anything existing two hundred years ago would remain today. With my destination only half a block ahead, I resigned myself to the fact that Bear Alley might be little more than a driveway.

At last, I came upon a small white-and-black placard marking an alleyway hidden between high-rise buildings: Bear Alley, EC4. The alley did indeed appear to be a service route for delivery trucks. Overfilled garbage cans cluttered one side of the alley while a mess of cigarette butts and fast-food containers littered the blackened pavement. Disappointment settled heavy on my chest; though I didn't expect a sign reading Apothecary Killer Was Here, I'd hoped there would be a bit more intrigue than this.

As I walked deeper into the alley, the street noise fading quickly behind me, I realized that behind the street-front concrete-and-steel buildings were older brick structures. Ahead of me, the alley stretched on for a couple hundred meters. I scanned the area to see a man leaning against the wall, smoking a cigarette and checking his phone — but other than him, the lane was empty. Despite this, I felt no fear; my adrenaline was high in anticipation of James's arrival.

I walked slowly between the brick build-ings, searching for anything interesting as I made my way to the end of the alley, but I only found more trash. I asked myself what I was searching for. It wasn't as though I needed proof that the vial, or the unnamed apothecary, had a connection to this alley. After all, I wasn't even convinced she existed; the hospital note could have been written by a deranged, hallucinating woman in the hours before her death.

But the *possibility* of the apothecary's exis-tence, the mystery of it, drew me deeper. The youthful, adventurous Caroline had begun to come alive again. I thought of my unused history degree, my diploma shoved away in a desk drawer. As a student, I'd been fascinated by the lives of ordinary people, those whose names weren't ac-knowledged and recorded in textbooks. And now, I'd stumbled on the mystery of one of those nameless, forgotten people — and a woman, no less.

If I was honest with myself, this adventure drew me in for another reason: I sought distraction from the message sitting in my inbox. Like the final day of a vacation, I longed for something, anything, to delay the inevitable confrontation to come. Placing my hand over my belly, I sighed. I also sought a distraction from the fact that my period still hadn't shown.

Disheartened, I approached the end of the alleyway. But then to my right, I spotted a steel gate, about six feet high and four feet wide, cracked and warped with age. Beyond the gate was a small square clearing, roughly half the length of a basketball court, unpaved and overgrown with shrubs. Discarded equipment littered the clearing: rusted pipes, metal sheeting and other trash that looked well suited for a colony of stray cats. The clearing was surrounded by the timeworn walls of the brick buildings around it, and I found it strange that a lot in obvious disuse was situated in such a popular commercial area. I was no real estate developer, but it seemed like a waste of perfectly good space.

I leaned into the gate, held in place by two stone pillars, and pushed my face up against the bars to better see the clearing. Though two hundred years had passed since the apothecary *might* have lived, my imagination grasped at the possibility that the tucked-away, abandoned clearing in front of me had remained unchanged. Perhaps she had walked this very ground. I wished badly the area wasn't so crowded with shrubs and weeds, because the walls surrounding it looked ancient, too. How long had these buildings even existed?

"Looking for a lost cat?" came a husky voice from behind me. I jerked my head away from the gate and turned around. About fifteen feet away, a man in blue canvas pants and a matching shirt stood watching me, an amused look on his face. A construction worker, possibly. A lit cigarette dangled from his lips. "Sorry, didn't mean to scare you," he offered.

"Th-that's all right," I stammered, feeling ridiculous. What good reason could I possibly give for peeking through a locked gate in an inconspicuous alley? "My husband is just around the corner," I lied. "He was going to take a picture of me in front of this old gate." Inside, I cringed at my own words.

He glanced behind him as though checking for my invisible husband. "Well, don't let me stop you, then. Creepy place for a picture, though, if you ask me." He snickered, taking a pull from his cigarette.

I appreciated that he kept a safe distance away, and I glanced up at some of the windows around me. Surely I was safe; as secluded as the alley felt, it was within sight of plenty of people in the buildings.

Feeling slightly more at ease, I decided to

use this stranger's arrival to my advantage. Perhaps I could glean some information from him. "Yeah, I guess it is creepy," I said. "Any idea why this clearing even exists?"

He stamped out his cigarette with his foot and crossed his arms. "No idea. A few years back, a *biergarten* tried to set up shop. Would've been perfect, but heard they couldn't get permits. It's hard to see from here, but there's actually a service door over there —" He pointed at the left end of the clearing, where a few bushes stood taller than me. "Probably just leads to a subcellar or something. Guess the folks who own the building want to keep this area clear in case they ever need to get in there." A buzzing noise suddenly came from his pocket, and he withdrew a small walkie-talkie. "That's me," he said. "Always a pipe to install or fix."

So he was a plumber. "Well, thanks for the info," I said.

"No worries." He waved while walking away, and I listened closely to the steady sound of his footsteps as they faded out of earshot.

I turned back to the gate. Using a dislodged stone on one of the pillars, I pulled myself up a few inches to get a better look over it. I directed my gaze to the left side of the clearing, where the plumber had pointed. From this higher vantage point, I squinted, trying to see past the branches.

Behind one shrub, I could make out what appeared to be a large piece of wood set into the aged brick building; the base of the wood piece was partially hidden amid tall, thick weeds. A rustle of breeze moved the branches ever so slightly, and then I caught the crumbling, reddish protrusion of something halfway down the wood. A rusty door handle.

I gasped, nearly losing my footing on the stone pillar. It was most definitely a door. And by the looks of it, it had not been opened in a very, very long time.

13
NELLA

As I opened the door for the woman whose arrival I'd been dreading, shadows threw her figure into silhouette, and her features were masked behind a sheer veil. I could make out only the width of her skirts and the delicate lace trimming around her collar. Then she took a hesitant step forward into the shop, a breeze of lavender floating behind her, and candlelight illuminated her form.

I covered a gasp; for the second time in a week, before me stood a customer unlike any that had been in my shop. First it had been a child, but now it was a grown woman who, by mere appearances, seemed more suited to the airy parlors of Kensington than my lowly, concealed shop. Her gown, a deep green edged with golden embroidered lilies, seized nearly a quarter of the space, and I feared a single turn may send half my vials to the floor.

153

The woman removed her veil and gloves, setting them on the table. Eliza seemed unsurprised by the visitor, taking the gloves immediately to the fire to dry them. The gesture was so obvious, and yet one that had not crossed my mind as I stood, stunned, observing the lady poised before me. If there was any doubt about her wealth, her status, it was gone now.

"It's so dark in here," she said, her cochineal-painted lips turned downward.

"I will add more wood to the fire," chirped Eliza. It was only her second time in my shop, and yet in some ways, she had begun to outwit me.

"Sit, my lady, please," I said, motioning to the second chair.

She lowered herself delicately into it and let out a long, shaky breath. She removed a small hairpin from the back of her head, adjusted a dangle of curls and re-pinned them into place.

Eliza stepped forward with a mug in her hand, setting it carefully on the table before the woman. "Warm peppermint water, miss," she said, curtsying.

I looked to Eliza, perplexed, wondering where she'd even found the spare mug, much less the crushed peppermint leaves. There was no chair for her, but I expected her to drop onto the floor or busy herself with the magick book I had given her.

"Thank you for the information in your letter," I said to the woman.

She raised her brow. "I didn't know how much to say. I took great lengths to protect myself in the event it was seized."

Yet another reason I didn't meddle with the rich: people always wanted what they have, their secrets most of all. "You said just enough, and I believe you will be pleased with the preparation."

A loud screeching sound interrupted us, and I turned to see Eliza dragging a wooden box across the floor. She pushed the box up to the table, between the woman and myself, and folded her hands in her lap. "I'm Eliza," she said to the woman. "We are so pleased to have you here."

"Thank you," the woman replied, her eyes softening as she took in the girl. "When I made my way over here today, I did not realize there would be two of you." She looked to me expectantly. "Your daughter?"

Oh, how I wished my daughter were by my side. But then we would not have been doing this at all, dispensing poisons and hiding in shadows. I choked over my response. "She helps me on occasion," I lied, unwilling to admit that Eliza had arrived without notice at the perfectly wrong time. There were only two chairs at the table for a reason, and I soon felt a cloud of regret in permitting Eliza to stay. I had spent a lifetime valuing discretion, and I saw clearly now the mistake in allowing her to intrude on the secrets exchanged between this woman and myself. "Eliza, perhaps you should take leave of us now."

"No," the woman said with the force of someone well accustomed to getting her way. "This peppermint tea is very good," she continued, "and soon I'd like more. Besides, I find the presence of a child to be . . . comforting. I don't have children of my own, you know, as badly as I want them and as much as we've —" She paused. "Oh, never mind that. How old are you, little Eliza? And where are you from?"

I could hardly believe it. This woman, surely an heiress to some great estate, shared something in common with me: we both desired the swelling of our bellies, the little kicks in our wombs. And yet, how lucky she was that her time had not yet passed. The skin around her eyes told me she could not be more than thirty years old. It was not too late for her.

"Twelve," Eliza said softly. "And I'm from Swindon."

The woman nodded approvingly while I, desperate to conclude the appointment, walked to one of my shelves and withdrew a small sheep horn jar. I motioned for Eliza to help me, and then I directed her to carefully spoon the beetle powder from the bowl on the table into the jar. As I had hoped, her hand was steadier than mine.

Once we finished, I set the uncovered jar before the woman for her to inspect. Inside, a lustrous green powder shimmered back at her, so fine it could run between her fingers like water. "Cantharides," I whispered.

Her eyes widened. "It is safe to be this close?" she asked. She scooted forward in her chair, her enormous skirts rustling around her legs.

"Yes, so long as you don't touch it."

Eliza leaned forward to peek into the jar while the woman nodded, her brows still lifted in surprise. "I have heard of it only once. Something about its use in the Parisian brothels . . ." She tilted the bowl slightly toward her. "How long did this take?"

The memory of crossing the River Thames — my coughing fit, the woman feeding her baby, Beatrice — seized me at once. "All night and into this morning," I breathed. "It requires more than just harvesting the beetles. They must be roasted over the fire and ground." I pointed to the mortar bowl and pestle across the small room; the bowl was as wide across as the woman's bodice. "I ground them up in that basin over there."

The lady, whose name I still did not know, lifted the jar of powder and shifted it in the light. "Do I simply drop the powder into a bit of food or drink? Is it really so simple?"

I crossed my ankles and leaned back in my chair. "You asked for something to incite lust. Cantharides are meant, foremost, to arouse. Blood will rush into the loins, and overtake —" I paused, aware that Eliza continued to listen closely. I turned to her. "This is not for your ears. Might you consider stepping into the storage room?"

But the woman placed her hand over mine and shook her head. "It is my powder, is it not? Go on. Let the girl learn."

Sighing, I continued, "The swelling of the groin is insatiable. This arousal will continue for some time, then will be accompanied by abdominal pain and mouth blisters. I suggest you brew something dark — a molasses liqueur, perhaps — and drop in the powder, then give it a good stir." I hesitated, choosing my words carefully. "A quarter of the jar, and he will not survive the night. Half of it, and he will not survive the hour."

There was a long pause as the lady considered this, and the only noise came from the clock ticking by the door and the snapping of the fire. I remained still, my previous unease of the woman's visit returning with a vengeance. She mindlessly touched the thin wedding band adorning her hand, her gaze locked on the low flame behind me, fire dancing in her eyes.

She lifted her chin. "I cannot kill him. I cannot have a child if I kill him."

At once, I feared I had not properly explained the danger of the powder. My voice began to shake. "I assure you, this is a deadly poison. You cannot safely administer a nonfatal amount —"

She raised her hand to stop me. "You misunderstand me. I do, indeed, seek a deadly poison. I only mean to say, it is not *him* I want to kill. It is *her.*"

Her. I flinched at this final word; there was nothing more I needed to know.

It was not the first request of its kind. Over the preceding two decades, I had been asked several times to dispense a poison that would be administered to another woman, but I had refused these customers without question. No matter the underlying betrayal, no woman would suffer at my hands. My mother founded the apothecary shop at 3

Back Alley to heal and nurture women, and I would preserve this until the day I died.

It was possible, of course, that some of my customers told me lies — that they kept their true intentions from me and meant to slip my tinctures to sisters or courtesans. And how could I stop them? It would have been impossible. But as far as I knew, my poisons had never been used against a woman. *Never.* And so long as I lived, I would not knowingly agree to it.

I considered how I might say this now — how I might tell this woman no — but her eyes were dark and I felt sure she sensed my desire to refuse her. She seized the moment of silence, my weakness, like I was a rabbit and she a fox. She squared her shoulders toward me. "You do not seem pleased by this."

I had regained some of my senses, and words no longer resisted. "I appreciate your efforts in seeking me out, but I cannot agree to this. I cannot send you away with this powder, if you mean to kill a woman. This shop is meant to help and heal women, not harm them. That remains the cornerstone. I won't dislodge it."

"And yet you're a murderer," she accused. "How can you talk about helping and healing anything, man or woman?" She glanced at the open jar of beetle powder. "Do you even care to know who she is, this *insect*? She is his mistress, his whore —"

The woman continued to explain, but her words deteriorated into a faint hum as I blinked slowly, the room growing dark around me. An old, shameful memory closed in: I had been a mistress once, too, though I hadn't known it at the time. An *insect,* a *whore,* according to this woman. I was the secret kept in the shadows — not someone to be loved, but a form of amusement. And no matter how I adored him, I would never forget the moment that I learned of Frederick's masquerade — his web of lies. It was a bitter thing to swallow, the realization that I'd been little more than an empty vessel for Frederick's lust.

If only this had been the worst of his transgressions. The worst of what he had done to me. Instinctively, I grazed my fingers across my belly.

This merciless woman was not worth another moment of my time; I would not tell her about my story, about the coward who sowed the first seed of the tainted legacy that brought her to my door. As the room continued to whirl about me, her chatter finally ceased. My unsteady hands sought the flat, hard safety of the table.

161

Unsure of how many seconds or minutes went by, I eventually became aware of Eliza shaking me by the shoulders. "Nella," she whispered, "Nella, are you well?"

My vision cleared and I saw the two of them, sitting across from me with troubled looks on their faces. Eliza, leaning forward to touch me, appeared concerned for my well-being. The woman, however, resembled a petulant child, fearful that she might not be given what she wanted.

Comforted by Eliza's touch, I forced a small nod, shaking loose the memories. "I am well, yes," I assured her. Then I turned to the lady. "It is my business only who I choose to help and who I choose to hurt. I will not sell you this powder."

She looked at me in disbelief, her eyes narrow, as though it was the first time she had been told no. She let out a single barking laugh. "I am Lady Clarence of Carter Lane. My husband —" She paused, looking at the jar of beetle powder. "My husband is Lord Clarence." She watched me closely, waiting for my surprised reaction, but I gave her no such satisfaction. "You cannot understand the urgency of this, clearly," she continued. "As I said in my letter, we are to have a party tomorrow eve. Miss Berkwell, my husband's cousin and mistress, will attend." Lady Clarence tugged at the hem of her bodice, rubbing her lips together. "She's in love with my husband, and he with her. It cannot continue. Month after month, I am sure that I am not with child because he has nothing left for me, having spent it all in her. I will take this powder," she said, reaching into a pocket sewn into her skirts near her waist. "How much do you want, anyhow? I'll give you twice what you want for it."

I shook my head, caring little for her money. I would not have it, just like I would not have a woman — mistress or not — dead on my account. "No," I said, standing from the chair and rooting my feet to the ground. "The answer is no. You may leave now."

Lady Clarence stood from her own chair, our eyes level.

Meanwhile, Eliza's head jerked back and forth as she looked at us on either side of her. She sat up straight, back rigid, lips pressed tightly together. When she asked to be my apprentice, I doubt she imagined an encounter like this one. Perhaps it would be enough to make her change her mind.

At once, there was a flurry of movement; I thought that Lady Clarence had dropped her money onto the table, for her hands darted around quickly. But then I realized, with horror, that one of her hands was reaching for the jar of powder, which Eliza and I had not yet corked, at the center of the table, and her other hand stretched open her pocket. She intended to take the lustrous green powder, no matter my wishes.

I lunged for the jar — snatching it from her fingertips at the last moment and bumping into Eliza with such force that she nearly fell off her box — and did the only thing that came to mind: I tossed the jar of poisonous cantharides powder into the flames of the fire behind me.

The flames exploded into a bright green flare, in an instant rendering the poison worthless. I stared at the fireplace in astonishment, hardly able to believe that a night and morning's worth of work had just been so readily destroyed. My hands shaking, I turned very slowly to see Lady Clarence, flushed and astounded, and little Eliza, eyes wide as eggs, staring back at me.

"I cannot —" Lady Clarence stuttered. "I can't —" Her eyes darted around the room like mice, searching for a second jar, more powder. "Have you gone mad? The party is tomorrow evening!"

"There is no more," I told her, before motioning to the door.

Lady Clarence glared at me, then turned to Eliza. "My gloves," she demanded. Eliza sprang into action, delicately lifting the gloves from the drying rack and handing them to Lady Clarence. She began to pull the gloves on, shoving her fingers deep into them one at a time. After several heavy breaths, she spoke again. "You can easily make me another batch, I'm sure," she said.

God, this woman was insufferable. I threw my hands up in dismay. "Is there not some physician that you can bribe? Why must you put this on me, after I've refused you twice?"

She draped her veil over her face, the delicate strands of lace reminding me of hemlock leaves.

"You fool," she retorted from behind her lace. "Don't you think I've considered every physician, every known apothecary, in the city? I don't want to be caught. Do you even know your own distinction?" She paused, straightening her gown. "It's been a mistake to place my trust in you. But there's little use in reversing my decision now." She glanced down at her gloved hands, counting off a few fingers. "You made the powder in only a day, is that right?"

I furrowed my brow in confusion. What did it matter at this point? "Yes," I muttered.

"Very good," Lady Clarence said. "I will return tomorrow, as I understand that is ample time to prepare the powder anew, and you will give me a bowl of fresh cantharides, identical in appearance and form to those which you just foolishly ruined. I will be here at half one."

I stared at her, dumbfounded, ready to push her out the door with Eliza's help if I must.

"If you do not have the powders ready for me as I've asked," Lady Clarence continued, "then you best gather your things and make haste, for I will go straight to the authorities and tell them all about your little shop, full of cobwebs and rat poison. And when I speak to them, I'll make special note to proceed through the storage room and check behind the wall at the back. Every secret within this squalid hole will come to light." She pulled her shawl tightly around her. "I'm the wife of a lord. Don't try any tricks on me." She yanked the door open and let herself out, slamming it shut behind her.

14
CAROLINE
PRESENT DAY, TUESDAY

With only a few hours left before James's arrival, I didn't have time to investigate the gated-off door, but my curiosity, piqued yesterday, now felt on fire. It seemed that every bit of information gleaned, beginning with the vial, then the cryptic hospital note about Bear Alley, and now the door at the back of the alley, presented a new piece of a tantalizing puzzle. I resolved to do more digging and return when I could.

As I made my way out of Bear Alley, the sun slipped behind a cloud, plunging me into a cool shadow. Assuming the apothecary did exist, I envisioned what she may have looked like: an elderly woman with white, scraggly hair, frayed at the ends from spending so much time over her cauldron, hurrying out of the cobblestoned alley in a black cape. Then I shook my head at my own imagination: she wasn't a witch, and this wasn't *Harry Potter*.

I thought back to the hospital note. Whoever wrote the note had said the *men* are dead — plural. It was frustratingly vague. And yet, if more than a few people had died because of the apothecary, there should be some reference, some record of the apothecary's renown, online.

As I turned back onto Farringdon Street, I pulled out my phone, opened up my browser search bar and typed London Apothecary Killer 1800s.

The results were mixed: a few articles on the eighteenth-century gin obsession; a Wiki page on the Apothecaries Act of 1815; and an academic journal page on bone fractures. I clicked on the second page of search results, and a website with an inventory of London's old criminal court — the Old Bailey — seemed the best search hit so far. I used my finger to scan the page, but it was terribly long and I had no idea how to do a document search on my cell phone. A moment later, the amount of data on the site froze my web browser. I cursed, swiping up on my phone to close the app altogether.

Frustrated, I sighed. Did I really think I could solve this with a simple web search? James would probably blame it on inadequate research techniques, which might have been better primed during undergrad if I'd read more textbooks and fewer novels during my long days at the university library.

The library. I jerked my head up and asked a passerby for the nearest Underground station, crossing my fingers that Gaynor would be working again today.

A short time later, I stepped inside the Maps Room, glad that I wasn't rain-drenched and covered in stink like last time. I spotted Gaynor immediately, but she was in the middle of helping someone at a computer, so I waited patiently for her to finish.

After a few minutes, Gaynor made her way back to the desk. Upon seeing me, she gave me a smile. "You're back! Did you learn anything about the vial?" she asked cheerily. Then she feigned a serious look. "Or did you go mudlarking again, and you've brought me another mystery?"

I laughed, feeling a surge of warmth toward her. "Neither, actually." I told her about the hospital papers and the note by the unknown author, alluding to the apothecary's involvement in multiple deaths. "The note was dated 1816. It mentioned a Bear Alley, which just so happens to be close to my hotel. I ventured over there this morning but didn't see much."

"You're a budding researcher," she said playfully. "And I would have done the exact same thing." Gaynor tidied a few folders sitting in front of her, then put them aside. "Bear Alley, you said? Well, the etching on your vial did resemble a bear, though it seems a bit of a stretch that the two might be connected."

"I agree." I leaned my hip against the desk. "The whole story seems a bit of a stretch, to be honest, but . . ." I trailed off, my eyes falling on a stack of books behind Gaynor. "But what if it's not? What if there's something to it?"

"You think this apothecary might really have existed, then?" Gaynor crossed her arms, looking at me inquisitively.

I shook my head. "I'm not really sure what I think. Which is part of why I'm here. I thought I'd see if you have any old maps of the area — Bear Alley, I mean — from the early 1800s. And I thought you might be better at a simple web search, too. I tried Googling an apothecary killer in London, but didn't turn up much."

Gaynor's face lit up at my request; as she'd told me when we first met, the old historical maps were her favorite. A subtle rush of envy seeped into me. With the passage of another day, I was that much closer to returning to my own job in Ohio — a job having nothing to do with history at all.

"Well, unlike yesterday," she said, "I think I can actually help you on this. We have some excellent resources. Come with me." She guided me over to one of the computers and motioned for me to sit. I felt, for the first time in a decade, like a student of history once again.

"All right, the best place to start is definitely with Rocque's map from 1746. It's a bit early for our time frame, but it was considered one of the most accurate and thorough plans of London for more than a century. It took Rocque a decade to survey and publish." Gaynor clicked on an icon on the computer's desktop and navigated to a screen covered in black-and-white boxes. "We can zoom into each square for a close-up of the streets, or simply type in a street name. So let's type in *Bear Alley,* since that's the street mentioned in the hospital note."

She hit Enter, and immediately the map jumped to the only Bear Alley on the map. "To orient ourselves," she explained, moving the map around, "let's look at the surrounding area. St. Paul's Cathedral is over here to the east, and the river's down here to the south. Does this seem to be the same general area where you went today?"

I frowned, not feeling confident. The map was more than two hundred and fifty years old. I read the surrounding street names and recognized none of them: Fleet Prison, Meal Yard, Fleet Market. "Um, I can't be sure," I said, feeling silly. "I'm not great with maps in general. I only remember Farringdon Street, the main road I was on."

Gaynor clicked her tongue against her teeth. "Brilliant. So we can overlay a present-day map on this Rocque map fairly easily." She pressed a few more buttons and instantly, a second map was displayed on top of the first one. "Farringdon Street," she said, "runs right here. It's called Fleet Market on the old map so, at some point, the name changed. No big surprise there."

With the second, current map on display, I instantly recognized the layout of the area — the present-day map even showed the intersection where the taxi nearly ran me over. "That's it!" I exclaimed, leaning forward. "Yes, it's definitely the right Bear Alley, then."

"Perfect. Let's go back to the old map and look around a bit more." She removed the current map from the overlay and zoomed in as much as she could onto Bear Alley, as displayed on Rocque's map.

"So this is interesting," she said. "See this?" She pointed at a tiny line, thin as a strand of hair, protruding off Bear Alley. The line was labeled Back Al.

I hardly noticed the unexpected cramp that had begun to tug at my lower belly. "Yes, I see it," I said. "Why is it interesting?" But as the words rolled off my tongue, my heart began to beat faster. *The door.*

"It's just such a tiny little thing," Gaynor said. "Rocque did a very good job with street size — the main thoroughfares are drawn widest, for example — but this is about as narrow as he would have drawn on the map. Must have been an unassuming little road, maybe no more than a walkway. Makes sense, as it's labeled Back Alley." She overlaid the current map yet again, clicking it on and off with the mouse. "And it definitely doesn't exist today. It's not un-common — thousands of streets in the city have been replaced, diverted or simply built over." She peeked over at me, and I pulled my hand from my mouth; I'd been absent-mindedly chewing my fingernail. "Some-thing's bugging you," she said.

Our eyes met. For a moment, I felt the almost uncontrollable desire to lean on her and unburden everything on my heart. But as heat began to prickle behind my eyes, I

173

shoved my hands under my legs and turned my face back to the computer. James hadn't arrived in London yet; this time was my own, and I wouldn't spend it sobbing over him.

Looking again at the map, I hesitated, debating whether to tell Gaynor that I saw a door in exactly the spot where, according to the map, the now-obsolete Back Alley jutted off Bear Alley. But it didn't mean a thing, right? As the plumber told me, the door led to a storage cellar in one of the buildings. Nothing more. "I'm all right," I said, forcing a smile and turning back to the screen. "So Bear Alley survived two centuries, but Back Alley wasn't so lucky. It must have been built over."

Gaynor nodded. "Happened all the time. Let's fast-forward to a hundred years after Rocque's map." She clicked a few more buttons and overlaid another map, this one with irregular shaded shapes throughout. "This is an ordinance survey map from the late nineteenth century," she explained, "and the shaded areas represent structures, so we can easily see what buildings were in place."

Gaynor paused a few moments, scanning the screen. "Okay, so this whole area was definitely pretty built-up by the mid-1800s.

What this tells us is that even though Back Alley existed in the eighteenth century, it had essentially disappeared by the nineteenth century. But —" She paused and pointed to the screen of the ordinance survey map. "There's a little jagged line here that seems to separate a couple of buildings, and it follows the path of Back Alley almost perfectly. Maybe even in the nineteenth century, Back Alley still existed as a walkway between the buildings. It's just impossible to know."

I nodded my head; despite my limited understanding of surveys and ordinances, I followed her logic. And with each passing moment, I felt myself more convinced that the narrow, jagged line representing Back Alley on the nineteenth-century map was related to the door I saw earlier today. The precise location of the door, relative to the two old maps that Gaynor had shown me, was simply too coincidental.

For the first time since finding the vial, I allowed myself to dream that I'd begun to unravel a significant historical mystery. What if something lay behind the door, something related to the hospital note, the vial, the apothecary? And what if I revealed the connection to Gaynor, and she thought it worthy of sharing more broadly with historians? Perhaps I'd be invited to assist with other research projects, or do a brief stint at the British Library . . .

I took a deep breath, reminding myself to follow the facts in slow, logical order. I couldn't get ahead of myself.

"It's pretty cool," Gaynor continued, "cross-referencing all these maps. But if you're looking to learn more about the apothecary, I'm not sure what these maps could tell you."

I couldn't disagree with her. "Okay," I said, ready to move on to my second request — which was perhaps the more important one. "So, if we want to verify that this apothecary actually existed, what would be the best way to do that? Like I said, my own online searches were pretty fruitless."

Gaynor nodded, unsurprised. "The internet is an invaluable tool, but the algorithms used by search engines like Google are a nightmare for researchers. It's just not really built for searching antiquated documents and newspapers, even if they've been digitized." She went back to the computer's desktop and clicked on a new icon that brought up the British Newspaper Archive. "Okay," she said, turning to me. "Let's give it a go. This will search every line of text in most British newspapers for the last few hundred years. If there's an article about the apothecary, it will be here, but the trick is searching the right keywords. What did you try earlier?"

"Something along the lines of *1800s, apothecary killer, London.*"

"Perfect." Gaynor typed in the keywords and hit Enter. A moment later, the page displayed zero results. "Okay, let's remove the date," she said.

Yet again, no results.

"Could there be something wrong with the search function?" I asked.

She laughed. "This is the fun of it — the longer and harder we search, the more rewarding it is at the end." As she continued to try new keywords, I considered the dual meaning of her statement. I was searching for a lost apothecary, yes, but a sense of sadness came over me as I acknowledged what else I sought: resolution to my unstable marriage, my desire to be a mother, my choice of career. Surrounded by a thousand broken pieces, a long and hard search stretched ahead of me, one that would require sifting through the pieces I wanted to keep and the ones I didn't.

Gaynor cursed under her breath, frustration clear on her face. "Okay, well, so far nothing has come up. It's no wonder your online search was unsuccessful. Let's try this another way." She typed one word into the search bar, apothecary, and then manually refined the search results on the left-hand side of the screen. She set the date to 1800 to 1850 and the region to London, England.

A few results appeared, and my heart jumped as I caught the headline of one newspaper article: "Offences of Deception and Murder, Middlesex." But the article, dated 1825, seemed too late — and it turned out to be about a male apothecary who'd been killed after stealing a horse.

My shoulders slumped. "What else could we try?"

Gaynor pursed her lips to one side. "Well, we can't give up on the newspaper search just yet. Maybe we need to nix the word *apothecary* and try some others, like *Bear Alley*. But there are countless other resources to search, too. For example, our manuscript database . . ." She trailed off as she flicked to a new webpage. "By definition, manuscripts include handwritten documents like journals, diaries, even family estate papers. It's often very personal information. But our manuscript collection also includes some printed material — typescripts, printed logs and so on."

I nodded, recalling this from my schooling.

Gaynor picked up a pen and began to twirl it between her fingers. "We have millions of manuscripts in our collection. But searching this collection poses its own problems. You see, the newspaper records are instantly available on-screen since they've been digitized, but the manuscripts must be ordered. You request them, wait in a queue, which may be a couple of days, and then the desk delivers the actual document for you to review."

"So digging into this could take days."

Gaynor nodded slowly, twisting her face, like a doctor delivering bad news to a patient. "Yes, if not weeks or months."

The magnitude of such a search was exhausting to even think about, especially given that the story of the apothecary was little more than myth as it stood; what if the entire search was in vain, because there wasn't even a real person to uncover? I sat back in my chair, defeated. It seemed I couldn't sort truth from lie in any part of my life.

"Chin up," Gaynor said, nudging my knee with her own. "You're clearly intrigued by this sort of thing, which is rare in and of itself. I remember well my first week working at the library . . . I had no idea what I was doing, but I loved the old maps more than anyone else here. People like us need to stick together and keep at it."

Keep at it. Though I didn't know what, exactly, I wanted to find — or if there was even anything *to* find — one thing couldn't be ignored: the door at the end of Back Alley aligned perfectly with the old maps. And whether the apothecary worked in the area or not, the idea of an old walkway or street, known only to those who lived two hundred years ago but still buried underneath the city, captivated me.

Maybe this was what Gaynor meant by the appeal of the search. I had no idea what lay behind the door — it was likely to be a crumbling mess of brick, filled with rats and spiderwebs — but if there was anything I knew about myself now that I didn't know a few days ago, it was that *looking inside* wasn't always comfortable. Which was exactly why I'd avoided thinking about James thus far, and why I hadn't yet told my parents or anyone other than Rose about what he'd done. It was, in fact, why I'd distracted myself with the lost apothecary in the first place.

Gaynor and I exchanged phone numbers, and I let her know that I would be in touch if I wanted to request any manuscripts or further search the digitized newspaper records.

As I left the library, my phone showed it was just after nine o'clock. James would be landing any minute. And though I was discouraged by the fruitless search, I breathed in the warm London air and steeled myself as I made my way toward the Underground and Ludgate Hill, ready to face head-on what I could no longer choose to ignore.

As distraught as I'd been in the last few days, I felt more alive in London — enveloped in an old mystery, an old story — than I could remember feeling in years. I resolved to continue digging. To push through the dark and look inside of it all.

15
ELIZA

After Lady Clarence rushed out of Nella's shop, the air in the small room felt humid and hot, like it often did in the kitchen. The hair on my arms stood on end; I'd never heard anyone speak in the tones Nella and Lady Clarence had exchanged a moment ago.

Nella's face twisted into a look of misery and fatigue. I could see how the weight of her work — and the demands of women like Lady Clarence — had carved lines into her forehead and sunk pockets into her cheeks. Faint wisps of smoke still curled in the air as she slumped to one side in her chair, concern splashed all over her face like spilled vinegar.

"Kill the mistress of a lord," she mumbled, "or swing from the gallows?" She rolled her head to look into the fire, as though searching for what remained of her beetles. "Each choice is more hideous than the other."

"You must remake the powder." She did not ask for my opinion, but the words came out of me before I knew what I was saying. "It is the only option."

She turned on me, her eyes crazed. "Easier than killing a woman? All my life, I have sought to help women. Indeed, it is the only part of my mother's legacy that I have maintained with any measure of success."

But Nella had shown me her register, and I knew the entries consisted of names and dates and remedies. Worse than this, I knew that Mr. Amwell's name, and my own, were listed within. Which meant that if Nella did *not* remake the powder and Lady Clarence sought revenge, I would be exposed.

All of us in the book, exposed.

I pointed my finger at her book. "You may find a way to avoid writing Miss Berkwell's name in there, but what about me? What about the others written in those pages?"

Nella looked down at the book and frowned, like she had not even considered this idea. Like she did not really believe that Lady Clarence would make good on her threat. She slowly read the last few rows.

"I haven't the strength," she whispered at last. "I spent all of last night in the field gathering the beetles, and until sunrise I roasted and ground them. When she comes back, I'll tell her such. I'll show her the swelling underneath my gown, the places I am unwell, if she insists on seeing them. I could not remake the powder, even if I wished to do so."

An opportunity now stood before me, if I could be smart about it. My fears about Mr. Amwell's spirit had not lessened, and now I was burdened with yet another misfortune: the bailiffs uncovering Nella's shop and register.

I retrieved the empty mugs on the table and took them to the washbasin, rinsing them out. "I will do it, then. I will gather the beetles, if you tell me how, and I will roast and grind them." After all, I was well accustomed to doing another person's dishonorable work. Whether it meant writing lies in letters for Mrs. Amwell or crushing poisonous beetles for Nella, I was no tattle. I could be trusted.

Nella did not answer for some time, so I continued to rinse the mugs long after they were clean. Her nerves seemed to have quieted for the moment, though I could not tell if it was because she felt hopeful at my offer to assist her or because she had resigned to her fate.

"The field is across the river," she said at last, leaning forward in her chair as though exhausted by the mere idea of returning. "It will be a long walk, but you cannot do it alone. I'll gather the strength. We will go after the sun falls. The beetles are easier to catch at night, when they rest." She coughed several times and wiped her hand on her skirts. "Until then, we may as well make use of our time. Earlier, you mentioned helping me with the labels on my vials." She gave me a sidelong glance. "It's not needed. I know them by heart, with a label or no."

"What if they get mixed up? Put out of order?"

She pointed first at her nose, then her eyes. "Scent, then sight." She motioned to the register at the center of the table. "But there's something else. I'll have you fix a few of the faded entries in my book. I've not the steadiness of hand to do it myself."

I frowned, pulling the broad book toward me, wondering how the names and dates in the register could possibly be more important than the vials on her shelves. In fact, I'd expect the opposite; this book held the names of everyone who had purchased Nella's poisons. It seemed to me the pages should be burned, not repaired.

"Why is it so important to fix the faded entries?" I asked.

Nella leaned forward and turned to a page

riddled with entries from 1763. She ran her hand over the bottom left corner; at one time, a liquid had doused the parchment, leaving many of the entries unreadable. She pushed a quill and inkwell toward me. At her direction, I lifted the pen and began to copy the faint strokes in the book with fresh ink, tracing the remedies — *sorrel, balsam, safflower* — as carefully as I traced the names of the customers.

"For many of these women," Nella whispered, "this may be the only place their names are recorded. The only place they will be remembered. It is a promise I made to my mother, to preserve the existence of these women whose names would otherwise be erased from history. The world is not kind to us . . . There are few places for a woman to leave an indelible mark." I finished tracing an entry, moving on to the next one. "But this register preserves them — their names, their memories, their worth."

It was a harder task than I imagined, this tracing and darkening. Copying words was not the same as writing words; it required me to move very slowly with the curves of someone else's hand, and I did not feel as proud of my work as I'd hoped. Yet Nella did not seem to mind, and I let my shoulders relax, which made the task go quicker.

Nella turned to a more recent page of entries made just a few months ago. At some point, the pages must have stuck together, damaging several lines of text. I began to trace the first one, reading as I went. *7 Dec 1790, Mr. Bechem, black hellebore, 12 gr. on behalf of his sister, Ms. Allie Bechem.*

I gasped, pointing at the word *sister.*

"I remember that one well," Nella said as I darkened the letters. "Ms. Bechem's brother was a greedy man. She discovered a letter — he meant to kill their father in a week's time, to inherit a great estate."

"She killed her brother, so he would not kill their father?"

"Precisely. You understand, Eliza, that no good comes of greed. Certainly, no good came of this . . . Ms. Bechem felt someone would end up dead. The question, then, was who."

I traced Ms. Bechem's first name, *Allie,* making long downward strokes. The quill moved easily over the rough parchment, as though the pen itself knew the importance of this effort, the importance of preserving Ms. Allie Bechem's name and what she'd done.

Then my eye caught her name again. Just several days later, on December 11, she'd returned to the shop.

"This time, I sold Ms. Bechem nerve-root for her mother," Nella explained. "The poor woman had just lost her son, and quite unexpectedly at that. Nerve-root is entirely benign, not harmful in any way. It is meant for hysteria."

"Poor lady. I do hope it worked."

Nella motioned to the register, urging me to finish the page. "Nerve-root is quite effective," she said, "though the truth about her son and his plot would have been the best remedy. Alas, I don't know if her daughter revealed it. No matter, her secret is safe in here." She ran her finger along the edge of the book, toying with the pages.

I understood, now, why Nella sold medicines in addition to her poisons. People like Ms. Bechem needed both.

Except I still did not know why Nella sold poisons at all. During my first visit to her shop, she'd said the hidden room didn't exist when she'd worked at the shop as a child with her mother. Why did Nella build the secret room and begin to brew terrible things behind it? I resolved to find the courage to ask her, and soon.

After I finished the entry, Nella flipped the pages again, landing on 1789. The year stood out in my memory; it was the year my mother had left me in London to work for the Amwell family. Only, the entries on this page appeared in good condition. I could not see any that needed work.

"Why, this was just before I arrived in London," I offered.

"I think you might like this page," Nella replied. "There is a name on here you should recognize."

At once, it became a game. I scanned my eyes over the entries, doing my best to ignore the dates and ingredients, searching instead for a name I knew. My own mother, perhaps?

Then I saw it: *Mrs. Amwell.*

"Oh!" I gasped. "My mistress!" Quickly, I read the rest of the entry. Had my mistress poisoned someone once before? "Indian hemp?" I asked Nella, pointing to the register.

"One of the most powerful drugs in my shop," she said, "but like the nerve-root, there is nothing harmful about it. Indian hemp is especially useful in the case of tremors or spasms." She looked at me, waiting. When I did not respond, she explained, "Eliza, your mistress came to my shop when the shaking in her hands first began. I'd forgotten about her visit, until you mentioned earlier today that you write her letters for her." She ran her fingers over the entry, a faraway look in her eyes. "The gentlemen's doctors could do nothing for her. She'd paid visits to a dozen of them. She came to me when she felt she had no options left." She briefly set her hand over mine. "Your mistress had never been here before. She only knew of it from a friend."

A sense of overwhelming sadness fell over me. I'd never considered that Mrs. Amwell had sought help from so many doctors. I'd never considered at all how she felt about her impediment.

"Did the Indian hemp help?" I asked, glancing again at the entry to ensure I repeated the words correctly.

Nella paused and looked down at her own hands as if ashamed. "Remember what I told you, Eliza," she finally said. "This is not a shop of magick. The gifts of the earth, while valuable, are not infallible." She lifted her head, shaking herself from her reverie. "But it's all right. For if the Indian hemp had worked too well, then your mistress would not need your help writing letters. And you would not be sitting here now, helping me with my register. And you remember what I said about the importance of the register, right?"

Aiming to impress her, I recited what

she'd said a few minutes ago. "The register is important because the names of these women might otherwise be forgotten. They are preserved here, in your pages, if nowhere else."

"Very good," Nella concluded. "Now, let's do a few more. The sun is falling fast."

How did she know? Without windows, and without glancing at the clock, I certainly could not tell the sun was falling fast. But I could not ask her, for Nella had already turned to another page, hovering her hand over an entry that needed attention.

I got back to work, eager to please my new tutor.

After sundown, I gathered my coat and pulled out my gloves, which had never sifted through shrubs or dirt or wherever it was that beetles made their home, and eagerly pulled them on.

My hands were sore already — the careful tracing had left them stiff — but I could hardly wait for the next adventure.

Seeing the spark in my eye, Nella raised her brows. "Don't expect your gloves to be so clean when we're done," she said. "This is dirty work, child."

We walked for more than an hour, eventually making our way to a broad, quiet field separated from the road by hedges that were taller than me. The air grew unbearably cold as darkness spread across the sky, and I could not help but think that if I were a beetle, I would have traveled south long ago to the warm, humid air of some seaside village. And yet, Nella assured me that the beetles liked the cold — that they preferred starchy root crops, like beets, where they could nestle in to dine on the sugar and then sleep.

There was only a sliver of moon to see by. Nella and I each held a linen sack, and I watched her closely in the dark as she got onto her hands and knees, located a bundle of green, veiny leaves, and brushed aside a thin layer of hay until she reached the shoulders of the beet bulb underneath.

"Here we have the fruit," she said, continuing to dig. "They prefer to eat the leaves, but this time of night, they will be burrowed in the soil." And then, out of nowhere, she withdrew a glossy little bug, no longer than her thumbnail. "Now this is very important," she said, dropping the squirming beetle into the bag. "Do *not* press them or crush them."

I wiggled my toes in my shoes, hardly able to feel them even though we had been in the field only a few minutes. "How can I get one from the ground without pressing it?" I asked, my interest in the whole activity suddenly waning. "When I find one, I will need to grab him before he runs off, and I cannot do that without pressing on him a bit."

"Let's do the next one together," she urged, patting the ground beside her. It seemed her aches and discomforts had lessened; perhaps the cold had numbed her. "Reach into that same spot, where I just put my hand. I'm sure I felt another set of legs."

I shuddered. I had expected we would use a tool — a net or spade — instead of our gloved hands. But I did as she asked, grateful that the dark sky prevented her from seeing the grimace on my face. I moved my hand around the hard, smooth bulb of beetroot, and then I felt it: something crawled against my fingers, something very much alive. Steeling myself, I twisted my hand in the dirt and cupped my fingers around it. I lifted a pile of soil to show Nella and, sure enough, a green striped beetle crawled out of the dirt as though to greet us.

"Very good," she said. "Your first harvest. Drop him in the bag and close it up, else he will make quick work of escaping back to his little beetroot. I'll start over there, on the next row. We need one hundred beetles. Keep count of yours."

"One *hundred*?" I glanced down at my single beetle, writhing around in the bag. "Why, we'll be here all night."

She cocked her head at me, her face serious. The moonlight reflected against her left eye, giving her a strange, two-faced appearance. "It's curious to me, child, that you'd complain of the effort in catching a night's worth of beetles — mere bugs — and yet you think nothing of killing a man."

I shuddered, wishing she hadn't reminded me of Mr. Amwell's ghost, still pressing inside of me, making me trickle blood.

"It is hard work," she said, "and harder for me, as of late. Go on, now, let's get to it."

The night passed, though how much of it, I could not in truth be sure. The moon moved a quarter of the way across the sky, but I was not wise enough to use it as my clock.

"Seventy-four," I heard Nella say from behind me, her feet crunching on the hay beneath us. "And you?"

"Twenty-eight," I replied. I had counted diligently, repeating the number in my head, lest I forget and be forced to reach in and

194

count the crunchy bugs again.

"Ah! We're finished then, and with two to spare." She helped me to my feet, for my knees were sore and my hands raw.

We began to walk toward the road when I grasped her arm, distress warming me in an instant. "There will be no coaches running this late," I gasped. "We do not have to walk all the way back, do we?" I could not do it, not for anything.

"You have two perfectly good legs, don't you?" she replied, but at the sight of my miserable expression, she broke into a smile. "Oh, don't despair. We will rest over there, in that shed. It's quite warm, in fact, and perfectly quiet. We will take the first coach in the morning."

Trespassing seemed a worse offense than harvesting deadly beetles, but I followed Nella willingly — excitedly, even, for I so desperately wanted to rest — as we went through an unlocked door into the wooden shed that was, as she had promised, warm, dark and quiet. It reminded me of the barn at home in the country, and I cringed at the thought of what my mother would say to me if she saw me now, awake in the middle of the night with a bag of deadly bugs in my hand.

It took my eyes several moments to adjust,

but eventually I could make out a wheel-barrow at the far end of the structure and, closer toward us, an assortment of tools for tending a field. Along the wall to our right, several haystacks were pushed neatly against one another. It was here that Nella stepped forward, nestling herself against one of the stacks.

"It's warmest here," she urged, "and if you pile up a bit of hay on the ground, it makes a decent bed. Watch out for the mice, though. They like it here as much as we do."

Looking back at the door, fearing that some angry grounds owner might come chasing after us, I reluctantly followed Nella and made my own spot. She sat across from me, our feet almost touching, then pulled a small bundle from underneath her coat and unwrapped a loaf of bread, a bit of cheese and a leather canteen of what I assumed to be water. The moment she handed it to me, I realized how desperately thirsty I was. As I drank, the beetles in the bag rustled next to me.

"Have as much as you want," she said. "There's a barrel behind this shed, full of rainwater." I realized that not only had she used the shed previously for shelter, but she had, apparently, explored the grounds for other resources.

I finally pulled the canteen away and wiped water from my lips with a long edge of my skirt. "Do you often go onto other people's farmland to get what you need?" I thought not only of this shed, which did not belong to us, but the field where we'd just spent almost an entire night.

She shook her head. "Almost never. The wild, uncultivated earth provides most of what I need, and she disguises well her poisons. You have seen a belladonna bloom, yes? It opens like a cocoon. It seduces, almost. It may seem rare and unusual, but the truth is that this sort of thing may be found everywhere. The earth knows the secret to disguise, and many would not believe that the low fields they tend, or the trellis vines under which they kiss, hold poison within their stems. One only need know where to look."

I glanced at the hay bales against which we sat, wondering if Nella had some trick, possibly, to extract poison from something as innocent as dried grass. "Did you learn all this from books?" In her shop, I had seen the stacks of dozens of books, some appearing worn and well used, and I began now to feel foolish for broaching the idea of a short apprenticeship. It must have taken her years to learn everything she knew.

Nella took a bite of cheese, chewing slowly. "No. My mother."

Her words were sharp and uninviting, but this only served to pique my curiosity. "Your mother who did not have the wall or poisons."

"That's right. As I've said, a woman does not need to hide behind a wall if she has no secrets and does no wrong."

I thought of my mistress and myself, sitting in the drawing room behind a closed door, pretending to write letters, while Mr. Amwell suffered upstairs.

"My mother was a good woman," Nella added, letting out a shaky breath. "She did not dispense a single poison in her lifetime. You may have noticed it while looking through the older entries in my book tonight. The older remedies are helpful, curative. All of them."

I sat up straighter, wondering if Nella might finally share her story with me. Bravely, I ventured the question. "If she did not dispense poisons, how did she teach you about them?"

Nella looked hard at me. "Many *good* remedies are poisonous in great quantities or when prepared a certain way. She taught me these quantities and preparations for my own safety, and for the safety of our patrons.

Besides, just because my mother did not use poisons against anyone does not mean she did not know how." She nestled farther into the hay bale. "I suppose this made her even more admirable. Like a dog with a mouthful of sharp teeth who never once attacks, my mother's knowledge was a weapon she never once used."

"But you —" The words tumbled out of me, and I snapped my mouth shut before I finished. It was clear that Nella had decided to use her own knowledge as a weapon. Why?

"Yes, me." She folded her hands in her lap and met my gaze directly. "Eliza, let me ask you something. When you set the plate in front of Mr. Amwell — the one with the larger eggs, which you knew would kill him that very day — what did you feel inside?"

I thought carefully, remembering that morning as though it had happened only moments ago: his hot gaze as I stepped into the dining room; my mistress's soft eyes, in quiet alliance with me; and the sensation of oily fingers trailing up the back of my knee and along the skin of my thigh. I thought, too, of the day Mr. Amwell, my once-trusted master, gave me the brandy while my mistress was at the winter gardens — and what might have happened if the footman had not called for him to come downstairs.

"I felt like I was protecting myself," I said. "Because he meant to do me harm."

Nella nodded eagerly, as she might if she were leading me down a path in the forest, encouraging me to follow. "And what were you protecting yourself from?"

I swallowed, nervous to share the truth; I had never told Nella why Mrs. Amwell wanted to kill her husband, and why I helped her do it. But I was the first to ask the prying question, so I owed her my own story, too. "He had begun to touch me in ways that I did not like."

Again, a slow nod. "Yes, but look deeper than that. His unwelcome touch, as much as it repulsed you . . . Why was it different than, say, a stranger on the street? I suspect you would not resort to murder if a stranger let his hand stray?"

"I do not trust most strangers on the street," I said. "But I trusted Mr. Amwell. Until recently, he gave me no reason not to." I paused, slowing my breath, and thought of Johanna. "I learned there are secrets in his house. Things he has destroyed, things he has kept hidden. I feared I was to be one of them."

Satisfied, Nella leaned forward and patted my foot. "First, there was trust. Then, there was betrayal. You cannot have one without the other. You cannot be betrayed by someone you do not trust." I nodded, and she leaned back again. "Eliza, what you have just described is the same heart-wrenching journey of every woman to whom I have sold a poison. And it is, indeed, the same path for me."

She frowned as if thinking of a long-buried memory. "I did not set out to brew poisons. It is not as though I came from the womb a born killer. Something happened to me, long ago. I was in love once, you see. His name was Frederick." She stopped suddenly, in spite of herself, and I thought she might cease her story. But she cleared her throat and went on. "I expected a proposal. He had promised it to me. Alas, he was a fantastic actor and liar, and I soon learned that I was not the only recipient of his affection."

I gasped and placed my hand over my mouth. "How did you find out?" I asked, feeling privy to the scandal and secrets typically reserved for girls much older than myself.

"It is a sad story, Eliza," she said. She nudged my foot with her own. "And you must listen very carefully to me. After we prepare the beetle powder together in the morning, I do not want to see you at my shop again. This is my work, my grief to bottle up and dispense." Disappointment and enthrallment tugged equally at me, but I nodded so she would go on.

And so she began her story, and though each word seemed to rise painfully to the surface like a boil, I also sensed that her words were a form of release. I might have been only twelve, but sitting together amid the hay bales, I felt as if Nella considered me a friend.

"My mother died when I was a young woman," she explained. "This was two decades ago, though the grief is still tender, like a bruise. Have you ever grieved?"

I shook my head. Other than Mr. Amwell, I'd never known someone who'd died.

Nella took a deep, steadying breath. "It is a terrible, exhausting, lonely thing. One day, at the very peak of my grief, a young man named Frederick arrived at the shop — which was not one of poisons, yet — and he begged for something to give to his sister, Rissa, to induce bleeding, for the cramping in her belly was unbearable and it had been half a year since her monthly course."

I frowned. I was not sure what *monthly course* meant, but no matter how Rissa played into the story, I could empathize with her belly pains. "He was the first man to step foot into my shop," Nella continued, "but he was so desperate! And if Rissa did not have a sister or mother to send, how could I refuse him? So I gave him a tincture of motherwort, an emmenagogue."

"*Motherwort*," I repeated. "Is it for mothers?"

Nella smiled and went on to explain that more than a century ago, Culpeper — the great healer — believed it to bring joy to new mothers and remove the melancholy so common in the days after childbirth. "But you see," she continued, "motherwort also settles the womb and stimulates the belly to shed what's inside. In doing so, it must be administered very carefully, and only to those who are positive they are not with child."

She pulled a stem of hay from the bale and began to twist it around her finger, like a ring. "The next week Frederick returned, vibrant and gentlemanlike, thanking me for returning his sister to her normal, healthy self. I found myself intensely drawn to him for reasons I didn't understand at the time. I thought it love, then, but now I wonder if it wasn't simply the emptiness of grief, seeking something to rush in and take away the barren feeling."

She exhaled. "Frederick seemed drawn to me, too, and in the weeks that followed, he promised me his hand. With each passing day, each promise, something in my heart came back to life. He promised me a house full of children and a beautiful shop with pink glass windows to carry on the memory of my mother. Imagine how that made me feel . . . What could I call it other than love?" She looked down at her hand, where the stem of hay was wrapped in a perfect circle around her finger. At once, she let go and it fell to her lap.

"I soon became pregnant. One would think I knew how to prevent such a thing, but that is not how it happened. Despite my grief, the new life inside of me gave me a great deal of hope. Not everything in the world had given up its last breath, like my mother. And when I told Frederick about our baby on that early-winter morning, he seemed overjoyed. He said we would get married the week after next, following Martinmas, before anyone else could see that I was with child. You may be young, Eliza, but you know enough to see that the sun does not shine so brightly on a child born out of wedlock."

Concern bubbled inside of me. Nella had never mentioned a child, grown or otherwise; where was the child now?

"Well, as you might suspect, I was not with child for much longer. It happens often, little Eliza, but that does not make it any less terrible. I hope that you never have to experience it." She pulled her legs up closer to her body and crossed her arms, as though protecting herself from what she was to say next. "It happened very late at night. Frederick meant to leave the city for a week to visit family, so we'd spent the entire evening together. He fixed us supper, helped with the repair of several shelves, read me a poem he'd written . . . a perfect evening, or so I thought. He left me with a long kiss, promising to return the next week." Nella shuddered and was silent a moment. "Hours later, the cramping began, and I lost my child. No words can describe the pain. Afterward, I needed nothing so much as the comfort of Frederick's embrace. In bed-ridden agony, I waited for the week to pass, repressing my grief until he returned and could help me with the burden of it. But he did not show — not after the second week, nor the third. I began to suspect something terrible, and I thought it very strange that the night I fell ill — the night I lost our girl — was the last night he'd shown his face.

"Frederick was familiar with many of the

shelves and drawers at my shop. And as I said, even the most benign remedies may be deadly in great quantity. I checked several bottles against my register, and to my horror, I saw that the motherwort was not at its recorded level. Frederick knew of its properties, since I had dispensed it to his sister, Rissa. I realized, then, that he had used my own tinctures against me. Against our child. We had spent so much time together, and it was not out of the realm of possibility that he had somehow disguised it and tricked me into ingesting it during supper. I felt sure, as the days passed, that the motherwort — meant to remove melancholy and bring joy to a new mother's soul — had taken the child right from my womb."

The back of my throat burned and tightened as Nella spoke. I wanted to ask how Frederick managed to deceive her — how he could have rooted through her things, slipped a single drop into her food or drink without her noticing — but I did not want to turn this against her, to make her feel any worse about it than she must already.

"Little Eliza, at last, there was a knock on my door. And who do you think it was that had come to see me?"

"Frederick," I said, leaning forward.

"No. His sister, Rissa. Except . . . she was

206

not his sister. She told me, without hesitation, that she was his wife."

I shook my head as though this memory of Nella's was happening now, right in front of my eyes. "H-how did she know where to find you?" I stammered.

"She knew of my mother's shop for women's maladies. Remember, she was the one who first sent Frederick to me, when she badly needed the motherwort. She also knew he had a *tendency,* you might say, to skirt around. She asked me to share the truth with her. This was merely four weeks after I had lost the baby. I was still bleeding, still in a great deal of heartache, and so I revealed everything to her. Afterward, she told me that I was not his first mistress, and then she began to ask questions of the bottles and brews on my shelves. I told her what I have told you — that in large quantities, nearly anything is deadly — and to my great surprise, Rissa asked for *nux vomica,* which can be used in very small doses to treat fever, even plague. But it is, of course, rat poison. The same thing that killed your master."

Nella spread her hands wide. "Upon her asking, I hesitated but a moment, then dispensed her a deadly quantity, free of charge, and advised her how to best disguise the flavor. Just as Frederick had slipped a poison to me, I instructed Rissa how to do the same. That, child, is how it began. With Rissa. With *Frederick.*

"After Rissa left, there was a sense of release within me. Vengeance is its own medicine." She let out a small cough. "Frederick was dead the next day. I read it that week, in the papers. Doctors blamed it on heart failure."

Nella's coughing grew louder and rose into a full-blown fit. She clutched her stomach, her breath hoarse, for several minutes. At last she leaned forward, gasping. "My mother, my child, my lover. And so it went — like a tiny leak, slow and hushed at first, word began to spread through the city. I do not know who Rissa told first, or who that person told next, but the web of whispers began to spread. At some point they started leaving letters, and I was forced to build a wall in my shop to remain unseen. I had not the heart to close up the place of my mother's legacy, no matter how I had spoiled it."

She patted the hay beside her. "I know what it is to watch my child fall from my body at the hands of a man. And while my story is terrible, every woman has faced a man's wickedness to some degree. Even you." She placed a hand on the floor, steadying herself as she began to tilt to one side. "I am an apothecary, and it is my duty to dispense remedies to women. And so over the years they have come to me, and I have sold them what they wish. I have protected their secrets. I have borne the brunt of their burdens. Perhaps if I had bled again after the loss, if my womb were not scarred, I would have stopped long ago. But the absence of bleeding has been a constant reminder of Frederick's betrayal and what he took from me."

In the darkness, my brow furrowed into confusion. The absence of *bleeding*? I presumed she misspoke on account of her fatigue.

Slowly, Nella fell onto her side, yawning and weak. I knew that her story was nearly over, but although she appeared exhausted, I was wide-awake.

"It cannot go on forever, of course," she whispered. "I am failing. And whereas I thought, long ago, that issuing such pain may ease my own, I was wrong. It has only grown worse, and my bones swell and ache with the passing of each week. I am sure that dispensing these poisons is destroying me from the inside, but how can I tear down what I have built? You heard Lady Clarence . . . My distinction is well-known."

She cleared her throat, licked her lips. "It is a strange puzzle," she concluded. "For as much as I have worked to fix women's maladies, I cannot fix my own. My grief has never gone away, not in twenty years." Speaking so quietly that I could hardly hear her, I wondered if she had not slipped into a sort of peaceful nightmare. "For this kind of pain, no such tincture exists."

16

CAROLINE

When I stepped into the lobby of La Grande, dread hardened in my chest. Though I'd mulled over the apothecary for most of the train ride to the hotel, now the more urgent concern — my husband's imminent arrival — pushed aside any thoughts of Bear Alley, the vial or the library documents.

Given the time needed to clear customs and catch a taxi, it seemed mathematically impossible for James to already be at the hotel. In spite of this, I hesitated in front of my room door, wondering if I should knock. *Just in case.*

No. This was my room, my trip. He was the interloper. I slid my keycard into the door and went inside.

Mercifully, the room was empty and everything inside was my own, albeit in tidier condition than I'd left it. The crisp white bed linens had been tucked neatly

211

against the mattress, the kitchenette had been refreshed with clean mugs, and . . . *shit.* A vase of beautiful, baby blue hydrangeas sat on the small table near the door.

I pulled the tiny envelope from the center of the flower posy and opened it, hoping it was only an unwitting display of congratulations from one of our parents.

It wasn't. The inscription was short, but I knew instantly who sent it. *I'm sorry,* the note began, *and I have so much to make up to you, to explain to you. I will love you always. See you soon. J.*

I rolled my eyes. James was an intelligent guy; he meant to do damage control in advance of his arrival, pulling whatever strings he could to ensure I at least opened the hotel room door for him. But if he thought we could talk this over in a single morning, then share a couple of mimosas and resume our lovebird itinerary as originally planned, he was sorely mistaken.

I didn't allow myself to feel guilty about this. I may not have been perfectly happy with our life, but I wasn't the one who'd thrown it away.

A short while later, I lay on the bed sipping an ice-cold water when there came a knock at the door. I knew instinctively that it was him. I could feel it, just like I could feel the exhilaration in his body when I stood across from him at the altar on our wedding day.

I took a single deep breath and opened the door, unwillingly inhaling the scent of him: the familiar aroma of pine and lemon, subtle remnants of the homemade soap he loved so much. We'd bought it together at an outdoor market a few months ago, in the days when my free time was spent peeking at fertility tips on Pinterest. Things seemed so much easier then.

James stood before me, a charcoal-gray suitcase against his leg. He wasn't smiling, nor was I, and if an unlucky stranger were to walk by at that very moment, they would have believed it the most awkward, unpleasant reunion they'd ever seen. As we stared dumbly at each other, I realized that, until just a moment ago, part of me didn't believe he'd actually turn up in London at all.

"Hi," he whispered sadly, still on the other side of the threshold. Though only an arm's length separated us, it felt like an ocean.

I opened the door wider and motioned for him to come in, like he was a bellman delivering my luggage. As he rolled in his suitcase, I walked away to refill my glass of water. "You found my room," I said over my shoulder.

James eyed the vase of flowers on the table. "My name is on the reservation, too, Caroline." He tossed a few travel documents — his passport and a couple of receipts — onto the table next to the flowers. His shoulders slumped and his eyes creased at the edges. I'd never seen him look so tired.

"You look exhausted," I said, my voice hoarse. My mouth had gone dry.

"I haven't slept in three days. Exhausted is an understatement." He touched one of the flowers, running his finger along the edge of a silky, baby blue petal. "Thank you for not turning me away at the door," he said, looking at me tearfully. I'd only seen him cry twice: once at our wedding reception, when he raised a glass of pink champagne to me, his new wife, and once after his uncle's burial ceremony, as we walked away from the gaping hole in the earth that was soon filled with dirt.

But his tears drew no sympathy from me. I didn't want to be around him, could barely look at him. I pointed to the sofa underneath the window, with its round arms and tufted upholstery. It wasn't meant for sleeping, but for lounging and easy conversation and lustful, late-night lovemaking — all the things James and I wouldn't be doing. "You should rest. There are extra blankets in the closet. The room service is quick, too, if you're hungry."

He gave me a confused look. "Are you going somewhere?"

The late-morning sun shone bright into the room, leaving pale yellow streaks across the hotel room floor. "I'm going out to get lunch," I said, taking off my sneakers and putting on flats.

The hotel room had listed a few suggestions in a binder on the table; there was an Italian place just a few blocks away. I needed comfort food, and maybe a glass of Chianti. Not to mention an Italian restaurant was likely to be low-lit. Perfect for someone like me who needed a discreet place to think, maybe cry. Seeing James now, in flesh and blood, had left a hard lump in my throat. I wanted to embrace him as much as I wanted to shake him, to make him tell me *why* he'd ruined us.

"Can I join you?" He ran his hand across his jawline, hidden under three days' worth of stubble.

I knew the misery that was jet-lagged heartache, and in spite of myself, I pitied him for it. And hadn't I decided to stop ignoring the discomfort in looking deeper? I might as well start by getting some things off my chest. I only hoped I could keep the

215

tears at bay. "Sure," I muttered, then I grabbed my bag and led the way out the door.

The restaurant, Dal Fiume, was just a block from the River Thames. The hostess took us to a small table at one corner of the restaurant, away from the other patrons; she probably assumed James and I were on a first date given the obvious distance we kept from one another. As though it were late in the evening, several vintage lanterns glowed throughout the dining area, and heavy scarlet curtains wrapped around the room like a cocoon. I would have found it intimate on any other day, but today it was stifling. Maybe this choice had been a bit *too* discreet, but we were both hungry and exhausted, and we let out a collective sigh as we sank into the leather armchairs on either side of the table.

The large menus offered a welcome distraction, and for a while neither of us spoke, except to the waitress who brought us water and, soon after, two glasses of Chianti. But as soon as she placed the glass in front of me, I remembered: my period. Still late. Alcohol. Pregnancy.

I ran my finger along the base of the glass, considering what, if anything, to do. I couldn't send the wine back — James would suspect something, and I would not share this with him. Not here, not in this godforsaken red room that threatened to suffocate us both.

I thought of Rose. Hadn't she had alcohol in the first few weeks of her pregnancy, before taking a test? Her doctor had had no concerns at that very early stage.

Good enough for me. I sucked down a gulp of the wine, then proceeded to skim the menu, seeing but reading none of it.

A few minutes later the waitress took our orders and left with the menus, and I instantly missed the protective barrier between James and me; there was nothing left to focus on except one another. We sat so close together, I could hear him breathing.

I looked directly at my husband, his face even more sunken in this light than earlier. I tried not to wonder when he last ate, as he seemed to have lost a few pounds. Taking a fortifying sip of wine, I began, "I'm so angry —"

"Listen, Caroline," he interrupted, intertwining his fingers like I'd seen him do on the phone with disappointed clients. "It's done. We're having her transferred to another department, and I let her know that if she contacts me again, I'll inform Human

Resources."

"So it's her fault, then? Her problem? You're the one on partner track, James. Seems to me that Human Resources might be more interested in *your* involvement." I shook my head, already frustrated. "And why is this even about your *work*? What about our marriage?"

He sighed, leaning forward. "It's unfortunate things came to light this way." An interesting choice of words; he meant to diffuse responsibility. "But maybe it's not all bad," he added. "Maybe there's some good to come of it, for us and our relationship."

"Some good to come of it," I repeated, astounded. "What good could possibly come of this?"

The waitress returned with large pasta spoons, delicately placing them before us, and the silence between the three of us was thick and awkward. She quickly left.

"I'm trying to level with you, Caroline. I'm here, now, telling you that I'll do counseling, I'll do soul-searching, I'll do whatever."

My solo trip to London was meant to be like a counseling session for me — until, of course, James showed up at my door. And his flippant manner angered me further. "Let's start the soul-searching now," I said.

"Why did you do it? Why did you let it continue after the promotion event?" I realized that despite my desire to know the gruesome *what* and *how,* what I most wanted to know right that moment was . . . *why?* A question struck me at once, something I hadn't considered before. "Are you scared of trying for a baby? Is that why?"

He looked down, shook his head. "Not at all. I want a baby just as much as you do."

A small weight lifted inside of me, but the problem-solving part of me wished he'd said yes; then we could hold the truth up like a diamond, set it in front of the light and address the real issue. "Then . . . why?" I resisted the urge to spoon-feed him any more possibilities, and I brought the rim of the wineglass back to my lips.

"I guess I'm just not entirely happy," he said tiredly, like the words alone exhausted him. "My life has been so safe, so fucking predictable."

"*Our* life," I corrected.

He nodded, conceding this. "Our life, yes. But I know you *want* safe. You want predictable, and a baby needs that, too, and —"

"*I* want predictable? *I* want safe?" I shook my head. "No, you have that all wrong. You didn't support me applying to Cambridge because it was so far away. You —"

219

"I wasn't the one to rip up the application," he said, his voice like ice.

Undeterred, I went on. "You didn't want kids early in our marriage because of the burden while working long hours. You begged me to take the job at the farm because it was secure, comfortable."

James tapped two fingers against the white tablecloth. "You accepted the job, not me, Caroline."

We fell silent as our waitress arrived with two bowls of pasta and set them in front of us. I watched her walk away, making careful notice of her perky, perfectly shaped ass, but James's eyes stayed solidly on me.

"You can never take back what you did to me," I said, pushing away my untouched plate. "Do you realize that? I will never forget. It will be a permanent scar on us, if we even make it through this. How long will it take us to be happy again?"

He grabbed a bread roll from the center of the table and shoved it into his mouth. "That's up to you. I told you, it's over and done with. A screwup on my part, one I'm now working to fix with you, my wife."

I imagined five or ten years from now. If James did indeed remain faithful to me, perhaps the other woman would someday seem little more than an old mistake. After all, I'd once heard that nearly half of marriages struggle with infidelity at some point. But I'd realized in recent days this woman wasn't the only source of unhappiness in my life. As we sat across from each other at the table, I considered sharing my feelings with him, but I didn't view him as an ally in whom I could confide. He remained an adversary, and I felt protective of the truths I had begun to discover on this trip.

"I came to London to apologize to you," James said. "I don't care what the rest of this trip looks like. Screw the original plans. We can hang out in the room and eat Chinese food for all I care —"

I held up my hand to stop him. "No, James." No matter how raw he felt, his feelings were the least of my concerns. My own were still terribly bruised. "I'm not at all happy you came out to London without asking me. I came here to process what you did, and I feel like you chased me here. Like escape wasn't something you allowed me to do."

He stared at me, dumbfounded. "Like I chased you here? I'm not a predator, Caroline." He pulled his eyes from mine and picked up his fork, his face growing flushed. He shoved a forkful of food into his mouth, chewed quickly and speared another bite.

"You're my wife, and you've been in a foreign country, alone, for the first time in your life. Do you know how panicked I've been? Pickpockets, or some creep realizing you're here alone —"

"*Jesus,* James, give me a little credit. I've got a bit of common sense." My wineglass was empty, and I waved the waitress over for a refill. "It's been just fine, actually. I've had no issues whatsoever."

"Well, good," he relented, his tone softening. He wiped the edges of his mouth with a napkin. "You're right. I should have asked you whether it was okay for me to come out. I'm sorry I didn't. But I'm here now, and the last-minute plane ticket cost me three grand. A second one to fly home wouldn't be cheap, either."

Three grand? "Okay," I said through thinned lips, further pissed that he'd spent so much money on a plane ticket he shouldn't have booked at all. "Can we agree, then, that at least for the next few days, I get time and space? I still have a lot to process." *Though I've processed enough to see how much of my old self has been buried,* I thought miserably.

He opened his mouth and blew out air. "We should be talking through the hard questions together, though, right?"

I shook my head gently. "No. I want to be alone. You can sleep on the sofa in the hotel room, but that's the extent of it. I came on this trip by myself for a reason."

He closed his eyes, disappointment all over his face. "Okay," he finally said, pushing aside his half-eaten meal. "I'll head back to the room. I'm exhausted." He pulled a couple of twenty-pound notes from his wallet, slid them across the table to me and stood up.

"Get some rest," I said, my eyes not leaving his empty chair.

He kissed the top of my head before he left, and I stiffened in my seat. "I'll try," he said.

I didn't turn around to watch him go. Instead, I finished my pasta and my second glass of Chianti. After a few minutes passed, I saw my phone screen light up on the table. Frowning, I read a new text message from an unknown number.

Hi Caroline! Did a bit more digging after you left & got some hits on our manuscript database. I've req a few, will take a couple of days. How long you in town for? Gaynor xx

I sat up straighter in my chair and texted her back immediately.

Hi! Thank you SO much. In town another week! What kind of doc? Does it look promising?

I leaned my elbows on the table, awaiting Gaynor's reply. While researching together at the library, she'd explained that manuscripts could be handwritten or printed material. Could she have located another letter, another "deathbed confession," about the apothecary? I opened her response the moment it came through.

Both search hits are bulletins — a type of periodical. Dated 1791. Not part of our digitized newspaper collection & pre-1800, which is why it didn't come up earlier. Metadata says one of the bulletins includes an image. Who knows? Will keep you posted!

I closed my phone. Intriguing news, yes, but as I stared at James's half-eaten plate and his dirty cloth napkin lying on the table, bigger issues tugged at my attention. The waitress offered a final glass of wine and I declined; two glasses with lunch were more than enough. I needed to sit and think for a few minutes with the steady din of conversation around me.

According to James, his infidelity came from a place of dissatisfaction with the safe, predictable nature of our lives. Was it possible we'd been equally discontent with the stagnant way of life back home and things had finally come to a shuddering halt? And if so, what did that mean for our desire to be parents in the immediate future? I wasn't sure any child would want us for parents now.

A child would also need a stable home, a good school system and at least one income-earning parent. There was no doubt that our life epitomized this, but James and I had both just shared our dissatisfaction with the paths we'd chosen. Where on the list was *our* fulfillment, *our* joy? Was it selfish to put our own happiness before the needs of another human being, one who didn't even yet exist?

Surrounded by London's weathered brick buildings, mysterious artifacts and obsolete maps, I'd been reminded why, so long ago, I found myself enamored of British literature and history's obscurities. The youthful, adventurous student in me had begun to resurface. Like the vial I'd dug out of the mud, I had begun to unbury something dormant inside of myself. And as much as I wanted to hold James accountable for keeping me in the States, at the farm, I couldn't blame it entirely on him; after all, as he'd said, I was the one to rip up the application for Cambridge's history graduate program. I was the one to accept the job offer with my parents.

If I was honest with myself, I wondered if looking forward to a baby had been a subconscious way of disguising the truth: that not everything in my life was how I imagined it would be, and that I hadn't lived up to my own potential. And worst of all, I'd been too scared to even try.

As I'd yearned for motherhood, fixing my attention entirely on my *someday,* what other dreams had been buried and lost? And why had it taken a life crisis to finally ask myself the question?

17
ELIZA

Just as Nella promised, the coaches began running again at daybreak. We took the first one back into London, empty except for us two ragged, dirty travelers and our filthy linen sacks full of beetles, many of which were still alive and nearing suffocation in their tightly tied bags.

Neither of us said much on the journey. For me, it was due to fatigue — I had hardly slept a minute — but Nella had slept well, I knew, for she'd snored loudly most of the night. Perhaps she remained quiet due to embarrassment at all she had revealed: her love for Frederick, the baby out of wedlock, the terrible loss of it. Was she ashamed she had shared too much with me, who she meant to send away and never see again?

The coach dropped us on Fleet Street, and we made our way to Nella's shop along the mud-packed street, passing a bookseller, a printing press and a stay-maker. I read a window advertisement for a tooth extraction — three shillings, including a complimentary dram of whiskey. I cringed, averting my gaze to a pair of young women in pastel morning gowns floating past, their pale faces heavily rouged. I caught the edge of their conversation — something about the lacy fringe on a new pair of shoes — and noticed that one of the women held a shopping bag.

I glanced down at my own bag, full of crawling creatures. The importance of our impending task brewed terror inside of me. Purchasing the eggs for Mr. Amwell had not scared me like this; a watchman would not question a young girl with eggs. But now, a quick glance in our linen bags would reveal an odd sight indeed and would surely prompt questioning. I, for one, did not have an explanation prepared, and I resisted the urge to look behind me at the cobbled lane, lest someone followed on our heels. The likelihood of detection must have been a heavy burden; how did Nella carry the weight of it each day?

We continued to walk quickly, stepping around tied-up horses and scurrying chickens, and I had little else to do but fear imminent arrest as I forced my feet forward.

At last we arrived at the shop, and I had

never in my life been so grateful for an alley empty of all but shadows and rats. We slipped into the storage room, made our way through the hidden door, and Nella immediately set a fire going. Lady Clarence was to arrive at half one, and we hadn't a moment to waste.

The room warmed in minutes; I let out a sigh, grateful for the heat on my face. Nella removed turnips and apples and wine from her cupboard and placed them onto the table. "Eat," she said. While I dug in hungrily, she continued to toil about the room, pulling out pestles and trays and buckets.

I ate so quickly that a terrible stomachache began to spread its way across my belly. I leaned forward, hoping to hide from Nella's ears the rumbles and growls coming from within me, wondering for a moment if perhaps she had poisoned *me.* It would, after all, be a convenient way to get rid of me. Panic rose in my chest as the pressure inside grew, but the feeling released with a belch.

Nella threw her head back in laughter, the first time I had seen real cheer in her eyes since the moment we met. "Feel better?" she asked.

I nodded, stifling my own giggle. "What are you doing?" I asked, wiping a bit of apple from my lip. She had taken hold of one of the beetle bags and now shook it forcefully.

"Stunning them," she said, "or at least those that are still alive. We'll pour them into this bucket first, and it's not easy reining them in if a hundred angry beetles try to crawl out at once."

I grabbed the other bag, mimicking her actions, and shook it with all my might. I could hear the bounce and fall of the insects inside the bag, and in truth, I felt a bit sorry for them.

"Now pour them in here." She slid the bucket toward me with her foot. I carefully untied the strings at the top of my bag, gritted my teeth and opened it. I had not yet had a clear look inside the bag, and I dreaded what I might find.

I estimated half the beetles to be dead already — they lay there like pebbles, but with eyes and tiny legs — and the other half showed little resistance as I poured them out, their greenish-black bodies tumbling into the tin bucket. Nella poured her bag in next, then lifted the bucket and walked it to the hearth, setting it onto the roasting rack over the fire.

"Now you roast them? It is as simple as that?" I asked.

She shook her head. "Not yet. The heat of the fire will kill the remainder of them, but we cannot roast in this bucket, or we will find ourselves serving up little more than beetle stew."

I cocked my head, puzzled. "Stew?"

"Their bodies have water inside them, just like you and me. Now, Eliza, you have worked in a kitchen. What would happen if you set a dozen fish into a small pan over the fire? Would the fish on the bottom be crispy and flaky, as your master might have liked?"

I shook my head, finally understanding. "No, it would be soggy and wet."

"And can you imagine trying to turn a soggy, wet fish into a powder?" At my grimace, she went on. "So it is with these beetles. They will steam if dumped in all at once. We will roast them on a much larger pan, only several at a time, to ensure they are crispy and dry."

Several at a time, I thought to myself. *And more than a hundred beetles?* That may take as long, if not longer, than the actual harvesting of the silly things.

"And after they are crispy?"

"Then, one by one, we will grind them up with a pestle, until the powder is so fine, you would not know it from water."

231

"One by one," I repeated.

"One by one. Which is why Lady Clarence best not return a moment too soon, as it will take us every last second to finish the task."

I recalled the moment when Nella threw her beetle powder into the fire, causing an eruption of green flame; what nerve it must have taken, to throw over a day's worth of work into the blaze. Until now, it had not been clear to me just how strongly she felt against murdering the mistress of a lord — how strongly she resisted aiding in the death of a woman.

I imagined the tediousness of the day ahead and willed myself to be cheerful about it. Nella had told me that she did not want me at the shop after this chore was complete. But perhaps if I performed it well, she would change her mind and permit me to stay. The idea of it energized me, because the hot, crimson bleeding from my belly had finally ceased, leaving in its wake a russet-colored shadow, and this could mean just one thing: Mr. Amwell's spirit had decided to make its way out of my body and lie in wait for me. But where? There was only one sensible place, the place where he knew I was soon to return: the lonely Amwell estate on Warwick Lane.

Oh, how I would have rather stayed and roasted a thousand beetles than step foot back into the dwelling place of my dead master. Who knew what ugly form he would take next?

With twelve minutes remaining until Lady Clarence's arrival, a terrible storm was unleashed outside. But we hardly noticed it, for both of us were bent over mortar bowls, grinding the beetles as finely as we could.

If Nella intended to send me away before Lady Clarence returned, it must have been a distant thought by now; it would have been impossible for her to finish the task without my help. With six minutes to go, Nella asked me to choose a vessel — any appropriately sized jar would do, she instructed. She remained head down, eyes focused and sweat on her forearms as she ground the pestle loudly against the mortar.

At half one, Lady Clarence arrived, not a tick of the clock late. No pleasantries were exchanged upon her arrival. When she stepped into the room, her lips formed a tight line and her shoulders were pulled taut. "You have it ready?" she asked. Rain droplets slid down her face like tears.

Nella swept underneath the table while I carefully poured the remainder of the powder into the sand-colored earthenware jar I had found in a lower cabinet. I had just finished securing the stopper and the cork was still warm from my fingers when Nella answered her.

"Yes," she said, while I gently, ever so gently, passed the jar into the care of Lady Clarence. She clutched it to her chest in an instant, hiding it underneath her coat. No matter who would ingest the poison — for my loyalties were not as rigid as Nella's — I could not help the pride that swelled within me on account of the many hours that went into the preparation of it. I did not recall ever being so proud, not even after composing lengthy letters on behalf of Mrs. Amwell.

Lady Clarence passed a banknote to Nella. I could not see how much, nor did I particularly care.

As she turned to leave, Nella cleared her throat. "The party is still tonight?" she asked. In her voice was a glimmer of hope, and I suspected that she prayed the whole affair had been canceled on account of the weather.

"Would I have rushed over here in the rain if it were not?" Lady Clarence retorted. "Oh, don't be so foul about it," she added, seeing the look on Nella's face. "You're not the one stirring it into Miss Berkwell's liqueur." She paused, pursing her lips. "I only pray she drinks it quickly so we may put this all to an end."

Nella closed her eyes as though the words sickened her.

After Lady Clarence left, Nella walked slowly to where I sat at the table, lowered herself into her chair and pulled her register toward her. She dipped her quill into the ink with a slowness I had not seen plague her before, as if the burden of the preceding hours had, at last, caught up to her. To think of the countless poisonous remedies she had dispensed, and yet this single one lay so heavy on her heart. I could not understand it.

"Nella," I began, "you mustn't feel so bad. She would have ruined you had we not made the beetles for her." Nella had done nothing wrong in my eyes. Indeed, she had just saved *countless* lives, my own included. How did she not see it?

Nella paused at my words, the quill in her hand. But without replying, she placed the nib to parchment and began to write.

Miss Berkwell. Mistress to, cousin of, the Lord Clarence. Cantharides. 9 February

1791. On account of his wife, the Lady Clarence.

On the last mark, she held the nib to the paper and exhaled, and I felt sure tears were imminent. Finally, she set the quill on its side, and a gentle roll of thunder rumbled somewhere outside. She turned to me, her eyes dark.

"Dear child, it is that —" She hesitated, considering her words. "It is that I have never had this feeling before."

I began to tremble, as if a chill had just entered the room. "What feeling?"

"A feeling that something is about to go terribly, terribly wrong."

In the quiet moments that followed — for I knew not how to reply to her frightening statement — I grew convinced that some nameless, unseen evil haunted us both. Could the spirit of Mr. Amwell have begun to haunt her, too? My eyes fell on the worn burgundy book still resting at the side of the table. *The book of magick.* Nella had said the book was meant for midwives and healers, but the inscription inside the back cover noted the address of the bookshop where it originated — a place where I might find more volumes of the same subject matter.

If my fear of Mr. Amwell's spirit was

236

reason enough to visit the shop, Nella's sense of impending doom was reason to make haste.

The muffled sound of rain continued; the storm had not yet let up. If Nella did indeed throw me out, I would be passing a long, wet night in the slick streets of London. I would not return to the Amwell house, not yet, and I doubted I had the bravery to sneak into a stranger's shed as Nella liked to do.

"I intend to visit the bookshop in the morning, once the rain has ended," I told her, pointing at the magick book.

She raised her brows at me, a skeptical look I was getting to know well. "And you still intend to seek a remedy to remove spirits from the house?"

I nodded *yes,* and Nella made a small grunting noise, then stifled a yawn with her hand.

"Little Eliza, it is time for you to go." She stepped closer to me, pity in her eyes. "You ought to return to the Amwell house. I know you fear it greatly, but I assure you, your fright is needless. Perhaps when you step through the door and declare that you have returned, any remnant of Mr. Amwell's spirit, real or imagined, will be released, and your heavy heart with it."

I stared at her, speechless. I had known all along that a dismissal was possible, but as she had now declared it so, I could hardly believe she had the gall to send me away so easily — and into the rain, at that. I'd ground more beetles than she did, after all; she could not have done any of it without me.

I stood from my chair, my chest hot and thumping, and felt the childish sting of tears forming. "You d-do not want to see me again," I stammered, letting a sob come forth, for I realized all at once that I was not as sad about being banished from this place as I was about never again seeing my new friend.

At least I knew she was not made of stone, for Nella stood from her own chair, shuffled toward me and wrapped me in a tight embrace. "I do not wish you a life of good-byes, as the one I have lived." She brushed away my stray hair with the back of her hand. "But you are unspoiled, child, and I am not the kind of company you want to keep. Go on now, please." She took the magick book from the table and placed it into my hands. Then she abruptly pulled away from me, walked to the hearth and did not look at me again.

But as I stepped through the hidden door

and away from her forever, I could not help but glance back once more. Nella's body bowed into the warmth of the fire, as though she might let herself fall into it, and amid her haggard breaths, I was sure I also heard her weeping.

18
CAROLINE

That evening, after dark, I exited the hotel room as quietly as I could, careful not to wake James as he slept soundly on the sofa. I left a short note next to the TV — *Gone out for late dinner. C* — and hoped he wouldn't wake to find the note anytime soon.

I closed the door softly behind me, waited impatiently for the empty elevator and hurried across the hotel lobby. Beneath me, the marble floors shone like a mirror, polished and bright. I chased after my own reflection, my face alight with a daring excitement I hadn't felt in years. I grabbed an apple and a complimentary bottle of water from a table in the lobby and stuffed them into my crossbody bag, but I didn't bother with pulling out my phone or a map; I'd walked this route once before.

Given the late hour, the streets were nowhere near as busy as yesterday; there were few cars and even fewer pedestrians. I made my way quickly into Bear Alley once again, the evening air calm and cool around me as I passed the same garbage cans and fast-food containers that I'd seen early this morning, each object frozen in time as though not even the breeze had ruffled it since my last visit.

Head down, I made my way to the end of the alley, and I found myself almost surprised to see it again: the steel gate flanked on either side by stone pillars, the overgrown clearing, and — I stretched my neck to see over the gate — yes, the door. It had taken on new importance already, given my time spent perusing the old maps with Gaynor at the British Library. I felt like I knew secrets about the area: that nearby, there once existed a tiny walkway called Back Alley; and just down the way was a place called Fleet Prison; and even Farringdon Street, the main avenue a few steps away, used to be called something different. Did everything reinvent itself over time? It was beginning to seem like every person, every place, carried an untold story with long-buried truths resting just beneath the surface.

This morning, I'd been grateful for the windows of the buildings surrounding Bear Alley, in case the plumber decided to come too close. But now, I didn't want to be seen, which was why I'd left the hotel after dark. The sky now was a charcoal gray, only a hint of the sun's last rays glowing from the west. A few windows of the surrounding buildings were lit, and inside one building I could see desks and computers and a stock ticker with bright red letters flicking across its screen. Thankfully, no late workers milled about within.

I looked down. At the base of the locked gate was a small red-and-white sign that I hadn't seen this morning: NO TRESPASS-ING. ORD. 739-B. The back of my neck prickled with nerves.

I let a minute pass; there was no sound or movement other than a pair of sparrows flit-ting by. I tightened the strap of my bag and stepped onto the loose rock foothold at the base of the stone pillar and heaved myself to the top, where I teetered precariously. If there was ever a time to change my mind, it was now. Even now, I could *still* manage an excuse or explanation. But once I swung my legs over and landed on the other side? Forget it. Trespassing was trespassing.

Keeping my center of gravity low so as not to slip, I awkwardly twisted my torso around so that my legs hung over the other side. Then, with a final glance behind me, I jumped.

It was a clean, quiet landing, and had I closed my eyes, I could have convinced myself that nothing had changed — except, of course, I'd now broken the law. But the decision had come and gone.

Even though it was dark, I crouched down a few inches and covered the distance of the clearing in a few long strides, heading for the shrub that stood directly in front of the door. The branches, void of any blooms or buds, were instead covered in prickly, brownish-green leaves and inch-long thorns. Cursing under my breath, I pulled my phone out of my bag and flipped on the flashlight feature. I knelt in the dirt, using one hand to gingerly spread apart the thorny branches.

A sharp prick stung my palm, and I snapped it back: a thorn had drawn blood, and I put my skin to my lips to soothe the sting while using the flashlight to look more closely behind the shrub. The ruddy bricks of the building's facade were weatherworn, and a mottled, green fuzz had staked its claim every few feet, but directly behind the shrub was the wooden door I had seen this morning.

Adrenaline surged through me. Since leaving the hotel and making my way here in the cover of darkness, a part of me believed this moment wouldn't actually happen. Maybe Bear Alley would be closed for construction, or it would be too dark to see the door, or I'd simply lose my nerve and turn the other way. But now I stood deep within the clearing, whether on account of my bravery or my stupidity, and the door was mere inches away. I didn't see a lock on it, and I could make out a single, crumbled hinge on its left edge. A good shove seemed all it would take to push it open.

My breath came faster now. Truth be told, I was scared. Who knew what was behind the door? Like the lead female character at the start of a horror movie, I felt sure the smart thing to do was run. But I was tired of doing what I was *supposed* to be doing, tired of taking the practical, low-risk, responsible route.

Instead, it was time for me to do what I *wanted* to be doing.

I still clung to the fantasy that I was on the path of solving the apothecary mystery. After discussing my job with James at lunch — and our unstable future — I couldn't help but imagine the opportunity that might present itself if I uncovered something newsworthy on the other side of this wall. I was motivated now by more than opening a door to the building; perhaps I'd be opening the door to a new career path, the one I'd envisioned so long ago.

I shook my head at the idea of it. Besides, the plumber said this door probably just led to an old cellar. Chances were this whole discovery would be anticlimactic, and I'd be grabbing a slice of pizza in twenty minutes. I looked back at the gate, hoping it would be as easy to climb up the stone pillar again from this side.

I decided that it was best to use my back and shoulders instead of my bare hands to push aside the thorny branches. I carefully maneuvered my way behind the bush, remaining mostly unscathed, then placed my hands on the cool wood of the door and paused. I slowed my breath, bracing myself for what I may find on the other side, and then gave the door a hard shove inward.

It budged a tiny bit, enough to tell me that the door was not locked. I gave it a second shove, and a third, and then I placed my foot against the door and exerted as much pressure as I could with my right leg. At last the door fell inward with a crusty, scratching sound. I cringed when I realized, too late, there was no way I'd be able to set it back into the same position once I'd finished.

As the door opened, a rush of dry, woodsy air enveloped me, and a few insects, disrupted from their slumber, skittered away. I lifted my phone to quickly scan the black, hollow opening, breathing a sigh of relief; no rats, no snakes, no dead bodies.

I took a tentative step forward, scolding myself for not having had the forethought to bring a real flashlight. But then again, I really didn't think I'd come this far. I checked the flashlight feature on my phone to see if there was a way to brighten it, and I cursed when I saw the upper right-hand corner of my screen: my battery, which was full upon leaving the hotel, was now at 55 percent. The flashlight pulled a heavy charge, apparently.

I shone the light into the black opening, frowning as I discerned a hallway stretching out in front of me. It appeared a lower-level corridor or cellar, just as the plumber had said. The hallway was only a few feet wide, but I couldn't determine how deep it stretched on, given my insufficient beam of light.

Glancing at the busted-open door to ensure it wouldn't somehow close, I took a few steps deeper inside, letting the light spread out before me.

At first, I couldn't help the disappointment that crept in; there was really not much to see. The corridor had a dirt floor with just a few stones scattered about, and it was empty of machinery, tools or anything else that the building's owners might have found necessary to store inside. But I thought back to the maps Gaynor showed me this morning, and the way that the old Back Alley ran a jagged course away from Bear Alley, turning at several sharp, ninety-degree angles, almost like stair steps. Ahead, I could see the faintly illuminated path made its own such turns; and though I had no desire to venture to the very back of the corridor, my heart thumped hard in my chest.

There was no doubt that this was Back Alley — or at least a remnant of it.

I smiled, pleased with myself, imagining what Bachelor Alf would say if he were beside me. He'd probably rush ahead, seeking old artifacts.

I felt it before I saw it — a draft of air brushing up against me — and I lifted my light in the direction from which it came. Another door stood ajar just ahead, the air of the room within being sucked out, presumably, by the vacuum I'd now created in opening the door at the entrance. The tops of my arms prickled with goose bumps, and

I jumped at the sudden tickle of a loose hair on my neck. Every muscle in my body tensed, ready to run or scream — or look closer.

Up to this point, my breaking-and-entering had led me on a mostly predictable journey. I knew the outside door existed, and I suspected it led to a jagged corridor — a built-over street or walkway, according to Gaynor — and I felt there was a good chance the corridor wouldn't be all too interesting once I got inside.

So far, true, true and true. But *this* door? This wasn't on the map.

I was desperate to peek inside, and I told myself that was all I would do. The door was already ajar — no more kicking and shoving — so I resolved to slide my phone's flashlight into the room, take a quick glance around and then leave. Besides — I checked my phone's battery life, which was now at 32 percent — I didn't have much time to stick around anyway, unless I wanted to be left in the dark.

"Christ," I muttered as I stepped to the door, sure that I'd gone clinically insane. This wasn't something normal people did, right? I couldn't even be sure this was about the apothecary anymore. Was I still chasing down her story, or was I one of those people

who went on reckless, adrenaline-high-seeking adventures after a big loss?

If something happened to me — if I slipped or got bit by a feral animal or stepped through loose floorboards — no one would know. I could lie here dead and undiscovered for who-knows-how-long, and James would surely think I'd left him once and for all. This realization paired with my quickly dying phone made it difficult to steady my beating heart. I resolved to look inside, then get the hell out.

I pushed the second door all the way open. It swung easily on its hinge, which wasn't warped and rusted like the exterior door and instead seemed to have remained fairly dry and intact. Standing just inside the threshold, I moved my phone in an arc in front of my body to more closely look at what lay within. The room was small, perhaps ten by twelve, and the floor was packed dirt, the same as the rest. Inside were no crates, no tools, no old building fixtures. Nothing.

But the back wall — there seemed something different about it. Whereas the walls on either side of the room were brick, similar to the building's exterior, the back wall was made of wood. Some shelves were affixed to the wall, like it had once been a built-in library or cupboard. I took a few steps closer, curious to see if there was anything on the shelves: old books or implements, any forgotten remnant of the past. Again, there was little of interest. Most of the shelves were warped and splintering, and a few had collapsed entirely and lay on the ground near the center of the room.

And yet, there was something odd about the arrangement. I couldn't quite place my finger on it, so I stepped back and considered the wall of shelves as a whole. A memory of the mudlarking tour came back to me, Bachelor Alf's eerie words: *You are not searching for a thing so much as you are searching for an inconsistency of things, or an absence.* I frowned, sure there was something strange about what I was seeing now. But what was it?

I noticed, with a start, that most of the fallen shelves had come from one section of the wall — the far left side. In this place, rather than being secured against the wall, most of the shelves had buckled and crumbled to the floor. I stepped closer, using the light to inspect the panel. Only one shelf on the left side of the wall remained in place, so I gripped it and wiggled it slightly; the shelf rattled easily in my hand, so loose that I felt sure I could yank it off without much difficulty. Why on earth would the left side of the wall have lost its shelves? It was as though these shelves weren't installed correctly, or the structure behind it was inadequate —

I gasped in realization, covering my mouth with my hand. The space where the shelves were dislodged was about my height and only slightly wider than me. Instinctively, I took a step back. "No," I said involuntarily, the word echoing in the tiny, empty room. "No, no, no. It can't be." And yet, I knew as I said the words that I'd stumbled on something. An interior door.

To men, a maze. The first sentence in the hospital note rushed forward in my memory, and I understood, at once, what it might mean: this door, if it did indeed lead somewhere, was meant to remain concealed within a cupboard-like structure. If anyone today — perhaps a building inspector — had reason to be in this room, I felt sure they would have noticed the oddity, like I had. But given the fallen shelves directly in front of me, it was clear not a soul had been down here in decades. And no one had discovered, much less opened, the inset door.

I crouched and searched for a handle, but saw none. I pushed my right hand against

251

the wall, jumping at the silky, sticky feeling of a cobweb against my fingers. I groaned, wiped my hand on my pants, and used the phone flashlight to illuminate the lone, intact shelf. Then I saw it: underneath the shelf was a tiny lever, visible only on account of the crumbling wood. I maneuvered it out of position and gave the wall another push.

Without so much as a croak or groan, as though grateful to be discovered at last, the hidden door swung open.

With one shaky hand against the wall, I clutched my dying cell phone and lifted it up. Ahead of me, the beam of light pierced the dark. Then, in breathless, disbelieving silence, I took in what lay before me: all that had been lost and buried for far too long.

19
ELIZA

I woke upon a dry, clear morning to the sound of a carriage rushing by, its iron wheels screeching against the cobblestone road. I'd slept a street away from Nella's shop in a protected crevice at the back of Bartlett's Passage. It was damper and less comfortable than the shed inside which I had rested two nights ago, but still better than my warm cot at the haunted Amwell home.

As soon as I woke, I clenched my teeth, waiting to see if the bloody belly pains had returned — if Mr. Amwell's spirit, no longer fooled, had made its way back to me. But that was not the case. The pains had now stayed away for a full day, the trickle of blood reduced to almost nothing. And though I was grateful for it, I felt sure it was because Mr. Amwell lay in wait for me elsewhere. The idea of it angered me; he may have been master over me in days past, but it was not so any longer. I was not his toy, his plaything in death.

I thought, too, of Lady Clarence's dinner party last evening. If all went as planned, Miss Berkwell should now be dead. A frightening vision, but I remembered what Nella told me about betrayal, and vengeance as medicine. Perhaps now, without the unwelcome presence of Miss Berkwell, Lady Clarence would find a way to tend her marriage and make a baby.

Unsteady on my feet, I lifted myself from the ground and pressed down my skirts, which were grimy and in need of a wash. My hand brushed the cover of the book inside my gown's pocket: the book of magick. Locating the address within was my most pressing task, for I had little else in which to hope, and no other way to rid the Amwell house of ghosts.

I began to make my way to the bookshop on Basing Lane. A night of poor sleep had left me feeling wild, like an animal. My hands shook and a headache beat behind my eyes as the people near me moved about in a watery haze. Messenger boys raced their carts against one another, fishmongers waved away the gulls, and an elderly man slapped the rear of his goat with a flimsy reed. As my toes pushed uncomfortably against my tight shoes, I could not ignore the momentary temptation of returning home, or even to the servant's registry office, where Mrs. Amwell first found me. I was a hundred times more desirable now than I was then. I was literate, for one; I could read and write and had been employed by a wealthy family. Surely my skills would be valued elsewhere, in a home not teeming with unsettled spirits.

I thought on this as I walked to the magick bookshop, but the idea quickly lost its hold as I considered the many reasons that I could not bear to run away — not least of which was my devotion to Mrs. Amwell. She would return from Norwich in a few weeks' time, and by then I hoped to have rid the house of Mr. Amwell — and Johanna — altogether. Besides, I could not imagine any other girl writing my mistress's letters. It felt a very special task, reserved only for me.

And a spirit could move, too; if the spirit of Mr. Amwell was able to seize me and follow me to Nella's shop, what was to stop him from haunting me all over London? Even leaving the city and returning to Swindon would not solve this, for there was no such thing as escape from something that could float through walls. If I could not run from his spirit, I must find a way to dispel it.

There was so much at stake in this very moment, and removing Mr. Amwell's spirit seemed all that mattered to me. So I was pleased, finally, to come upon Basing Lane, and I hoped to find the bookshop without trouble. But my joy did not last long; my eye passed from one storefront to another — a haberdashery and a baker, among others — and I frowned. The bookshop was not there. I walked another block, retraced my steps and even looked for the shop across the street. As I searched, I felt plagued by endless discomforts: tears pricking my eyes, frigid air burning my throat, a blister stinging and wet on the bottom of my foot.

Walking again to the end of Basing Lane, the whistle of wind rushing between buildings caught my attention. Set back from the lane was a shoulder-width alley, and at one side of this was a building with a wooden sign: Shoppe of Books and Baubles. I gasped; the bookshop, which I'd walked right past several times, was tucked behind the other storefronts, as though it meant to disguise itself. If Nella were here, she would have been disappointed that I had not unraveled the mystery sooner.

I placed my hand on the doorknob and stepped into the shop. It was not a large place, about the same size as Mrs. Amwell's drawing room, and it was deserted save a single young man at the counter, his face buried in the spine of a thick book. This gave me a moment to take in my surroundings, which consisted of several shelves of dusty children's trinkets and trifles at the front of the store, and a small area of books at the back behind the store attendant. The shop was humid and smelled of yeast, probably on account of the bread bakery nearby. I closed the door and the bell jingled softly.

The attendant looked up at me over his eyeglasses, eyes widening. "May I help you?" His voice cracked on the last word. He was young, only a few years older than me.

"The books," I said, motioning to the shelves. "May I browse them?"

He nodded, then returned his attention to his book. I crossed the room in only four or five strides. As I stepped closer to the shelves, I saw that each shelf had a small sign identifying its subject. Eagerly, I read them: History and Medical Arts and Philosophy. I scanned quickly, wondering if the book on midwife magick might have come from the Medical Arts section, or if there might also be a shelf with books on the occult.

I made my way to a second case of books. Squatting low to better read the small signs at the base of the bookshelves, I let out a gasp; there, at the very bottom on a single half shelf, was a sign that read Magickal Arts. There were only a dozen or so volumes on the subject, and I intended to inspect them all. I began with the book on the far left, letting it fall open in my hands, but I cringed at the images printed onto the first few pages: large blackbirds with massive swords through their hearts; triangles and circles in a variety of strange patterns; and a long passage written in a language I could not understand. I carefully placed it back on the shelf, hoping for better luck.

The next book was half the size, both in height and width, with soft, sand-colored binding. I turned several pages until I found the title, printed in a small, even font: *Spells for the Modern Household.* I was pleased to find that it appeared written entirely in English — no strange symbols in this one — and the first few pages revealed a wide assortment of everyday "recipes," although not the sort required to make a pudding or a stew:

Elixir to Extract Child's Tendency to Lie

Brew to Assign Infant's Gender In Utero

Tincture to Create Great Wealth Within a Fortnight

Brew to Reduce Age in the Woman's Body

On and on they read, each stranger than the last, but I felt it possible that here within this book, I might locate something useful. I found a more comfortable seated position and tucked my legs underneath me. I continued to read each and every recipe, sure not to overlook a single one, and I searched especially for anything in reference to spirits or ghosts.

Concoction for Erasure of Memory, Specific or General

Philter to Instill Affection in Object of Desire, Even Inanimate

Elixir for Restoring Breath to the Deceased Infant's Lungs

I paused, bumps forming on my skin, as I felt a warm breath against the back of my neck.

"My own mother used that spell," came the young voice, mere inches behind me.

Ashamed of the book in my hands, I snapped it shut.

"Sorry," he continued, his voice backing away from me. "I didn't mean to frighten you."

It was the shop boy. I turned to face him, seeing now more clearly the pimples on his chin and the roundness of his eyes. "It's okay," I mumbled, the book lying limp in my lap.

"A witch, then, are you?" he asked, a sly grin at the edge of his lips.

I shook my head, embarrassed. "No, just curious, is all."

Satisfied with this response, he nodded. "I'm Tom Pepper. Pleasure to have you in the shop."

"Th-thank you," I muttered. "I'm Eliza Fanning." And though I wanted badly to open the book once again and continue my search, I found that Tom, up close, was not so unpleasant to my eyes.

He glanced down at the book. "I wasn't lying, you know. That book was my mother's."

"So your mother is a witch, then?" I was only teasing, but he didn't laugh as I'd hoped he would.

"She was not a witch, no. But she lost her babies — one after the other, nine of them before me — and in her desperation, she used the elixir on the page you just closed. May I?" He motioned to the book, waited for my nod and gingerly took it from my lap. He flipped to the page I had just been reading and pointed to it. " 'Elixir for Restoring Breath to the Deceased Infant's Lungs,' " he read aloud. Then, looking up at me, he added, "According to my father, I was born dead, like all the others. This spell brought me back to life." He tensed, as though the revelation pained him to share. "If my mother were still alive, she could tell you about it herself."

"I'm sorry," I whispered, our faces close.

Wetting his lips, he looked to the front of the shop. "This is my father's shop. He opened it after my mother died. The front, where you came in — those baubles all belonged to her. Things she collected for the babies over the years. Most of it never touched or used."

I could not help but ask, "When did your mother die?"

"Soon after I was born. Later that week, in fact."

I covered my mouth with my hand. "So you were her first baby that lived, and then she did not . . ."

Tom picked at a fingernail. "Some say that is the curse of magick. Why books like the one you're holding should be burned." I frowned, not understanding what he meant, and Tom went on. "The curse of magick, they believe, is that for every reward, there is a great loss. For every spell that goes right, there is something else — in the real, natural world — that goes terribly wrong."

I looked at the book in his hands. It would take a great while, a couple of hours, at least, to read every spell within. And even then, who knew if I would find something that might prove useful? "Do you believe in the curse of magick?" I asked.

Tom hesitated. "I don't know what I believe. I only know that this book is very special to me. I would not be here without it." He then set the book gently in my lap. "I would like you to have it. You may take it for free, if you like."

"Oh, I can pay you, surely —" I reached a sweaty hand into my pocket, fumbling for a coin.

He put out a hand but did not touch me. "I'd rather it go to someone I like than a complete stranger."

At once I felt hot, almost unwell, as my stomach turned loops inside of me. "Thank you," I said, hugging the book close to my chest.

"Just promise one thing," he said. "If you find a spell in there that works, it will be two for two. Promise me you will stop by and tell me of it."

"I promise," I said, untangling my tingling legs to stand. And though I did not want to go, I had no reason to stay. Making my way toward the door, I turned back a final time. "And if I try a spell and it does not work?"

This seemed to take him by surprise. "If the spell does not work . . . Well, then the book cannot be trusted, and you must come back to exchange it for another." His eyes glinted mischievously.

"So either way, then —"

"I'll be seeing you. Good day, Eliza."

I walked out the door in a dizzy haze, feeling a strange, new feeling, one I had not felt in my twelve years of life. It was foreign and nameless to me, but I felt sure it was not hunger or fatigue, for neither of those things had ever made my step so light and my face so warm. I hurried west, eventually walking along the south edge of St. Paul's churchyard, to find a bench in the soft, quiet frontage of the church. A place where I could read every single spell and, perhaps, find one to take to the Amwell house today.

With all my might, I wished to find the perfect spell inside this book of maybe-magick. Something not only to remove spirits and mend all that was broken, but something that would permit me to share the good news with Tom Pepper as soon as possible.

20
NELLA

The demon who decided, long ago, to crawl its way through my body — crunching and curling my bones, hardening my knuckles, wrapping its fingers around my wrists and hips — had begun, finally, to move upward into my skull. And why wouldn't it? The skull is made of bone, just as what might be found in the hand or the chest. It is as susceptible as anything else.

But whereas this demon inflicted tightness and heat on my fingers and wrists, in my skull it took another form: an agitation, a tremor, a persistent *tap tap tap* inside of me.

Something was approaching, I felt sure of it.

Would it come from within, my bones melting into a single, hardened mass, leaving me crippled on the floor of my shop? Or would it come from the outside, dangling in front of me like a rope at the gallows?

I missed Eliza the moment I sent her away, and now, as I picked rosemary leaves from the stem, the lack of her companionship was as sticky and sharp as the residue on my fingers. Had it been cruel of me to dismiss her, no matter how petty I considered her fears? I did not truly believe the Amwell estate swarmed with ghosts, as Eliza seemed to think — but did my beliefs carry any weight if I was not the one sleeping at the place?

I wondered how she felt, returning to the Amwell house last night with a gown made filthy by our efforts, and gloves worn through, and a silly book on magick that couldn't possibly remove ghosts that existed only in her colorful imagination. I hoped, in time, she would learn to replace such fanciful thoughts with real matters of the heart: a husband to love, children to feed, all the things I would never have for myself. And I prayed Eliza woke this morning anew, never to think of me again. For as much as I missed her pleasant chatter, longing was something with which I was well acquainted. I would manage just fine.

I had made my way through four stems of rosemary when there was a sudden commotion in the storage room: a panicked cry, then the incessant hammering of a fist against the hidden wall of shelves. I peeked out of the cleft to see Lady Clarence, her eyes wide as saucers. Given my heavy sense of foreboding over the course of the preceding day, I could not say I was all that surprised by her unexpected arrival. Still, her manner alarmed me.

"Nella!" she shouted, her hands flinging wildly about in front of her. "Hello? Are you in there?"

I opened the door quickly and ushered her in, no longer taken aback by the untarnished silver buckles on her shoes and the scalloped edges of her taffeta gown. But as I gazed over her, I noticed the material at the bottom edge of her skirt was smudged, as though she had traveled part of the way on foot.

"I have not more than ten minutes," she cried, nearly falling into my arms, "and when I left, it was under pretense, something about the estate."

I frowned at her nonsensical words, confusion surely writ all over my face.

"Oh, something has gone terribly wrong," she said. "God, I will never . . ."

As she dabbed at her eyes, choking over her words, my mind raced with possibilities. Had she accidentally disposed of the powder? Had she managed to rub some in her eye or on her lips? I searched her face for blisters, pockets of pus, but saw none.

"Shhh," I said, quieting her. "What has happened?"

"The beetles —" she hiccuped, like she had just sucked down something bitter. "The beetles. It all went awry."

I could hardly believe my ears. Did the beetles cause no harm? I was sure that Eliza and I had gone to the correct field and harvested the blister beetles, rather than their harmless, bluish cousin. Yet it had been so dark, and how could I know for sure? I should have tested a few of them for the familiar burn upon the skin before roasting them.

"She is still alive?" I asked her, my hand on my throat. "I assure you, they were meant to be fatal."

"Oh." She laughed, a twisted grin upon her face, fat tears spilling down her cheeks. I could not make sense of it. "She is very much alive."

My heart surged for a moment. Intermingled with the dismay that my poison failed, I was greatly relieved, too, that a woman did not die at my hands. Perhaps this gave me another chance to change Lady Clarence's mind. But as I considered this, a knot formed in my belly. What if Lady Clarence thought I'd given her a false poison? What if she meant to reveal my shop to the authorities, as she had originally threatened?

Instinctively, I took a step back toward my register, but she went on. "It is *him*. My husband." She let out a wail and covered her face. "He is dead. Lord Clarence is dead."

My mouth dropped open. "H-how?" I stammered. "Did you not watch your lady's maid give it to the mistress?"

"Don't blame this on me, woman," she snapped back. "My maid put it into the fig dessert liqueur, just as planned." Lady Clarence fell into the chair and took a steadying breath as she unraveled her story for me.

"It was after dinner. Miss Berkwell sat some ways away from me and my husband, the Lord Clarence, was at my right. I watched from across the room as Miss Berkwell took a sip, a single sip, of the fig liqueur from her pretty crystal glass. Within seconds, she reached her hand to her throat, a lascivious smile on her face. She began to cross and uncross her legs — I could see it all, Nella! I could see it so clearly, what was happening to her — but I began to fear that someone might catch me looking, and so I turned to my left and began to speak with

269

my dear friend Mariel, and she told me all about her recent visit to Lyon, and on and on she went, until after a short while I dared to look over at Miss Berkwell again."

Lady Clarence sucked in a breath, her throat rattling. "But she was gone, and my husband, too, and the crystal glass of liqueur with them. I could not believe I'd missed it — that he'd stepped away with her in that short time, and I had missed it. I was sure, in that moment, I would never lay eyes on her face again, and I imagined the two of them running off to his library or back to the carriage house for the final time. I took comfort in this, you know."

As she told her story, I remained still, envisioning it all before me: the dinner table of puddings and evening gowns, the fig liqueur, the fine green powder hiding in the viscid shadows of it.

"But then I grew anxious," Lady Clarence continued, "thinking perhaps it was all happening a bit too fast, and I worried that in her state of lust, she may forget the liqueur altogether and not drink the required amount." She paused, looking around. "Might I have some wine to calm my nerves, please?"

I rushed to my cupboard, poured her a glass and set it in front of her.

"I began to panic, Nella, and considered searching them out, confronting them, asking her to join the ladies in the drawing room. Instead, I remained frozen at my seat while Mariel continued to spout on about Lyon, and I prayed that at any moment my husband would come into the room, telling me something terrible had happened to her, his dear cousin." Lady Clarence looked down at the floor and suddenly wrapped her arms around herself, shivering.

"Then I saw a ghost approaching from the corridor. The ghost of Miss Berkwell. Oh, how I nearly cried out! I stifled it, thank heavens — how strange that would have seemed to the dinner guests — but I soon learned it was no ghost. It was her, in flesh and blood. I knew it by the mole on her neck, red and inflamed, as though my husband's lips had just been on it."

A small moan left her throat. "She came out with such a look of fright. She is just a young thing, and so small. She nearly collapsed into the arms of the first person she saw, Lord Clarence's brother, who is a physician. Immediately, he rushed down the corridor from which she'd just come. There were people everywhere, running this way and that in a complete uproar. From down the hall, near the library, I heard shouts and cries, something about his heart having stopped, and I rushed to see him. He was still clothed, thank God. And as I suspected, on a small table next to the chaise was the empty crystal glass. He must have drank the entire thing. Oh, Nella, I did not know it would happen so quickly!"

"I told you half the jar would kill him in an hour. How much was in the glass?"

The look of anguish on Lady Clarence's face fell away, transformed into something like guilt. "I believe my maid used all that was in the jar." She let out a cry, slumping forward in her chair, while I gasped in disbelief; it was no wonder he died within moments.

But Lady Clarence seemed as distraught about Miss Berkwell's behavior after the fact as she was about her dead husband. "Would you believe that as I sat there looking at his dead body, Miss Berkwell approached me and placed her arms around me, and began to cry? 'Oh, Lady Clarence,' the girl wailed, fig fruit stinking on her breath, 'he was like a father to me!' And I thought it a sick thing to say, and I had half a nerve to ask her if she liked to prig her own father, too!"

Lady Clarence let out a final, hideous laugh, her eyes sunken as though spent from the telling of her tale. "And now I am the widow of a wealthy man and will never want for anything except for the thing I most want, which is a child. How utterly bitter on the tongue, even to say it! I will never have a child, Nella, never!"

A statement with which I could well relate, yes. But something about her story began to tug, to worry me. "You say his brother, a physician, was the first to administer to him?"

She nodded. "Yes, a kindly man. He declared my husband dead not five minutes after Miss Berkwell came into the dining room in a mad fright."

"And he did not seem worried by the empty glass sitting next to the chaise?"

Lady Clarence shook her head, sure of herself. "He asked about it, to which Miss Berkwell immediately claimed it as her own. She said they'd been in the library so he could show her a newly acquired tapestry, as she claims some recent interest in the textile arts. And she could hardly reveal that he shared of her drink, could she? For then it would be clear they were doing more than just enjoying his *art*."

"And the jar?" I asked. "You hid it somewhere, or destroyed it?"

"Oh, yes. My lady's maid put it on a shelf

at the very back of the cellar. Only the cook has any reason to go digging back there. I'll dispose of it as soon as I am able to sneak down there. Tonight, perhaps."

I exhaled a small sigh of relief, grateful that the canister remained hidden. But even if it were found, not all would be lost; this was precisely why the jars and vials about my shop were naked, save for the small engraving of the bear. "Though it is not traceable to me," I urged, "best to get rid of immediately."

"Most certainly," she said, chastised. "Anyhow, I thought it curious you would have engravings on the jar." She delicately wiped her nose, composing herself. A lifetime of rigid manners could not be so easily forgotten.

"Just that of a little bear," I said, pointing to a small canister on a nearby shelf. "Like that one. So many jars are similar in appearance. Imagine if someone were to administer a drop from the wrong bottle, and the wrong person —" I stopped myself, ashamed of what had nearly slipped from my tongue, given the story she had just told.

But she didn't seem to notice as she frowned and walked to the shelf. She shook her head. "My jar had this image, but there was something else." She lifted the jar and turned it on its side. "No, these aren't the same. My jar has something on the other side of it. Words, I'm sure of it."

A faint rumble crawled through my belly, and I let out a nervous laugh. "No, you must be mistaken. What words would I dare place on a jar of poison?"

"I assure you," Lady Clarence said. "There was something written on it. Jagged letters, as though it had been etched into the clay by hand."

"A scratch, perhaps? Or dirt, just rubbish," I suggested, the pressure in my stomach rising upward into my chest.

"No," she insisted, irritation in her voice now. "I know words when I see them." She threw me an exasperated glance and returned the jar to its shelf.

Though I was listening to her words, I did not fully hear them; the *tap tap tap* was too loud, and the story which Lady Clarence had just shared no longer seemed her crisis alone. Like I had just sipped from the crystal glass of cantharides myself, I choked out her name: "Eliza."

A memory began to crystallize. Yesterday afternoon, just before Lady Clarence arrived to retrieve the poison, Eliza had selected the jar that would hold the powder. I hadn't paid any attention to the jar she selected, for any within easy reach were etched with the bear logo and nothing more. Only those deep in the back of my mother's cupboard were marked otherwise.

"Eliza, yes, where is she today?" Lady Clarence asked, unaware of the storm brewing inside of me.

"I must find her immediately," I gasped. "The cupboard . . ." But I could not speak another word, much less explain myself to Lady Clarence, for I could not think about anything except making haste to Warwick Lane, where I would find the Amwell estate. Oh, how I prayed she was there! "And you," I said to Lady Clarence, "go, now! Get the jar immediately and bring it to —"

"Your eyes are that of an animal," she cried. "Whatever is the matter?"

But I was already moving out the door, and she followed close behind. As I stepped outside, I did not feel the cold against my skin or the tightness of my shoes against my swollen ankles. Ahead, a flock of blackbirds took flight; even they were scared of me.

At some point, Lady Clarence went her own way — to retrieve the jar, I prayed. I continued onward, rushing up Ludgate Street, the cathedral rising high above me. The Amwell estate was very close now, only a couple of blocks ahead.

As I neared my turnoff to Warwick Lane, I spotted a small, shrouded figure on a bench ahead, near the churchyard. Were my eyes playing tricks on me? My heart surged as I observed the light, playful manner in which this mysterious figure turned the pages of the book in her lap. I was close to the Amwell home; it would not be out of the realm of possibility to encounter Eliza at any moment.

My hopes were soon confirmed: it was undoubtedly her. Not an hour ago, I feared the child may be fear-stricken and morose, but that did not seem the case whatsoever. For, as I drew closer, I saw indeed that as the girl perused the book she wore a wide smile, as fresh and bright as a bloom.

"Eliza!" I shouted when we were only meters apart.

She jerked her head toward me. Her smile fell, and she clutched the book to her chest — but it was not the book I gave her. This one was smaller, and the cover a lighter color. "Eliza, oh, do listen to me, for it is very urgent."

I reached for her, bringing her into a hesitant embrace, yet she remained stiff in my arms. There was something odd with her; she was not pleased to see me. This morning, I had wished to be a distant memory of hers, yet now I found myself offended by it. And what of her smile a moment ago? What had happened recently that left her in such a gleeful state?

"You must return to the shop with me, child, for there is something I need to show you." In fact, I needed *her* to show *me* from exactly which cupboard she withdrew the jar.

Her gaze was flat, unreadable, but her words were not. "You sent me away. Remember?"

"I do remember, but I also remember telling you that I feared something terrible was about to happen, and it has. I want to tell you all about it, but —" I glanced at a man walking close by, and lowered my voice "— I cannot do so here. Come with me now, I need your help."

She clutched the book tighter to her chest. "Yes, fine," she mumbled, glancing at the dark clouds building overhead.

We made our way back to the shop, Eliza silent next to me, and I sensed she was not only confused by my stealing her away, but irritated that I had seized her attention from whatever she busied herself with a moment ago. As we drew close to the shop, I hoped to find Lady Clarence inside, returned with the cursed jar in her hand — and indeed if that were the scene we came upon, my question for Eliza would be unnecessary. But could I really send her away again so soon? It was of no matter, for the shop lay empty and Lady Clarence had not yet returned. I sat down at the table, feigning calm, and wasted not a moment. "Do you remember putting Lady Clarence's powder into the canister?"

"Yes, ma'am," Eliza said quickly, her hands neatly folded in her lap, as though we were strangers. "Just as you said, I retrieved a proper-size jar from the cupboard."

"Show me," I said, a small tremble in my voice. I followed Eliza one, two, three steps across the small room, and she crawled onto her knees, opened a lower cupboard, and leaned her little body in. She reached to the very back and I clutched my belly, fearing I may vomit.

"Back here," she said, her voice distorted as the sound echoed inside the wooden cabinet. "There was another one just like it, I think . . ."

I closed my eyes, terror finally rising in me and seizing my throat, my tongue. For this cupboard, the one in which Eliza now found herself halfway inside, was full of my mother's things, including treasures with which I could not bear to part, old remedies

279

of which I'd had no need, and yes, a terrible, shuddering yes, several of her old containers that I knew for certain were engraved with the address of her once-reputable apothecary shop.

The address of *this* shop, which was not so reputable anymore.

Eliza's tiny body slithered out of the cupboard, and in her hand was a cream-colored jar — about four inches high, one of a pair, *3 Back Alley* hand-engraved onto the side of it. Without her saying another word, I knew its mate was in the cellar of Lady Clarence's stately home. A familiar, sour burn rose in my throat, and I placed my hand on the cupboard to steady myself.

"It was like this," Eliza said, her voice hardly more than a whisper, her eyes downcast. "The one with the powder looked like this." She slowly, bravely looked up at me. "Have I done something wrong, Nella?"

Though my hands itched with the urge to strangle her, what did the girl know? It was a terrible misunderstanding — the room was full of shelves, and was it not my own fault for asking her to choose a canister? Was it not my own fault for bringing the girl into this shop of poisons in the first place? — and so I resisted the urge to slap her flushed face, and instead, I placed my

280

arm around her. "Did you not read the jar, girl? Did you not see the words on it?"

She began to cry and sucked in a breath full of snot and tears. "It hardly looks like words," she hiccuped. "See here, just a few messy etches. I cannot even properly read what it says." And while she was correct — the impression was old, nearly illegible — it remained nevertheless a terrible oversight on her part.

"But you know words from a picture, don't you?" I said.

She nodded slightly. "Oh, I am so sorry, Nella! What does this say?" She squinted as she attempted to read the words on the jar. I slowly traced the fading outline of the words, running my finger along the fat loops of the 3 and the letter B.

"Three B —" She paused, thinking. "Three Back Alley." She set down the jar and crumbled into my arms. "Oh, can you ever forgive me, Nella?" Her shoulders heaved as she sobbed uncontrollably, tears dropping to the floor. "If you are arrested, it will be all my fault!" she said through her hiccups.

"Shhh," I whispered. "Shhhhh." And as I rocked her forward and back, forward and back, I was reminded of baby Beatrice. I closed my eyes and put my chin on Eliza's head, and thought of how my own mother had done this after she'd grown very ill; how she had comforted me when I was sure her end was near. I had cried so hard with my face nuzzled into her neck. "I will not be arrested," I whispered to Eliza, though I did not entirely believe it. Lord Clarence was dead, and the weapon — with my address on it — was still in his cellar.

The *tap tap tap* had not left me, and the demon in my skull was not yet at rest. I continued to rock Eliza back and forth, hushing her tears away, thinking of the lies my own mother told me about her illness and the severity of it after she fell sick. She had sworn she would live many more years.

And yet she had died in only six days. As a result, I had spent a lifetime wrestling with the abruptness of that grief, the incompleteness of it. Why didn't my mother tell me the truth and use her last days to prepare me for a lifetime alone?

Eliza's dewy tears began to dry. She hiccuped once, twice, then her breathing slowed as I continued to rock her back and forth. "All will be well," I whispered, so quietly that I could hardly hear my own words. "All will be well."

Two decades after my mother's death, I found myself reassuring a child exactly as my mother had reassured me. But to what end? Why did we go to such lengths to protect the fragile minds of children? We only robbed them of the truth — and the chance to grow numb to it before it arrived with a hard knock on the door.

21

CAROLINE

PRESENT DAY, WEDNESDAY

Within the recesses of Back Alley in the subcellar of an old building, the hidden door
swung open, revealing the tiny space behind
the wall of crumbling shelves. I lifted my
phone and shone the light around, reaching
my hand to the wall, suddenly unbalanced.
It was so dark in this room-within-a-room,
darker than anywhere I'd ever been.

My single beam of light illuminated the
details around me: several wall-mounted
ledges sagged under the weight of milky,
opaque glass containers; a wooden table
with a buckled leg dipped at a slant in the
center of the room; and just to my right
stood a counter with a metal scale and what
appeared to be boxes or books laid out on
its flat work surface. The room looked very
much like an old pharmacy of sorts —
exactly the type of place an apothecary
might keep her shop.

My phone beeped. I frowned and looked

at the screen. *Shit.* The battery was at 14 percent. I was shaking and terrified and exhilarated and I couldn't think clearly, but I'd be damned if I stayed in this place without a light to guide me out.

I decided that I better make it quick.

With trembling hands, I flipped off the flashlight and opened my camera app, turned on the flash, and started taking pictures. It was the only logical thing I could think to do at the moment, given I'd just found something which, truly, could be worthy of international news. "London Tourist Solves 200-Year Old Murder Mystery," the headline might read, "Then Returns Home to Begin Marriage Counseling and Start New Career." I shook my head; if there was ever a time to remain rational, it was now. Besides, I'd solved nothing.

I snapped as many pictures as I could, each time the room bursting alive under the glare of the bright white flash. As I took the first few pictures, the flash provided a rapid, fraction-of-a-second view of the room: there was a hearth, I thought, at one corner, and a single mug lay on its side underneath the table. But after the first few shots, the camera flash left white, floating dots in my vision; the effect disoriented me, and soon I could hardly keep myself standing upright.

Nine percent. Vowing to leave when the battery hit 3 percent, I considered how to best use the remaining battery life. I looked again to my right and snapped a picture of the counter — the flash helped me confirm that it was books, not boxes, that I saw a moment ago — and then I opened the largest book, which was lying flat on the work surface. Some of the words within appeared to be handwritten, but I couldn't be sure. In the black cover of absolute darkness, I opened the book to a dozen random pages, taking pictures of each one. I might as well have been blindfolded, because I had no idea what I was taking photos of. Would the words even be in English?

Within the book, the pages of parchment were thin as tissue and I handled them as delicately as I could, cursing when the corner of one page fell away completely. I flipped to the back of the book and took a few more pictures, then I closed it, pushed it aside and grabbed another book. I opened the cover of this one, pressed the shutter button on my phone's camera, and — *dammit. Three percent.*

I groaned, maddeningly frustrated at this unbelievable discovery and the short amount of time I'd had to explore it. But given how quickly the flashlight and camera had drained my battery, I gave myself sixty seconds to get out, maybe less. I flipped the flashlight on again, backed my way out of the room and swung the hidden door closed as best I could. Then I backtracked, quickly crossing the first room and stepping once again into the corridor. Ahead, the subtle glow of moonlight crept inside from the third and final door.

As expected, my phone died within seconds of stepping outside. Still hidden behind the thorny shrub, I did my best to blindly set the exterior door back into position, but I felt sure I did a terrible job of it. I scooped up some dirt and leaves with my hands and tossed them haphazardly around the base of the door to give it the appearance of being undisturbed. Then I pushed my way past the shrub and turned around to look at my work; the door certainly didn't look as snug as when I first discovered it, but it was still quite inconspicuous. I could only hope that no one had been paying as close attention to the area as I had.

I rushed back to the locked gate and heaved myself onto one of the pillars, though not without a great deal of straining and heavy breathing. Pulling my legs over the pillar, I jumped to the other side. I wiped my hands on my pants and looked up to the glass windows above me. Still, nothing moved; as far as I could tell, no one knew I was here, much less what I'd done.

It was no wonder the apothecary had remained a mystery; her door was well hidden by the wall of shelves, and only the passage of two centuries had deteriorated things enough for me to find it. That, and a little bit of recklessness and lawbreaking on my part. But if there was any doubt about her existence, it was gone now.

I walked out of Bear Alley aware that I'd just committed a crime for the very first time in my life. I had dirt underneath my fingernails and a dead cell phone full of incriminating photos to prove it. Yet guilt eluded me. Instead, I was so anxious to plug my phone into a charger and review the photos that I had to resist running back to the hotel.

But *James.* As I slipped quietly into the hotel room, hoping not to wake him, my heart sank. He was awake on the sofa with a book.

We didn't speak to one another as I crawled into bed and plugged in my phone. I yawned, my adrenaline having melted into an aching fatigue, and peeked over at him. He seemed entirely engrossed in his book, as alert as I'd been at bedtime last night.

The curse of jet lag.

Frustrated, I turned my body away from him. The pictures would have to wait until morning.

I woke to the sound of the shower running and a narrow strip of daylight searing its way through the curtains and onto my face. The bathroom door stood slightly ajar, steam rushing out of it, and on the sofa, James had folded up his blanket and set it neatly beside the spare pillow.

I picked up my phone — fully charged — and resisted the urge to dive immediately into the photos. Instead, I pushed my face against the pillow, trying to ignore my full bladder, counting the minutes until James left the hotel so I could begin my day in peace.

At last, he walked out of the bathroom, wearing nothing but a beige towel around his waist. It was so normal, the sight of my husband half-naked, and yet something inside me grew tense. I wasn't ready, not now or anytime soon, for "normal." I turned my face away.

"Late dinner last night," he said from across the room. "Anything good?"

I shook my head. "Just grabbed a sandwich, took a walk." It wasn't like me to tell little white lies, but I wasn't about to tell him — or anyone — what I'd really done last night. Besides, he'd lied to me for months about something much worse.

Behind me, James let out a raspy cough. He walked over to the couch, leaned down and grabbed a box of tissues from the floor. I hadn't seen them earlier, but he must have had them next to him all night. "Not feeling a hundred percent," he said, putting the tissue against his mouth and coughing again. "Throat hurts, too. Dry air on the plane, I guess." He opened his suitcase and pulled out a T-shirt and jeans, then dropped his towel to the floor as he began to dress.

I kept my eyes off his naked body by looking at the vase of flowers on the table near the door, a few of which had begun to wilt slightly. With my hands on top of the duvet, I noticed last night's dirt under my fingernails, and I shoved my hands under the covers. "What's your plan for the day, then?" I pleaded silently that he planned to explore the city or go to a museum or just . . . leave. I wanted nothing more than to be here alone with my phone, the Do Not Disturb sign hanging from the door.

"The Tower of London," he said, threading his belt around his waist. *The Tower of*

London. The ancient castle was one of the sites I'd been most excited about — it was the home of the Crown Jewels — and yet it now seemed a mere children's museum compared to what I found last night hiding behind Bear Alley.

James let out another cough, patting his chest with the palm of his hand. "Got any DayQuil, by chance?" he asked.

In the bathroom was my bag of toiletries, filled with makeup, floss sticks, deodorant and a few essential oils. I knew I had a few spare Tylenol, but I hadn't thought it worth the added space to bring every possible medicine for any given ailment. "Sorry," I said. "I've got eucalyptus oil?" It had long been my go-to remedy anytime I felt a cold coming on; as one of the ingredients in Vicks VapoRub, eucalyptus worked wonders on congestion and coughs. "In the white bag on the counter," I said, pointing to the bathroom.

As James went in, a small chirp caught my attention: my phone, beeping about something trivial, an unnecessary reminder that last night's discovery sat inches from my face. My heart began to thump hard in my chest while James rustled about in the bathroom.

He came out with a grimace on his face.

"Strong stuff."

I nodded in agreement; even from a few feet away, I could smell the pungent, medicinal odor of it.

Since he was dressed and looked ready to go, I did my best to avoid any chance of further conversation. "I'm gonna try to lie back down for a bit," I said, kicking my feet around in the sheets. "Enjoy your sightseeing."

He nodded slowly, a sad look on his face, and hesitated as though wanting to say something. But he didn't, and after grabbing his wallet and cell phone, he made his way out of the room.

The moment the door clicked shut, I lunged for my cell phone.

I typed in my password and navigated to my photos. There they were, about two dozen of them. I opened the first couple; they were shots of the room — the table, the hearth — but I was disappointed to see that the photos were blurry. I cursed, fearing the entire set may be the same. But once I got to the close-up shots of the book, I breathed a sigh of relief; these photos were sharp. The air in the room had been dusty, and I supposed the camera flash had been unable to cut through the minuscule particles to focus on anything except the fore-ground.

I bolted upright at a noise just outside the hotel room door. I clicked off the phone and rushed to the peephole, just in time to see a hotel employee with a clipboard walking past. He wasn't coming to my room, but it reminded me to put up the Do Not Disturb sign.

Once back on the bed, I opened the pictures again and studied the first photo of the book. Holding my breath, I used two fingers to zoom into the picture and move around the screen. I sat in utter disbelief at what lay before me.

The words in the book were, in fact, handwritten, with fat ink spots scattered and smeared on the page. The text was neatly lined in rows and each entry was written in a similar format, with what appeared to be names and dates. A log or register of some kind, then? I flipped to the next picture. It was similar in nature, though the ink was darker, heavier, like a different person wrote this page. I flipped to the next, and the next, my hands shaking harder with each swipe. I wasn't entirely sure what the book was, but I felt confident that its historical value was immeasurable.

Most of the photos of the book were clear,

although the edges of some were overexposed and so the borders were white and indecipherable. And yet, despite the clarity of the pictures, I was faced with another maddening frustration: I couldn't understand much of the text. Not only did it seem to be written in shorthand, but the cursive handwriting was at such a slant — and so hastily written in places — that parts of it may as well have been in a foreign language. In one photo, I could understand only a portion of one row toward the top:

Garr t Chadw k. Marl bone. Op um, Prep. lozenge. 17 Aug 1789. On acc nt of Ms. Ch wick, wife.

As my brain struggled to fill in letters and make sense of the text, I felt like I was playing one of those missing-letter word games. But after a few minutes, I realized that the v's and s's and d's — which were indistinguishable at first — were looped in a certain way, and my brain began to recognize them so that I was better able to make out the subsequent pages:

Mr. Frere. S uthwark. Tobacco leav s, prep. oil. 3 May 1790. On acct of Ms. Am er, sister, friend of Ms. M nsfield.

Ms. B. Bell. Raspb rry leav, crush'd plaster. 12 May 1790.

Charlie Turner, May air, NV tincture. 6 Jun 1790. On acc of Ms. Apple, servant-cook.

I set my chin in my hand, reading certain entries again, discontent welling inside of me. *Raspberry leaves? Tobacco?* There was nothing dangerous about these, though I had once heard that nicotine was toxic in large amounts. Perhaps it was the quantity of a non-poison that proved deadly? And as for some other references in the book — like *NV tincture* — well, I had no idea what they even meant.

I tried to decipher the way the entries were formatted, too. Each one began with a name, then listed an ingredient — dangerous or not — followed by a date. Some entries included a second name at the end with the designation, *on account of.* I assumed this meant the first name was the intended recipient of the ingredient, and the second name was the person who actually bought it. So Charlie Turner, for example, was meant to ingest *NV tincture* — whatever that was — and it was likely purchased by Ms. Apple.

I grabbed a pen and my notebook from

the nightstand and jotted down a few things to research later:

Quantities of non-poisons needed to kill
Opium — lozenge?
Tobacco — oil?
NV tincture — what is NV?

I spent the next fifteen or so minutes cross-legged on the bed, furiously writing down questions and words, some familiar, some not. *Nightshade.* Wasn't that a plant? *Thorn apple.* Never heard of it. *Wolfsbane.* No idea. *Drachm, bolus, cerate, yew, elix.* I wrote all of it down.

I flipped to another photo and gasped as my eyes fell on a word that I knew, without doubt, to be deadly: *arsenic.* I wrote it down in my notebook, putting an asterisk next to it. I zoomed farther into the photo, hoping to decipher the rest of the words in the row, when I heard another noise outside.

I froze. It sounded like someone had stopped just in front of the door. I silently cursed whoever it was; didn't they see the Do Not Disturb sign? But then I heard the keycard slide into the door. Had James returned already? I shoved the phone underneath my pillow.

A moment later, James walked in — and I

knew immediately that something was very, very wrong. His face was pale and clammy, his forehead dripping wet, and his hands shook badly.

Instinctively, I stood from the bed and rushed toward him. "Oh, my God," I said as I approached him; I could smell his sweat and something else, sweet and acidic. "What's wrong?"

"I'm fine," he said, rushing for the bathroom. He leaned over the sink, taking deep breaths. "Must be yesterday's Italian food." He looked up to the mirror in front of the sink, making eye contact with me even though I stood behind him. "I'm such a fucking mess, Caroline. First you, and now this. I got sick outside, on the sidewalk," he said. "I think I just need to get all this out. Would it be okay if —" He paused, swallowing something down. "Would it be okay if I have the room to myself for a bit until this is out of my system?"

I didn't hesitate for a second. "Of course, yes." I'd known for years that James hated being sick in front of other people. And, truthfully, I wanted the privacy, too. "You sure you're okay, though? Do you need juice or anything?"

He shook his head, starting to close the bathroom door. "I'll be fine, I promise. Just give me a bit."

I nodded, put my shoes on and grabbed my bag, tossing my notebook inside. I set a water bottle just outside the bathroom door and told James I'd be back soon to check on him.

I remembered there being a café a block down the road so I headed that way, intending to finish looking at the photos on my phone. But as soon as I stepped outside, my phone started to ring. I didn't recognize the number, and thinking it might be James calling from the hotel, I answered it quickly. "Hello?"

"Caroline, it's Gaynor!"

"Oh, oh, my gosh, hi, Gaynor." I stopped in the middle of the sidewalk, and a pedestrian threw me an irritated glance.

"I'm sorry for calling so early, but the manuscripts I texted you about last night came in. Are you able to meet me at the library, like, ASAP? I'm not technically working today, but I stopped in a few minutes ago to check out the documents. You're not going to believe it."

I squeezed my eyes closed, trying to remember what she'd said yesterday about the documents. So much had happened in the last twenty-four hours and her text messages had, admittedly, been relegated to the back of my brain, given last night's adventure — and now James's illness.

"I'm so sorry, Gaynor. I can't come now, I need to stay in this part of town in case —" I paused. Despite our long research session together, I still didn't know Gaynor well enough to start on about my unfaithful husband who was now vomiting in my hotel room. In fact, I hadn't even told her I had a husband — we hadn't discussed our personal lives at all. "I just can't make it over there right now. But I'm about to grab coffee, if you want to join? You could bring the documents with you?"

I heard her laugh on the other end of the line. "Taking them out of the building is a hell of a way to lose my job, but I can make copies. Plus, I could use a coffee."

We agreed to meet in a half hour at the café near my hotel, and I passed the time at a small table in the corner of the café, eating a raspberry croissant and analyzing the photos of the apothecary's book as best I could.

When Gaynor walked through the glass door at the front of the café, I flicked off my phone and closed my notebook, shoving it safely inside my bag. I reminded myself to play it cool; I couldn't let it slip that I knew anything more about the apothecary than I did yesterday while at the library. I hardly knew Gaynor, and sharing this information would reveal that I not only broke the law, but that I infringed upon what might be a valuable historical site. As an employee at the British Library, it was possible she'd be bound by a professional commitment to report me.

I nibbled on the final bite of my croissant, the irony not lost on me; while I came to London because I was hurt by someone else's secrets, now *I* was the one hiding things.

Gaynor slid into the chair next to me and leaned in excitedly. "This is . . . unbelievable," she began, pulling a folder from her large purse. She withdrew two sheets of paper, black-and-white copies of what looked very much like old newspaper articles, divided into several columns with a header toward the top. "The bulletins are dated only a couple of days apart." She pointed toward the top of one page. "The first one is February 10, 1791, and the second one is February 12, 1791." She set the earlier bulletin, from February 10, on top, and leaned back in her chair to look at me.

I looked closer at the bulletin and gasped.

"Remember yesterday," Gaynor explained,

"when I texted you that one of the documents contained an image? That's the image." She pointed toward the center of the printout, though it was unnecessary; my eyes were locked on the page. There was a drawing of an animal, so rudimentary it looked like something a toddler scribbled in sand, but there was absolutely zero doubt in my mind that I'd seen the image before.

The image was a bear — identical to the tiny bear etched on the light blue vial I'd plucked from the mud of the Thames.

22
ELIZA

It was after eight o'clock in the evening, and though Nella had worked ceaselessly over the last few hours, she would not let me help. Instead, she strained under the effort of pushing corks as far into their bottles as they would go, nesting the empty boxes as tightly as they would fit and scrubbing a few of her gallipots with all her might. She tidied and organized as though she meant to leave — if not permanently, then at least for a long while — and it was due entirely to my careless mistake.

Of all the errors, great and small, I had made in my twelve years of life, I believed that taking the jar from the lower cabinet was my greatest offense of all. How could I have overlooked the address etched into the jar? I'd never before made such a mess of things, never in my life.

Oh, how I wished I could turn back the hours. And to think I was once merely *use-*

less to Nella. At present that seemed a dream; with my mistake, I might have doomed her and all of us within the pages of her book. I thought again of the many names I'd traced in the register a couple of days ago. I had darkened the ink strokes in order to preserve and protect the names of the women, to give them a place in history, just as Nella had explained. Now, I feared I hadn't preserved and protected anything at all. Instead, my mistake with the canister might expose the countless women in the book. Might ruin them.

I considered any practical ways to repair my wrongdoing but could think of none. Only the reversal of time could fix this, but it seemed a daunting thing to ask, even of magick.

And yet, Nella had not sent me away. Did she mean to kill me? Force me to account for my mistake? The room in which we sat, not speaking to one another, was thick with her frustration. I aimed to be as quiet as possible so as not to further agitate her, and I shrank in shame near the fated cupboard, hunched over myself, only three things before me: the book of household magick from Tom Pepper, lying open in my lap; the book of midwives' magick from Nella, set aside; and a candle that was nearly spent. I had not the heart to ask Nella for a new candle, and would be forced soon to put away the books and — what? Fall asleep with my head against the stone wall? Wait for Nella to issue her punishment?

I lifted the dying candle above the open page before me. In the dim light, the printed words of Tom Pepper's magick book seemed to dance and move on the page, and it took great effort for me to focus on a single line of text. This frustrated me greatly; if there was ever a time to rely on magick, what with its ability to give breath to stillborn baby Tom, it was now. I needed to find a spell to fix it all, and it couldn't happen a moment too soon. Whereas this afternoon I sought a potion to unburden me of a man's spirit, now I wished to remove the burden I had unwittingly placed upon Nella and myself and many others: the threat of arrest, condemnation and perhaps even execution.

With my finger, I traced each sentence and continued to run through the list of spells within Tom's book.

Oil of Transparency, vis-à-vis Playing Cards

Tincture to Reverse Bad Fortune

Amid the clamor of Nella hammering a nail into a wooden crate, my eyes widened. *Tincture to Reverse Bad Fortune.* Well, I could be sure that no good fortune had found me whatsoever in recent days. My hand began to shake, the flame of the candle with it, as I read the spell, which claimed to be more powerful than "any weapon, any court, any King." I studied the required ingredients — venom and rosewater, crushed feather and fern root, among others — and I swallowed hard, growing feverish. They were strange things, yes, but Nella's shop was full of strange things. And I already knew that two of them, the rosewater and fern root, were on her shelves.

But what about the others? There was no way to move about the shop unnoticed; how could I collect the ingredients I needed, much less prepare them as indicated in the book? I would need to reveal my plans to Nella, for there was no other way —

At once, there came another striking noise. I had believed it a moment ago to be Nella's hammer, but now I saw she had set the hammer down. As understanding came over me, I nearly dropped my candle; someone was at the door.

Nella, toiling by the hearth, looked to the door, her manner calm. She gave no sense of fear, showed no nerves. Did she wish it to be the authorities? Perhaps an end to all of this would be a welcome relief. Meanwhile, I remained frozen in terror. If a constable had come to arrest Nella, what would become of me? Would Nella reveal what I had done to Mr. Amwell? I would never see my mother or my mistress again, never get the chance to tell Tom Pepper of the spell I meant to try . . .

Or what if the newcomer was something even worse? The thought of Mr. Amwell's hollow eyes and the idea of his milky, hazy ghost seized me, clutched my very heart. Perhaps he grew tired of waiting and had returned for me at last. "Nella, wait —" I cried.

She ignored me. With no hesitation in her step, Nella approached the door and opened it. I tensed, setting Tom Pepper's magick book aside, and leaned forward to better see around the door. There was only one person in the shadows. I sighed in relief, for surely a constable would not arrive without his partner.

The visitor, covered in loose black fabric,

wore a hood over their face. Their shoes were caked in mud — the stench hit me instantly, horse urine and turned-over earth — and from where I sat across the room, the guest appeared little more than a shrouded, trembling shadow.

A pair of black-gloved hands extended forward. Held between them was a jar: the jar I had filled only yesterday with the deadly beetle powder. It took me a moment to fully comprehend what was happening before me. The jar! Nella's death sentence was no more!

The visitor unwrapped the black fabric around their face, and I gasped in recognition. It was Lady Clarence. Oh, I had never been so relieved to see anyone in all my life.

Nella reached a hand to the wall to steady herself. "You have the jar," she said, her voice hardly more than a whisper. "Oh, how I feared this would not be the case . . ." She leaned forward, her other hand on her chest, and I worried she might fall to her knees. I stood at once and moved toward her.

"I came as quickly as I could," Lady Clarence told us. A hairpin hung loose against her neck, ready to dislodge at any moment. "You must understand the flurry of activity at the estate. I have never seen so many people in one place. It's as if another dinner party is imminent, though a more somber one at that. And the questions they continue to ask! The attorneys, worst of all. The activity was too much for my lady's maid — she left me. This morning, before dawn rose, off she went without a word. Told only the coachman that she had resigned and planned to leave the city. I suppose I cannot blame her, given recent events. She did play a part in the whole thing, putting the powder into Miss Berkwell's glass. Though she has left me greatly inconvenienced."

"Heavens," Nella said, but in her voice I heard apathy; she did not care a whit about Lady Clarence's lady's maid or lack thereof. She reached for the jar, spun it round in her hands and let out a sigh. "This is the one, yes. This is the exact one. Oh, how you've saved me from ruin, Lady Clarence . . ."

"Yes, yes, well, I told you I would dispose of it, and returning it to you here has been quite a chore, but your look this afternoon gave me such a fright. All is well now, I trust, and I see little reason to stay even a second longer than necessary, as it is growing late and I've not had a moment for a proper cry."

Nella offered her tea before she took leave,

but Lady Clarence declined.

"One more thing," she said, briefly glancing at me and then trailing her eyes across the tiny room, void of the luxuries with which she must have been well accustomed. "I am not entirely sure what arrangement you've given the girl, but in the event you'd consider it, please do keep in mind that I'm now seeking a new housemaid." She motioned to me like I was a piece of furniture. "She's younger than I'd prefer, but not unreasonably so, and she's obedient enough, the type to keep her mouth closed, yes? I'd like to fill the vacancy by the end of the week. Please do let me know as soon as possible. As I said, I'm on Carter Lane."

Nella stammered over her reply. "Th-thank you for letting me know," she said. "Eliza and I will discuss this. Such a change may be a welcome idea."

Lady Clarence nodded and made her way out, leaving Nella and me alone.

Nella set the jar on the table and sank into a chair, the necessity of her organizing and packing efforts now removed. I glanced to Tom's magick book, still on the floor; the candle beside it had expired at last. "Well," Nella began, "there is no immediate crisis now. You may stay here tonight on account of this fortunate event. In the morning, I do suggest you consider the idea of visiting Lady Clarence. It may be a good post for you, should you remain fearful of the Amwell house."

The Amwell house. The very words reminded me that not every curse upon me had vanished with the return of the jar. My error that had put Nella at risk might be gone, but that left me in the same spot I'd been earlier today. And I had no desire for a post with the Lady Clarence; I did not trust her and her manner was cold. I desired only to return to the service of my mistress. This meant returning to the Amwell house, so the importance of the Tincture to Reverse Bad Fortune still existed. Of the hundreds of spells I had read in the book, it was the only one that, with a bit of imagination, seemed able to vanquish Mr. Amwell's lingering spirit.

Grateful for a place to lay my head, my heart now thumped in hopeful anticipation about the tincture. But if I intended to attempt the spell, then I must either tell Nella of my plans in the hope that she would permit me the use of her vials, or I must think of a way to gather the ingredients without her knowing — like Frederick did, so very long ago.

Yet even if I chose the first option, this

310

exact moment did not seem the wisest; we were both tired, Nella so much so that her eyes were pink. For now, we both needed a few hours of sleep.

Tomorrow would come soon enough, and then I would find a way to try my hand at this thing they called magick. I tucked the book beneath my head and used it as a makeshift pillow. And as I fell asleep, I could not help but fall into an easy dream of the boy who'd given it to me.

23
NELLA

If the poisons I dispensed, and the deaths they subsequently caused, were indeed rotting me from the inside out, then I felt sure the death of Lord Clarence hastened the decay. Was it possible the consequence upon me increased with the renown of the victim?

It was of only some significance that the Lady Clarence returned the damnable jar, for the immediate crisis of the gallows was averted, but the slow rotting within me did not cease. A thick, bloody trickle in my throat had plagued me the last day, and while I would have liked to blame it on the late nights in the beetle field, I feared something worse: that whatever plagued my bones and skull had moved into my lungs.

Oh, how I cursed the day that Lady Clarence dropped her rose-scented letter into the barley bin! And how maddening that none of my own concoctions could resolve this. I hadn't the name of the disease, much less the remedy for it.

I could not sit in my shop another moment, turning to stone, and I needed a block of lard besides. And although I had not the heart to send Eliza away immediately after Lady Clarence's visit, the next morning I had no choice. As I prepared to depart for the market, I told Eliza, once and for all, that it was time for her to leave.

She asked me how long I planned to be gone. "No more than an hour," I said, and she begged me to let her rest another thirty minutes, claiming a deep ache in her head on account of yesterday's anxieties. Admittedly, I suffered a bad headache myself, and so I gave her an oil of herb prunella to rub into her temples and told her she could rest her eyes just a few minutes more. We said goodbye, and she assured me she would be gone by the time I returned.

I gathered my tendrils of strength and made my way to Fleet Street. I kept my head down, fearing as always that someone might look into my eyes and discern the secrets I kept within, every murder as clear as the crystal glass from which Lord Clarence drank to his death. But no one paid me any mind. Along the avenue, a hawker woman offered lemon confections, and an artist sketched lighthearted caricatures. The sun began to peek out of a cloud, its heat wrapping around my tired, sore neck, and around me floated the safe, relaxed din of conversation. No one seemed interested in me; no one even noticed me. I could not help, therefore, but think it a good day, or at least better than yesterday.

As I passed a newspaper stand, I found myself tangled up with a small boy and his mother. She had just bought a newspaper and now attempted to wrestle him back into his coat as he ran in circles around her, making a game of it. Since my head was down, I could not properly see, much less avoid, the chaos, and I found myself stepping straight into the little boy's path.

"Oh!" I exclaimed. My market bag flew forward and gave the boy a good knock in the head. Behind him, his mother lifted her newspaper and gave him a firm smack on the bottom.

Under attack from two women, including one stranger, the young boy relented. "Fine, Mama," he said, and stuck his arms out like a featherless bird, waiting for his coat. The mother, victorious, handed the newspaper to the person nearest her — which happened to be me.

Yesterday's evening newspaper, headlined *The Thursday Bulletin,* fell open in my

314

hands. It was thin, unlike the stacks of *The Chronicle* or *The Post,* and I glanced down at it with disinterest, expecting to return it to the woman as soon as she had a free hand. But an insert, a hastily printed advertisement, had been stuffed within, and my eye caught several words toward the bottom.

Like black, inky beasts, the words read "Bailiff Searching For Lord Clarence's Murderer."

I froze, rereading the words and covering my mouth lest I retch onto the clean pages. My nervous state must be playing tricks on me. Lady Clarence had returned the jar and all was perfectly well — certainly no one was suspected of murder. Why, I must have misread the text. I forced myself to pull my eyes off the page and look at something new — the purple, ribbon-adorned hat sitting atop the lady across the street, or the blinding glimmer of sunshine on the mullioned window of the milliner's shop behind her — and then I returned my gaze to the page.

The words had not changed.

"Miss," came a soft voice. *"Miss."* I looked up to see the mother, holding the hand of her now-obedient son, resplendent in his thick coat, waiting for me to return the paper to her.

"Y-yes," I stammered. "Yes, here you are." I handed it over, the paper trembling as it passed from my fingers to hers. She thanked me and stepped away, after which I rushed immediately to the newsboy at the stand. *The Thursday Bulletin,"* I said. "You have more copies?"

"A few." He gave me one of two remaining copies on his table.

I dropped him a coin, shoved the paper into my bag and rushed away from him lest the terror on my face betray me. But as I fled to Ludgate Hill, forcing one foot in front of the other with as much speed as I could muster, I finally began to fear the worst. What if the authorities were at my shop right that moment? Little Eliza, she was there alone! I crouched between two rubbish bins at the side of a building, opened the paper and read it as quickly as I could. It was printed overnight; the ink was fresh.

At first, I found the article so impossible to believe, I wondered if I'd been given a prop in some performance, one in which I acted the unwitting performer. And perhaps I could have been convinced it was mere theatrics if the details did not tie together so well.

The lady's maid, I learned, did abruptly

resign from her post, just as Lady Clarence said — but she must have put two and two together about Lord Clarence's sudden death, for she went to the authorities with a wax impression of my mother's engraved jar. At this revelation, I nearly cried out; it was of no consequence that the jar now rested safely in my shop, for the maid took a damned impression of it! She must have done it before Lady Clarence seized the canister from the cellar. Perhaps the maid was fearful of taking the jar itself on account of being found out and labeled a thief.

According to the article, the wax impression revealed a partially legible set of letters — B ley — and a single, thumbprint-size drawing, which appeared to authorities to be that of a bear on all fours. The lady's maid told authorities that her mistress, the Lady Clarence, instructed her to put the contents of the canister into the dessert liqueur that was ultimately ingested by Lord Clarence. The maid presumed it a sweetener; only later did she realize it was poison.

I continued reading and clasped my hand over my throat. The authorities went to Lady Clarence's home late last evening — it must have been soon after she had returned the jar, which would explain the hours-old ink on the hastily printed insert

— but Lady Clarence vehemently denied the maid's claim, insisting no knowledge of any poison or canister whatsoever.

Upon turning the page, I learned that the identification of the *origin* of the poison was now of utmost importance, as the "dispenser" (at this, I let out another small cry) might serve to resolve the conflicting stories of Lady Clarence and her maid. The bailiff hoped that, in exchange for a reasonable amount of clemency, the dispenser would identify who actually purchased the poison that was used to kill Lord Clarence.

And yet, the utter peculiarity of it! Lord Clarence was not meant to suffer a sure and sudden death at all. Miss Berkwell was the one who was meant to drink the cantharides, and yet she escaped the entire thing unscathed — she was not so much as a suspect in her lover's death, her name not even mentioned in the article. I had mourned the possibility of her death all along, but by God, how things had swung in her favor!

At the end was a crude image: a hand-drawn copy of the wax impression provided by the lady's maid. If the canister itself was hardly legible, this drawing-of-a-drawing certainly wasn't any better. That, if nothing else, gave me a moment of ease.

I tore my eyes from the page. My damp, hot fingers had smudged the ink in several places, and the flesh of my inner arms and my groin was damp. I stood in the narrow alley between the two bins of rubbish, breathing deep, sucking in the odor of decay.

As I saw it, there were two possibilities: I could return to my shop and blow out every candle, lest the authorities locate 3 Back Alley and I must rely on my final disguise — the cupboard wall — to protect me and the secrets housed within. But even if it did protect me, for how long would I subsist under the relentless grasp of my illness? Only days, I feared. And oh, how I did not want to die while trapped inside of my mother's shop! I had spoiled it enough with my killing; need I ruin it further with the decay of my body?

The second possibility, of course, was that the cupboard wall might not protect me. As safe as I'd felt behind it in years past, my shop's address had never been exposed in such a blatant way. The disguise was not infallible; the authorities might arrive with hounds at their heels, and the dogs would surely smell my scent of fear through the wall. If the authorities broke their way through and arrested me, what legacy was left to preserve from prison? The lingering trace of my mother was delicate enough; memories of her came easily as I moved about my shop, but these precious recollections would not follow me to Newgate.

That wasn't to say I would find myself alone; I expected the constables would soon bring in the countless other women whose names were in my register. Women I intended to aid, to comfort, would then be alongside me behind the iron bars, and we would be accompanied only by the unwanted groping of the prison guards.

No, I refused it. I refused both possibilities, because there was one more alternative.

This third and final choice was to lock up the shop, leave the register safely behind the false wall, and hasten my own death: to dive into the icy depths of the River Thames, to make myself one with the shadows of Blackfriars Bridge. I had thought of it many times, most recently while crossing the river with baby Beatrice in my arms, as I'd gazed at the waves lapping against the creamy white stone pillars and felt the film of mist on my nose.

Had all of my life led me to this destiny, that fateful moment when the cold water would braid around me and pull me under?

But *the child*. Eliza was at the shop, just

where I left her, and I could not leave her alone to suffer the inquisition of a bailiff that might find his way to 3 Back Alley. What if Eliza heard a commotion, peeked out of the door and unwittingly exposed what lay behind the false wall? She'd made one grave mistake already; if she made another and found herself facing an angry constable, I could not ask the poor child to defend all that I'd done.

It had hardly been fifteen minutes since I left her. Stuffing the newspaper back into my bag, I stepped out of the alley to return to my shop of poisons. I could not choose a certain death. Not yet, anyhow.

I had to go back for her. I had to go back for little Eliza.

I heard her before I saw her, and fury rose inside of me. Her careless noisemaking could have ruined us, if the drawing in the newspaper didn't do it first.

"Eliza," I hissed, closing the cupboard door behind me. "I can hear your clatter from halfway across the city. Have you no —"

But my breath caught at the scene before me: at the table in the center of the room, Eliza sat before numerous jars, bottles and crushed leaves of all colors, sorted into separate bowls. There must have been two dozen vessels in all.

She looked up at me, pestle in hand, a look of concentration frozen into her brow. Her cheek was smeared with reddish pigment — merely beet powder, I prayed — and the strands of hair above her forehead jutted out in all directions, as though she'd been boiling water over the fire. For a moment, I was returned to this same scene thirty years ago, but it was me at the table and my mother stood over me, her eyes patient if not a bit vexed.

The memory lasted only an instant. "What is all of this?" I asked, fearing that the crushed leaves that littered my table, floor and instruments might be deadly. If so, the cleanup of such a virulent mess would be dreadful.

"I — I'm working on some hot brews," she stammered. "Remember the first time I visited? You gave me — ah, it was called valerian, I think. Here, I found some." She pulled a dark reddish jar toward her. Instinctively, I glanced to the third shelf from the bottom of the back wall; the spot where the valerian should be was indeed empty. "And here, too — rosewater and peppermint." She thrust the vials forward.

Where to begin with this ignorant child?

Had she no sense? "Eliza, don't touch another thing. How on earth do you know that none of these may kill you?" I rushed to the table, my eyes scanning each jar. "You're to tell me that you began pulling things from my shelves without any knowledge of what they may do to you? Oh, heavens, which ones have you tasted?"

Panic rose inside of me as I began to consider antidotes to my most lethal poisons, cures that could be quickly blended and administered.

"I have been listening very closely in recent days," she said. I frowned, not believing I'd had any recent need for things such as rosewater and venom and fern root, the last of which was clearly marked on the wooden box balancing precariously at the edge of the table. "And I also referenced a couple of your books over there." She pointed at the books, but they appeared untouched, meaning that Eliza was either lying about this, or she had the sleight of a well-practiced thief. "I've prepared a couple of the teas here, for us to try." She bravely pushed two cups toward me, one of them brimming with liquid of a deep indigo color and the other, a pale brown resembling the inside of a chamber pot. "Before I leave for good," she added, her voice trembling.

I had no interest in her hot brews and I had a mind to tell her as such, but I reminded myself that Eliza hadn't read the news article that left me with such taut nerves. Now, more than ever, I needed to remain diligent and discreet — and it would be prudent to resume tidying the shop once and for all. Though I had no aim to return, I could not bear to leave it disheveled.

"Listen very closely to me, girl." I set down the market bag, empty except for the newspaper. "You must leave. Right now, without a moment to waste."

Her hand fell into a pile of crushed leaves on the table. Defeated and heartbroken, she seemed in that moment more a child than I'd ever known her to be. She glanced at the cupboard where the canister stood, the one that Lady Clarence had returned to us. How confused Eliza must have been by my forcefulness and the sudden necessity to make haste.

Still, I would not tell her my reasoning — I would not tell her what I knew. I meant, even then, to protect her.

I tilted my head, pitying the both of us. I wished I could send her to Lady Clarence's, but knowing that the authorities were there, asking questions, it was much too close for my comfort. "Please go back to the Amwell house, child. I know you fear it so, but you must go. It will be safe, I promise."

Surrounded by crushed leaves and colorful spills, Eliza gazed over the jars and bottles in front of her as she considered my request. At last, she nodded and said, "I will go." Then she wrapped her fingers around something I could not see and stuffed it into her dress. I did not care enough to question her about it; let the child take what she wants. Greater concerns awaited me.

After all, our very lives were at stake.

24

CAROLINE

At the back of the coffee shop, Gaynor and I leaned close together, the two articles about the apothecary spread on the table in front of us. They'd been published in a paper called *The Thursday Bulletin,* which, Gaynor explained, was not a widely circulated periodical and ran only between 1778 and 1792. According to her brief research that morning, the paper eventually shut down due to lack of funding, and the library's archive carried only a fraction of the published issues, none of which had been digitized.

"Then how did you find these?" I asked her, taking a sip from my coffee.

Gaynor grinned. "Our dates were all wrong. If the hospital note was indeed a deathbed confession, the author was probably referencing something that had happened earlier in her life. So, I searched the manuscripts and expanded my search to the late 1700s. I also added the keyword *poison,* which seemed logical for an apothecary who helped kill people. The search returned this article, and of course I spotted the image of the bear immediately."

Gaynor lifted the earlier bulletin, dated February 10, 1791. The headline read "Bailiff Searching for Lord Clarence's Murderer."

Since Gaynor had already read it, she went to the counter to order a latte while I picked up the article and skimmed it quickly. By the time she returned, I'd moved to the edge of my seat, mouth agape. "This is scandalous!" I told her. "Lord Clarence, Lady Clarence, a maid serving the dessert liqueur at a dinner party . . . Are you sure this is real?"

"More than sure," Gaynor said. "I checked the parish records on Lord Clarence. Sure enough, his date of death is recorded as February 9, 1791."

I pointed to the image in the article again. "So the maid made a wax impression of the bear on the jar, and . . ." I ran my fingers over the printed image. "And it's the same as the bear on my vial."

"One and the same," Gaynor confirmed. "It makes sense, the more I think about it. If the apothecary really did dispense poisons

327

to multiple women, maybe the bear was her logo, her mark that she put on all her vials. In which case, your finding one in the river is still incredible, but not as coincidental as we originally thought."

Gaynor lifted the article and reread a portion of it. "And here's where things get a bit unfortunate for our dear apothecary. The wax impression didn't just have the image of the bear. It had a few letters, too." She pointed to the section indicating that the police were looking to decipher the letters *B ley.*

"Police suspected this was part of an address. Obviously, we know from the hospital note that this meant Bear Alley. But at the time of this printing, police didn't know it." Gaynor lifted the lid from her cup to let her latte cool, and I held my breath, envisioning the door I'd gone through last night. I suspected *B ley* didn't mean Bear Alley at all. It probably meant *Back Alley,* the walkway leading to the apothecary's concealed room.

"It seems wild that she would put her address on any of her vials, doesn't it?" Gaynor shrugged. "Who knows what she was thinking. Maybe a careless mistake." She reached for the second article. "Anyway, I also brought the other bulletin with me, and it's this one that identifies the woman as an apothecary. And more than that, an *apothecary killer.* I suspect that soon after the first article was printed . . ." Gaynor trailed off. "Well, let's just say it was the beginning of the end for her."

I frowned. "The beginning of the end?"

Gaynor flipped to the second article, dated February 12, 1791. But I didn't have the chance to read it because my phone, sitting on the table in case James called, began to ring. I checked the screen, my heart lurching when I saw that it was him. "Hi — are you okay?"

I heard his haggard breathing first, a slow intake of a breath followed by a shaky, wheezy exhale. "Caroline," he said, his voice so quiet that I could hardly hear him. "I need to go to the hospital." I pressed my hand to my mouth, sure that my heart had stopped. "I tried dialing 911, but it's not going through."

I closed my eyes, vaguely recalling a pamphlet at the hotel check-in desk with the emergency number for the United Kingdom. But in my moment of disoriented terror, I couldn't remember the number.

The sensation of vertigo hit as panic rose inside of me; the coffee shop, buzzing with chatter and the hiss of an espresso machine, shifted on its axis. "I'll be right there," I choked out, sliding out of the chair and grabbing my things.

"I have to go," I told Gaynor, my hands shaking fiercely. "I'm sorry, it's my husband, he's sick —" At once, my eyes welled with tears. Despite what I'd felt toward James in recent days, I was now so terrified that my mouth had gone dry; I couldn't even swallow. On the phone, James had sounded like he was struggling to breathe.

Gaynor looked at me, confusion and concern on her face. "Your *husband*? Oh, God, yes, okay, go. But —" She picked up the two articles and handed them to me. "Take these. The copies are for you."

I thanked her, folded the pages in half and shoved them into my bag. Then, offering her a final apology, I rushed out the door and started running to the hotel, hot tears finally breaking through and rolling down my cheeks for the first time since I'd arrived in London.

When I entered the hotel room, the stench hit me first: the sweet, acidic odor that I had smelled on him earlier. *Vomit.*

I tossed my bag onto the floor, ignoring the water bottle and notebook that fell out, and rushed into the bathroom. I found

James on his side in a fetal position, knees tucked up against his chest, white as a sheet and trembling terribly. He must have removed his shirt at some point because it lay rumpled near the door, soaked through with sweat. This morning I couldn't bear the sight of him without a shirt, but now I dropped to my knees alongside him and placed my hand on his bare stomach.

He looked at me with sunken eyes, and a scream rose into my throat. There was blood on his mouth.

"James," I cried. "Oh, God —"

It was then that I looked inside the toilet. More than just vomit, it looked as though someone had splashed it with crimson watercolor paint. Unsteady on my feet, I ran to the hotel phone and asked for the front desk's help calling an ambulance. I hung up and rushed back into the bathroom. This wasn't food poisoning from Italian food, that much was clear. But I had zero medical knowledge of any kind; how was it that James had only a mild cough this morning, and now he was vomiting blood to within an inch of his life? Something didn't make sense.

"Did you eat anything after you went out this morning?" I asked him.

From where he lay on the floor, he shook

his head weakly. "I've had nothing. I haven't eaten anything."

"No water, no nothing?" Perhaps he drank something he shouldn't have, or —

"Just the oil you gave me, which I'm sure came up a long time ago."

I frowned. "There's nothing to come up. You just rub it on your throat, like you've done before."

James shook his head again. "I asked if you had DayQuil and you said no, you had yucca oil or something."

The color drained from my face. "Eucalyptus?"

"Yeah, that one," he groaned, wiping his mouth with his hand. "I took it like I would take DayQuil."

The bottle sat next to the sink, and the label affixed to it was clear: the toxic oil was meant for topical application only. Not to be ingested. And if the danger wasn't obvious enough, the label also stated that ingestion may cause seizures or death in kids.

"You *drank* this?" I asked incredulously, and James nodded. "How much?" But before he could answer, I lifted the vial up to the light. Thank God, it wasn't empty — not even half empty. But still, he drank a mouthful of it? "James, this is fucking toxic!"

He responded by hugging his knees closer

into his chest. "I didn't know," he mumbled in a soft voice. It was so pathetic, I wanted to crawl on the floor next to him and apologize, even though I'd done nothing wrong.

There came an abrupt knock at the door and a shout from the other side. "Medics," said a deep male voice.

The next few minutes passed in a blur as I was told to stand aside while the paramedics evaluated James. Including a pair of hotel managers who'd just appeared, there must have been ten people in the room, a merry-go-round of spinning, concerned faces.

A young woman in a well-kept, navy blue uniform stood near me — *La Grande* was embroidered on her shirt — and she offered me tea, a biscuit, even a sandwich tray. I declined them all, instead trying to listen to the thick British accents flying around as everyone made an effort to treat my husband. They asked him question after question, only some of which I could understand.

The medics pulled equipment from a heavy canvas bag: an oxygen mask, blood pressure cuff and stethoscope. The hotel bathroom soon resembled a trauma room, and the sight of the equipment was like a slap in the face as I wondered, for the very first time, if this might be a matter of life and death for James. *No, I shook my head, don't even go there. It won't happen. They won't let it happen.*

When I left for London without James on our "anniversary" trip, I expected emotional turmoil, but not of this kind. Now, with my own wounds still so raw, I found myself hoping desperately that James didn't die on the bathroom floor in front of me, even if I'd had such fleeting, dark notions about killing someone in the hours after learning of his affair.

Soon, James told the medics about the eucalyptus oil, and one of them lifted the bottle to look at it, just as I'd done. "The bottle is forty mil, but it's still half-full," the medic said in an authoritative voice. "How much of this did you have?"

"Just a swallow," James muttered as someone shone a small light into his eyes.

One of the paramedics repeated this into the cell phone he held at his ear. "Hypotension, yes. Significant vomiting. Blood, yes. No alcohol, other medicines." They all paused a moment, and I assumed that someone on the other end of the line was plugging things into a database, perhaps to determine urgent treatment methods.

"How long ago was it ingested?" the paramedic asked James, holding an oxygen mask to his face. He shrugged, but I saw in his eyes that he was terrified, confused and struggling even now to breathe.

"Two and a half, three hours ago," I offered.

Everyone turned to look at me, like it was the first time they'd noticed my presence.

"Were you with him when he drank it?"

I nodded.

"And does the oil belong to you?"

Again, I nodded.

"Right, then." The paramedic turned back to James. "You'll be coming with us."

"T-to the hospital?" James muttered, lifting his head slightly from the floor. Knowing James, he wanted to fight this, to magically make himself well, to insist that he'd be fine if only they'd give him a few minutes.

"Yes, to the hospital," the paramedic confirmed. "While the risk of seizure has likely passed at this point, central nervous depression is common for several hours after ingestion, and the delayed onset of more serious symptoms is not atypical." The medic turned to me. "Very unsafe, this one," he said, holding up the vial. "If you've got kids, I suggest you toss it altogether. Isn't the first time I've dealt with accidental ingestion of this stuff."

As if I didn't feel guilty and childless enough.

"Mr. Parcewell." In the bathroom, one of the paramedics took hold of James's shoulder. "Mr. Parcewell, sir, stay with me," the medic said again, his voice urgent.

I rushed into the bathroom and saw that James's head had lolled to one side and his eyes had rolled back. He was unconscious. I lurched forward, reaching for him, but a pair of hands held me back.

At once there was a flurry of activity: unintelligible messages relayed on radios, the shriek of steel as a gurney was brought in from the hallway. Several men lifted my husband from the floor, his arms drooping on either side of him. I began to sob, and the hotel staff stepped into the hallway to clear the space; even they looked fearful, and the woman in the navy blue suit trembled slightly as she nervously adjusted her uniform. A quiet soberness fell over the room as the paramedics, well trained, made quick work of getting James onto the gurney and out of the bathroom.

They rushed James into the hall and toward the elevators. In a matter of seconds, the space had emptied, leaving just me and a single medic. A moment ago, he'd been on a phone call at the edge of the room, near the window. Now, he kneeled on the floor near the table and unzipped the front pocket of a large canvas bag.

"I can go with him, in the ambulance?" I asked through tears, already making my way to the door.

"You can ride along with us, yes, ma'am." This gave me a measure of comfort, though something in his cool tone concerned me, and he appeared hesitant to look me in the eye. Then, my breath caught. Next to the medic's bag, I saw my notebook, which had fallen open to a page of my notes from earlier that morning. "I'll be bringing this along," he said, lifting my notebook from the floor. "We have two officers waiting at the hospital. They'd like to discuss a few things with you."

"O-officers?" I stammered. "I don't under-stand —"

The medic looked hard at me. Then, with a steady motion of his hand, he pointed to my handwriting at the top of the notebook page:

Quantities of non-poisons needed to kill.

25
ELIZA

Nella was meant to be gone for an hour, and I was horrified when she returned in less than half that. It was time enough to find and blend the ingredients as needed for the Tincture to Reverse Bad Fortune, but not enough to tidy my mess and replace the vials on the shelves.

Once inside, she found me with filthy hands and two hot brews, which served only as disguise, just as she taught me — something to show her in the event she returned early, because I did not want her to know I had used her vials to try magick. The hot brews were meant to deceive her and so I couldn't help but feel somewhat like Frederick, who had also blended tinctures behind Nella's back. But whereas he meant to use them against her, I meant her no harm.

Something seemed to worry Nella, and despite the mess upon which she'd stumbled, she was not as angry with me as I would have expected. Breathless, she stated that I must leave at once and begged me to return to the Amwell house.

No matter. Most of my work was complete. Just moments before she stepped inside, I poured the newly mixed potion into two vials, both of which I found sitting out with the other empty containers on the surface of her main workspace. I thought it prudent to prepare two vials, in case one slipped and shattered. Only four inches high or so, the vials were identical in all but color. One was the color of soft daylight — a pale, translucent blue — and the other, a pastel, rose-colored pink.

I had been sure to check twice, three times: the vials were etched only with the image of the bear — no words. The vials were now tucked inside my dress against my chest.

Nella seemed relieved when I agreed to comply with her wishes and leave the shop. But I did not intend to return immediately to the Amwell house, as she believed. According to the magick book, the tincture must cure for sixty-six minutes, and I finished the blending only four minutes ago, at exactly one o'clock. For this reason, I could not go to the Amwell house. Not yet.

I offered to clean up the mess I'd made,

but she shook her head, calling it a worthless task as things now stood. Though I
wasn't sure what she meant by this, I placed
my hand over my chest, where the vials were
secured. Soon, I hoped things would return
to normal. In only weeks, my mistress would
return from Norwich and we could resume
our long, comfortable days together in her
drawing room, free of Mr. Amwell altogether — in any form.

And so for the second time in two days,
Nella and I parted ways. There was no
doubt in my mind that, after today, I would
not see her again. She did not want me
there, and whether the magick tincture
worked or not, it would be unwise to return.
Despite this goodbye with my newfound
friend, my heart felt light — the vials were
cool against my skin, and full of possibility
— and I was not so sad as the last time we
said goodbye. I did not cry, and even Nella
seemed distracted, like her heart was not as
raw.

As we hugged a final time, I checked the
clock behind her. Eight minutes had passed.
I stuffed Tom Pepper's magick book into an
inner pocket of my gown. Although the
tincture was now mixed and I had no need
of the book, I could not bear to part with
his gift. And I meant, someday very soon,

to return to the shop. Perhaps we could open the book and try another spell or two together. The idea of it made the tips of my fingers tingle.

Though I could not return to the Amwell house with my tincture for another hour, I headed west because the route to the Amwells' took me close to another place I was curious to see: the Clarence estate. While I had little interest in accepting Lady Clarence's vacancy, my curiosity was piqued by the unseen place where Lord Clarence met his end. I walked toward the breathtaking dome of St. Paul's, eventually turning onto Carter Lane, where Lady Clarence had said she lived.

Before me lay a half dozen terrace homes, identical in appearance, and on any other day I would have had no idea which one belonged to the Clarence family. But that was not the case today; the house at the far end, like a honeypot of bees, swarmed with people, and the buzz of uneasy conversation floated all about. I knew, instinctively, that this was the Clarence home — and something was awry. I stiffened, afraid to move closer.

Standing behind a row of hedges, I observed the scene. Indeed, there must have been more than twenty people running about, half of them constables in dark blue tailcoats. I did not see Lady Clarence anywhere. I shook my head, not understanding the reason for such excitement. I had seen, last night, the jar that Lady Clarence returned to Nella. She had given no hint of a crisis, and her greatest concern of the moment was that her lady's maid had left abruptly. If she had been suspected of a crime, she would have mentioned it last night. Had something else happened at the house?

My courage built, and an idea struck me at once: I would approach the house, pretend interest in Lady Clarence's vacancy, and perhaps learn the reason for so many visitors, so many constables. I stepped away from the shrub and walked casually toward the house like I was ignorant of the fact that a man died there, victim of a poison I prepared with my own hands.

Several men stood near the entry of the house. As I approached the front steps, I began to overhear fragments of their hushed, hurried conversation.

"He's in the drawing room — came straightaway —"

"— image on his vial matches the maid's wax impression, an identical match —"

My skin felt suddenly dewy with sweat,

and one of the vials slipped deeper into my gown. I made my way slowly up each stair, remembering my feigned purpose for coming to the Clarence estate. No matter what I might see or hear, I could not forget myself. I approached the front door. No one minded me as they continued to converse.

"— have been reports of other deaths, similar in nature —"

"— repeat killer, perhaps —"

I stumbled, one foot tripping the other, and began to fall forward. Two arms appeared to catch me, and a constable with a scar on his left cheek lifted me back into a standing position.

"Lady Clarence," I gasped. "I have come to speak with her."

He frowned. "And for what purpose?"

I paused, my mind a cluttered mess of herbs and names and dates, like a page from Nella's register. *Repeat killer.* The words echoed in my mind as though someone whispered them behind me. A bright light flashed behind my eyes and I feared I may collapse to the floor, but the man continued to hold me. "Maid —" I stammered. "I am here to speak with her about the vacancy for the housemaid."

The man tilted his head at me, still frowning. "The lady's maid left only yesterday.

Has Lady Clarence already posted a vacancy?" Then he turned to look behind him, as though wanting to ask it directly of the mistress. "Come with me," he said. "She's in the parlor."

We went in together, the constable leading me through the overcrowded foyer smelling of sweat and sour breath. Several more officers stood in a circle, discussing what appeared to be a drawing in a newspaper, but I could not make out the image. Above a side table lacquered in black-and-gold paint, an enormous mirror reflected the horror in my eyes. I turned my face away, wanting badly to escape this place of angry, red-faced men. I shouldn't have come at all.

Lady Clarence sat in the parlor with a pair of constables. The moment she recognized me, she stood and let out a great breath of relief. "Oh, heavens," she said. "Have you come about the vacancy? Come, let's discuss and —"

One of the constables raised his hand. "Lady Clarence, we are not yet finished."

"I won't be but a few minutes with the child, sir." She gave him not another word before wrapping her arm around me and rushing me from the room. Her skin felt damp and sticky; sweat beaded on her brow.

Quickly, she pulled me up the stairs to the second story and took me into one of the rooms. It was pristinely arranged, the four-poster bed stiff as if never used. A cabinet, recently polished, reflected the buttercream light from the window.

"It is all very bad, Eliza," she whispered after she had shut the door. "You must go back to Nella immediately and tell her to leave. Both of you, as soon as possible, for she will be arrested and hanged — and you, too, possibly. They will not spare you on account of your age — oh, how impossible this whole thing is."

"I do not understand," I said, my lips trembling, words tumbling out. "You returned the jar and said all was well —"

"Oh, but it all fell apart last evening! You see, when my maid left yesterday, little did I know that she first divulged much to the constables. She told them I instructed her to put the contents of the jar into the glass, and she gave them a wax rubbing of the jar — it shows the little bear and the address. The address, thank heavens, has not yet been discerned, though I fear it is only a matter of time. And little use in returning the jar to Nella when the maid had already taken an impression of it, isn't it? How terrible that maid is, and how cowardly! If she had any smarts, she would have stolen the jar itself to give to the police, but I suppose she was scared someone might walk in and catch her stuffing it into her gown."

Lady Clarence sat on the bed and smoothed her skirts. "The image was printed overnight in a bulletin and put into the papers this morning, and shortly thereafter, a gentleman from St. James's Square went straight to the authorities. Several weeks ago, following the unexpected death of his grown son — which they believed, first, to be gaol fever — he found a vial underneath the bed where his son died. He'd thought nothing of the vial at the time, until seeing the image in the newspaper. The exact image of the bear was on the vial he'd found!"

Lady Clarence paused to breathe, looking helplessly toward the window. "No address was on that man's vial, thank heavens. I know little more than this, Eliza, but I have heard whispers between officers that there is another person, perhaps two, who came forward with something similar, look-alike containers that they discovered with the same little bear etching, and each of them has an account of an unexpected death among their close circles. Who knows how many there will be! But now there is talk of a repeat killer, and a great rush to identify the illegible address. They have deciphered a couple of the letters, so it is only a matter of time before they muster the mapmakers and trace every street."

She ran her hand over the top of the dresser next to us, which was spotless until her fingerprints left an oily smear. "This matters greatly to me, of course," she said, lowering her voice even further. "Late last evening, the bailiff confronted me about my maid's claim that I killed my husband. And what could I do except deny it? So now, the illegible address is even more important to the authorities, as they intend to speak to the dispenser of the jar to determine who purchased it. And I am so glad you came, for how could I now escape such prying eyes to tell Nella of this? Would she give them my name? Oh, go now, and convince her otherwise! Tell her she must leave in an instant, otherwise they will find her and employ whatever tricks they must until she gives up her secrets."

Lady Clarence shivered and wrapped her arms around herself. "And to think I threatened to reveal her after she threw the powder in the fire! My God, how it has all turned against me. Go now, or we will all find ropes around our necks by nightfall."

Of further questions, I had none. I did not care to know more about the man in the drawing room with the matching vial, or where the deceiving lady's maid had run off to, or whether the poor Lord Clarence had even been laid yet in the ground. I knew all there was to know: it was more than Mr. Amwell's spirit that haunted me now. The shadow of my mistake, which I thought removed only hours ago, had now returned with a vengeance. I must make haste to Nella's at once. Except —

"What time is it?" I asked. The Tincture to Reverse Bad Fortune was, now more than ever, of utmost importance. Nothing else could save Nella, and me, from this predicament.

Lady Clarence gave me a surprised look. "There is a clock in the corridor," she said. But as we made our way out of the room, I exhaled in frustration. The clock said it was not even half one; only twenty-eight minutes had passed since I stoppered the vial.

Out of the house I ran, pushing past the many uniformed men milling about in the foyer. Several of them watched as I left, and I overheard Lady Clarence tell them she turned me away for the vacancy. I dared not look behind me until I made it to Dean's Court, and I was greatly relieved to see that no one had followed. To be very sure, I took a complicated, winding route back to the shop. When I reached 3 Back Alley, I shoved open the storage room door, and I did not even give Nella the courtesy of a knock on the hidden wall of shelves. Instead, I reached for the hidden lever and slid the door open.

Nella stood at her table, her register in front of her. She had turned it toward the middle. Her body was bent over the table, as though she meant to read one of her entries from long ago. At my abrupt entrance, she looked up at me.

"Nella, we must leave," I cried. "Something terrible has happened. Lady Clarence's lady's maid, she told the authorities that —"

"You saw the paper," Nella interrupted, her voice so thick that I wondered if she hadn't taken a heavy dose of laudanum. "The maid gave them the wax rubbing. I know all about it."

I stared back at her, stunned. She already knew of it? Why had she not yet left?

I looked at the clock by the door. Thirty-seven minutes had passed. I rushed forward to the shelf above the table, the contents of which I was now familiar, and I pulled down the jar filled with tear-shaped drops, resin of frankincense. I had seen Nella take them once before, after rubbing at her swollen fingers.

"There is more," I said. "Take some of these while I tell you." I explained that I had passed by the Clarence home and heard it all from the mistress herself. After the papers were printed, another person — perhaps two or three or more — came forward with vials that were engraved with the same bear. All the vials were found in the days or weeks following untimely deaths, and now authorities believed the vials might be associated with a repeat killer.

"I had not heard that," Nella said, her face calm. Had she gone mad? Did she not understand the urgency, and what this all meant? Only minutes ago she was the one telling *me* to make haste; why did she not do it herself?

"Nella, listen to me," I pleaded. "You cannot stay. Remember the night when you helped me with the beetles? Somehow, you drew together your strength. Do it now, please!" Then I was struck by an idea. "We can go to the Amwells' until we determine what to do next. It is the perfect place. No one will bother us there." So long as Nella was with me, I felt I could stand to be inside the home while waiting for the tincture to finish curing. Mr. Amwell's spirit would not harm me with her so close, would it?

"Easy, child," Nella replied, putting a handful of resin pills into her mouth. "I do not intend to stay here." She pushed the jar of frankincense aside. "I know where I am going, and I was about to leave, anyhow. But you mustn't come with me. I will go alone."

If my agreement was what she needed, she had it. I smiled at her and helped her with her coat. As I did so, I was reminded of my first visit to the shop, only a week before. How much had happened in recent days, and none of it good. I remembered sitting at the chair across from her, hesitant to drink the valerian hot brew, while Mr. Amwell and Lord Clarence were still alive and ignorant of the plans laid out before them. I remembered, too, my second visit — pleased with the success of the poisoned eggs but plagued with a new terror and crouching forward in pain as my belly bled.

At once, a memory struck me. "Nella, after we harvested the beetles and you told me about Frederick, you said that if you'd *bled again,* you might have stopped this long ago."

Nella looked sharply away, as though my question had just struck the side of her face.

351

"Yes," she said between clenched teeth. "Perhaps I would have. But you are too young to understand what I meant, so you may forget I said it at all."

"When will I be old enough to understand?"

"There is no set age," she said, checking the buttons on her coat. "When your womb is ready to carry a baby, you will begin to bleed, once each month as the moon makes her route across the sky. It is a passage, child. Into maturity."

I frowned. *As the moon makes her route across the sky.* Didn't Mrs. Amwell say something similar on the night I began to bleed, the night we killed her husband? "How long does the bleeding last?" I asked.

Nella looked at me strangely, her eyes narrowed, as though reconsidering me. "Three or four days, sometimes more." She lowered her voice. "Did your mother, or Mrs. Amwell, never tell you any of this?"

I shook my head.

"Are you bleeding now, child?" she asked.

Suddenly embarrassed, I said, "No, but I did a few days ago. It hurt very much — my belly felt swollen and cramped."

"And it was the first time?"

I nodded. "It happened right after Mr. Amwell's death. I feared he did it to me —"

352

Nella raised her hand and smiled softly at me. "A mere coincidence, child. You are blessed, and more so than me. I only wish you'd told me sooner. I could have mixed something up to ease the cramping altogether."

I wished I'd told her sooner, too. For the first time since the death of Mr. Amwell, I allowed myself to consider the possibility that the bleeding might not have been his wicked spirit taking hold of me. Could it have been simply the monthly bleeding of which Nella just spoke? A passage into maturity? I had never thought of myself as a woman — only a child, a girl.

I wished to think on it longer, but there was no time. We should have left long ago.

Nella's register was still open on the table, and I glanced down at it. She had opened it to the year 1770, more than twenty years ago. The page was badly damaged; a dark red stain, like wine, smeared across the side.

Why had Nella returned to this old entry? Perhaps she meant to turn back the pages of her life — to remember the early days, before it all began. When this page was written, Nella's heart was not yet scarred. Her joints were not yet swollen and stiff. Motherhood, and her own mother, had not yet been taken from her. Perhaps she'd revisited the entry because she meant to remember these things: the honorable work she once did, the sort of apothecary she could have been, the virtuous woman her mother wanted her to be.

All of it, thrown aside in the bitter wake of Frederick's betrayal.

Nella caught me looking, then closed the book with a loud *snap* and led us to the door to go our separate ways.

26
CAROLINE

In a dingy, windowless room on the third floor of St. Bartholomew's hospital, I sat across from two male police officers, my notebook between us. A nauseating odor permeated the airless room — antiseptic and floor cleaner — while a fluorescent light buzzed and flickered above us.

The lead officer spun my notebook to face him, tapping his finger on the incriminating words: *Quantities of non-poisons needed to kill.* I braced myself, fearing what else he might see on the page of my hastily jotted notes. The word *arsenic* was asterisked, for God's sake.

I wanted desperately to search for James, who'd been rushed down the long corridor leading to the critical care unit. But instinct told me this would not be wise; the unshaven officer sitting in front of me would slap handcuffs on me before I even made it to the hallway. Leaving was not an option.

Suddenly, I had a lot of explaining to do.

I held my breath, praying the officer didn't look farther down the page. If he did, how could I begin to tell him the truth? Where would I even start? Would I begin with my unfaithful husband arriving in London unplanned, or my breaking-and-entering into a serial killer's apothecary shop, or my reason for having eucalyptus oil in my toiletry bag at all? Every scenario stood against me; every explanation seemed either too implausible or too coincidental.

I feared my version of events would do more harm than good; I was emotionally wrecked and unable to form a clear thought, much less a coherent sentence. But given James's condition only a short while ago, time was of the essence. I needed to find a way out of this, and quick.

As the second officer excused himself out of the room for a call, the first cleared his throat and addressed me. "Ms. Parcewell, do you care to explain what's in this notebook?"

I forced myself to focus. "These notes are related to a historical research project," I insisted. "Nothing more."

"A research project?" He didn't hide the dubious expression on his face as he leaned back in his chair and spread his legs apart. I stifled the sudden urge to vomit.

"About an unsolved mystery, yes." At least that much was true. It dawned on me that maybe the whole truth wasn't necessary — maybe the partial truth was enough to get me out of this predicament. "I'm a history major. I've been twice to the British Library, investigating an apothecary who killed people a couple hundred years ago. The notebook contains my research notes about her poisons, that's all."

"Hmm," he mused aloud, crossing one leg over the other. "Seems a fitting story."

This was precisely my concern. I stared at him, dumbfounded, resisting the desperate urge to throw up my hands and say, *Okay, asshole, come with me and I'll show you a few things.* He pulled a notebook and pencil from his pocket and began to scribble down words, some of which he underlined with rough, chalky strokes. "And you began this research when?" he asked, not looking at me.

"Just a couple of days ago."

"And you're visiting from where?"

"The States, Ohio."

"Have you ever faced criminal charges?"

I spread out my hands in disbelief. "No, never. Nothing." The back of my neck began to itch. *Not yet, anyway.*

357

Just then, the second officer returned to the room. He leaned against the wall and tapped his boot on the floor. "We understand you and your husband are having a bit of a . . . rough patch."

My jaw fell open. "Who —" But I steadied my voice; the more defensive I appeared to these men, the worse off I'd be. "Who told you that?" I asked, feigning calm.

"Your husband has been slipping in and out of consciousness; the charge nurse —"

"So he's okay?" I restrained myself from lunging out of my chair and making my way to the door.

"The *charge nurse,*" the officer started again, "has begun to ask him a few additional questions as they get him hooked up to his IV."

Heat rose to my face. James told the nurse we're having a rough patch? Was he trying to have me arrested?

But I reminded myself: so far as I knew, James was unaware of the predicament I now found myself in. Unless the police had told him that I was under interrogation, he had no knowledge of the terrible turn of events that had landed me in front of these officers.

The lead officer tapped his pencil against the table, waiting on my response to James's

358

claim. To improve my own situation, I considering rejecting it, insisting James had lied about our rough patch. But wouldn't it look even worse if I accused James of being a liar? The officers were inclined to believe the person in the critical care unit, not the healthy wife with the suspicious notebook — so if James told them we were having marital struggles, I couldn't deny it. The reality of the situation hardened around me like the steel bars of a jail cell. Maybe it was time to start thinking about an attorney.

"Yeah," I relented, preparing to unleash my only line of defense: James's infidelity. It was unfortunate for him that, just as I'd begun to process the reality of what had happened, I found myself wanting to use it against him. "I found out last week that he —" But I stopped myself. It was no use to reveal to these two men that James had cheated on me. It wouldn't turn them on him, I felt sure of that; it would only serve to make me look vengeful and, perhaps, emotionally unstable.

"James and I learned, last week, that we have a few things we need to work through. I came to London to get away for a few days. I meant to be here alone. Call the hotel and ask the registration desk. I checked in by myself." I straightened, looking the second officer in the eye. "In fact, James showed up in London unplanned, with almost no warning. Go ask the nurse. James can't deny it."

The two officers eyed one another warily.

"Let's finish this conversation over at the station," the officer across from me said, glancing toward the door. "I sense there's something you're not telling us. Perhaps our sergeant will have more success."

My stomach clenched; a sour taste flooded my mouth. "Am I —" I paused, gasping. "Am I being arrested?" I looked around helplessly for a trash can in case I needed to vomit.

The second officer placed his hand on his hip, near the dangling handcuffs. "Your husband — with whom you are having marital problems — is down the hall, fighting for his life after ingesting a harmful substance that you gave him. And your 'research notes,' as you call them, mention substances 'needed to kill.' " He emphasized the last three words as he unlatched the handcuffs from his hip. "Those are your words, Ms. Parcewell, not mine."

27
NELLA

If the departure from my shop was to be a temporary one, I would have reached into the cabinets — beginning with my mother's, along the side wall — to withdraw certain sentimental items I wanted for safekeeping.

But death was permanent. What earthly objects, then, did I need?

I could not tell this to Eliza, of course. After she helped me with my coat — my strength, mercifully, had returned for the moment on account of the frankincense — we stood together at the threshold, ready to leave, and I was forced to give appearance that I would come back to this place after the crisis had passed.

My eyes fell on the line that Eliza had drawn in the soot on her first visit and the clean, unblemished stone hiding underneath the filth. My breath caught. From the moment of her arrival, this child had unwittingly begun to unravel me, to expose something inside of me.

"Is there nothing you want to take? Your book?" She pointed at the register in the center of the table, the one I had just slammed shut. Contained within were the thousands of remedies I had dispensed over the years, harmless draughts of lavender alongside deadly, arsenic-laced puddings. But more important were the names of the women recorded inside. I could open the book to any page at all and easily recall the memories of the women within, no matter their ailments, betrayals or boils.

The book was evidence of my life's work: the people I had helped and the people I had hurt, and with what tincture or plaster or draught, and how much and when and on account of whom. It would be wise for me to take it, so the secrets could sink with me to the bottom of the Thames; the words smeared, the pages dissolved, the truth of this place destroyed. In this way, I could protect the women within the register.

Yet to protect them was to erase them.

These women were not queens and great heiresses. Rather, they were middling women whose names would not be found in gilded lineage charts. My mother's legacy embodied the brewing of potions to ease maladies, but it also meant preserving the memory of these women in the register — granting them their single, indelible mark on the world.

No, I would not do it. I would not erase these women, obliterate them as easily as I'd done with the first batch of cantharides powder. History might dismiss these women, but I would not.

"No," I said at last. "The book will be safe here. They will not find this place, child. No one will find this place."

A few minutes later, we stood in the storage room. The hidden door to my shop was closed and the lever latched. I placed my hand on the top of Eliza's head, her hair soft and warm against my fingers. I was grateful that the frankincense had numbed more than just my bones, for my innermost turmoil had also been tempered. I was not breathless or forlorn, nor did I await the rushing water with any sense of dread.

I considered it fitting that in the final moments of my life, I was aided by one of the many vials on my shelf. In life and in death, I relied on the palliative nature of what sat inside those glass bottles, and I was reminded, then, of more good memories than bad: more births than murders, more blood of life than of death.

But it was not only the frankincense that

gave me comfort in this decisive moment; it was also the company of little Eliza. Despite the fact that her error had brought all of this upon us, I chose not to harbor ill feeling toward her, and instead I regretted only the day that Lady Clarence left me her letter. Indeed, if it weren't for her renown and her scheming lady's maid, I would not be in the predicament I now found myself.

Yet, there was no use in looking back. In the face of this hard goodbye and, very soon, my own departure from life, Eliza's inquisitive spirit and youthful energy were salves upon my heart. I never met my own daughter, but I suspected she would have been much like the girl standing next to me. I put my arm around Eliza's shoulder and pulled her close to me.

With a final glance behind us, I led Eliza out the storage room door. We stepped into the alley, the cold air wrapping around us, and began to walk. "Up here —" I motioned to where Bear Alley opened up to the avenue "— you will continue on to the Amwell house, or wherever it is you choose to go, and I will go my own way."

In the corner of my vision, Eliza nodded. I moved closer to her, as a final, invisible goodbye.

We did not make it but twenty steps

before I saw them: three constables wearing dark blue coats, walking straight toward us, their faces grim. One of them carried a rod in his hand, as though the shadows of the alley scared him, and I could faintly make out a scar across his left cheek.

Eliza must have seen the men at the same time — for, without speaking a word or exchanging a glance, we began to run. Together we instinctively headed south toward the river, away from them, our sharp breaths in harmony with one another.

28
CAROLINE

As the officer unlatched the handcuffs from his belt, a cell phone rang from somewhere in the small room. I remained frozen, waiting for one of the officers to answer it, then the hazy disorientation cleared from my brain; the phone ringing was mine.

"It might be about James," I said, lunging for my purse, not caring if the officers tried to slap the cuffs on me before I could answer it. "Please, let me take it." I put the phone to my ear, bracing for the worst. "Hello?"

On the other end of the line was a cheery, if not slightly concerned, voice. "Caroline, hey, it's Gaynor. I'm just calling to check on things. Is your husband doing okay?"

God, what a dear she was. If only the timing wasn't so terrible. The lead officer watched me closely, bouncing his foot lightly on his knee. "Hi, Gaynor," I replied, my voice stiff. "Things are okay. I have —"

I paused, aware that my every word was being closely monitored, maybe even recorded. "I'm dealing with a situation right now, but I promise I'll call you back as soon as I can."

I gazed at the nearest officer, the one with handcuffs out and ready. My eyes fell on his badge affixed to his left hip: a sign of his position, his authority. Suddenly, like a rush of fresh air in the room, it dawned on me that Gaynor's position at the library might work in my favor.

"Actually, Gaynor . . ." I pushed the phone harder to my ear ". . . perhaps you could help me with something."

"Yes, of course," she said. "Anything."

"I'm at St. Bartholomew's," I told her, drawing an odd look from the officers.

"The hospital? Are you okay?"

"Yes, I'm fine. I'm on the third floor, near the critical care unit. Could you possibly make your way over here? It's quite a long story, but I'll explain when I can."

"Okay," she said. "I'll head that way in a few."

My shoulders sagged with relief. "The woman on the phone is a colleague and friend," I told the officers after I'd hung up the phone. "She works at the British Library, and she's been helping with my research. Whether you decide to arrest me

367

or not, I hope you'll hear what she has to say first."

The men glanced at each other, and the one across from me made another note in his book. After a few minutes, he checked his wristwatch and drummed three fingers on the table.

It was a last-ditch effort. Gaynor had no knowledge that I'd broken into the apothecary's shop or snapped pictures of the register, and at no point in our research together did we take notes on things like opium, tobacco or arsenic. I prayed the officers wouldn't show her the notebook, but I had to accept the risk. I'd rather come clean with Gaynor than get arrested for something I didn't do.

Eventually, one of the officers found Gaynor in the waiting area; she stepped into the small room with a terrified look on her face, probably thinking the presence of officers signified that something tragic had happened to James. I hadn't meant to cause her such alarm, but it would be impossible now to share any private words with her.

"Hi," she said upon seeing me. "What's going on? Are you all right? Is your husband okay?"

"Why don't you have a seat with us," the lead officer stated.

He motioned to an extra chair, and Gaynor lowered herself into it, clutching her purse closely to her side. Her eyes fell on my notebook, but it was far enough across the table that I thought it unlikely she could read anything on its pages.

"We were about to bring Ms. Parcewell to the station for further questioning," the officer explained, "regarding a harmful substance her husband ingested earlier today, and some unusual notes we found in her notebook, possibly related to the incident."

I shook my head, my courage strengthened now that Gaynor sat close to me. "No, *not* related, as I said."

Gaynor moved her hand toward me, as though reaching for my own — whether to comfort herself or me, I wasn't sure.

The officer leaned toward Gaynor, his hot, tobacco-tainted breath wafting across the table. "Ms. Parcewell said you may be able to explain some things for us." At this, Gaynor's demeanor changed in an instant; whereas a moment ago, she seemed to pity me, now her shoulders stiffened defensively. "We understand you work at the British Library?"

Gaynor's eyes darted at me. "What does this have to do with my job?"

At once, remorse wrapped around my

throat. I'd asked Gaynor to come to the hospital because I needed help — I needed saving. Now I realized the foolishness in it; I'd dragged someone else into my mess. God forbid Gaynor thought I tricked her into this. She hadn't done a single thing wrong, and yet now I'd maneuvered her into sitting next to me as I was questioned by two police officers.

I took a deep breath. "They don't believe I've been researching the apothecary. That's why I told them you worked at the library." I then faced the lead officer. "I've been to the library twice. I've looked through maps, I looked online . . ." I purposely said *I,* not *we,* because I meant to remove Gaynor from this — to place as much distance between her and my mess as I possibly could.

I exhaled as a clock on the wall ticked forward, another minute passed. Another minute stuck here, trying to explain myself, while James fought for his life. "These officers," I said to Gaynor, "seem to think I'm somehow involved in my husband's illness. He came down with a cold today, and I suggested he use a bit of eucalyptus oil. He was supposed to rub it into his chest, his skin, but he actually ingested it. Unfortunately, it's highly toxic." I eyed my notebook warily, wishing it would dissolve into thin air — wishing, in many ways, I hadn't found the vial or learned about the apothecary at all.

I placed my hands on the table in front of me, ready to ask Gaynor what I needed of her. "The medics found my research notes and called the police. Can you please assure these men that you do work at the library, and that I've been twice to research the apothecary? That this isn't just some lie I've made up on the spot?"

For a moment, Gaynor's reaction put me at ease. I watched it unfold, her slow understanding of the coincidence, the terrible timing of it all. The fluorescent light above us continued to flicker as we all waited for Gaynor to speak. Perhaps she would come to my defense without asking anything about the research notes — without reading the notebook at all. Then, I wouldn't have to explain the omission to her.

Gaynor took a breath to speak, but before she could say anything, the officer across from us placed his hand on my notebook and — to my horror — spun it around to face her.

I wanted to lunge across the table, throw the notebook aside and strangle him. He knew Gaynor had nearly come to my defense; he could see it as well as I could, and he'd saved his final trick for the eleventh hour.

There was nothing to do now but accept the inevitable. I watched carefully as Gaynor's eyes flicked left and right on the page. This was it: the truth, at last, coming to light. The names of obscure poisons, copied from the apothecary's register; random dates and names scribbled in the margins of the page, none of which Gaynor and I had researched together at the library; and, of course, the most incriminating line of all: *Quantities of non-poisons needed to kill.*

This was, I knew, the beginning of the end for our friendship. Gaynor would deny helping me with this level of research; any sane person would. Her confusion would only throw further doubt on my story in the eyes of the police, and that would be the end of it for me. I sat motionless, awaiting the cold, hard metal that would soon snap around my wrists.

Gaynor took a long, shaky breath and gazed at me, as though she meant to communicate something with just her eyes. But my own were welling quickly with tears, and my remorse was such that I almost wanted to be taken away in handcuffs. I wanted out of this goddamned room, away from the disappointed faces of these officers and my new friend.

Gaynor reached into her bag. "Yes, I can validate all of this research." She pulled out her wallet, then withdrew a card. Handing it to one of the officers, she said, "Here's my employee card. I can confirm that Caroline's been to the library twice in recent days to research the apothecary, and I can request the camera footage if it's needed for your investigation."

I could hardly believe it. Gaynor had come to my defense, even after surely understanding there was something I hadn't yet told her. I gaped at her, my body going limp in the chair. But I couldn't offer an explanation yet, or even say *thank you.* That, by itself, would seem suspicious.

The officer at the table ran his thumb over Gaynor's employee card as though checking the expiration and validity of it. Satisfied, he tossed it onto the table, where it slid several inches. Something buzzed in his pocket, and he withdrew a cell phone.

"Yes?" he said tersely into the device. I could hear a woman's faint voice on the other end of the line, and the officer's face hardened. I braced myself for news as he hung up the phone. "Mr. Parcewell would like to see you," he said, standing from the chair. "We'll show you to his room."

"H-he's okay then?" I stammered.

Gaynor reached again for my hand, giving it a gentle squeeze.

"I wouldn't say that quite yet," the officer replied, "but he's fully conscious, at least."

With Gaynor remaining in the room behind us, the officers ushered me out, one with his hand near my lower back. I stiffened, saying, "I can find James's room myself, thanks."

He smirked. "Not a chance. We're not quite finished yet."

I paused. This did nothing to ease my worry about an impending arrest. What had the nurse told the officer on the phone? Whatever it was, he felt he needed to accompany me.

As we made our way down the hospital corridor, silent other than the heavy stomping of the officers' boots, my spirits remained low. James's room was just ahead, and it was with a sense of dread that I awaited what he meant to say to me — and the officers flanking my sides.

29

ELIZA

My legs began to burn soon after leaving the alley, and my left foot started to blister, the swollen skin rubbing against my worn shoe with each stride. I gasped for air and a sharp pain, like an ice pick, left me clutching my rib cage. Everything in my body begged me to *stop, stop.*

The constables were twenty strides from us now, perhaps less. How had they found us? Had they followed me from Lady Clarence's estate, even though I took a winding, complicated route? There were only two of them; the third constable must have stayed behind, or perhaps he could not keep up. They chased after us, this pair of wolves, like we were rabbits — their supper.

Where was the wolfsbane now?

But we stayed ahead of them. We did not carry rings of iron on our uniform or have stomachs heavy with ale. And even in her weakened state, Nella was faster than the constables. As they pursued us, the distance grew greater by three, five, six strides.

With the instinct of prey, I motioned for Nella to follow as I made a sharp turn left onto a small alley. We raced to the very back — the constables having not yet come around the corner to see where we'd gone — and found ourselves at a cobbled walking path leading to another alley. I grabbed Nella's hand and pulled her forward. She winced at some pain, but I ignored it. There was no room for pity in my fear-stricken heart.

I wanted desperately to look behind us, to see if the constables had turned onto the alley and were quick on our heels, but I resisted. *Forward, forward.* A stinging sensation crawled across my collarbone. Not slowing my steps, I glanced down, expecting to see a bee or some other biting insect. Instead, it was one of the vials pressing uncomfortably against my skin as I ran, as if I needed a reminder that the minutes were passing too slowly, and it was not yet time for the tincture.

Ahead, situated behind a carriage house, I spotted a stable: dark, covered, with several haystacks forming a boulder that stood twice as tall as me. I aimed straight for it, still urging Nella along, but her grimace told me that she was in real pain. Her face, which a moment ago was a beating, angry red, had gone pale.

Nella and I passed by the carriage house and slithered through a wooden gate leading to the stables. There was a horse in the center stall and he exhaled nervously at our approach, as though sensing danger. We made our way to the stall at the far left, halfway hidden by the carriage house.

Here, at last, Nella and I crumbled to the ground, which was covered mostly in remnants of loose hay. It felt like being back in Swindon again, inside the stables where I used to fall asleep instead of doing my chores. I avoided a spot toward the center with a pile of horse dung, but Nella paid no attention to where she sat.

"You are well?" I asked between my own desperate breaths.

She nodded her head weakly.

Crouching down to seek out an opening in the wall where I could peek out, I found a penny-size hole so close to the ground that I had to kick aside a pile of soiled hay and lie on my belly. Peering through the hole, I was relieved to see nothing awry. No officers searched the area, no dogs sniffed the scent of a newcomer, there was not so much as a stable attendant doing chores.

But I was not so naive to believe we were out of harm's way, so I held my position on the damp ground. For the next few minutes, I alternated between deeply inhaling in order to catch my breath, checking the peephole for any movement outside and glancing at Nella, who remained very still and had not spoken a word to me since we left the shop.

As I lay there and watched her slowing breath and the way she brushed an unruly curl from her face, I remembered the very moment that brought us to this one, the night we slept in another stable after beetle-hunting. That was the night that Nella had revealed so much to me: her love for Frederick, his betrayal of her and everything that led her to live a life as a poisoner of brothers, husbands, masters, sons.

Peeking out again, movement caught my eye. Given the tiny hole through which I looked, I tried to move my eye around the narrow field of vision, to little avail. I waited, my heart thundering in my chest.

"They may find us yet, Eliza," came a hoarse whisper behind me. I winced at the strain in Nella's voice. "If they do, you must deny knowing me. You must deny ever setting foot into my shop. Do you understand? This is not yours to face. Say that I threatened you, forced you into this stable, and —"

"Shhh," I hushed her. My God, she looked weak — the resin drops were fading fast. And ahead, near the carriage house, a small gathering had formed. I could not make out everyone in attendance, but several young men chatted animatedly and waved their hands, pointing around the edges of the stables where we now waited with bated breath. Given my position on my belly, my arms bore most of my weight and began to shake, but I could not release the weight without also pulling my eye from the peephole.

If the men searched the stables, they would find us within seconds. I looked to the back of the stable; the walls were roughly a meter and a half high, and I felt confident that I could scale it and escape from the back if necessary. Though a touch of color had returned to her face, I was not so confident about Nella. I could escape now if I wanted and leave her to be caught alone. But I brought her into this, and I must now try to fix my wrongdoing.

"Nella," I said to her, my voice a mere whisper, "we must escape over the back wall there. Do you have the strength?" Without answering, she began to lift herself from the ground. "Wait," I said, "stay low. There are people just by the carriage house."

She must not have heard me, for she began to crawl up the wall. Before I could stop her, she lifted herself over it and collapsed onto to the other side, then she began to run as best she could.

I heard a man yell from behind us, and I was at once furious with Nella for her recklessness, which had drawn the attention of the men. Without looking behind me, I scaled the wall easily, landed on two feet and ran after Nella, who was already several strides ahead of me. She hurried south down a short pathway between two houses, limping all the while, and ahead I saw the cool, glimmering, dark River Thames. She was heading straight for it.

Unlike a few moments ago when I pulled her along, there seemed now a renewed strength in Nella, some primal fear, and it was me who followed her. The river drew closer, closer, and when she turned onto Water Street, I believed her to be making her way to Blackfriars Bridge.

"No!" I yelled at her as she skirted the shadowy edge of a building. "We will be in clear view!" I had not the breath to explain my logic, but with the men a short distance behind us, I knew that our chances of escape were best if we remained hidden by shadows and alleys. Perhaps we could find an unlocked door to run into; London was big enough to aid many a criminal in escape, as Nella well knew from a lifetime of secrecy. "Nella," I said, a cramp suddenly seizing my side, "it is too open, like being onstage." Ignoring me, she drew near Blackfriars Bridge, which swarmed with children, families and couples walking hand in hand. Had Nella lost her mind altogether? Surely some bold man would see the constables chasing us and take it upon himself to stop us, overpower us with his strength. Had Nella thought of none of this? She kept running, running, not looking back.

Where was it that she meant to go? What was it that she meant to do?

Near the center of the bridge, a clock tower seized my attention. I squinted, looking at the tip of the small hand; it was ten minutes after two. *Seventy minutes!* Enough time had passed; the tincture was ready.

I turned my head back to see that, indeed, the officers had followed us onto the bridge. I reached into the bodice of my gown, my fingers wrapping around the two smooth vials near my breast. I'd prepared two vials in case one slipped from my dress, but I realized this decision had been wise for another reason: both Nella and I now found ourselves in a desperate position.

In my effort to carefully remove the first vial from my gown, I failed to notice that Nella had come to a complete stop in the middle of the bridge, chest heaving, her hands on the railing. I slowed, now just inches behind her. Dozens of people dressed in black and gray moved all around us, unaware.

Capture was imminent. I gave the officers fifteen, maybe twenty seconds before they were upon us.

I uncorked the pale blue vial. "Take this," I pleaded, handing it to Nella. "It will fix everything." I wished for the spell to give her wise words to say to the constables or form lies on her tongue; any kind of powerful magick, like that which had brought breath back to Tom Pepper's lungs when he was an infant.

Nella looked to see what was in my hand. At seeing the vial, she showed no surprise. Perhaps she suspected I hadn't really been making hot brews when she went off to the market; perhaps she knew, all along, that they were a disguise.

Her shoulders trembled violently. "We must part now," she said. "Go into the crowd, little Eliza, and disappear like you're one of them. *Run,*" she breathed, "and let the men follow me into the river."

Into the river?

All this time, I had wondered why she made her way straight to the Thames. But how could I not have seen it? I understood, now, exactly what she meant to do.

The constables grew nearer, fighting against the mass of people around us, pushing them aside. One of the men was close, only seconds from us; I could see the chapped skin of his lips and the angry scar on his left cheek, which I recognized instantly. He was one of the constables I had seen at Lady Clarence's.

He pushed toward us, staring directly at me, and the look of vengeance in his eyes said, *This is where it ends.*

30
CAROLINE
PRESENT DAY, WEDNESDAY

As the two officers and I approached the closed door to James's hospital room, the charge nurse — sifting through paperwork posted outside of the door — informed us that his condition had stabilized. They were arranging to move him out of the critical care unit, but James had insisted on seeing me first.

I slowly opened the door, unsure what would greet me on the other side, and the officers followed me in. I exhaled as I spotted James, tired-looking but with color in his face, propped against several pillows in the hospital bed. But if I looked surprised at his improved condition, it must have been nothing compared to his own look of astonishment when he noticed the uniformed men following close behind me.

"Um, is there an issue?" He looked at the nearest officer.

"They think I poisoned you," I said before

384

the officer could reply. I walked to the edge of the hospital bed and leaned a hip against it. "Especially since you told the medics we're having marriage issues." I scanned the IV drips hooked to his arm, the gauze keeping the needles in place. "Did you not see the warning label on the side of the bottle? Why on earth did you drink it?"

He blew out a long breath. "I didn't see it. I guess it serves me right." Then, turning to face the officers: "Caroline had nothing to do with this. The whole thing was an accident."

My knees went weak; they couldn't arrest me now, surely. One of the officers raised his brow, and a look of boredom fell over his face, like his hot lead had just gone lukewarm.

"Are we done here," James asked, "or do I need to sign a statement?" Frustration and fatigue were clear on his face.

The lead officer reached into his shirt pocket and withdrew a small business card. He made a show of tapping the card against the table at the front of the room, then headed for the door. "If anything changes, Mr. Parcewell — or if you want to share something with us confidentially — call the number on that card."

"Right," James said, rolling his eyes.

Then, without so much as an apologetic glance in my direction, the officers left the room.

With the agony of the preceding hour now lifted, I lowered myself gratefully onto the edge of James's bed. "Thanks," I mumbled, "and good timing. If you'd waited much longer, I might have been calling from a jail cell." I glanced at the monitors next to him, a blinking screen of scraggly lines and numbers I couldn't decipher. But his heart rate looked steady, and no warning alarms flashed. I hesitated to admit it, but I set my pride aside and said it anyway. "I thought I might lose you. Like, *really* lose you."

James's mouth turned upward in a soft smile. "We're not meant to be apart, Caroline." He squeezed my hand, an expectant look on his face.

A long pause passed as both of us held our breaths, our eyes locked. It seemed the entirety of our future depended on my response — my agreement with his statement.

"I need some air," I said at last, tearing my gaze away. "I'll be back in a bit." Then, gently dropping his hand from mine, I stepped away and out of the room.

After leaving James's hospital room, I

ventured down the hall to the empty waiting room and settled onto a sofa at the far corner of the room. A vase of fresh flowers sat on a table next to an oversize box of tissues. I'd be needing them; tears had begun to prick my eyes like needles.

I leaned back against a pillow and let out a small sob, pushing a tissue into my eyes to soak up not only the tears, but all the other things pouring out of me: relief at James's wellness, coupled with the continued sense of betrayal about his infidelity; the unfairness of the officers' questioning, and the knowledge that I didn't tell them the full . . . truth.

The truth.

I wasn't exactly blameless.

Was it really just last night that I'd dug my way into the depths of Back Alley? It felt like a lifetime ago. How did James manage to hide his infidelity for months? I'd kept my secret from James, Gaynor and two police officers for only a matter of hours, but it had proved almost physically impossible.

Why did we suffer to keep secrets? Merely to protect ourselves, or to protect others? The apothecary was long gone, dead for more than two hundred years. There was no reason for me to stand guard over her.

Like two guilty children in a playroom, there they stood, side by side: James's secret, next to my own.

As tears continued to soak through the tissue, I realized my grief was richer and more nuanced than what lay on the surface. This was about more than the burden of the apothecary, more than James's infidelity. Intermingled in the mess was another, subtler secret that James and I had hid from each other for years: we were happy, yet unfulfilled.

It was possible, I understood now, to be both at the same time. I was happy with the stability of working for my family, yet unfulfilled by my job and burdened by the things I hadn't pursued. I was happy with our desire to someday have children, yet unfulfilled by my achievements apart from family life. How had I only just learned that *happiness* and *fulfillment* were entirely distinct things?

I felt a gentle squeeze on my shoulder. Startled, I lowered my soaked-through tissue and looked up. *Gaynor.* I'd almost forgotten that we'd left her alone in the small interrogation room. I composed myself enough to force a weak smile and take a few deep breaths.

She handed me a small brown paper bag.

"You should eat something," she whispered, taking a seat next to me. "At least a bite of the biscuit. They're quite good." I peeked inside the bag and found a neatly wrapped turkey sandwich, a small Caesar salad and a chocolate chip cookie the size of a dinner plate.

I nodded in appreciation, tears threatening once again. In a sea of strange faces, she had proved a true friend.

Not a crumb remained once I finished. I drank half a bottle of water and blew my nose with another tissue, steeling myself. This wasn't how, or where, I imagined sharing everything with Gaynor, but it would have to do.

"I'm so sorry," I began. "I didn't want to drag you under with me. But when I was with the police and you called, I thought you might be the only person able to help me."

She folded her hands in her lap. "Don't apologize. I would have done the same thing." She sucked in a breath, choosing her words carefully. "Where has your husband been the last few days? You haven't mentioned him once."

I looked down at the floor, concern about James's health now replaced with shame over everything that I'd hid from Gaynor.

"James and I have been married ten years. This trip to London was meant to be our anniversary trip, but last week, I learned he'd been unfaithful. So, I came alone." I closed my eyes, raw with emotional fatigue. "I've been running from the reality of it, but James showed up yesterday unannounced." At Gaynor's look of surprise, I nodded. "And as you know, today, he unexpectedly fell ill."

"It's no wonder the police were suspicious." She hesitated, then said, "Probably not the anniversary celebration you expected. If there's anything I can do . . . ." She trailed off, as lost for words as I was. The situation, after all, wasn't remedied. James might have been on the mend, but *we* were not. I envisioned us together in Cincinnati again, trying to undo the tangled knot he'd brought into our lives, but the vision was murky and unsatisfying, like an ill-fitting resolution at the end of an otherwise decent movie.

Gaynor reached into her bag and pulled out my notebook. When I'd left the interrogation room with the police, I hadn't even noticed that the notebook remained in the center of the table, right in front of Gaynor. "I didn't look through it," she said. "I thought I'd give you a chance to . . .

explain." Her face twisted as though she didn't want to know the full truth — as though her ignorance would keep us both safe.

This was my last chance to escape unscathed; my last chance to salvage a remnant of our friendship. By falsifying a story about my own research, I could avoid admitting to the worst wrongdoing of all, which was that I'd breached a precious historical site. If I told her, who knew what she may do? She might chase after the two officers and report the offense; she might cash in on the incredible, newsworthy discovery; or she might reject me altogether and tell me to never contact her again.

But this wasn't about what Gaynor would or would not do with the information. This was my burden, and if there was anything I'd learned in recent days, it was that secrets wreaked havoc on lives. I needed to let out the truth about my trespassing — which now seemed minor, relative to the murder charge I'd nearly faced — and I needed to let out the truth about the unfathomable discovery I'd made.

"There's something I need to show you," I said at last, checking to ensure the waiting room remained empty. I pulled out my cell phone and navigated to my photos of the lost apothecary's register. Then, with Gaynor peeking eagerly over my shoulder, I began to unveil the truth.

When I returned to James's bedside, it was midafternoon. Little had changed — only now, he slept soundly. When he woke, later, there were a few things I needed to tell him.

Before settling myself into the chair near the window, I made my way to the restroom. Suddenly I froze, looking down at myself with wide eyes: I'd felt that unmistakable, leaking sensation from between my legs. Clenching my thighs together, I rushed into the cold bathroom in James's hospital room and sat down on the toilet.

Thank God, I finally had my answer: I was not pregnant. I was very much *not* pregnant.

The bathroom was well-stocked with pads and tampons, the latter of which I eagerly tore open. When I was done, after washing my hands at the sink, I peered up at myself in the mirror. I pressed my fingers to the glass, touching my reflection, and smiled. No matter what would come of my marriage, there was no baby to complicate things. No innocent child to stand by helplessly as James and I redefined ourselves, both as individuals and as a couple.

I returned to my seat next to James and

leaned my head back against the wall, considering whether I might be able to catch a short nap in such an uncomfortable position. In the moment of warm, satiated respite, a memory slipped toward me: this morning, in the coffee shop, with Gaynor. She'd given me the two articles about the apothecary, but I hadn't yet read the second one.

I frowned, reaching into my crossbody bag and pulling the articles out. Why on earth didn't I show *these* to the officers earlier, when they threw doubt on my research claims? In truth, I'd forgotten about the articles entirely, given the more immediate concerns at hand.

I unfolded the two pages; the earlier article, dated February 10, 1791, was on top. It was the article about Lord Clarence's death and the wax impression of the bear logo. Since I'd already read it, I moved it to the back, and my eyes settled on the second article, dated February 12, 1791.

I gasped as I read the headline. This article, I understood now, explained what Gaynor meant at the coffee shop, when she referred to Lord Clarence's death as the *beginning of the end* for the apothecary.

The headline read "Apothecary Killer Jumps from Bridge, Suicide."

The article began to tremble in my hands, like I'd just read the death announcement of someone I knew all too well.

31
NELLA
FEBRUARY 11, 1791

Eliza and I stood together on the bridge, the constable no more than three strides behind us. Death was close — so close that I could feel the chill of its outstretched arms.

The seconds preceding my death were not as I expected. Within me, there arose no memories of my mother, my lost child or even Frederick. There was only one memory, a single, young one, hardly formed: little Eliza and the first time she appeared at my doorstep in her threadbare cloak, her poor excuse of a hat, yet her cheeks so young and dewy, like a newborn. In the truest sense of the word, she was a *disguise*. The perfect murderer. For many a servant had murdered her master in the city of London, but who would believe a twelve-year-old served a poison-laced egg at the breakfast table?

No one would believe it. Not even me.

And so it was that I fell into disbelief

again. For, as we stood on the bridge together and I prepared to jump, just as the word *run* had tumbled off my tongue, the girl lifted her thin legs over the railing of Blackfriars Bridge. She glanced back at me with a gentle gaze, the edges of her skirt whipping in the breeze that pushed up against her from the River Thames.

Was this a trick? Or were my eyes deceiving me, perhaps under attack by the demon inside me, ravaging me of this valuable sense in my final moments? I heaved my weight forward to grab her, but she slid away from me along the railing, my efforts no match for her nimble movements. This left me furious, as her little game had taken precious seconds from me. Somehow, I must find the strength to lift my own bones over the metal railing before the officer seized me.

One hand on the railing, Eliza's other hand clutched the tiny blue vial that she had just offered me. She lifted it to her lips, sucked the liquid from it like a starving infant and tossed it into the water below.

"It will save me," she whispered. Then her fingers, one by one, slid from the railing like ribbons.

Everything placed unto the body removes

something from it, calls it forth or represses it.

My mother taught me this simple lesson, the power of earth-borne remedies, when I was a child. They were the words of the great philosopher Aulus, of whom little was known. Some, in fact, doubted his very existence, much less the veracity of this claim.

His words flooded over me as I watched Eliza's body fall. I had never before experienced the strangeness of this vantage point, to watch someone fall directly below me. Her hair pulled upward as though I had an invisible hold on it. Her arms crossed over her chest as though she meant to protect something inside. She looked directly ahead, her gaze on the river outstretched before her.

I clung to the promise of Aulus's words. I knew that, placed unto the body, oils and tinctures and draughts could remove — indeed, unweave and destroy — the creation of one's womb. They could remove the thing one most desired.

I knew, too, that they could call forth pain and hatred and revenge. They could call forth evil within oneself, the rotting of bones, the splitting of joints.

Yet placed unto the body, these things could repress . . . what? Could they repress death?

By the time my fearful, racing heart understood what had happened, Eliza had disappeared into the water, the death I had dreamed of as my own. But animal instinct begged me away to the more urgent crisis before me: the constable mere inches away, his arms reaching, as though he, too, wanted to grab hold of the falling girl — for by jumping from the bridge, she had implicated herself, and the constable must have surely believed that only she could solve the mystery of who slipped the poison into the liqueur that killed Lord Clarence.

All around us, movement: a distraught-looking woman carrying a basket of oysters; a man herding a small flock of sheep south; several young children scattered about like rats. They all closed in, dressed in dark, morbidly curious.

The constable turned his gaze on me. "Were you in it together?" He motioned to the water.

I could not respond, so shattered was my still-beating heart. Below me the river toiled, as though angry with its newly claimed victim. It should not have been her. It should have been me. My desire to die was what brought us to the peak of this bridge, anyhow.

The constable spat at my feet. "Bloody

mute, are we?"

I leaned onto the railing, my knees no longer serving me, and gripped the iron.

The second officer, brawnier than the first, came up behind him, his cheeks red and his chest heaving. "She jumped?" He peered around in disbelief before finally turning to appraise me. "This can't be the second one, Putnam," he shouted. "She can hardly stand. The two we saw running, they were dressed like anyone else." He looked over the crowd, presumably searching for another cloaked figure with more vigor in her face than me.

"Damn you, Craw, it is, though!" Putnam yelled back, like a fisherman about to lose a valuable catch. "She can stand fine, she's only shocked at the loss of her friend."

I was, indeed. And I felt as though he meant to dig the fishhook as far into my flesh as it would go.

Craw stepped closer and leaned into his partner, lowering his voice. "You sure she's not just one of the crowd, then?" He motioned around him. The mob of bodies, all dressed in similar dark coats as my own, had grown around us. By mere appearances, I blended in with them. "You're sure enough to let her swing? The poisoner's dead, sir." He glanced over the edge of the bridge.

"Buried in muck by now."

A flash of doubt crossed Putnam's face, and Craw seized it like a dropped coin. "We chased the rat out of her hole and we both saw her jump. It ends here. This is enough to satisfy the papers."

"And the dead Lord Clarence?" Putnam screamed, his face red. He turned on me. "Do you know anything about him? Who bought the poison that killed him?"

I shook my head and heaved out the words like vomit. "I don't know who that is, or of any poison that killed him."

A sudden commotion silenced the men as another office ran up the bridge. I recognized him as the third constable from the alley. "There's nothing there, sirs," he said.

"What the hell do you mean?" Putnam asked.

"I broke through the door where the women came out. Not a thing inside. A dry storage bin full of rotted grain."

Amid the distress of the moment, I felt a singular sense of pride. The register, and the countless names within, were safe. All of those women, safe.

Putnam jerked his hand at me. "Does this woman look familiar? Was she one of the two we saw?"

The third constable hesitated. "Hard to

tell, sir. We were quite the distance."

Putnam nodded as though he, too, hated to finally admit to this. Craw gave him a stiff pat on the back. "Your case against this woman is losing its legs, good sir."

Putnam spat at my feet. "Get out of my face, wench," he said. The three men gave a final glance over the railing, nodded at one another, and headed back down the bridge.

After they had gone, I peered over the edge, my eyes searching desperately for the swirling fabric of a soaked gown or the creamy paleness of skin. But I saw nothing. Only the muddy, unsettled churn of the river.

She needn't have done it. Her little heart must have thought that by bringing the devastation upon us with her mistake, she must be the one to take the fall. Or perhaps it was something more, like her fear of spirits. Perhaps she feared *my* spirit, haunting her after my death, cursing her for bringing this upon us. Oh, how I wished I'd been gentler with her about the ghost of Mr. Amwell! How I wished I had softened my tone, gained her trust, convinced her of what was real and what was not. I wanted more than anything to reverse time and pull her back upward to me. I stumbled backward a step, my knees weakened under the suffocating sense of regret.

Regret, but also discontent.

I meant to be the one down there. I meant to be the one to die. Could I live another day bearing this new agony, too?

The crowds had mostly dispersed; they no longer pushed inward, curious. And if I forced aside the memory of Eliza's fall, I could almost convince myself that nothing had changed. It was just me, alone with the end I had always imagined.

I squeezed my eyes shut and thought of all that I had lost, and then I stepped toward the railing and leaned over the hungry black waves.

32

CAROLINE

James lay still next to me, his breaths slow and even, while I sat in the chair by the head of his hospital bed. The article rested in my lap. After reading it a moment ago, I could only lean forward and put my head in my hands. Though I didn't know her name — I knew the woman only as the *apothecary* — her self-chosen death tugged at me, uncomfortable in the way of a slow-building headache.

Of course, she lived two hundred years ago; I'd known from the first moment I learned of her that she was no longer alive. The shock was *how* she died.

Maybe it was that I'd been to the River Thames, where the woman jumped, and I could picture the whole event in my mind. Or maybe it was that I'd been inside the apothecary's hidden shop, the discreet and shadowy place where she lived and breathed and mixed her potions, however menacing

403

they were, and so I felt a sense of solitary connection to her.

With my eyes closed, I imagined the events set out in the second article: the family and friends of previous victims — those who died before Lord Clarence — coming forward after seeing the first article, bringing with them their own vials and jars, all of them bearing the same logo of the little bear.

The police understanding, at once, that they were hunting a serial killer.

The mapmakers enlisted late in the night; every instance of *B ley* in the city turned over, inspected, considered.

The three officers descending on Bear Alley on the eleventh of February, their arrival so abrupt that a woman began to *run* and did not stop until she was standing at the top of Blackfriars Bridge.

The article mentioned Back Alley, too, albeit briefly. After the woman began to run, the third and most junior officer remained in the area to inspect the door from which he thought the woman had come. It was the door at 3 Back Alley. But upon entering the room, he found only an old storage cellar: a wooden bin of rotted grain and empty shelves at the far end of the room, but little else.

This place, I knew, was the very same in

which I'd stood last night — the room with the crumbling shelves at the back. It served as the apothecary's cover, her facade, akin to the mask one might hold over their face at a masquerade. Meanwhile, behind the room lay the truth: the shop of poisons. And though the two-hundred-year-old article assured the public that police would continue to dig until they uncovered her name and place of work, the untouched space I found last night told me that they never did. The apothecary's facade had been resolute.

But there was something odd. Although the article seized a fair amount of space on the page, the author glossed over the most significant part of the whole event: the woman who jumped. Her description and features were not discussed, not even the color of her hair; it only said she wore dark, heavy clothing. The article did not reveal whether any words were exchanged with the woman and noted the whole affair had been rather disorderly. A number of spectators had descended upon the immediate vicinity, the confusion and chaos such that the officers briefly lost sight of the woman before she stepped over the railing of the bridge.

According to the article, there was no doubt the woman was an abettor in the death of Lord Clarence, and officers were certain the string of murders associated with the woman they'd dubbed the *apothecary killer* had come to an end. The River Thames was hostile that day, swift and frigid, littered with ice. After the woman jumped, police monitored the area for a long while. But she did not surface. She did not reappear.

Her identity, according to the article, remained unknown.

As twilight fell over London and nightfall neared, James began to stir. He turned over in the hospital bed, facing me, then slowly opened his eyes. "Hi," he whispered, a smile pulling at his lips.

Sobbing in the waiting room had been more cathartic than I realized, and after fearing this morning that I might lose James, something within me had softened. I was still desperately angry with him. But in this moment, at least I could bear to be close to him. I reached for his hand and took it in my own, wondering if this might be the last time we would hold hands in a very long time — or perhaps forever.

"Hi," I whispered back.

I put a few pillows behind James's back so he could more comfortably sit up, then handed him the menu for the hospital's cafeteria. I insisted it was no problem to go out and order him real food, but the hospital's menu wasn't half bad.

After he placed his order, I prayed he wouldn't ask more questions about the police, like *why* they thought I poisoned him. If James asked what prompted the interrogation, he'd want to see the notebook himself. But for now, I meant to keep it between Gaynor and myself.

After I'd shared the photos with Gaynor, she agreed not to divulge what I'd told her. She realized my life was chaotic enough given the situation with James, and since she had not been directly involved in the discovery of the apothecary shop, she didn't feel it her place to dictate my next steps. That said, she did ask me to think very carefully about what I would do with this information, given the precious historical nature of what I'd found. I could hardly blame her; she worked at the British Library, after all.

Now, the reality was that only two of us knew the full truth; only Gaynor and I knew about the workplace of the murderous apothecary who lived two hundred years ago, and the unbelievable source of information she left buried deep within the bowels of an old cellar. Once this present crisis was behind me, I would have to make a few difficult decisions about what to reveal, and how, and to whom — and how this played into my own, recently resurfaced passion for history.

To my relief, James didn't seem interested in reliving what had happened a few hours ago. "I'm ready to get back," he said, taking a sip of water while I perched on the side of his bed.

I raised my eyebrows. "You just got here last night. The flight home isn't for another eight days."

"Trip insurance," he explained. "A hospital stay is more than enough reason to file a claim on the cost to get home. As soon as I'm out of here, I'll rebook my flight." He toyed with the edge of the bedsheet, then looked at me. "Should I book you a seat, too?"

I blew out a sigh. "No," I said gently. "I'll take the original flight home."

Disappointment flashed in his eyes, but he quickly recovered. "Fair enough. You need space, I get that. I shouldn't have come out here at all. I realize that now." A few moments later, a member of the hospital staff appeared with a tray and set James's dinner in front of him. "It's only eight days, at least," James added, digging ravenously into his meal.

My breath quickened. *Here we go*, I thought. Sitting cross-legged at the end of his bed, a corner of his bedsheet over my lap, it almost felt like we were back in Ohio, back into our normal routine. But we would never know our old "normal" again.

"I'm quitting my job at the farm," I said.

James paused, a bite of potato suspended in front of his mouth. He set the fork down. "Caroline, a lot's going on. Are you sure you don't want to —"

I rose from the edge of the hospital bed, standing tall. I could not fall victim to this talk of reason, not again.

"Let me finish," I said softly. I looked outside, my gaze scanning the London skyline. A panorama of new against old: trendy shopfront windows reflected the pearl-gray dome of St. Paul's Cathedral, and red tour buses sputtered past long-standing landmarks. If there was anything that the last few days had taught me, it was the importance of shining new light on old truths hidden in dark places. This trip to London — and finding the light blue vial, the apothecary — had exposed them all.

I turned away from the window to face James. "I need to choose me. I need to

409

prioritize me." I paused, wringing my hands together. "Not your career, not our baby, not stability and not what everyone else wants of me."

James stiffened. "I'm not following."

I glanced at my bag, inside of which were the two articles about the apothecary. "At some point along the line, I lost a part of who I am. Ten years ago, I envisioned something much different for myself, and I'm afraid I've abandoned that vision altogether."

"But people change, Caroline. You've grown up in the last ten years. You've prioritized the right things. It's okay to change, and you —"

"It's okay to change," I interrupted, "but it's not okay to hide, to bury parts of ourselves." I didn't feel the need to remind him that he'd hidden a few things about himself, too, but I refused to address the other woman at this exact moment. This conversation was about my dreams, not James's mistakes.

"Okay, so you want to quit your job and wait for a baby." James took a shaky breath. "So, what do you plan on doing?" I sensed he meant not only with my job, but also with our marriage. And though James's tone wasn't condescending, it was laced with skepticism — just like ten years ago, when he first asked me how I planned to land a job with my history degree.

I now stood at a crossroads, and I didn't dare look back at the road behind me — the road littered with monotony, complacency and other people's expectations.

"I'm going to stop hiding from the truth, which is that my life isn't what I want it to be. And to do that —" I hesitated, knowing once I said my next words, I could never take them back. "To do that, I need to be alone. And I don't mean for eight more days in London. I mean *alone,* for the foreseeable future. I intend to file for a separation."

James's face crumpled as he slowly pushed away his dinner tray.

I sat next to him again and placed my hand on the white cotton sheet, warm from his body beneath. "Our marriage has disguised too much," I whispered. "You clearly have a lot to figure out, and so do I. We can't do these things together. We'd end up on the same trail, making the same mistakes that got us here in the first place."

Covering his face with his hands, James began to shake his head back and forth. "I can't believe it," he said through his fingers, a clear IV tube still dangling from the back of his hand.

I motioned around the dim, sterile room. "Hospital or not, I haven't forgotten that you had an *affair,* James."

With his face still buried in his hands, I could hardly make out his reply. "On my deathbed," he mumbled, and a moment later, "no matter what I do —" He broke off, the rest of his sentence unintelligible.

I frowned. "What do you mean, 'no matter what you do'?"

He finally pulled his face from his hands and gazed out the window. "Nothing. I just need . . . time. This is a lot to take in." But he seemed hesitant to look at me, and a quiet, interior voice told me to dig further. I sensed he wasn't being entirely forthcoming, like he'd done something that hadn't resulted in the intended outcome.

I thought back to the vial of eucalyptus oil, the toxic warning label on the outside. Like a rush of cold air in the room, a question presented itself. And as unfair as the accusation might be if I was wrong, I forced myself to spit the words out.

"James, did you ingest the oil on purpose?"

The idea of it had never entered my mind, but now it left me aghast. Was it possible I'd undergone police interrogation and the fear of my husband's imminent death, all because James had knowingly swallowed the toxin?

He turned his head in my direction, his gaze clouded with guilt and disappointment. I'd seen this look before not long ago; it was the same look on his face when I'd found his cell phone with the incriminating text messages. "You don't know what you're throwing away," he said. "This is fixable, all of it, but not if you've pushed me away. Let me back in, Caroline."

"You haven't answered my question."

He threw his hands up, startling me. "What does it matter at this point? Everything I do pisses you off. What's one more screwup? Add it to the list." Using a finger, he made a checkmark motion. An admission, etched right beneath his infidelity and his uninvited arrival in London.

"How dare you," I whispered, my tone belying the fury coursing through me. Then I asked the same question I'd been asking for days: *"Why?"*

But I already knew the answer. This was yet another ploy, another tactic. James was a calculated, risk-averse person. If he'd swallowed the oil despite knowing its dangerous effects, he must have thought it a last-ditch effort to win my favor. Why else would an unfaithful husband put himself in

413

harm's way? Perhaps he thought my concern for his physical well-being would trump my heartbreak; that my pity for him would expedite my forgiveness.

It had almost worked, but not quite. Because now, having distanced myself physically and emotionally from this man, I was able to see through him to his real nature, and it reeked of deceit and unfairness.

"You wanted me to pity you," I said quietly, standing again.

"The last thing I want is your pity," he said, his voice cold. "I just want you to see straight, to understand that you'll regret this someday."

"No, I won't." My hands shook as I spoke, but I went on without mincing words. "You've managed to twist so much blame onto me. Blame about your unhappiness, your mistress, now this 'illness.'" He grew pale as my voice rose. "A few days ago, I thought nothing good would come of this anniversary trip. But that couldn't be further from the truth. I know, now more than ever, that I'm not the cause of your errant ways, your unhappiness. I've learned more about our marriage while apart from you than I ever did when we lived under the same roof."

A light tap at the door severed the conversation. It was just as well, for I feared I might collapse to the sticky, tiled floor if I went on much longer.

A young nurse stepped into the room and smiled at us obliviously. "We're about ready to move you to your new room," she told James. "Almost ready to go?"

James nodded stiffly; he suddenly looked extraordinarily tired. And as my adrenaline began to recede, I felt the same. Not unlike the night I arrived, I found myself longing for my pj's, take-out food, and my low-lit, empty hotel room.

While the nurse unhooked James from the monitors, he and I said an awkward goodbye. The nurse confirmed he was queued up for discharge the next day, and I promised to return first thing in the morning. Then, having mentioned nothing of the apothecary or her shop to James, I made my way out, closing the heavy door behind me.

Back in my hotel room, nestled in the middle of the bed with a take-out carton of chicken pad thai in my lap, I could have cried tears of relief. There were no people and no police and no beeping hospital equipment . . . and no James. I didn't even turn on the TV. Between mouthfuls of noodles, I just closed my eyes, leaned back my head and savored the silence.

The carbs energized me somewhat, but it wasn't even eight o'clock. After I finished my meal, I lifted my bag from the floor and grabbed my phone, then pulled out my notebook and the two articles from Gaynor. I spread them out around me, flipping on the second bedside lamp for better light to reread the articles about the apothecary and look more closely at the pictures on my phone.

I returned to the first few images in the set, the photos of the shop interior. They were terribly grainy and overexposed, and even after playing with the exposure and brightness, I was unable to see anything beyond the foreground. It seemed the camera's flash brought into focus only the flecks of dust floating about in the room; I supposed that was the downside of using a cell phone to capture images of a once-in-a-lifetime event. I could have kicked myself. Why hadn't I brought a proper flashlight?

I flicked over to the next few photos, those of the apothecary's book — her register. There were eight photos of the register, pictures I hastily took at random: a couple from the front, a few toward the middle, and the rest from the back of the book. These were the pictures that got me into trouble; they were clear enough that I was able to jot down notes, and those same notes nearly had me thrown in jail.

The final photo in the set was a picture of the inside cover of another book that was on the shelf. I could only make out one word: *pharmacopoeia.* I plugged this into my browser's search bar, and the results told me this second book was a directory of medicinal drugs. So, a reference guide then. Interesting, but not as much as the apothecary's handwritten register.

I returned to the last image of the apothecary's register. As I zoomed into the photo, I noticed the familiar format of the entries, which included the date and to whom the remedy was dispensed. I read the entries closely, and it dawned on me that since this was the final page of the register, these entries would have been made in the days or weeks immediately preceding the apothecary's death.

At once, my eyes fell on the name *Lord Clarence.* I gasped aloud, reading the entirety of the entry:

Miss Berkwell. Mistress to, cousin of, the Lord Clarence. Cantharides. 9 February

1791. On account of his wife, the Lady Clarence.

I lunged forward on the bed, reaching for the first article that Gaynor printed for me — the one dated February 10, 1791. My heart racing, I cross-checked the names and dates between the register entry and the article related to the same incident, Lord Clarence's death. And though I'd believed all along that the shop belonged to the murderous apothecary, this was proof. This picture of the register from inside the shop was proof that she had dispensed the poison that killed him.

But I frowned, reading the entry more closely. The first name in the entry, the person meant to ingest the poison, was Miss Berkwell. Lord Clarence, who actually ingested it, was mentioned only in reference to Miss Berkwell; she was his cousin. And the final name listed, the purchaser of the poison, was the Lady Clarence. His wife.

I reread the end of the first newspaper article and it did not even mention a Miss Berkwell. The article stated, very clearly, that Lord Clarence was dead, and doubt existed as to whether it was his wife or someone else who had slipped poison into his drink. Yet the apothecary's register entry

418

implied he wasn't supposed to die at all. The intended victim was Miss Berkwell.

According to what lay in front of me, the wrong person had died. Did anyone, besides Lady Clarence and the apothecary — and now me — even know it? I might not have had an advanced degree in history, but pride swelled within me at the monumental discovery I'd made.

And as for the motive? Well, the entry made that clear, too; it identified Miss Berkwell as not only Lord Clarence's cousin, but his mistress. It was no wonder Lady Clarence set out to kill her; Miss Berkwell was the other woman. I remembered well enough learning about James's infidelity and the immediate urge within me to seek revenge on the other woman. In this way, I could not blame Lady Clarence, though I wondered how she felt when her plan went awry and her husband died instead. Things certainly did not happen as she intended.

Did not happen as she intended . . .

The hospital note. Hadn't it said something similar? Hands shaking, I navigated back to the digitized image of the note from St. Thomas' Hospital, dated October 22, 1816. I reread the line I'd remembered:

Only, it did not happen as I intend'd.

Could it have been that the author of the hospital note was Lady Clarence? I covered my mouth with my hands. "Impossible," I whispered aloud to myself.

But the last sentence of the hospital note fit the possibility, too: *I lay blame unto my husband, and his thirst for that which was not meant for him.* Had this clue been both literal and figurative — referring to Lord Clarence's thirst for a poisonous drink that was meant for Miss Berkwell, *and* his thirst for a woman who was not his wife?

Without giving it a moment's thought, I texted Gaynor. At the coffee shop, she'd mentioned that she'd confirmed the date of Lord Clarence's death in the parish records. Perhaps she could do the same for Lady Clarence, to validate whether the woman had indeed penned the hospital note. Hi again! I texted Gaynor. Could you check the death records one more time? Same surname Clarence, but a woman. Any death record around October 1816?

Until Gaynor replied, it would be useless to waste any more time on this idea. I took a long drink of water, tucked my legs against my body and zoomed into my phone to better read the final entry — the *closing* entry.

Before I even read it, bumps prickled on my skin. This entry was the last record the

420

apothecary made before running from the police and jumping to her death.

I read the entry once, but I frowned; the handwriting of this final entry was less steady, as though the author had been trembling. Perhaps she'd been ill or cold or even hurried. Or perhaps — I shuddered as I considered it — someone else made this entry.

The heavy curtains of my window were open, and across the street in another building, someone flipped on a light. I suddenly felt on show, so I stood from the bed to close the curtains. Below, the streets of London churned with movement: friends heading to the pub, suited men leaving a late night at work, and a young couple pushing a baby stroller, walking slowly toward the River Thames.

I took my seat again on the bed. Something did not feel quite right, but I couldn't place my finger on it. I reread the final entry, clicking my tongue against my teeth as I considered each word, and then I saw it.

The entry was dated 12 Feb 1791.

I picked up the second article — the one that described the apothecary jumping to her death — and it said the woman jumped from the bridge on the *eleventh* of February.

The phone tumbled from my hands. I sat back on the bed, an eerie sensation floating over me, as though a ghost had just settled herself in the room, watching, waiting, as exhilarated as I was that the truth had been unveiled: that no matter who jumped from the bridge on the eleventh of February, someone had returned to the shop, alive and well.

33
NELLA

FEBRUARY 11, 1791

Before I lifted my own leg over the railing, I paused.

All that I've lost. It weighed on me now, a lifetime of misery, like the raw earth pressing into an open grave. And yet — this precise moment of breath, the light breeze at the back of my neck, the distant call of some hungry waterfowl on the river, the taste of salt on my tongue — these were all things I had not lost yet.

I stepped back from the railing and opened my eyes.

All that I'd lost, or all that I hadn't?

Eliza jumped in my place. A final offering to me, her last breath an effort to fool the authorities and implicate herself as poisoner. How could I possibly throw her gift back into the water to sink alongside her?

As I stood on the bridge and looked east over the River Thames, another person came to mind: Mrs. Amwell, Eliza's beloved

423

mistress. She would return to her estate in coming days, only to find Eliza . . . gone. Disappeared. No matter the pretense and feigned grief Mrs. Amwell displayed now at the loss of her husband, once she discovered Eliza missing, the grief would no longer be a ruse. It might haunt her for a lifetime, this belief that the child had abandoned her.

I must tell Mrs. Amwell the truth. I must tell her that Eliza had died. And I must comfort this woman the only way I knew how: a tincture of *scutellaria,* or skullcap, which would ease the piercing ache of her heart when she learned that little Eliza would write her letters no more.

And so, I turned away from the railing of the bridge, willing the sob in my throat to delay until I was alone — until I was back in my shop of poisons, which I had meant never to see again.

Twenty-two hours had passed since the moment Eliza jumped — an entire night and day, during which I'd prepared and bottled the skullcap I meant to deliver to the Amwell estate — and yet still my hands felt the chill of the empty air as I reached for her. Still I heard the plunge of her body, the sucking of the water as it took her in.

After I left the bridge and returned to 3

Back Alley, I could smell traces of the constable in the storage room — the sweaty, filthy scent of a man snaking about the room, looking for something he would not find. He had not found, either, the new letter in the barley bin. It must have been left only recently, perhaps when I went to the market and Eliza busied herself with her tincture.

I held the letter now in my hands. No scent of lavender or rose wafted up from the paper. The hand was not particularly fine or neat. The woman gave little detail, identifying herself only as a housewife, betrayed by her husband.

This final request, hardly different than the first.

The preparation would be uncomplicated. Indeed, a glass bottle of prussic acid sat within my arm's reach; I could dispense it with minimal effort in less than a minute's time. And perhaps this final poison, this *last* one, would finally grant me the peace I'd sought since my baby fell from my belly at the hand of Frederick.

Healing by way of vengeance.

But no such thing existed; it never had. Hurting others had only injured me further. I took the letter, traced the words with m finger and stood from my chair. Bend'

425

forward, I stretched one weak leg in front of the other, my breath raspy, and approached the hearth. A low flame ate away at a single scrap of wood. Gently, I set the letter into the dancing peak of the light, watching as the paper ignited in an instant.

No, I would not grant this woman what she wanted.

No more death would go forth from this room.

And with that, my shop of poisons existed no longer. The single flame in the hearth sputtered out, the final letter crumbled to ash. No balms left to simmer, no tonics left to blend, no tinctures to agitate, no plants to uproot.

I leaned forward and began to cough, a clot of blood making its way out of my lungs and onto my tongue. I'd been coughing up blood since yesterday afternoon — since running from the bailiffs, falling over the back wall of the horse stable and watching my young friend fall to her death. I'd expended a year's worth of effort in mere minutes; the bailiffs, by way of chase, drove me closer to death than I'd realized.

I spit the blood clot into the ash, without even a desire to take a drink and wash the sticky residue from my tongue. I felt no thirst, nor hunger, and I had not urinated in nearly a day. I knew this did not bode well; when the throat ceases to beg, when the bladder ceases to fill, it is nearly over. I knew this because I had experienced it — I had watched it happen — once before.

The day my mother died.

I knew I must go to the Amwell estate, and soon. I would leave the letter and tincture with a servant, for Eliza said the mistress may be gone some weeks, and I did not expect her to be in. Then I would go to the river, sit along its silent banks and wait for a certain death. I did not expect the wait to be a long one.

But before I left my shop for good, a single task remained.

I lifted my quill, pulled the open register toward me and diligently began to record my final entry. Though I did not dispense the potion and I knew not what ingredients it contained, I could not leave without confessing the life of her, the loss of her.

Eliza Fanning, London. Ingr. unknown. 12 Feb 1791.

As the nib scratched along the paper, my hand shook terribly, and the words were so sullied that the handwriting appeared not even my own.

Indeed, it was as though some unknown spirit refused to let me write the words — refused to let me record the death of little Eliza.

34

CAROLINE

I read the final entry again, my hand over my lips.

Eliza Fanning, London. Ingr. unknown. 12 Feb 1791.

The twelfth of February? It didn't make sense. The apothecary jumped from the bridge on the eleventh of February, and the article said the river was "littered with ice." Even if someone survived the fall, it seemed unlikely they would have lasted more than a minute or two in the frigid water.

It was curious, too, that just one name was listed: *Eliza Fanning.* The entry did not say she was "on account" of anyone else. She must have come to the shop by herself, then. Did she have any idea that she was the final customer? And did she play any role in the apothecary's demise?

I pulled a blanket over my legs. Admittedly, this final entry left me a bit spooked.

429

I considered the possibility that the discrepancy was an error; perhaps the apothecary simply got her dates mixed up. Could this something really be nothing?

And it was also strange that the entry said *Ingr. unknown* — ingredients unknown. It seemed impossible. How could the apothecary have dispensed something of which she had no knowledge?

Maybe it wasn't the apothecary at all. Maybe someone else made the entry. But the shop was well hidden, and it seemed unreasonable that someone would have entered the shop the day after the apothecary jumped in order to write down such a cryptic, final message. It only made sense that it was the apothecary's own entry.

But if she made the entry, then who jumped?

More questions than answers had presented themselves in the last few minutes, and my curiosity melted into frustration. Nothing matched up: the victim in the first article didn't fit with the victim in the entry about Lord Clarence; the final entry was cryptically written, with its strange handwriting and the reference to *unknown* ingredients; and most significant, the date of the final entry was a day after the apothecary had supposedly died.

430

I spread out my hands, at a complete loss. How many secrets did the apothecary take to her grave?

I walked to the minifridge and pulled out the bottle of champagne that the hotel had stocked in the suite. I didn't think to pour the chilled wine into a glass; instead, once I'd popped off the cork, I lifted the rim to my lips and took a deep drink directly from the bottle.

Instead of fortifying me, the champagne left me fatigued, almost dizzy. My curiosity about the apothecary had worn down for the day, and the idea of further research was not appealing.

Tomorrow, perhaps.

I resolved to write down my questions about everything I'd learned today, and I would revisit them in the morning, or once James left. I grabbed a pen and my notebook and flipped to a clean page. I had a dozen or more questions about what I'd read. I prepared to list them all.

But as I held the pen in my hand and considered what to write down first, I realized that there was one question I most wanted to know. It was the most intrusive, the most insistent of them all. I sensed the answer to this question might solve some others, like why the entry was made on the twelfth of February.

I pressed the tip of my pen to the page and wrote:

Who is Eliza Fanning?

The next morning, after James had been discharged from the hospital, we sat at the small table near the door of the hotel room. I wrapped my hands tightly around a cup of weak tea as he held his cell phone close, searching the airline's website for flights home. Housekeeping hadn't yet come to the room so a half-drunk bottle of champagne sat near the coffeepot, and I had the headache to show for it.

He reached into his pocket and withdrew his wallet. "Found one that leaves Gatwick at four," he said. "Gives me enough time to pack up and catch a train there. I'll need to leave by one."

The vase of baby blue hydrangeas sat between us; most had wilted and now tumbled over the edge of the glass. I slid the vase to the side and looked at him more closely. "You think you'll be okay? No dizziness or anything?"

He put down his wallet. "None at all. I'm just ready to get home."

A short while later, James stood near the window with his packed luggage beside him

— as though we'd rewound the trip and he had only just arrived. I remained at the table, where I'd been half-heartedly perusing the photos of the apothecary's book, keenly aware that the minutes were counting down. If I planned to reveal to James the truth about my own activities in recent days, I'd better do so quick.

"I think I'm good," James said, patting his jeans to make sure his passport was in place. Between us was the unmade bed in which I'd slept — alone — for the past several nights. It was a force between us now, a white, billowy reminder of everything we were meant to share on this trip, yet hadn't. Only days ago, I'd hoped desperately that our baby would be conceived in this bed. But now, I couldn't fathom making love to the man standing across the room ever again.

What I imagined for this "anniversary" trip had been nowhere close to reality, but I felt this horror story had been a necessary lesson. After all, what if I hadn't discovered James's infidelity, and we'd gotten pregnant, and the truth had come out after the baby's arrival? Or what if both of us developed a slow-burning resentment — for our jobs, our routine or each other — and the result was a cataclysmic end of our marriage and the ripping apart of our maybe-family-of-three? Because this wasn't just about James. I'd been just as dissatisfied with life as he was, and I'd buried those feelings deep inside of myself. What if *I* had been the one to snap? What if I had been the one to make an irreversible mistake?

I checked the time; it was five till one. "Wait," I said, setting down my phone and standing from my chair. James frowned, his fingers clutching the handle of his luggage. I leaned over my own suitcase, shoving aside the sneakers I wore while mudlarking, and reached for something that had been hidden at the bottom. It was so small, it fit easily in the palm of my hand as I lifted it out.

I wrapped my fingers around the cool, hard object: the vintage box meant for James's business cards. It was my ten-year anniversary gift to him, which I'd kept tucked away since that fateful afternoon in the bedroom closet.

I crossed the room. "This isn't forgiveness," I said softly, "or even a path forward. But it belongs to you, and it's more fitting now than I could have dreamed when I originally purchased it." Then I gave him the box, which he accepted with a trembling hand. "It's made of tin," I explained. "It's the traditional gift for ten-year anniversaries because it represents strength and —" I took a deep breath, wishing I could see into the future. In five or ten years, what would our lives look like? "Strength, and the ability to withstand a fair amount of damage. I bought it to symbolize durability in our relationship together, but that's not the important thing anymore. What's important is strength on our own. We both have a lot of hard work ahead of us."

James wrapped me in a tight hug; we stood that way so long, I felt sure the clock ticked past one, and then some. When he finally released me, his voice shook. "I'll see you soon," he whispered, his fingers still clutching my gift.

"See you soon," I said in return, and an unexpected quiver made its way into my own words. I walked James to the door and we glanced at each other a final time, then he left and shut the door behind him.

Alone, again. And yet the freedom was so penetrating and real that I stood motionless, almost stunned, for a moment. I gazed at the floor, waiting with dread for the inevitable wave of loneliness to wash over me. I waited for James to run back, asking for another chance to stay. I waited for my phone to ring, the hospital or police calling with news, bad news, *more* bad news.

I waited, too, for the stab of regret; I did not tell James about the apothecary. I didn't tell him that I broke into a hidden subcellar. I didn't tell him about Gaynor or Bachelor Alf or the serial killer whose secrets I still held safe.

I didn't tell him any of it.

I stood in front of the door a long while, waiting for guilt, or regret, to rush its way into me. But nothing of the sort plagued me. Nothing festered, and no scores were left to be settled.

As I turned away from the door, my phone dinged — a text from Gaynor. Sorry for the delay! she said. Parish records show a Lady Bea Clarence died at St. Thomas' hospital, edema, on 23 Oct 1816. No surviving children.

I stared at my phone, dumbfounded, and lowered myself onto the bed. The hospital note was indeed a deathbed confession, written — perhaps with a guilty conscience — by Lord Clarence's widow twenty-five years after his death.

I picked up the phone to call Gaynor and tell her what I'd learned.

After I explained the existence of Miss Berkwell, the mistress — who I knew about not from the articles Gaynor printed for me, but from the entry in the apothecary's

436

register — Gaynor was quiet for some time.

There was only one thing I hadn't told her, and this was about the register entry made the day after the apothecary supposedly died, bearing the name Eliza Fanning. I kept this to myself.

"This is astounding," Gaynor finally said through the phone. As I pondered how utterly unbelievable the entire thing was, how utterly spectacular the whole thing was, I could imagine Gaynor shaking her head in awe at all that I'd solved. "And all of this due to a little vial in the river. I can't believe you pieced it all together. Excellent detective work, Caroline. I do believe you'd be an asset to any PI team."

I thanked her, then reminded her I'd been a little too close to the police force in recent days.

"Well, if not a PI team," she replied, "then maybe you could join the research crew at the library." I felt sure she meant it in jest, but she'd struck a tender nerve. "I've seen the spark in you," she added.

If only I didn't have to return to Ohio in a matter of days. "I wish I could," I said, "but I've quite the mess to sort out back home . . . starting with my husband."

Gaynor took a breath. "Look, we're new friends, and I won't offer advice on your

437

marriage. Though if we go for cocktails, I'll start in on that without issue." She chuckled. "But if there's one thing I do know, it's the importance of chasing dreams. Believe me, if you want something different, the only person holding you back is you. What is it you love to do?"

I blurted it out without missing a beat. "Dig into the past — dig into the lives of *real* people. Their secrets, their experiences. In fact, I almost applied to Cambridge after graduation to study history . . ."

"Cambridge?" Gaynor gasped. "Like, the university an hour from here?"

"One and the same."

"And you almost applied but didn't, why?" Her tone was gentle, inquisitive.

I gritted my teeth, then forced the words out. "Because I got married, and my husband had a job back in Ohio."

Gaynor clicked her tongue against her teeth. "Well, you might not be able to see it, but I do — you're talented, you're intelligent, you're capable. You also have a new friend in London." She paused, and I imagined her crossing her arms, a determined look on her face. "You're cut out for more. And I think you know it."

35

NELLA

As I approached the Amwell estate, my vision began to twist and spin, colors bright like a child's toy, the city of London unsteady around me. I tucked a bloodied rag into the pocket of my skirt and looked at the faces walking past — some sharp with concern about the dried blood on my lips, others hazy and obscure and unseeing, as though I did not exist at all. I wondered if I'd entered a realm of ghosts. Was there such thing as a half world, an in-between place, where the dead and the living mingled together?

In another pocket of my skirt was the package: the skullcap tincture and a short letter, in which I'd explained to Mrs. Amwell that Eliza would not be returning — and not for a lack of affection, but because of a heroic act in which Eliza was selfless and brave. I also advised the mistress of the suggested dosage of the skullcap, just

439

as I did when she came to my shop long ago, seeking a remedy for her trembling hands. I would have written more — oh, how much I could have written! But time did not permit, as indicated by a smudge of my blood at the corner of the letter. I hadn't even had time to record the skullcap, my last remedy, in my register.

The estate loomed ahead: three stories of mottled, bloodred brick. Sash windows, twelve panes each, or maybe sixteen; I could not be sure of anything, not in these final minutes. It was all so hazy. I urged my feet forward. I must only reach the front steps, the black door, and set down the package.

I glanced up at the gabled roof, tilting and bending beneath the clouds. No smoke bled from the chimney. As suspected, the mistress was not home. This came as a great relief; I had not the strength to talk to her. I would drop the package and go. Crawl away, south, to the nearest set of riverbed stairs. If I could manage to make it so far.

A child scurried by, laughing, nearly tangling herself in my skirts. She spun about me once, twice, playing a game of my senses, reminding me of the baby that fell from my belly. She ran off as quickly as she'd appeared. As my vision blurred with tears, her face seemed to melt away, obscure and indistinct, a phantom. I began to feel a fool for doubting Eliza's claim that ghosts resided all around her. Perhaps I'd been wrong when I told her these spirits were only remnants of memories, creations of an invigorated imagination. They all seemed so vibrant, so corporeal.

The package. I must drop the package.

A final glance upward, to the dormer windows, where the servants would be. I hoped one would see me drop the paper-wrapped bundle on the porch, just steps ahead, then retrieve it for safekeeping until Mrs. Amwell returned.

Indeed, yes, a servant spotted me! I saw her clear as day behind the window, with her thick black hair, and her chin held high —

I stopped short on the walkway, my fingers loosening on the package; with a soft *thunk,* it fell to the ground. This was no servant behind the window. It was an apparition. *My little Eliza.*

I could not move. I could not breathe.

But then a flash, a movement, as the shadow pulled away from the window. I fell to my knees, the urge to cough rising within me again, the colors of London turning to black, everything turning black. My last breath, only seconds away . . .

And then, in my final, coherent moment, the color around me returning: little Eliza with the bright, youthful eyes I knew so well, floating out of the house in my direction. *A rosy flash of glass.* I frowned, trying to focus my vision. Clutched in her hand was a tiny vial, so similar in size and shape to the one she'd offered me on the bridge. Only that vial had been blue, and this one was seashell pink. She uncorked it as she ran toward me.

I reached for her bright shadow, finding it all so strange and unexpected: the flush in her cheeks, the inquisitive grin, as though this was not a ghost at all.

Everything about her, so lifelike.

Everything about her, just as I remembered in the moments before her death.

36

CAROLINE

The next morning, I stepped into the British Library for the third time. I walked along the familiar path, past the reception desk, up the staircase, and made my way to the third floor.

The Maps Room now felt as familiar and comfortable to me as the underground train stations. I spotted Gaynor near one of the stacks toward the center of the room, rearranging a pile of books at her feet.

"Psst," I whispered, sneaking up behind her.

She jumped and turned around. "Hi! You can't stay away, can you?"

I grinned. "As it turns out, I have news."

"More news?" She lowered her voice and said, "Please tell me you didn't break down another door." At seeing the smile still on my face, she breathed a sigh of relief. "Oh, thank God. What is it, then? Something more on the apothecary?" She grabbed a book from the floor and pushed it into place on one of the shelves.

"This news is about me, actually."

She paused, suspending another book in midair as she looked at me. "Do tell."

I took a deep breath, still in disbelief that I'd done it. *I'd done it.* After all the outrageous things I'd done in London this week, it was this that most surprised me. "I applied to grad school at Cambridge last night."

In an instant, Gaynor's eyes filled with tears, catching the reflection of the lights overhead. She set the book down and placed a hand on each of my shoulders. "Caroline, I am so completely proud of you."

I coughed, a knot in my throat. I'd called Rose a short while ago to tell her the news, too. She'd burst into happy tears, calling me the bravest woman she knew.

Brave. It wasn't a label I would have given myself back in Ohio, but I realized now that she was right. What I'd done *was* brave — even a bit mad — but it was authentic and true to the real me. And despite how different my life looked from Rose's now, her support reminded me that it was okay for friends to venture down different paths.

I looked at Gaynor, thankful for this unlikely friendship, too. I thought of my very first time in this room; rain-drenched, grieving and directionless, I'd approached Gaynor — a total stranger — with nothing but a glass vial in my pocket. A glass vial and a question. Now, I stood before her again, bearing almost no semblance to that person. I was still grieving, yes, but I'd uncovered so much about myself, enough to propel me in another direction altogether. A direction I felt I was meant to pursue long ago.

"It's not a history degree, but a master's program in English studies," I explained. "Eighteenth century and Romantic studies. The coursework includes various antiquated texts and works of literature, as well as research methods." I felt the degree in English studies would bridge my interest in history, literature and research. "I'll submit my dissertation at the end of the program," I added, though my voice shook at the word *dissertation.* Gaynor raised her eyebrows as I explained, "The lost apothecary — her shop, her register, the obscure ingredients she used — I'm hoping to make these the subject of my research. An academic, preservationist approach to sharing what I've found."

"My God, you sound like a scholar already." She grinned, then added, "I think it's absolutely brilliant. And you won't be so far at all! We should plan a few weekend getaways. Maybe hop over to Paris on the train?"

My stomach flipped at the thought of it. "Of course. The program starts after the first of the year, so we've got plenty of time to plan a few ideas."

Though I could hardly wait to get started, in truth it was probably best the program didn't start for another six months. I had some difficult conversations ahead of me — my parents and James, to start — and I'd need to train my replacement at the family business; secure student housing at Cambridge; and complete the paperwork for a marital separation, which I'd initiated online last night . . .

As if reading my thoughts, Gaynor wrung her hands together and asked in a hesitant voice, "It's really none of my business, but does your husband know yet?"

"He knows we need to be apart for a time, but he doesn't know I plan to return to the UK while we sort out our lives. I'm calling him tonight to tell him that I've applied."

I also intended to call my parents and tell them, finally, the truth about what James had done. Whereas a few days ago, I'd meant to protect them from the news, now

I realized how unreasonable that was. Gaynor and Rose had reminded me of the importance of surrounding myself with people who supported and encouraged me and my desires. This encouragement had been missing for far too long, and I was ready to reclaim it.

Gaynor resumed placing books on the shelf, looking over at me as she did so. "And the program, how long is it?" she asked.

"Nine months."

Nine months, the same amount of time I had so desperately wished to carry a baby. I smiled, the irony not lost on me. A child might not have been in my immediate future, but something else — a long-lost dream — had taken its place.

After saying goodbye to Gaynor, I made my way to the second floor. I hoped she wouldn't spot me turning into the Humanities Reading Room. Admittedly, at this very moment, I meant to avoid her; for this task, I wanted to be alone and away from any prying eyes, however well-intentioned they may be.

I walked to one of the library-issued PCs at the back of the room. It was only a few days ago that Gaynor and I sat together at an identical computer upstairs, and I hadn't yet forgotten the basics of navigating the library's search tools. I opened the main British Library page and clicked Search the Main Catalogue. Then I navigated to the digitized newspaper records, where Gaynor and I had attempted our own fruitless search on the apothecary killer.

The whole day lay empty in front of me, and I expected to be here a long while. I settled into my chair, pulled one leg up underneath me and opened my notebook. *Who is Eliza Fanning?*

It was the one question, the only question, I'd jotted down two nights ago.

In the search bar for the British Newspaper Archive, I typed two words: Eliza Fanning. Then I hit Enter.

Immediately, the search results returned a handful of entries. I scanned them quickly, but only a single record — the one at the very top of the page — appeared to be a match. I opened the article and, since it had been digitized, the full text was displayed in an instant.

The article was published in the summer of 1802, by a newspaper called *The Brighton Press.* I opened another tab in the browser to search for Brighton, learning that it was a seaside city on England's south coast, a couple hours south of London.

The headline read "Eliza Pepper, née Fanning, Sole Inheritor of Husband's Magick Book Shoppe."

The article went on to say that twenty-two-year-old Eliza Pepper, born in Swindon but a resident of the outskirts of Brighton since 1791, had inherited the entirety of her husband Tom Pepper's estate, including his wildly successful book shoppe at the north end of town. The shoppe carried a wide assortment of books on magick and the occult, and customers hailed regularly from all parts of the continent seeking remedies and cures for the most unusual of ailments.

According to the article, unfortunately Mr. Tom Pepper himself could not seem to conjure an antidote for his own troubles; he'd recently fallen ill, believed to be pleurisy of the chest. His wife, Eliza, was his sole caregiver until he met his untimely end. But as tribute to the life and success of Mr. Pepper, a celebration was held at the shoppe; hundreds were in attendance to pay their respects.

After the event, a small group of reporters interviewed Mrs. Pepper about her intent for the shoppe going forward. She assured the men that it would remain open.

"Both Tom and I owe our very lives to the magick arts," she told the reporters, before explaining that long ago, in London, her very own magick blend saved her life. "I was only a child. It was my first tincture, but I risked my life for a special friend, one who still encourages and counsels me to this very day." Mrs. Pepper then added, "Maybe my youth was to blame, but I had not an ounce of fear when the moment of death presented itself. Indeed, I found the little blue vial of magick to be feverish against my skin, and after swallowing the tincture, the heat of it was so powerful that the frigid depths were a welcome respite."

The article stated that the reporters questioned her further about this last bit. "The 'frigid depths'? Do explain, Mrs. Pepper," one of the men asked. But Eliza only thanked the men for their time and insisted she was needed back inside.

She then reached out her arms on either side of her, taking the hands of her two young children — a boy and a girl, twins, aged four — and disappeared with them into her late husband's store, the Blackfriars Shoppe of Magick Books & Baubles.

I left the British Library less than an hour after I arrived. The afternoon sun shone hot and bright above me. I bought a bottle of water from a street vendor and settled on a

bench in the shade of an elm tree, considering how best to spend the rest of the day.
I'd intended to spend the entire afternoon
at the library, but I'd found what I was looking for in almost no time at all.

I understood, now, that the apothecary
was not the one who jumped from the
bridge. It was her young friend, Eliza Fanning. This explained how the apothecary
made an entry in the register on the twelfth
of February. It was because, contrary to
what police believed, the apothecary was
not dead. But neither was Eliza; whether on
account of her tincture or sheer luck, the
girl survived her fall.

But the article about Eliza didn't explain
everything. It didn't explain why the ingredients of the tincture were unknown to the
apothecary, or whether the police ever knew
of Eliza's existence. The article didn't state
whether the apothecary subscribed to
Eliza's same beliefs about the efficacy of
magic, nor did it expand on the nature of
Eliza's relationship with the apothecary.

And still, I did not know the apothecary's
name.

There was something poignant, too, about
young Eliza's involvement. Shrouded in
mystery was the role she played in the
apothecary's life and death; she'd only

revealed to the papers that she'd *risked her life for a special friend,* one who still *counseled* her to that day. Did this mean the apothecary lived another decade and had left London to join Eliza in Brighton? Or had Eliza been referring to something else — the apothecary's ghost, perhaps?

I would never know.

Perhaps I would glean more information about these missing details, someday, when I began my research work and returned to the shop with a proper light and a team of historians or other academics. Undoubtedly, a wealth of unexplored possibility existed inside that tiny room. But these sorts of questions — especially those about the subtle, mysterious interactions between two women — would likely not be found in old newspapers or documents. History doesn't record the intricacies of women's relationships with one another; they're not to be uncovered.

As I sat underneath the elm tree, the soft twitter of larks somewhere above me, I mused on the fact that after learning the truth about Eliza, I hadn't gone back upstairs to tell Gaynor. I hadn't told her the name of the person who *really* jumped from the bridge on February 11, 1791, and lived to see another day. To Gaynor's knowledge, it was the apothecary who jumped from the bridge and committed suicide.

It wasn't that I felt the need to hide this fact from Gaynor, so much as I felt a protectiveness over Eliza's story. And even though I meant to further explore the apothecary's shop and her lifetime of work, I intended to keep Eliza to myself — my lone secret.

Sharing the truth — that Eliza, not the apothecary, jumped from the bridge — could very likely catapult my dissertation work to the front page of academic journals, but I didn't want the renown. Eliza had been only a child, but like me, she'd found herself at a turning point in her life. And like me, she'd gripped the light blue vial between her fingers, hovered above the frigid, unwelcome depths . . . and then she'd jumped.

While sitting on the bench outside the library, I pulled my notebook out of my bag, but I flipped backward, past the notes about the apothecary, to the first page. I reread the original, planned itinerary with James. My handwriting from weeks earlier was loopy and whimsical, interspersed with miniature hearts. Only a few days ago, this itinerary had left me nauseated, and I'd had no desire to see the sights that James and I meant to experience together. Now, I found myself curious about all the places I'd waited so long to see: the Tower of London, the V&A Museum, Westminster. The idea of visiting these places by myself wasn't as distasteful as it was a few days ago, and I found myself eager to explore. Besides, I felt sure Gaynor would be happy to join me on a few outings.

But visiting a museum could wait until tomorrow. There was something else I needed to do today.

I took the Underground from the library to Blackfriars station. As I exited the train, I headed east toward Millennium Bridge, strolling along the narrow riverfront walkway. The river, to my right, rolled calmly along its well-worn path.

I followed along the knee-high stone wall for some time, then I spotted the concrete steps leading to the river. They were the same steps I'd taken a few days earlier, just before the mudlarking tour. I made my way down them, then stepped carefully over the smooth, round stones along the river. The silence struck me, as it did my first time here. I was grateful to see that there were no people milling about on the rocks — no sightseers, no children, no tour groups.

Opening my bag, I pulled out the light

blue vial; the one, I now knew, which had contained Eliza's magic tincture. It had rescued her, and in some strange way, it had done the same for me. According to the apothecary's register, the contents of this vial two hundred years ago had been *ingredients unknown.* The unknown had once been an unpleasant concept to me, but I realized now the opportunity in it. The excitement in it. Clearly, it had been the same for Eliza.

For both of us, the vial marked the end of one quest and the beginning of another; it represented a crossroads, the abandonment of secrets and pain in favor of embracing the truth — in favor of embracing *magic.* Magic, with its enchanting, irresistible appeal, just like a fairy tale.

The vial looked exactly as it had when I'd found it, albeit a bit cleaner and smudged with my own fingerprints. I traced the bear with my thumbnail, thinking of all the vial had taught me: that the hardest truths never rest on the surface. They must be dredged up, held to the light and rinsed clean.

A movement in my peripheral vision caught my attention: a pair of women, upriver a long way, walking toward me. They must have come down another set of steps. I paid them no mind as I prepared for my final task.

I clutched the vial to my chest. Eliza must have done the same while standing on Blackfriars Bridge, not far from here. Raising the vial above my head, I thrust it forward to the water with as much strength as my arm allowed. I watched as the bottle made an arc upward and over the water, then splashed gently in the far depths of the Thames. A single ripple made its way outward before a low wave overtook it.

Eliza's vial. My vial. *Our* vial. The truth of it remained the one secret I would not share.

I remembered Bachelor Alf's words on the mudlarking tour, about how finding something on the river was surely fate. I hadn't believed it at the time, but I now knew that stumbling upon the tiny blue vial *was* fate — a pivotal turn in the direction of my life.

As I stepped onto the concrete steps to make my way up and out of the riverbed, I glanced once more upriver, toward the two women. This stretch of river was long and straight; they should have been closer to me now. But I frowned, studying the area, and then smiled at my own wild imagination.

My eyes must have been playing tricks on me, for the two women were nowhere to be found.

NELLA CLAVINGER'S APOTHECARY OF POISONS

Excerpt from dissertation submitted by Caroline Parcewell, MPhil candidate in eighteenth century and Romantic studies, University of Cambridge

Annotations & assorted remedies as recovered from the journals at Bear Alley Farringdon, London EC4A 4HH, UK

HEMLOCK JULEP

For a gentleman of exceptional intelligence and command of language. These qualities will remain until the very end, which may be useful when needing to extract a confession or account of events.

Fatal dosage: six large leaves, though an especially large male may require eight. Initial symptoms are vertigo and the sensation of being very cold. Recommended preparation is a decoction or julep, similar to thorn apple. Extract juice from fresh leaves, crushed and drained.

ORPIMENT (YELLOW) ARSENIC

Because this remedy takes on the consistency of flour or fine sugar, it is suited for the especially gluttonous gentleman, one who may enjoy a sweet lemon or banana pudding.

A most curious mineral. Note: highly soluble in hot water. Fumes smell like garlic; hence, do not serve warm. Used to kill household varmints of many kinds, human or animal. Lethal dose is three grains.

CANTHARIDES BLISTER BEETLE

When arousal before incapacitation is desired, such as at the brothel or in the bedchamber.

These insects may be found in low-lying fields in cool weather, near root crops; best harvested under a new or young moon. So as not to confuse with harmless beetles similar in appearance, crush a single male (will excrete milk-like fluid) to test for burn upon skin before full harvest. To prepare, roast then grind in wide basin until thin. Dispense in dark, thick liquid — wine, honey, syrup.

BLACK BUTTERCUP, HELLEBORE

For the gentleman prone to spells of madness or hallucination, possibly due to overconsumption of drink or laudanum drops. He will believe hellebore poisoning symptoms are the result of his own demons.

Seeds, sap, roots — all poisonous. Look for black blooms and roots, which prevent mix-up with other species in the buttercup family. Initial symptoms are dizziness, stupor, thirst and sensation of suffocation.

WOLFSBANE, OR MONK'S HOOD

For the most devout, who may feign the wrath of God in their final moments by way of physical outburst. Wolfsbane acts upon the nerves of the limbs, calming them; such theatrical reactions will be impossible.

Cultivation notes: flowering plant is very easy to grow, soil must be well drained.

Harvest when root is half-inch thick at base of plant. Handle with gloves. Dry the plucked root for three days. Shred root fibers with two sharp knives; dispense in mustard root sauce such as horseradish. Excellent when supper courses are to be served individually (avoid buffets).

NUX VOMICA, POISON NUT

The most reliable of remedies, as quick-acting as it is irreversible. Suitable for administration to all men, regardless of age, proportion or intellect.

For extraction of agent, grind finely the brown bean, also known as crow fig. In very low doses, may be used to treat fever, plague, hysteria. Be warned, very bitter! Produces a yellowish color when stewed. Victim will experience severe thirst as first symptom. Egg yolk is preferred preparation.

DEVIL'S SNARE, OR THORN APPLE

Due to immediate delirium, even the cleverest conspirator will be caught unaware. Ideal for attorneys and estate executors.

Note: egg-shaped seeds are not rendered

benign by drying or heating. Thorn apple produces greater delirium than other nightshades. Animals, wiser than men, will avoid the weed due to its taste and disagreeable odor. Find the plant in undisturbed areas.

GRAVEYARD YEW

Yew trees are said to lust after corpses; an ideal remedy to speed along death in an already-ailing or older gentleman.

Poison agent resides in seeds, needles and bark (needles least preferred, very fibrous). Often found in medieval village graveyards — trees upward of 400 to 600 years old. Seek younger trees for most desirous seeds. Preparation: bark bolus or suppository. Caution against dispensing to undertakers or cemetery groundsmen; familiar with the odor of the evergreens, they may thwart an attempt at administration.

PHALLUS FUNGUS

Death may be delayed five days or more. Best administered when a will or final testament must be amended in the presence of a witness or family member who needs time to arrive at the victim's sickbed.

The deadliest mushroom, appearing at the base of certain trees in the second half of the year. Cooking does not render the fungus benign. A reliable toxin, though very difficult to obtain. An evasive remedy, as victim will believe he is nearing recovery. This indicates imminent death.

HISTORICAL NOTE

Death by poison is, at its very nature, an intimate affair: an element of trust generally exists between victim and villain. Such closeness is liable to be abused, as demonstrated by the fact that throughout England in the eighteenth and nineteenth centuries, the largest population of accused poisoners consisted of mothers, wives and female servants, between the ages of twenty and twenty-nine. Motives ranged widely: grudges against employers, the removal of inconvenient spouses or lovers, death benefits or the inability to financially support a child.

It was not until the mid-nineteenth century that early toxicologists were able to reliably detect poison in human tissue. Thus, I set *The Lost Apothecary* in late-eighteenth-century London; even fifty years later, Nella's disguised remedies might have been easily detected during an autopsy.

The number of individuals (across all social classes) who died by poison in Georgian London cannot possibly be established. Forensic toxicology did not yet exist, and whether accidental or homicidal, poisoning deaths tend to be little more than a footnote in eighteenth-century bills of mortality. Certainly, the lack of detection methods contributed to this. Given how easily these agents can be disguised and administered, I'd venture the number of poisoning deaths is significantly higher than reported in these records.

In data gathered from 1750 to 1914, the most commonly cited poisons in criminal cases were arsenic, opium and nux vomica. Deaths due to plant alkaloids like aconitine — found in the Aconitum plant, also known as wolfsbane — and organic poisons of animal origin, such as the aphrodisiac cantharidin from certain species of beetles, were not uncommon.

Some of these poisons, like household rat poison, were readily accessible. Others were not, and their origins — the shops at which such toxins might have been purchased — have not been well established.

RECIPES

Tom Pepper's Hot Brew

To soothe the throat or otherwise ease a long day.

1.4 drachm (1 tsp) local raw honey
16 drachm (1 oz) scotch or bourbon
1/2 pint (1 cup) hot water
3 sprigs fresh thyme

Stir honey and bourbon at bottom of mug. Add hot water and thyme sprigs. Steep five minutes. Sip while warm.

Blackfriars Balm
for Bugs and Boils

To subdue angry, itchy skin caused by insect bites.

1 drachm (0.75 tsp) castor oil

1 drachm (0.75 tsp) almond oil
10 drops tea tree oil
5 drops lavender oil

In a 2.7 drachm (10 ml) glass rollerball vial, add the 4 oils. Fill to top with water and secure cap. Shake well before each use. Apply to itchy, uncomfortable skin.

ROSEMARY BUTTER BISCUIT COOKIES

A traditional shortbread. Savory yet sweet, and in no way sinister.

1 sprig fresh rosemary
1 1/2 cup butter, salted
2/3 cup white sugar
2 3/4 cup all-purpose flour

Remove leaves from rosemary and finely chop (approximately 1 Tbsp or to taste).

Soften butter; blend well with sugar. Add rosemary and flour; mix well until dough comes together. Line 2 cookie sheets with parchment paper. Form dough into 1.25-inch balls; press gently into pans until 0.5-inch thick. Refrigerate at least 1 hour.

Preheat oven to 375°F. Bake for 10–12

minutes, just until bottom edges are golden. Do not overbake. Cool at least 10 minutes. Makes 45 cookies.

ACKNOWLEDGMENTS

This book would not be in your hands were it not for my fierce agent and advocate, Stefanie Lieberman. She minces no words, makes no promises, and yet works magick behind the scenes. Thank you also to her fabulous team, Adam Hobbins and Molly Steinblatt.

To my editor at Park Row Books, Natalie Hallak. In such a powerful industry, she reminds me that at its core, publishing is about good people who enjoy good books. I am so appreciative of her warmth, optimism and vision. To the phenomenal team at Park Row Books and Harlequin/HarperCollins: Erika Imranyi, Emer Flounders, Randy Chan, Heather Connor, Heather Foy, Rachel Haller, Amy Jones, Linette Kim, Margaret O'Neill Marbury, Lindsey Reeder, Reka Rubin, Justine Sha and Christine Tsai, you are all rock stars! Thank you all, as well as Kathleen Carter, for working tirelessly to

469

sell and promote books in the strangest of times.

To Fiona Davis and Heather Webb, both of whom offered me invaluable, unbiased guidance at important junctures in my writing career: my sincerest thanks. Truly, writers are the nicest bunch around. You both inspire me to pay it forward.

To Anna Bennett, Lauren Conrad, Susan Stokes-Chapman and Kristin Durfee, for their feedback on early drafts. And to Brook Allen, for her friendship and always lending an ear.

To my sister, Kellie, and my mother-in-law, Jackie, for their endless support and love. To Pat and Melissa Teakell, for the "writer's block" block and their never-ending encouragement.

To Catherine Smith and Lauren Zopatti, whose support allowed me to balance my day job with my daydream.

To my lifelong comrade, the only woman who wouldn't blink an eye at my internet search history: Aimee Westerhaus, thank you for stumbling through life with me. And to four beautiful women, my Florida friends and early readers: Rachel LaFreniere, Roxy Miller, Shannon Santana and Laurel Uballez.

For those of you interested in writing

historical fiction: you know you're on the right path when you can't set down the research material. To Katherine Watson, author of *Poisoned Lives,* and Linda Stratmann, author of *The Secret Poisoner,* thank you for keeping me spellbound as I researched and drafted this novel.

To the many mudlarkers who read my first chapter long ago and encouraged me to keep at it, including Marnie Devereux, Camilla Szymanowska, Christine Webb, Wendy Lewis, Alison Beckham and Amanda Callaghan. And to Gaynor Hackworth, whose enthusiasm was so zealous, I renamed a character in her honor! And to "Florrie" Evans, whom I met while mudlarking on the River Thames in the summer of 2019 . . . thank you for teaching me how to spot real delftware. Follow her on Instagram: @flo_finds.

To booksellers, librarians, reviewers and readers: you are what keep books alive, and we need you more than ever. On behalf of authors everywhere, thank you.

To my husband, Marc. I think of the many hours you waited patiently in the other room while I typed away at a dream. You know the journey better than anyone. Thank you for always believing in me; this wouldn't be any fun without you.

Lastly . . . this book begins and now ends with a dedication to my parents.

To my mom: there is a certain joy and enthusiasm that only a parent can offer, and I am forever thankful to have you alongside me on this wild ride. I appreciate our closeness now more than ever. And to my dad, who passed away in 2015: countless things that go into my work — the tenacity, the stubbornness, an appreciation for language — are gifts you passed along to me. I will forever embrace them. Thank you both.

ABOUT THE AUTHOR

Sarah Penner is the debut author of *The Lost Apothecary,* to be translated in eleven languages worldwide. She works full-time in finance and is a member of the Historical Novel Society and the Women's Fiction Writers Association. She and her husband live in St. Petersburg, Florida, with their miniature dachshund, Zoe. To learn more, visit her online at SLPenner.com.